THE

HEART

OF

THORNTON

CREEK

THE
HEART
OF
THORNTON
CREEK

A NOVEL

BONNIE LEON

Revell

Grand Rapids, Michigan

Published by Fleming H. Revell
a division of Baker Publishing Group
P.O. Box 6287, Grand Rapids, MI 49516-6287

Printed in the United States of America

Library of Congress Cataloging-in-Publication Data
Leon, Bonnie
    The Heart of Thornton Creek : a novel / Bonnie Leon.
        p.   cm. — (Queensland chronicles; bk. 1)
    ISBN 0-8007-5896-X (pbk.)
    1. Pioneers—Fiction. 2. Queensland—Fiction. I. Title. II. Series: Leon, Bonnie. Queensland chronicles; bk. 1.
    PS3562.E533H43 2005
    813'.54—dc22   2004016966

Scripture is taken from the King James Version of the Bible.

Acknowledgments

No story is ever written without the help of others. This book is no exception. There are many who gladly shared their insights and knowledge with me.

I met some great blokes not far from home—Richard and Becky Gamble. They own and operate a specialty shop called the Ozstralia Store in Bend, Oregon. It's wonderful—packed with treasures from the Land Down Under. Richard is an Aussie, born and raised. He and Becky answered my many questions as well as provided videos and books that helped me find my way.

Mark Viney, who not only grew up in Australia but also lived among the aborigines, visited Bend. He spoke to a roomful of Australia enthusiasts and the following day was a special guest at the Ozstralia Store. While he spoke I furiously took notes and did my best to soak in his enthusiasm and knowledge of Australia and its people. I was also privileged to visit with him at the Ozstralia Store, where he graciously answered my questions.

I would be greatly amiss if I were to omit my online Aussie friends. I regularly spent time chatting with some fine people who live in Australia. We had many interesting and fun exchanges while visiting online. They knew me as "the Yank" and graciously included me in their conversations and answered my endless questions. Thanks, mates.

And when I needed to know how to harness horses to a wagon, Steve Bruce came to my rescue. Thank you. If not for you, Rebecca would never have figured out how to harness that wagon.

And finally, I must say thanks to my editor, Lonnie Hull DuPont. You knew my first draft could be better, and your contributions and guidance made it so.

1

Rebecca Williams knew life had more to offer her than a position of docile wife and mother. However, it seemed that only while on her roan mare's back did she truly believe it.

Wind snatched at her hat and ballooned the skirt of her riding habit, yet the young Bostonian kept a light hold on the reins and leaned farther over Chavive's neck. The mare was sure-footed and reliable. Rebecca felt no anxiety, only confidence and pleasure amid the explosive energy and blast of air.

The horse charged past the broad trunk of an oak, then strode toward a wooden fence. Rebecca leaned closer to the mare, gripping the tall pommel at the front of the saddle. When the horse's feet left the ground, the young woman's delight intensified and a sensation of power and freedom surged. Rebecca felt a true sense of liberty.

Chavive landed and, without missing a step, moved on, her hooves tearing up damp sod. The prior evening's rain had left its moist signature, and Rebecca breathed in the rich, heady fragrance of earth and vegetation.

Moving into a grove of maple and heavy underbrush, Rebecca slowed Chavive to a walk. The mare's sides heaved, and she blasted air from her nostrils. She tossed her head, and the silver bit and headpiece jangled. Rebecca stroked the animal's neck and spoke quiet words of gratitude.

Rebecca's thoughts turned to home and the morning's dispute with her father.

"If my own father won't engage me, what am I to do about a career?" she'd demanded. "My education is worthless. Absolutely wasted! I don't understand. I've worked beside you for years. I'm well trained, better than most men are when they obtain their first placement. I'm highly qualified. My schooling is completed, and I'm ready to step in and become part of the firm."

"No man will be interested in a woman with a career!" her father had countered in an uncharacteristically cruel tone.

"I don't care about a husband. I want more from life than a man and a flock of children."

Rebecca had meant it. Since girlhood she'd spent countless hours at her father's office, at first watching him work, then tidying files and such. But in more recent years she'd worked with him, puzzling over cases and discovering creative angles for a defense. She'd treasured the hours laboring alongside him.

There were almost no opportunities for women in the field of law. Still, she could have sought out a position in another firm. There were rare courageous women who had managed to find placements. She wanted to be one of them, but the only prize she truly wanted was to work with her father. Why couldn't he understand that not all women were meant to be wives and mothers?

She'd been certain he would accept her into the firm. When he'd turned her down, Rebecca had been stunned. It was his nature to give her what she wanted. He'd always been compassionate and overindulgent with his only child.

His closed door had closed all others. Charles Williams was a well-known and respected attorney, and if he wouldn't engage his own daughter, no other practice would violate his decision.

She rested on Chavive's neck, stroking her damp coat. Still breathing heavily, the horse glistened with sweat and her nostrils flared with each breath. The ride had been demanding. Rebecca straightened, removed her hat pin, repositioned her felt hat, and attached it more securely. *I must be a sight*, she thought, brushing damp strands of dark hair off her forehead and smoothing the tendrils clinging to her neck back into place.

Patting Chavive, she thought, *I know my father thinks I'm intelligent. I was top of my class. And how many times has he told me that it was only my sharp mind that saved a case?* She smoothed her gloves. *It's time I had a career. I don't fit in Boston society. I must make Father understand.*

Rebecca studied the broad valley dotted with farms. Her eyes wandered to Massachusetts Bay with its waters glinting like finely cut gems. This place usually soothed her, but she felt only a scrap of peace. Today even with God's creation laid out before her, she couldn't rid herself of the sense of strangulation pressed upon her by society.

I don't understand, Lord. You know my heart, and your holy Word says you will give us the desires of our hearts. You created me as I am. Why, then, would you restrain me from fulfilling my passion?

Chavive stomped a foot and tossed her head. Rebecca pulled up on the reins. "All right. We're off." She nudged the mare forward and turned her toward home. *I'll talk to Father again. I'm sure I can make him understand. He's always been a fair man.*

Their need for a good run satiated, horse and rider leisurely followed a trail through the forest and into an open field splashed with color. More than once Rebecca was tempted to stop and pick from summer's last offerings. There were blue lobelia, scarlet trumpet creepers, dainty bluebells, and other flowers she couldn't name. But she didn't dally. The closer she came to home, the more urgently she felt the need to speak with her father. Passing through the final gate, which led to a broad pasture beside her home, she caught the heavy, sweet fragrance of honeysuckle. Rooted along the fence, the plant embraced the weather-battered planks.

The sprawling, three-story house peeked out from behind trees and shrubbery. Rebecca pulled on the reins and stopped to study her home. An expansive, well-trimmed lawn dappled by gardens bursting with color surrounded the house. Brick steps led to a covered front entrance framed by broad pillars supporting a second-story balcony. White-trimmed windows gazed out on the serene surroundings.

The home had always felt like a sanctuary to Rebecca, and the sight of it provided an inner quiet. She'd had many good days here.

Her eyes rested on a window on the second floor. Someone stood there, gazing out. It must be her aunt Mildred watching for her. Rebecca smiled. Mildred was always watching, always concerned. A spinster, she'd filled the role of mother since Rebecca's mother, Audrey, had died of pneumonia. Rebecca had been only five years old.

Though she'd been young at the time, she had memories of her mother's warm smile and her energy. Rebecca's father had always said she was the spitting image of her mother not only in her looks but in her feisty spirit as well. Rebecca liked that—she remembered the vibrant brown eyes that had said, "I love you." She sighed. Her mother's absence was a grave loss.

Rebecca gently tapped Chavive's hindquarters with her

riding crop and cantered across the field and to the stables. Jimmy, the stable hand, greeted her with his usual open smile.

"Did you have a good ride?" he asked, taking hold of the halter.

"We certainly did." Rebecca lifted her right leg over the sidesaddle horn and attempted to slide from the horse. However, instead of making a graceful dismount, she fell forward when her dress caught on the saddle horn, and she nearly toppled on the boy as he attempted to break her fall.

"Dash it all!" Rebecca sputtered. As she pushed herself upright, her eyes met Jimmy's. "Er . . . I mean, land sakes." Rebecca detested profanity, but on certain occasions she forgot her own mouth.

"Give it no mind, miss. I've heard lots worse. Even from my own father." He grinned.

"Well, I'm sorry for my irritation." She yanked the last of her cumbersome black skirt free and smoothed it over her hips. "Dungarees would be so much more practical."

"Trousers, ma'am?"

"Yes." Rebecca straightened her hat. "And don't call me ma'am. We've known each other too long for that."

"Well, my father told me . . ."

"I know. I'll talk to him." Rebecca glanced about. "In fact, I'm going into town. Could you find him and tell him I'll need the surrey?"

"Yes, ma'am . . . Rebecca." He took Chavive's reins. "And then I'll cool your horse down and give her a good brushing."

"Thank you," Rebecca said and briskly walked to the house, stopping only to pluck a yellow rose from the garden. Mildred stepped onto the front porch just as Rebecca took the steps. "For you," Rebecca said, holding out the rose.

"Why, thank you." Mildred took the flower and smelled it. "Mmm. There's no finer fragrance, don't you agree?"

"I do, absolutely. I think we should plant more." Stepping indoors, Rebecca sniffed the air. "Smells wonderful. Fresh bread and one of your amazing stews?"

"Yes." Mildred smiled, and her narrow face rounded slightly. Her heels clicking on the vestibule tiles, she marched toward the dining room, where her steps were quieted by an elegant woven rug. "Did you have a nice ride?"

"Yes. Lovely. I never tire of riding, especially not Chavive. She seems to know my mind."

"It was rather chilly this morning."

"Fall isn't far away." Rebecca followed Mildred into the kitchen. "So did you give the cook the day off again?"

Mildred dusted flour from a cabinet. "You know I don't need her."

"Yes, you do. You work too hard." Rebecca took a small hand-painted vase from a cupboard and filled it with water. She took the flower from Mildred and plunked it in the vase. "You're a wonderful cook, but there's no harm in having someone to help." She set the vase on a small mahogany table in a kitchen alcove. "I'm going into town to see Father. Is there anything you need me to get for you?"

"No." Mildred pursed her lips. "You're not going to continue this morning's dispute are you?" She pressed the palms of her hands together. "I do hate it when you two quarrel."

"We weren't quarreling. But we didn't finish our . . . discussion. I'm not certain he really understands my point of view. However, I'm convinced that once he realizes how important all this is to me, he'll come to a more reasonable conclusion." Rebecca hurried toward the stairway. "I'll just change and be on my way."

"All right, then," Mildred said with a sigh. "Dinner will be ready at six o'clock sharp. Don't be late."

"I promise," Rebecca said. Then, deciding her aunt needed reassurance, she turned, retraced her steps, and planted a kiss on Mildred's cheek. "I'd never miss one of your superb meals," she said with a smile, then hurried upstairs.

Rebecca's mind clipped along at a much swifter pace than the steady clomping of the horses' hooves against brick. As if preparing a case, she thought over just what to say and decided forthrightness was best, no waffling. She considered demanding that her father show her the respect due someone who had given so much time to his business and who had worked so hard to reach a noteworthy goal. She would certainly remind him that if she weren't his daughter he would surely give her consideration. He'd always been clear about providing everyone a fair hearing.

Confident she would have her way, Rebecca gazed at the buildings of Boston's business district. She liked the tidy look, the brick construction and rows of framed windows, but it was the lively activity of industrious businessmen and careful consumers that she enjoyed the most. It was stimulating, nearly as much so as riding Chavive.

Amid important business ventures, men sporting smart-looking suits and puffing on cigars stood and talked about shipping ventures or politics. Women wearing the latest fashions, which always included their finest hats, strolled along the sidewalks, stopping occasionally to consider a window display or to chat.

Rebecca loved the city and hoped to one day live in a modern downtown apartment. That way she'd be in the center of activity. Of course, it would mean she'd either have to move Chavive to a stable nearby or travel out of town to ride. Neither idea appealed to her. Her mind wandered back to the woods and open fields surrounding her home, then to the house itself. She would miss it awfully. Maybe visiting and working in the business district would be enough.

"Good day." A woman's trill cut into Rebecca's musings.

She focused on the origin of the voice. Mrs. Hewitt waved and smiled, bobbing her head, crowned by a black velvet bonnet trimmed in soft faille. It had pink roses in front and a white ostrich plume scooping down in back. Rebecca preferred simpler, more practical bonnets.

"Good morning," Rebecca said. "How nice to see you. Is your family well?"

"Yes, very. Yours?"

"We're all fine."

Inwardly, Rebecca sighed at the superficial exchange. It was always the same. Mrs. Hewitt was a kindly enough person, but nothing in her life was remotely interesting to Rebecca.

"Wonderful to see you," Mrs. Hewitt chimed. "Have a lovely day."

Rebecca nodded. A sudden breeze caught at her bonnet, and she firmly held it down. Open carriages were immensely more comfortable in warm weather, but they did have their drawbacks.

Mrs. Hewitt bustled away, looking as if she'd been cinched up so tightly she might pop. Rebecca didn't believe in allowing her stays to be tight; the constriction was uncomfortable, and her slim figure didn't require it. She'd have been just as happy to forgo her corset altogether. However, Aunt Mildred would never allow it. Rebecca smiled at the thought, deciding that one day she would escape the house, unlaced and free.

The carriage stopped, and Tom Barnett, the coachman, climbed down and opened the door for her. She stepped onto the sidewalk.

"I shouldn't be long," Rebecca said before briskly taking the steps at the front of her father's office.

She sauntered down a dimly lit corridor and stopped at the door leading to his suite. After smoothing her skirt and tucking in a loose strand of hair, she swept into the room.

Rebecca removed one glove and waved it at a plump woman sitting behind a flat-topped desk cluttered with papers and files. "Hello, Miss Kinney. I'm here to see my father."

Stripping off the other glove, she strode across the room to the door leading into her father's office. Before Justine Kinney could speak, Rebecca breezed through the door.

"I have . . ." She stopped. Her father scowled at her. A good-looking, young man sat in the chair in front of his desk. "Oh, I'm sorry, I—"

"I'm busy at the moment," Charles Williams said, standing and still wearing a frown. "Could you—"

"No. Please." The young man stood, swiping back a thatch of blond hair. "Quite all right, 'ere. We've accomplished a fair bit already, eh, Mr. Williams? We've been working hard. How 'bout we give it a go again tomorrow?"

"I'd be more than happy to finish up here."

"Seems fair I give you some time with the . . . missus?"

Charles grinned. "No, no. She's not my wife. She's my daughter." He moved out from behind the heavy oak desk. "Daniel, may I introduce my daughter, Rebecca. Rebecca, Daniel Thornton—a client."

"A pleasure," Daniel said. He smiled, and a dimple creased his left cheek while his sky blue eyes crinkled at the corners.

Rebecca felt a slight flush. He was very handsome. "It's nice to meet you, Mr. Thornton. I'm sorry I interrupted your meeting. I'll wait until you've finished your business."

"No. It's no problem, not a bit. We've finished, wouldn't you say, Mr. Williams?" He grinned and patted Charles on the back, then looked at Rebecca. "It's nice to meet one of the local ladies. I've had little opportunity." He glanced at Rebecca's father. "I mean . . ."

Charles chuckled. "I know how it can be while away from home." He turned to Rebecca. "Mr. Thornton is from Australia. And he's been here only a few weeks."

"Oh, I wondered," Rebecca said. "I mean . . . I noticed the accent. I suppose you must miss your home."

"Yes, some, but it's all right. I've never been to the States before, so it's an adventure."

Charles cleared his throat. "I'll excuse the intrusion this time," he said with a grin. "But you, young lady, must check with Miss Kinney first or at least remember to knock rather than barging in."

"I apologize, Father. I just feel so at home here, I forgot. It won't happen again." She turned to Daniel. "I am sorry. I've worked alongside my father for so many years, this feels like *my* office."

Her eyes fell upon a bookcase crowded with weighty, academic-looking books. "In fact, I've spent so many hours in this room, I've probably read every book on the shelves."

"All those?" Daniel raised an eyebrow. "I'd say any woman who can wade through all that has a bit of brass to her. And a good mind. More brains than any bloke on our place." He grinned at Charles. "I'd say you're right smart to put her to work for you."

"If only he would," Rebecca said, folding her arms over her bodice and settling challenging eyes on her father.

"Now's not the time," Charles warned.

"No. Of course it's not. My apologies."

"I'm starved. Anyone else ready for a go at lunch?" Daniel asked.

"I am a little hungry," Charles said. "Rebecca?"

"I'd love to. I had a vigorous ride this morning, and I am hungry."

"A rider are you, then?"

16

"Yes. You?"

"Where I come from we live on horseback." Daniel moved toward the door. "There's a fine eatery just down the street. There's usually quite a mob there. S'pose that means it's good, eh?" He offered Rebecca an enticing smile.

Rebecca liked this Australian. She returned the gesture. "Australia's an awfully big country. Just where are you from exactly?"

"Queensland, actually. We've a cattle station out on the flats northwest of Brisbane." Daniel offered Rebecca his arm.

Rebecca rested her hand on Daniel's sleeve and glanced at Charles. "You ready, Father?"

2

Studying her reflection in the mirror, Rebecca fingered a bow on the bodice of her evening gown. "I abhor bows," she said with disgust, stripping off the dress, then flinging it on her bed. She glanced at the mantel clock. Daniel would be here any time, and she still hadn't decided what to wear. Nothing seemed quite right for this fascinating man from the other side of the world.

With a sigh she returned to her closet and scanned the remaining dresses. She touched a rose-colored silk gown. It was lovely, but the bodice was cut deeply. "Too daring," she said. Her eyes moved to a dark blue princess polonaise with a tall, tightly cinched collar lined with pearl buttons. Her eyes rested on the collar. "Too virtuous."

Folding her arms over her bodice, she stared at the gowns without actually seeing them. *Why do I care what he thinks? He's nothing more than a temporary distraction. I'll see him this once; then I'm sure he'll be off to his ranch in Queensland. It makes little difference what I wear.*

But it did matter. And Rebecca hated that it did. Daniel had unsettled her, and she'd found herself wishing he'd remain in Boston.

With a heavy sigh she picked a pale blue gown with soft

white faille trim. Its squared neckline and silk bodice was feminine but not vulgar. It *was* the latest from Paris. She stepped into the dress, slipped on its overskirt, and smoothed the waist.

A knock sounded at the door. "It's nearly time," Aunt Mildred called softly. "May I come in?"

"Yes."

Mildred stepped inside.

"You're just in time. I need help with my buttons."

"It's taken you an awfully long time to get ready. Daniel will be here any moment."

"I couldn't decide what to wear," Rebecca said, embarrassed at her indecision.

"Hmm. And since when did you care whether or not you were wearing just the right gown?" Mildred offered a small smile, then quickly looped the buttons at the back of the dress.

"I'm out of sorts," Rebecca said, stepping in front of the bureau mirror. "Actually, I've been considering not going at all. I may be coming down with something."

"Perhaps . . . if you're not feeling well."

Rebecca sighed, remembering Daniel's handsome face and sky blue eyes, which turned down slightly at the outer corners. She thought they looked a bit sad. "He's a foreigner and probably lonely. It doesn't seem proper to cancel." Rebecca picked up her hairbrush and pulled it through her dark curls. "I really ought to go." She expertly twisted and pinned up her hair, allowing a few soft tendrils to fall loose. "I think the floral wreath would be best, don't you?" She picked up the decorative comb and pinned it. "The blue matches the dress perfectly, don't you think?"

"A hat is proper." Mildred studied Rebecca. Her eyes turned tender. "However, you do look lovely just as you are."

Rebecca studied her reflection. Her dark brown eyes were

vibrant. *It must be the blue in my gown,* she thought and gently pinched her cheeks.

The bell rang downstairs. "That must be him," she said, feeling a surge of anticipation.

"You wait here. You don't want to look too eager."

"Well, and I'm not. In fact, I really couldn't care less if I see him or not."

"Is that so?" Mildred asked rather smugly.

🖉

Daniel swept off his hat and stared at the Williamses' front door. Why was he here? As beautiful and charming as Rebecca was, she could be nothing more than a diversion. His purpose for being in the States was a wretched one—to settle his brother's estate; that was all. And although he needed an amusement, he felt a bit like a gadabout. His brother was barely in the grave, and he was making merry.

His mind captured Rebecca's essence. She seemed more than a diversion. She was exceptional—not just beautiful but . . . more. He was setting himself up for disappointment. There could be no future for the two of them. She was too fine a woman to follow a bloke like him across the world to a piece of dry ground in the middle of the flats. *I barely know her,* he told himself. *I'm being carried away by a pretty face—empty passions can carry no long-term assurances.*

Daniel considered retreating. The doorknob turned. It was too late to change his mind. He straightened and tugged on the front of his waistcoat.

The door opened. "Good day. May I help you?" asked a buxom middle-aged woman wearing a frilled apron.

"I'm 'ere to see Miss Rebecca Williams."

"She's expecting you," the woman said with a smile, opening the door to reveal a spacious tiled entry. "Please, come in." She held out her hand. "May I take your hat?"

Daniel handed her the hat. "It's a fair night, eh?"

"Yes. Very." She set the hat on an ornate hall tree. "Right this way."

Daniel followed the woman to a heavy mahogany door.

She stopped and turned to Daniel. Her ruddy cheeks rounding with a smile, she asked, "Would you like a cup of tea while you wait?"

"A cuppa would suit me fine."

Her eyes momentarily held a question, then seemed to comprehend. "Fine, then. I'll be right back with it." Pushing the door open, she said, "Mr. Williams, Miss Rebecca's guest has arrived."

"Ah, Daniel." Charles sat behind a heavy mahogany desk. He pushed himself out of his chair and strode across the room to shake the young man's hand. "Good to see you."

"My pleasure, sir."

The maid quietly left.

"So it's the Boston Symphony tonight?"

"Yes. I heard it's grand. Does Rebecca like music?"

"The music, yes, but she considers the socializing that goes along with it balderdash." A heavy ornamental carpet cushioned Charles's steps as he returned to the chair behind his desk. He sat down and reclaimed a pipe smoldering in an ashtray. "Do you smoke?"

"No, sir. Never took a liking to it. Not that I mind . . ."

Charles chuckled. "My name's Charles. Relax. No inquisition tonight. I think I know you well enough. Have a seat."

Wondering just what he was doing there, Daniel lowered himself into a heavy brocade parlor chair.

There was a knock at the door.

"Come in," Charles said.

The buxom woman who had met Daniel at the door stepped

into the study, carrying a tray with tea and two cups with saucers. Setting the tray on the desk, she said, "Tea, sir."

"Fine. Thank you, Flora."

With a smile, Flora walked out and closed the door softly.

"I don't care for tea," Charles said. "Coffee's more to my liking. But help yourself."

Daniel filled a cup.

Charles leaned back in his chair and crossed his right leg over the left. "Actually, I'm surprised my daughter accepted your invitation."

"Why is that, sir . . . er, Charles?"

"She's never taken much to Boston society. She's more interested in my next 'big' case."

Charles picked up a newspaper lying on his desk. Shaking his head, he said, "Bad fire in Chicago."

"Too right, sir. A lot of good blokes were killed. Families and businesses overcome. Sorry to hear 'bout that one," he said. His mind was still on Rebecca's uncommon acceptance of his invitation.

Charles folded the paper. "I hear you get some fierce fires in Australia."

"We do. Sometimes things get right dry, and then the wind comes up and it can get bad, especially if it makes a run—then we've a mess on our hands. At Douloo we've been spared, but there've been fellas in the district who were hard done by fire." He sipped the tea.

Charles relit his pipe and sucked on it until the coals reddened and smoke drifted toward the ceiling. "Around here we get regular spells of rain. I doubt we'll ever see a fire like the one in Chicago."

Daniel nodded and glanced toward the door. In spite of his misgivings, he was anxious to see Rebecca.

"You can't rush her. She has a mind of her own."

Daniel felt his cheeks redden. "Yes, sir. I'm sure she does."

"So." Charles puffed and gazed through a haze of smoke. "Is the cattle business a profitable one?"

"We've done all right. It's hard work, a hard life. I'd say it's a fair day when none of the mob dies from heat or snakebite and you get in before dark." He grinned.

The rustle of skirts preceded Rebecca. Daniel set down his cup and stood as she stepped into the room. Unfamiliar emotions charged through him as her brown eyes held his gaze.

Rebecca casually crossed to Daniel. "How nice to see you again, Mr. Thornton."

He offered a slight bow. "It's an honor. You look grand, Miss Williams." He smiled. "I'll be the envy of every gent at the theater."

"Why, thank you." Rebecca pulled on her gloves. "We won't be late, Father." Glancing at Daniel, she said, "We should hurry. The orchestra will begin soon."

"Right." With a short bow toward Charles, Daniel said, "It was good to see you, sir."

"Nice to see you as well, Mr. Thornton."

Daniel offered Rebecca his arm and escorted her to the entrance, where the maid he'd met earlier slipped a cape over Rebecca's shoulders.

"The night air is chilly, miss."

Mildred joined them. "Good evening, Daniel."

"Evening, Miss Williams."

"I'll be escorting you, of course." Mildred moved toward the door.

"Of course," Daniel said, taken by surprise. He hadn't realized they'd have a chaperone. He quickly stepped up and opened the door, then followed Mildred and Rebecca out.

After helping both women into the carriage, Daniel took

a seat opposite them. He'd expected an evening alone with Rebecca and felt disappointment and relief as the horses took off at a brisk gait. For several moments no one spoke.

Finally Mildred asked, "So, Daniel, how do you like Boston?"

"It's a beautiful city. I haven't had enough time to see much of her, though. Been settling my brother's estate," he added, again feeling guilt over his merry making.

"Yes. I heard about your brother. I'm very sorry."

"It shook up my mum pretty badly."

"I'm so sorry," Rebecca said.

Daniel nodded. Silence settled over the threesome. Gazing out the window at a large, round moon, Daniel finally said, "It's a right lovely evening."

Rebecca leaned forward and stared at the moon. "Winter will be upon us soon. I'm looking forward to it, actually. I'm weary of summer heat and ready for cold weather and snow."

"We've never had snow at the station. During the winter, though, it cools off some."

"You've never had snow?" Rebecca asked incredulously.

"No. And from the sounds of it, I'm right glad of it." He grinned. "Seems a bother."

ⅅ

Rebecca liked the way Daniel's rounded words spilled casually from his mouth. And though she'd tried, she couldn't disregard his good looks. When he smiled his left cheek dimpled and warmed his expression. Although his blond hair could do with a cut, she thought its casual style suited his natural ruggedness.

Daniel pulled out a pocket watch and glanced at it. "We ought to get there just in time."

Rebecca searched for something more to say, but her mind was empty. This was something new—no man had ever left her at a loss for words. Finally she asked, "So, Mr. Thornton, how are things in Australia?" *What a stupid thing to say,* she scolded herself.

Wearing a soft smile, he said, "No worries. Australia's getting along quite nicely—no floods, no fires."

"That's good to know. Do those kinds of things happen often?"

"In Queensland you can expect most anything. During the summer months we sometimes have violent storms. The rivers fill and overflow their banks. When we get into a pattern of rain, you're liable to find most blokes at the pub, downing their grog and hoping their places stay above water. Nothin' much more the poor blokes can do. They've got no control over the weather."

He rested his arm on the window casement. "Usually the summer weather's hot and dry. The rivers are low, and some have no water at all; the land turns gold and brown. We fight dust. Mum is forever trying to clear it from the house."

"Sounds dreadful," Mildred said.

Daniel chuckled. "Yeah, maybe, but there's something about the open spaces that grabs hold of you. Sometimes I almost think I've taken a liking to dust." His grin softened into a smile. "And there's more—red and gold sunsets all soft like someone painted the sky, and sometimes the hills off in the distance look blue and misty. The night sky holds a massive number of stars—not like 'ere." He grinned. "When I was a lad I used to try to count them. Never managed though."

Rebecca was touched by the wonder she heard in Daniel's voice. "Tell me more. What's life like in Australia?"

"Depends on where you are. It's kind of like your United States 'ere. Some places have trees and some don't. Some have people, some don't."

"And where you live?"

"Our station is on the flats. Just south is the Downs. There's good farmland down that way. 'Round our place is grasslands. We mainly stick to raising cattle; some blokes have sheep. There's plenty of grass a good portion of the year. I quite like it, but I don't guess you'd see it as being very pretty."

Rebecca settled back and folded her hands in her lap. "Any place can be lovely if one's willing to look for the beauty."

"Too right." Daniel grinned, then turned his eyes outside and studied passing trees. "I miss it. 'Round 'ere you're all closed in by trees and buildings." He looked at Rebecca. "I don't s'pose you'd like it much out on the flats, eh?"

"I try hard not to set my mind against anything without first seeing it, Mr. Thornton. The Lord created all the earth, and it would seem ungrateful of us not to appreciate his work."

Daniel smiled. "Well said, miss."

"You may call me Rebecca if you'd like."

"Rebecca it is, then." He offered an appreciative smile. "And why don't you call me Daniel, then, eh?"

"Of course, Daniel." The beat of Rebecca's heart picked up slightly. She wasn't certain just why. She found Daniel attractive and very nice but felt no real passion.

꧁

The theater was crowded by the time Daniel, Rebecca, and Mildred found their seats. Daniel stood while Mildred sidestepped to her place and Rebecca followed. Gratefully he sank into a cushioned, pile seat. He felt as if he'd been introduced to half of Boston, or at least the upper crust of Boston. Rebecca and her aunt seemed to know just about everyone. Daniel tugged at his snug collar. He was overly warm and was beginning to think this hadn't been a good idea.

Rebecca leaned close, and Daniel caught a whiff of expensive perfume.

She whispered, "You've just met the best of Boston society, you know. And they find you very interesting," she added with a chuckle. "Personally, I think they're a bunch of snobs." She rested a hand on his arm. Then, seeming to notice her indiscretion, she quickly removed it and turned to watch the curtained stage.

Daniel stared at the stage but was not unaware of the touch of Rebecca's silk sleeve against his arm or her soft musical voice as she chatted with Mildred. He wanted to spend more time with her. For a brief moment he imagined what life would be like with more of her in it. He felt protective and tender toward the charming American.

Reality replaced his whimsy. He envisioned a hot, dusty, isolated cattle station. She didn't fit. With regret he promised himself this evening would be their only outing. No reason to take the friendship further. It would only become a cruel association. With a glance her way, he told himself, *She's nothing more than another sheila*. But even as the thought moved through his mind, he didn't believe it.

Heavy curtains opened, revealing a full orchestra. They began the performance with the soft, haunting strings of Tchaikovsky's "1812 Overture." Immediately Daniel was drawn from his fantasies and into the splendor and magnificence of the music, which swelled and then sped into an emotional and turbulent masterpiece.

The symphony moved on to Beethoven and Schubert; the theater resonated with the thrilling compositions of the masters. He thought of his mother and wished she could hear the beauty of Beethoven's Fifth. Instruments echoed one another. Growing louder and more insistent, they fought for prominence.

When it was over he realized he'd forgotten everything

except the music. With the last chord came disappointment. He wanted more. More to take home with him, more to share with his mum, more to carry him to heaven. Along with others in the theater, he spontaneously stood and clapped. He glanced at Rebecca and drew in her enthusiasm. Her cheeks held a blush, and her eyes glistened with tears.

"Wasn't it wonderful!" she said in a hush, brushing away a tear.

"I imagine we'll have orchestras in heaven, eh?"

Rebecca nodded.

"That was lovely," Mildred said. "Simply spectacular."

The applause died down; the spell was broken as people surged into the aisles. Daniel tucked his hat under one arm and offered the other to Rebecca. "My mum would have loved this. Wish we had music like it back home."

"You don't?" Rebecca asked.

"No. We'd have to travel to Brisbane or Sydney. We have bush music at the station."

"What's that?" Rebecca allowed him to steer her toward the exit.

"Oh, it's nothing. Something the blacks do."

"Blacks?"

"The blacks, aborigines. They have their own music they play on the didgeridoo. It's made out of a hollowed-out log, and they blow into it. It has a deep, throaty sound that echoes across the open lands. It's not an orchestra, but it's right pretty."

"Sounds interesting," Rebecca said.

Daniel helped Mildred and Rebecca into the carriage, then took his place across from them. *Strange custom, having an escort*, he thought.

The carriage stopped in front of the Williamses' mansion.

"I had a lovely evening," Mildred said, stepping onto the porch. She waited at the door.

"It *was* lovely." Rebecca glanced at her aunt, then asked Daniel, "Would you like to come in for tea and cake?"

Although he'd decided spending time with Rebecca would be ill-advised, Daniel heard himself say, "I'd like that." *You fool*, he thought. *You're only asking for trouble.*

He followed Rebecca inside.

The lights had been turned down, and a hush embraced the house. Daniel helped Rebecca with her cape, then quickly stepped back. The closeness was too much of an intoxicant. Turning away so Rebecca couldn't see the flush in his cheeks, he draped the wrap on the hall tree.

Rebecca stripped off her gloves and, with a glance in the entrance mirror, tucked in a loose strand of hair. The dark curl found its way back to her bare shoulders. "My hair is such a bother," she said with exasperation. "I'd love to have straight hair rather than all these curls."

"Your hair's perfect," Daniel said. "And it's not too curly. I'd say it's more . . . wavy." He wished he could touch the soft curls.

Mildred moved toward the kitchen.

"I can take care of our refreshments, Auntie."

Mildred stopped and stared at her niece, then with a sigh said, "I suppose." She took a step, then hesitated. "All right, then. I'll just go on up to bed." She settled serious, suspicious eyes on Daniel. "I won't be far. If you need anything . . ."

"I'm sure we won't," Rebecca said. "We'll be just fine. Good night." She hurried to her aunt and kissed her cheek. "Thank you for accompanying us."

"It was my pleasure. Good night, then." Mildred turned, and with a rustle of stiff skirts, she walked up the staircase.

As soon as her aunt was out of sight, Rebecca giggled. "I think a twenty-two-year-old is old enough to chaperone herself, don't you?"

"Too right," Daniel said with a grin.

Rebecca headed for the kitchen. "Would you like tea or coffee?"

"A cuppa's fine."

Rebecca looked at him. "A cuppa?"

"Oh. Where I come from 'cuppa' usually means tea, sometimes coffee. With my mum it's always tea."

"Tea it is, then."

"Right."

Wearing a smile, Rebecca set about making tea.

Daniel took a chair at a small mahogany table in a kitchen alcove, where he enjoyed watching Rebecca.

She set tea and cake on the table and sat across from him. "I had a delightful time this evening. Thank you for taking me. I suppose my father told you I rarely go out."

"He did mention it. I'm honored you allowed me to accompany you." Daniel knew he was being bold but continued, "I'd say we're a fine fit, eh?"

A worry line creased Rebecca's forehead. "I doubt I truly fit with anyone."

☼

For more than an hour the two chatted, discovering they had many common interests, one of them being music, although this was a new attraction for Daniel. They also loved reading books and horseback riding.

Daniel admitted his favorite book was *The Last of the Mohicans*. "I guess I've still got a bit of the pioneer spirit in me."

Rebecca rested her chin in her hand. "I'd like to be a pioneer, I think. I'm not sure I'd be very good at it though.

I've lived a very comfortable life." Her eyes traveled to the fine china resting in a mahogany cabinet in the dining room. "Of course, striving for a career is rather advanced thinking, almost like pioneering."

"What is it you want to do?"

"I hope to be an attorney and work with my father." She studied her tea. "I doubt it will happen." She added with a sigh, "In this time and place there's little room for women in *any* kind of business." She sat straighter. "However, I intend to try. I'm not giving up."

"I admire your spirit."

Rebecca leaned an elbow on the table. "Tell me about your family."

"There's not much to tell." Daniel's family was a subject he would rather not discuss, not tonight anyway. "My brother's gone, as you know. There were only the two of us, so my father's counting on me to carry on. His family emigrated from England two generations back. My mum came over when she was twelve." Wearing a soft smile, he continued, "She's still got a lot of England in her. She tries to keep a bit of it with her. She's even got a flower garden very like the one her mother had in England."

Daniel tapped the edge of his cup with the tip of his finger. "Well, then, it's getting late. I suppose I ought to be going." He stood. *It would be unwise to see Rebecca again*, he told himself, then asked, "Would you like to picnic tomorrow?"

"I'd love to. What time should I expect you?"

"I'll pop by 'round eleven o'clock?"

"Wonderful. I'll pack a lunch."

Daniel wanted to stay. "Tomorrow, then."

3

A soft rap sounded at Rebecca's door. "Yes, who is it?"

"Just me," Flora, the housemaid, said.

"Come in."

Her face flushed, Flora peeked inside the room. "Mr. Thornton's here, ma'am," she puffed, winded from climbing the stairs.

"I'll be right down."

"Yes, ma'am." Flora ducked out and quietly closed the door.

Rebecca moved to the mirror and tidied her hair, then pinned on her riding hat. She knew meeting with Daniel wasn't a good idea. There was no future for them. *I'm only making life more complicated for him,* she told herself, remembering the admiration she'd seen in his blue eyes. She'd have to make her plans clear to him. There was no room for a man in her life, especially not someone from the other side of the world.

Spine straight and shoulders back, she left the room. Her hand barely touched the wooden banister as she gracefully glided down the staircase. Daniel stood in the foyer, his eyes watching her appreciatively.

"Good morning. How nice to see you again, Mr. Thornton."

"G'day." Daniel offered an uneasy smile.

He knows this venture will come to naught, Rebecca thought. "I hope you don't mind, but I selected a horse for you."

"Don't mind at all. I trust your judgment."

"I've packed a lunch, but I'll have to get it from the kitchen." Rebecca retreated, feeling somewhat disappointed that the casual familiarity of the previous evening seemed to have vanished. *I ought to make my excuses.*

Mildred sat in the breakfast nook, sipping tea. "So you're off, then?"

"Yes. We shouldn't be long." Rebecca picked up a picnic basket.

"Be careful and have a nice time." Mildred set her cup on its saucer with a whispered clink. "You really ought not to be traipsing about without a chaperone, you know."

"There isn't anyone to join us." Rebecca's smile held a challenge. "Unless, of course, you'd like to come along?"

"I'm far beyond my riding days," Mildred said.

"Well, then I guess you'll have to trust me."

"I trust *you*." Mildred eyed Rebecca. "I know you're a proper young lady in spite of your high spirits." Her eyes darted toward the front entrance. "It's him," she whispered. "We know almost nothing about him. He may be a wild thing. Who knows what kind of life he lives in Australia."

Unable to keep the teasing lilt from her voice, Rebecca said, "What kind of life do you suppose?"

Mildred pursed her lips. With a sigh she said, "Never mind. Go along. I'll be praying for you."

"I'll be fine," Rebecca said, realizing her headstrong disposition had prevented her from taking advantage of a suitable justification to remain home. Then again she wasn't certain she actually wanted to stay home. She rather enjoyed Daniel's company.

☞

Rebecca strode toward the stables, her riding crop whisking the skirt of her riding habit with each brisk swing of her arm.

Daniel walked alongside her, carrying the basket. His silence made Rebecca uneasy. During their first two meetings, he'd been talkative and friendly. Was something troubling him?

Jimmy met them at the stable door, horses in tow. "Good morning. I'll take that," he said, handing off a large black stallion to Daniel and reaching for the basket.

"G'day, lad."

"Jimmy, can you please put the food in the saddlebags?" Rebecca asked.

"That's what I figured, ma'am."

Rebecca took Chavive and ran the palm of her hand over the horse's velvety nose. Jimmy transferred the lunch into two bags, then swung them up behind the cantle of Daniel's horse and secured them.

Daniel patted the animal's neck. "He's a beaut."

"And a handful," Jimmy added. "You gotta watch him." He grinned. "Sure you can handle him?"

Rebecca settled a mischievous look on Daniel. "Is it going to be a problem for you?"

"'Ere, I've been riding since I was a lad. No worries."

"His name's Tomlin."

"Interesting name."

"He's a twin," Rebecca explained. "He was born last and was the smaller of the two. His name means 'little twin.'"

Daniel took a step back and studied the animal, which

34

stood a good seventeen hands. "If he's the smaller of the two, I'd like to see his brother."

Rebecca moved to Chavive's side. "His brother's just down the road. He's a real beauty, but not as nice as our Tomlin." Jimmy gave her a foot up, and Rebecca settled on the saddle, then tidied her skirts.

Daniel mounted, casually seating himself on the stallion's back. Tomlin sidestepped and tossed his head. "'Ere, come on now," Daniel said gently. The horse quieted but chewed on his bit. "The saddle feels a bit queer. Not like what we've got back home."

"It's a gentleman's saddle, sir," Jimmy said. "I can change it if you like. I think we have a western saddle. I just thought . . ."

"No, no. I'll have a go with this one."

Chavive pulled on the reins. "She's ready. How about you?" Rebecca teased.

"Too right. You lead the way."

Rebecca and Chavive moved toward the pasture. Rebecca felt more relaxed and knew Daniel did too. There was no reason they shouldn't ride and enjoy the last warm days of summer.

"It's a perfect day to be out." Rebecca tipped her face up to catch the full warmth of the sun. Chavive pranced. "She wants to run," Rebecca said with a laugh.

Daniel's horse blasted air from his nostrils and tossed his head. "Shall we give them their way, then?"

Rebecca leaned forward and tapped Chavive's flanks with her riding crop. Immediately the mare stepped into a gallop. Daniel's horse strode out. Riders and horses tore across the open field and through the gate. Rebecca guided Chavive to the right and up a trail leading into the woods.

Daniel moved alongside. "He's not happy trailing behind. He's needing his head. I'm going to let him go. You mind?"

Rebecca laughed. "Absolutely not. Do as you wish." She leaned over Chavive's neck, and the horse charged ahead. "See if you can keep up," she called, hearing only the creak of leather, the pounding of hooves, and the labored breath of the horses.

Tomlin quickly pulled alongside Chavive. Daniel's expression was one of intense delight as he flew past, the stallion's hooves flicking up bits of sod.

Rebecca kicked Chavive's side and drove her on. She felt complete, free—elated! Her hat flew off, but she paid no heed even though her hair was quickly becoming a mass of dark tangles. All she knew was the power of the animal beneath her and a surging sense of liberation.

Breaking out of the trees, Daniel pulled up. His horse danced, huffing. "Which way?"

"Follow me," Rebecca called, barely slowing as she sped past. Boldly they moved along a ridge. They tempted peril, driven by the appeal of danger and liberty.

Finally, reluctantly, Rebecca pulled hard on the reins at the top of an embankment. Her horse trembled and panted; her sides heaved. The smell of leather and horse was heady.

Daniel reined in Tomlin.

Stroking Chavive's damp neck, Rebecca gazed at the lush valley with its farms, and then she turned her eyes to the distant bay reflecting a misty sky and smoldering sun. "This is it. My place."

Daniel stared at the open land. "Quite beautiful."

"I've been coming here since I was a girl." Rebecca glanced at Daniel, pleased to see he was impressed. "We can rest here and have a bite to eat if you like."

"I'm starved." Daniel dismounted and moved to Rebecca's side to lend her a hand down.

For a brief moment she was caught between Chavive and Daniel. His eyes sought out her thoughts. It wasn't exactly unpleasant, but she quickly stepped free of the unintended embrace. "We can tie the horses here." She led Chavive to a nearby tree and secured the reins to a low-hanging branch.

Daniel tied Tomlin nearby. "I've missed riding." He stroked the animal's face, caressed his neck, then ran his hand across his flanks. A tremor moved through the animal. "Outstanding steed. Wouldn't mind introducing him to some of the brumbies that come down from the hills. They'd produce spectacular foals."

"Brumbies?"

"The wild horses that range in the district."

Rebecca studied Tomlin. "My father would never let him go. I think he loves Tomlin as much as I do Chavive."

"If he were mine I'd keep a steady hand on him too."

Rebecca took a small quilt from a pack and spread it out over the wild grasses. "I hope you like chicken sandwiches."

"I do."

She sat gracefully, arranging her skirt about her.

Daniel hefted the saddlebags. "These feel right heavy. Got to be more than sandwiches in 'ere."

"I made cheesecake and also brought along apples and lemonade."

Daniel handed her the bags. "You cook?"

"A little. I enjoy it." She removed the contents from the bags and set them out, then handed Daniel a sandwich, taking one for herself as well. Carefully she unwrapped two crystal glasses swathed in embroidered napkins. "Actually, I'm quite a good cook. My aunt taught me." She filled the stemware with lemonade. Taking a sip, Rebecca gazed out over the rolling hills and farmland; then her eyes rested on a sailing ship gliding across the bay. "I always feel better when I'm here."

"I've a private spot back home too. Wish you could see it." His eyes lingered on Rebecca.

Unwilling to retreat from his gaze, she held his eyes. "I'd like to. Maybe one day I'll visit your . . . station."

"It's settled, then, eh? You'll be visiting." Daniel grinned, and his dimple appeared.

Rebecca liked this Australian. "I love to travel," she said nonchalantly. "It's been a long while since my last trip, more than three years. My father and I visited London and Paris. We had a lovely time."

For several moments they sat quietly. Rustling leaves, the munching of the horses, and birdsong spoke to them. There was no need for conversation. Like old friends, they sat comfortably and ate. Rebecca finished her sandwich, then leaned back and rested on one hand. "What's it like in Australia, at your home, I mean?"

Daniel thought while he started on another sandwich. "Not like 'ere. It's mostly flat. There are mountains, but they're a great distance away. And the seasons . . . well, they're not like yours either. During winter it's cooler but not cold. Sometimes there's quite a bit of rain and even the bushies find cover." He grinned.

"I've never heard of a bushie."

"Those are solitary types who live in the bush." He glanced at the horses. "And then there's the summer months. We get storms, but the sun turns hot. Real hot, not like 'ere." His eyes roamed over the lower hillsides. "The land is big and seems to go on forever. A man feels free there."

"Do you have a lot of cattle on your ranch?"

"Oh yeah. Thousands."

"How do you possibly take care of so many?"

"For the most part, they take care of themselves. But we've a fair number of chaps working for us. We've a right sizable number of drovers, and there are blacks to look after the house and crops."

"It's hard to imagine such a place. Are there a lot of other ranchers where you live?"

"In the district, yeah, but our places are spread out. It's open lands, like I said."

"That seems strange. We've always had neighbors, and of course, we're not far from the city."

"I like it quiet. Not much out on the flats—a few dingoes, a roo now and then, and once in a while a goanna might run across your trail." His gaze moved to the valley. "This is right pretty 'ere, but a chap feels a bit closed in." His eyes settled on the distant bay. "Have to admit though, this is a real beautiful spot." He plucked a piece of dry grass and placed it between his teeth.

"And what about birds? There are so many different kinds here." She glanced up into a tree and watched a pair of finches play tag.

"Oh, we have birds. They might seem strange to you though. Some make a bit of a racket, and others have brightly colored feathers, so much so they're startling to look at."

The peace of the woodlands enfolded the pair.

"I'm sorry about your brother. It must have been difficult to have him living so far from home and then . . . lose him."

"Yeah. It's especially hard on my mum." Daniel's voice had taken on a hard edge. "But I think he was happy. Elton came searching for a new life, and he found one." Daniel's words were positive, but his voice sounded sad. "How about you? What are your plans?"

"Well, like I told you last night, I want to be a lawyer."

"From what you said, that won't be easy. How do you figure to go about it?"

Rebecca sat upright. "I've completed my education, and I've worked alongside my father for years. I'm well prepared. I'm determined to convince my father to take me on." She compressed her lips, then continued, "If not for the archaic views about women in this city, I'd already be working."

Daniel picked up an apple and polished it on his pants leg. "It would be a hard go—working and taking care of a family."

"You sound like my father." She emptied her glass, then smoothed the rim with her index finger. "A woman must choose—family or career." She set down the glass. "I've always wanted to work with my father. He's a fine man, and the kind of work he does is quite stimulating." She met Daniel's eyes. "I've decided not to marry."

Daniel looked slightly unnerved. He bit into the apple, and juice squirted. Wiping his lower lip, he studied Tomlin. "I believe God created men and women for different roles."

Rebecca prepared herself for the customary lecture about how women were unable to sustain themselves in the uncompromising world of enterprise. Anger swelled.

"It's not that women can't have a family and a career," Daniel said. "They're smart enough, and some are tough enough, that's certain. But men haven't the tender touch for children the way women have." He brushed a piece of apple from his shirt. "We bully our way through life. If women were working and the raising of children were left up to us men, we'd make a mess of things. Can you imagine someone like me changing a nappy? Or soothing a fussy babe?" He smiled, his blue eyes crinkling at the corners. The wind caught hold of his blond hair, then dropped it onto his forehead. Rebecca was tempted to smooth it back.

"A woman can do anything she sets her mind to." He stopped and thought a moment. "But if women give up being mums, I'm afraid we'll have a world full of misfits. Children need their mums. Not to say fathers aren't important. They are. But they just don't have the touch with little ones."

Rebecca's heart softened toward Daniel. He understood.

40

An ache burrowed beneath her breast. She'd never have all she wanted.

"I fear if a woman tried to care for a family and have a career, it would be too much for her. Her family would be shorted. And so would she. Plus, she'd be plain worn out." Daniel shrugged. "I s'pose you're right. A woman would have to choose."

Rebecca had always been certain she would one day work beside her father. Not until this moment had she ever even considered any other alternative.

4

Rebecca followed the aroma of frying bacon to the kitchen. "I'm starving," she said. "And that smells wonderful."

Mildred flashed her a smile.

Rebecca glanced at the kitchen table where her father sat, a cup of tea cradled in his hands. "I know it's not a holiday, and you never miss work. Why are you still home?"

"He's not feeling well," Mildred said.

"You do look pale." Rebecca sat beside him. "Are you all right?"

"I'm sure it's nothing, just a bit of a stomach ailment." He winced, then sipped his tea. "Mildred's ginger tea will make things right."

Mildred forked a slice of bacon onto a plate. "He needs to see the doctor. He's feverish and hasn't been able to hold anything down."

"You worry too much. I'll be fine." Charles tried to stand but swayed. He pressed his hands on the table.

"Charles?"

"Just a bit of dizziness," he said weakly.

Mildred hurried to support her brother, then helped him sit. "Just the same, I'm sending for the doctor." She rested a hand on his damp forehead. "Flora," she called shrilly.

Almost immediately the stout maid appeared. "Yes, ma'am?"

"Have Jimmy run into town for the doctor, and tell Tom to come in here. We'll need a hand getting my brother upstairs to bed."

Flora seemed rooted in place, evidently stunned at Charles's illness. He was rarely sick.

"Please, Flora, now."

"Yes. Of course. Right away." Flora hurried out of the room.

"How long have you been ill, Father?" Rebecca rested a hand on his arm. She didn't like the look of him. His coloring had gone gray, and he was sweating heavily.

Charles slowly let out his breath. "Sometime in the night I noticed a pain in my right side—it was just a twinge at first. Now it feels as if my insides are on fire."

"Dr. Martin will know what to do," Rebecca reassured him. "Try to drink a little tea. It might help."

With a slight nod, Charles obeyed.

A few moments later, Tom strode in through the back door. "You needed me?" His gaze settled on Charles.

Charles offered Tom a half smile and said as jovially as he could manage, "That I do."

Mildred moved close to Charles. "My brother's quite ill and needs assistance getting to his room."

"I'm the one, then. I've a good strong back." He studied his employer. "Hope it's nothing serious."

"I'm sure it's not."

Tom crossed to Charles, and grasping one of his arms, helped him to his feet.

Immediately new droplets of sweat sprang out on Charles's face.

Rebecca leaned close to her father. "Let me help." She draped his other arm over her shoulders.

43

Charles groaned, wincing.

"Oh, I'm sorry. Did I hurt you?"

"No. It's not you. It's whatever's eating at my gut."

With Mildred following close behind, Rebecca and Tom managed to get Charles up the stairs and to his room. Mildred hurried inside and folded down his bedding. Tom and Rebecca helped lower him to the bed and lay him back.

"There you are," Mildred said, removing his shoes and jacket, then pulling the blankets over him. "I'm sure just a little rest and you'll be right as rain." The words were cheerful, but her voice sounded tight.

※

Dr. Martin placed a stethoscope on Charles's chest and listened. "Sounds a bit fast but strong." He moved the stethoscope to his stomach. His brow furrowed. He palpated Charles's abdomen, and Charles groaned. "Sorry, but it's necessary." The doctor continued probing. "Let me know where it hurts most."

"There. There," Charles said between clenched teeth. "I've never felt anything like this before. What is it?"

Dr. Martin's expression was grim. "Don't know just yet. We'll make you more comfortable though." He took a bottle of medicine from his bag, then lifted a glass of water from the nightstand. "Is this fresh?"

"Yes. We just brought it up," Mildred said.

He opened the bottle and measured two spoonfuls into the water and stirred. "Drink this," he said, holding the glass to Charles's lips. "It will ease the pain."

Charles sipped the mixture and grimaced. "Bitter," he said, lying back on the pillows.

"It will probably make you sleepy," Dr. Martin said, setting the medicine on the nightstand. He glanced at Mildred.

"Measure out two teaspoons as he needs it for pain. No more often than every three hours," he cautioned. He closed his bag and stood. "I'll be back to see you tomorrow," he said, giving Charles's arm a pat. He smiled, but his eyes were cheerless.

Mildred and Rebecca followed him out of the room.

"What's wrong with him, doctor?" Rebecca asked.

"Typhlitis, I believe."

"He'll get well, won't he?"

The doctor didn't respond immediately. "Sometimes these things resolve themselves."

"Sometimes?" Mildred asked. "And what about the rest of the time?"

Dr. Martin, who was quite tall, looked down on Mildred and rested a large hand on her shoulder. "I'm sorry, but in most cases the patient doesn't recover."

Mildred sucked in her breath and clapped a hand over her mouth.

"We'll just have to wait and see," the doctor added.

Standing board stiff, Mildred asked, "What can we expect?"

"He may gradually get better and recover. But often the patient has a spell with less pain, but it will return and become more intense. There will be nausea, increased fever, delirium . . ."

"There's nothing we can do?" Mildred asked.

"I'm sorry. Keep him as comfortable as possible. The laudanum will help him sleep."

Rebecca felt as if someone had hit her across the chest. "It's just a stomach ailment."

Dr. Martin's grave expression settled on Rebecca. "I wish I could tell you that he'll be fine, but I can't."

"How long, then?"

"A few hours. A few days. Every case is different."

As the circumstances became real, sorrow burrowed inside

45

of Rebecca. She grabbed the doctor's arm. "Please, there must be something. A specialist . . . or . . ."

"I'm sorry, there's nothing." He closed his hand over hers. "We have a mighty God. I would pray." He walked toward the staircase. "I'll let myself out."

*

Rebecca sat beside her father's bed, clasping his hand in hers. The weather had turned cold, and the chill seeped into the room. Two days had passed since the doctor's first visit. Her father's condition had not resolved itself. Instead, he'd grown sicker and now moved in and out of consciousness.

Charles opened his eyes and looked at his daughter. His voice barely more than a whisper, he said, "It's not so bad, this slipping into the Father's arms."

"Please don't talk like that. You're going to get well."

"No, I'm not." His eyelids drooped. "I've missed your mother. She's there waiting for me."

"Father, no. You're not going to die."

Charles focused on Rebecca. "Our time here is not our own. God brings us into the world, and he sees us out." He released his breath slowly with a slight moan.

"Do you need more laudanum?"

"No. I need . . . my senses about me." He struggled to concentrate. "There's something I . . . must speak to you about."

"Daddy . . ."

"Hush, now. Listen. Things aren't as . . . they seem." His breath was labored. "I've debts, serious debts."

"We can talk about all that later . . . when you're better."

"I'm not going to get better," he said with surprising ferocity.

46

Over the past two days, the light in his eyes had faded. Rebecca knew he was leaving her.

"I'm sorry," he said.

"About what?"

"I made some . . . bad investments." He sucked in a shallow breath. "I thought there would be . . . time . . . to make things right again. And now . . ." He shook his head slightly. "I'm about to leave you . . . penniless."

"I don't care about money. I just care about you. Please don't leave me." Rebecca pressed his hand to her cheek.

"I should have let you come to work for me. I'm sorry about that. At least you . . . would have had a way to make a living. Now I've left you at the mercy of society."

"You're still here. You haven't gone anywhere."

"You could teach, or marry well." He moaned and clenched his teeth.

"Daddy?"

He gazed at her. "I'm so sorry."

After that Charles slept. For two more days he seemed half in this world and half in the next. Mildred and Rebecca kept watch. The ticking of the mantel clock counted off the minutes of his life.

$$\mathcal{D}$$

The bedroom door opened with a whisper. "Rebecca, Mr. Thornton is here to see you," said Flora.

"Go ahead," Mildred said.

Rebecca gazed at her father. The laugh lines and worry lines in his face were now deeply etched. His breathing was shallow and hesitant. What if he slipped away while she was gone? "I'd rather stay."

"It's time you got some air. You've been here for hours."

Mildred looked at Flora. "Make sure she has something to eat."

Rebecca kissed her father's cheek. His skin felt damp and cool. She followed Flora out of the room. "Please don't make me anything to eat. I just couldn't manage any food right now."

"You haven't had a bite in nearly two days. You need to keep up your strength." Flora eyed Rebecca seriously. "Your father would disapprove." She stopped at the top of the stairs. "At least have a bit of broth. It will do you good."

"All right. After I speak with Daniel I'll have a little."

The tall, blond Australian stood in the foyer, hat in hand. "Rebecca. I'm so sorry to hear about your father. How is he?"

"Not well." Rebecca barely got the words out before the tears flowed. Pressing a handkerchief against her face, she whispered, "I can't stand to just sit by and watch him die. What will I do without him?"

Daniel rested a hand on her arm.

Her defenses stripped away, Rebecca grasped his hand and wept. When the tears subsided, she stepped back, embarrassed at her display. "I'm sorry. I shouldn't have done that. This isn't your affair."

"It is. I care about you and your father." He glanced at Flora as she moved past and on up the stairs. "Will you walk with me? It's a bit cold but quite refreshing. The sun and air will do you good."

Greeted by a cool breeze, Rebecca allowed herself to be escorted outside. The last of the roses had darkened and drooped as if nodding off to sleep. Only one had escaped the damage of the freezing air. Rebecca stopped and smelled it, but the fragrance had grown feeble.

"I'm right sorry, Rebecca."

"He's been everything to me." Fresh tears welled up, and she wiped them away. "I can't imagine life without him."

"If there's anything I can do . . . I want to help."

Rebecca looked at him, anger flaring at the futility of the offer. "Thank you, but you can't *do* anything. There's nothing any of us can do." She glanced at the house. "I'd better go back. Thank you for coming."

Daniel acted as if he would say more, but instead, he simply tipped his head in quiet acknowledgment, and Rebecca returned to the house.

✦

It seemed all of Boston turned out for Charles's funeral. He'd been well liked and respected. Words of comfort and affection could not ease Rebecca's pain. In a mournful fog she moved through the day, doing what was required of her.

In spite of her sorrow, she had to face her father's financial deficiencies. Sitting across from the family attorney, she discovered that a large number of her father's clients had never paid him, and although he was a fine lawyer, he was not a skilled financier and had made a number of bad investments. The Williams estate was in ruins.

The house and property would be sold, the family possessions auctioned off.

✦

Rebecca wandered to the stables. When she approached Chavive's stall, the horse thrust her head out over the gate. Her large brown eyes seemed to understand Rebecca's heartache. Rebecca reached into a pocket and pulled out a quartered apple and offered it to the mare. Head bouncing, Chavive munched, then nuzzled Rebecca, who pressed her forehead against the mare's face. The ever-present pain in her chest intensified. Tomorrow Chavive would go to her new family. "I will miss you so much," she whispered.

Daniel scanned the telegram a second time. "Urgent. Red water. Return home immediately." It was signed "Bertram Thornton."

Daniel clenched his teeth in frustration. Red water was a devastating disease that could destroy their herds, but his presence wasn't vital. There were others who could help. He squared his jaw and folded the telegram.

I have to go. He'll accept nothing less. But what about Rebecca? She needs me. For days his mind had been filled with nothing but her. In the weeks since her father's death, he'd sought her out on several occasions, and he believed they'd formed a true and lasting friendship. He'd hoped that in time something more might develop between them. He wasn't certain that he didn't already love her. He admired her—not just her beauty but her strength, knowledge, and indomitable spirit.

His mind returned to his father. He'd wanted Daniel to marry Meghan Linnell. Although they had been friends since childhood, Daniel had never thought of her as a good match. If he brought home a bride, he'd be free of his father's expectations.

Rebecca had no future in Boston. She and her aunt now lived with Mildred's sister and brother-in-law and their five children. Rebecca was trying to make the best of it, but he knew she felt wretched. Her father and her dreams had been snatched from her, leaving few options—marry well or become a teacher or a companion.

He slid the telegram into his coat pocket and settled his

hat on his head. He needed more time. "Lord in heaven," he said, "I can't stay and I can't go. Tell me what to do." He closed his eyes. Rebecca didn't love him, and he wasn't certain his feelings were anything more than infatuation, yet they complemented each other. He was certain they could make a go of it. He could offer her better than Boston.

Rebecca was used to the best. How would she see Queensland? Living on the station wasn't grand, but she'd be free of the societal constraints of Boston and the misery of being a poor relation taken in out of necessity. She would be good for the station—bringing innovation and a new depth of knowledge to Douloo.

His mind flickered to his father. He'd be angry. And the constraints he could press upon Rebecca might be worse than what she now faced. He hadn't even acknowledged his eldest son's death. Still, Daniel hoped he could do better by her. He was certain that the longing he felt for Rebecca would only intensify if a continent and an ocean lay between them.

He would marry her. He had to make her see that there was no other alternative.

5

Daniel stepped over a log that had washed up on the beach, then took Rebecca's hand to assist her. She stopped and stood atop the bleached-out tree, gazing at the curl of fog moving ashore.

Daniel felt the ache that showed on her face but was helpless to relieve her sorrow. Such grief could only be privately reconciled.

Finally, clutching her skirt in one hand, Rebecca stepped off the log and onto the rocky beach. Her breath fogged in the cold bay air as she moved along the seashore. With a shiver, she huddled deeper into her fur-lined coat.

"You cold?" Daniel asked. "We can go back if you like."

"No. I'm fine. It's difficult to believe that yesterday it was fair and warm. Today it feels like winter."

"Back home in Queensland it's heating up. We're coming into summer."

"Strange to realize our seasons are opposite each other." Rebecca bent and picked up a smooth, flat stone. "Thank you for rescuing me from my cousins." She nearly smiled.

"Tough, eh?"

"Yes. It's not that they're ill-mannered, but sometimes the house is in pandemonium. At those times, I'd like to be almost anywhere else." She tossed the stone into the surf. "Sometimes I feel as if I've been thrown into prison. My aunt and uncle are good people, but five children in such a small house is simply too much." She sighed. "The idea of teaching and living in a boarding house . . ." She shook her head. "I can't stay where I am. In spite of their kindness, I know I'm a burden to them."

"I dare say, you'll be better off when you can find an appointment of your own."

"The word *appointment* sounds horrid. I have a vision of ending up as a nanny for some upper-class family with a handful of spoiled children." She shuddered. "And poor Aunt Mildred. What's to become of her? She hasn't any alternative but to stay."

"I'm sorry, Rebecca." Daniel pulled the telegram out of his pocket. "I . . . heard from my father. He needs me at home. So I'll be on my way soon."

"You're leaving?" Rebecca's voice held true disappointment.

Daniel nodded, wondering if she might care for him more deeply than he'd thought.

"I'll miss you. You've been a good friend to me these last weeks." Her eyes filled with tears. "My father liked you—he told me so."

Using his thumb, Daniel gently wiped moisture from her cheeks. "He was a fine bloke."

Managing a tremulous smile, Rebecca turned and continued walking.

"So you'll go into teaching, then?"

"I don't suppose I have any other choice. It's the only thing a woman can do other than be a seamstress or nanny. And no one would want something I'd sewn." She sighed. "It's not fair—being a woman. Our choices are made for us, and even those are few."

"You're right there." Daniel stopped. "There might be another choice for you."

Rebecca stared at him, her dark eyes wide. "And what might that be?"

"Come to Queensland."

"What? But I couldn't . . ."

"Marry me. I'll take care of you. Douloo is a fine place. You'd be happy there. Women still struggle some like they do everywhere, but I'd say they're given a fair go of it. And there's enough open country that everyone can feel free."

"You're serious?"

"Never more."

"But, Daniel, we're . . . only friends."

"I care for you deeply. And in time . . . Well, in time one never knows. I've not known anyone like you—educated and genteel but gutsy—like a true Australian. You'd do well there."

"Australia? I must say, the idea has appeal. But what will I do about my aunt Mildred? I can't leave her."

"We can take her along."

"Oh no. She'd never go. She was born in New England, and she'll die here."

Rebecca turned serious eyes on Daniel. "I think very highly of you . . . but I don't love you." She picked up a small, broken shell and studied it. "We'd have a marriage of convenience. Is that what you want?"

"How do you know it would be like that? We're grand friends, and maybe we could be more. We've had a fine time together."

"I can't decide just like that. I need time."

"I haven't much time to give you. My father's counting on me to come right away."

Rebecca took a deep breath. "Can I let you know tomorrow?"

"Of course."

⑤

Rebecca was thankful for the quiet of the garden. Living among such a large family meant there were few moments of serenity. She walked beside her aunt Mildred, wondering just how she would tell her about Daniel's proposal. It seemed outlandish, and yet marriages of convenience happened every day. She might as well just come out with it.

"Auntie," Rebecca said softly, "Daniel's asked me to marry him."

Mildred raised an eyebrow and continued walking. "It's lovely having the children away at school."

"Yes." Rebecca placed a hand on her aunt's arm. "I'm not sure what to do."

Mildred stopped. "Do you love him?"

"No. I like him very much though."

Mildred moved toward a heavy-bodied oak. "Love is too highly rated." She brushed leaves from a bench and sat. "Daniel's a fine man."

Rebecca sat beside her. "If I did marry him, would you consider coming with us? I can't imagine going off to the other side of the world and leaving you here. I know he'd welcome you. In fact, he suggested that you might like to join us."

"No. I won't leave Boston. This is my home. I'll do quite well right here with my sister. She needs me, what with all the children and her charity activities." Mildred reached for Rebecca's hand. "It's your turn for an adventure. You'll be off to a new land, a new life." Her eyes turned sad. "I'll miss you, but . . ."

"I don't even know if I want to go. All I do know is that I don't want to depend on my aunt and uncle, and I don't want to become a schoolteacher or some woman's companion. I want more."

"You always have."

Rebecca looked at her hands. "Why did Father have to die?"

"Death is part of life—a preset engagement each of us has with our Creator. Who are we to argue with providence?" Mildred smiled. "I miss Charles, but I know he's right where he belongs. And I believe he would have approved of a marriage between you and Daniel. He thought a lot of that young man. His father's holdings are extensive—so you would be well married. That would be a comfort to your father and to me. Charles always admired your mother's sense of adventure—this would be your adventure." She studied Rebecca. "Audrey was beautiful and headstrong, just like you."

"I never truly planned on marrying. Whenever it did enter my mind I always thought that if it happened it would be with someone I love."

"Many couples begin without love, but over time it can grow. There's no reason to believe that won't happen for you and Daniel."

"I'd be so far away. I'd miss you terribly."

Mildred compressed her thin lips. "And I'd miss you. But there is one fact we cannot change in this life—we're women, and we must be practical. I would say you should count your blessings—a handsome man who is financially well off and clearly well mannered and kind wants to marry you. It could be worse."

"So you're saying I ought to marry him?"

Mildred watched a bee move among the fading garden. "I believe you should consider it. But . . . only you can decide what is right for you." She circled an arm around Rebecca's shoulders and offered a sympathetic smile. "However, necessity is often our guide."

⌘

Rebecca loathed her lack of choices. It was all so unfair. She should have been born a man. She tried to imagine life as Daniel's wife. The picture wasn't so terrible. He was handsome and kind. The time they'd spent together had been pleasant. Mildred's words echoed in her mind: *You could do worse.*

Maybe women in Australia have more freedom to be who they are, she thought. She looked about the comfortable but tiny room with its flowered wallpaper and very small window that peeked out from beneath the eves. She walked to the window and looked down on the tidy yard. It wasn't her yard, and this wasn't her house. The idea of an Australian adventure was appealing. If she lived in Queensland, she wouldn't be restricted by Boston's societal guidelines.

Her thoughts wandered to Daniel. As her husband he would have the right to rule her life. The idea grated. But what better prospects did she have? He'd told her life at Douloo wasn't dull; at least she would have something to look forward to. Rebecca closed her eyes. *Father, what should I do?* The sting of his absence brought tears. *I need to know what to do. Please tell me.*

⌘

Rebecca sat on a garden bench, fall sunshine warming her, and waited for Daniel to finish speaking to her uncle. She imagined the meeting in the library—her serious-minded uncle grilling Daniel while hoping for a way out of his obligation to his niece. And Daniel—would he present a case of devotion or pity? She cringed inwardly. If only there were some other way.

Footsteps clicked on the cobblestone walkway. Rebecca didn't look up. She knew it was him. Shiny black boots stopped directly in front of her. She forced her eyes upward.

Daniel looked down at her. "May I sit?"

"Yes, please." Rebecca scooted to the left of the bench to offer more room. Her heart thudded. She still wasn't certain what her answer would be.

"I might as well come right to it, then. I spoke to your uncle, and he's given me his blessing."

Rebecca willed herself to look at Daniel. He was quite handsome, with a strong, square jaw, startling blue eyes, and blond hair that needed a cut. He looked at her with compassion. *He's asking me out of pity. Well, I won't have it.*

"Will you marry me?"

"Why do you want to marry me, Daniel?"

He hesitated, then said, "I think highly of you—your strength of character is admirable. You'll make a fine wife and a good mother to my children."

"I have nothing of consequence to bring into a marriage."

"You have yourself. And that's enough."

Rebecca pulled out a handkerchief that had been tucked inside her sleeve. "I've given your proposal much thought." She twisted the handkerchief. "And I find myself in a quandary. As you well know, I never planned to marry—I had much higher aspirations. I doubt I'll make a good wife."

"You belittle yourself unnecessarily. I will be proud to have you on my arm." Daniel offered a warm smile.

For a moment Rebecca thought maybe she could love Daniel. She squared her shoulders. "I won't be told what to do."

"I believe God asked husbands to love their wives, not order them about. I will do my best to respect your ideals."

58

Rebecca turned her attention to a tiny bird flitting from branch to branch on a nearby bush. Why hadn't he flown south? Soon winter would arrive and he'd be trapped here, dependent on the few crumbs offered by the kindhearted. What of her? If she remained while Daniel sailed away, would she face the same kind of cruel reality?

She looked straight into his eyes. "All right. I'll marry you. And I'll do my best to honor you as a wife."

☉

Even with a sleeper car, the nine-day trek across the States was exhausting and agonizing to the body. The tiny bed was lumpy and hard, the room cramped, and the food barely tolerable. But Rebecca dared not complain, not even to herself, for each time she made a trip to the dining car she was reminded of her good fortune. Passengers in coach sat on hard benches with no place to lay their heads, and many of the women tended fidgety, cranky children.

Mile after mile clipped by. For the first time Rebecca understood the vastness of America. She'd never traveled so far overland, and the immensity of the country astonished her. When Daniel explained that the empty plains reminded him of home, she was not reassured. The open prairies gave her an uncomfortable sensation of space and lack of restraint. Strangely, these were things she'd always thought she wanted.

Beyond the plains, the train chugged over rugged mountains, rattled across wooden trestles, and clattered through dark forests. In spite of the circumstances, Rebecca found herself eagerly studying antelope, buffalo, and a strange-looking bird called a prairie chicken. They hadn't yet left the United States, and already the adventure had begun.

Although she didn't love Daniel, she believed it wrong to

59

withhold any part of herself from him. The vows exchanged were made before God and were not to be taken lightly. She'd faced their first evening together as husband and wife with trepidation, but the intimate bonding with Daniel had taken her by surprise. It had not been altogether unpleasant, and she'd been amazed to discover a passionate part of herself she'd not known existed. Still, she continued to feel awkward and unlike a wife.

When they arrived in San Francisco, Rebecca was too exhausted to take in the sights of the impressive city. She went straight to their hotel room and slept—fourteen hours straight. However, before boarding the ship, they walked the streets of the largest city on the West Coast, rode a cable car to the top of Nob Hill, where impressive mansions looked down on San Francisco Bay, and dined at an exquisite restaurant overlooking the harbor. She'd never expected San Francisco to be so cosmopolitan.

As the days passed, Rebecca tried to pry more information from Daniel about his family, but he said little, especially about his father. She felt a growing anxiety about her father-in-law. She wanted and needed a father now and was curious about the man who was to take that role in her life. Was Daniel hiding something? Fear of what that might be settled in the back of Rebecca's mind, where it lay coiled like a snake waiting to strike.

✲

The day to sail arrived, and Rebecca felt a tug of fear and sorrow. Now that her new life prepared to carry her away, she didn't feel ready to say farewell to the old one. She wished she hadn't married Daniel. What was she stepping into?

The steamer that would carry them across the Pacific sat

alongside the pier, looking magnificent. It gleamed beneath a bright California sun.

"This is amazing," Rebecca said as they boarded.

"Only the best for my wife."

"Passage must be very expensive."

"It is. But no worries. We've plenty of money."

"As you have said. But I'm becoming more and more curious about the station and our home. Is it so lavish?"

"The house is grand but not as extravagant as this. We have the finest cattle in the district and the best horses. You won't be disappointed." He grinned.

"You said it's called Douloo. What does that mean?"

"It's Greek, a biblical term. My grandfather was very religious. It means 'to be subjugated to,' like a bond of mutual support, or it can mean 'bondage.' We and the land belong to each other. We try to make the land submit, but in truth it's us who must submit to it."

"That's very interesting," Rebecca said, feeling unsettled.

Rebecca and Daniel followed a porter to their room. It was the most luxurious ship Rebecca had ever seen. She'd traveled abroad before but never on such a beautiful ocean liner. The promenade deck was wide and spacious, with lounge chairs lined up along the bulkhead. She managed to peek inside a dining saloon as they passed. It was elegant and large. Crystal had been set out on lace-covered tables surrounded by red velvet, cushioned chairs. There were pilasters and brackets of teak, which had been notched with gold leaf, and crystal lamps bathed it all in a soft glow.

Their spacious stateroom was tastefully furnished and was supplied with hot and cold running water. Putting her hand under a stream of warm water, Rebecca chuckled. "Why, I never! I can't wait to write Aunt Mildred."

"I'm happy it suits you," Daniel said. "The advertisement said it was built to indulge the tastes of the very wealthy."

Rebecca turned off the tap, wondering just what waited for her in Queensland. How rich was Daniel's family? She felt a shiver of trepidation. She'd been raised well, but her father had worked to earn his position. There was no powerful family behind him. The kind of wealth Daniel seemed to have shouted of old money, which often came with strong family ties. What would they think of their son marrying a woman without means?

When the ship steamed out of San Francisco Bay, Rebecca and Daniel stood on deck, the wind catching at their hair and salt spray wetting their lips. Daniel rested an arm about Rebecca's waist. She wished he wouldn't. The gesture felt possessive. She fought the impulse to pull away. After all, he had a husband's right to hold her.

The city grew small and finally disappeared into the hill-sides. Sudden fear swept away her excitement at the thought of a new beginning. She had a sense of being cut off from her world. What if she wasn't up to the trials ahead? What if she hated being Daniel's wife? And what of Daniel's family? Why wouldn't he talk about his father?

Their first night at sea revealed a more relaxed Daniel. It was as if he became Australian the moment his feet left American soil. After seating himself across from Rebecca at an elegantly laid table, he talked about Australia and life on the station.

"It's a land like none you've ever seen. Queensland has everything you could want. Along the coast there are tropical forests with brightly colored and noisy birds. Brisbane and Sydney are grand cities. Sydney's a fair way to travel though, so we rarely go there.

"Brisbane's on the east side of the mountains, and once we move west from the coast there are lots of eucalypts and pines. I fear the pines won't last. Blokes are cutting 'em down nearly as fast as they sprout." He picked up a cup of tea. "On the other side of the mountains are the flats—broad, open plains. The station's out there. We can ride often."

"I would like that." Rebecca stirred sugar into her tea. It was stronger than what she was used to.

"We've a mob of horses to choose from. You can pick your own."

"That will be nice. But I can't imagine ever replacing Chavive. I miss her," she said, suddenly finding herself holding back tears.

Daniel leaned across the table and took her hand. "You'll soon have another horse. I promise."

Rebecca didn't like the contact and pulled her hand free.

Daniel straightened. "I'm sorry. I don't mean to be forward."

"It will just take time, Daniel. I'm not used to having a husband." Using her handkerchief, she dabbed at her eyes. "And just the thought of Chavive brought back memories." She took a deep breath. "I'm sorry."

"No need to apologize. It hasn't been that long since you lost your father and everything that mattered to you. And of course you aren't used to being a wife."

"I'll try to do better." She brushed away the wetness on her cheeks.

"No worries. You'll soon fall in love with Australia. You'll see."

"I hope you're right."

"Mum will make you feel right at home. She has a way about her."

"I can't wait to meet her . . . and your father."

Daniel made no reply, but a shadow touched his eyes, leaving Rebecca wondering why.

$\mathcal{D}$

She couldn't pinpoint the exact day the weather warmed or when the color of the sea changed. Maybe it had happened so gradually that one wouldn't have noticed. But Rebecca liked the transformation—wraps were no longer necessary while strolling the promenade, and the seas were an iridescent blue.

One morning while wandering along the deck, she spotted land. So did many others, and anticipation spread throughout the ship. People gathered, watching and waiting.

Daniel stood beside Rebecca, but he didn't touch her. They gazed at the tropical foliage hugging the shoreline and reflecting off the blue sea. The colors were vibrant.

"You didn't tell me it was so beautiful. I had no idea." Leaning on the railing, Rebecca looked down through clear waters and studied sea plants swaying in the currents and bright fish darting among foliage and rocks.

When they entered Moreton Bay, porpoises danced alongside the ship, chattering. Their merriment eased the last of Rebecca's jitters.

"Where is Brisbane?" she asked Daniel.

"It's up the river a ways," he said, pointing to a river that flowed into the bay.

Anchor chains clanked while being lowered. Closing her eyes, she breathed deeply. *Lord, I pray I've done the right thing.* She looked skyward. A white-breasted sea eagle soared. Its heavy wings beat the air, and it glided upon invisible currents.

Only miles away her new life waited. It was time to begin.

6

A crewman lifted the oars out of the water, and the boat glided toward the dock. "'Ere we are, safe and sound, eh?"

Moving toward the bow of the boat, Daniel made his way through other passengers. "I'll tie 'er up for you." He grasped a rope secured to the front of the boat and waited until the small craft bumped the pier, then reached out and grabbed hold of a wooden pylon, quickly looped the rope around it, and tied it off. He leapt onto the dock, caught another rope tossed by the oarsman, and secured the back of the boat.

"Ya do that as if ya'd been out ta sea a bit of yer life, lad."

"I've made this trip often enough." Daniel straightened and gazed at the opposite bank of the Brisbane River. A brisk wind buffeted foliage crowding the shore. "Glad to be home . . . well, nearly home."

Daniel helped passengers disembark while Rebecca patiently kept her seat. Finally, when all the others were off, Daniel smiled at his wife and offered her his hand. "Right, then. Let me give you a hand, ma'am." He grinned.

Holding her bonnet secure, Rebecca allowed him to assist her from the pitching boat. Once planted on the wharf, she was obligated to keep hold of him. She felt as if she were still rocking, and her legs were wobbly.

"I suppose it will take me a while to get used to being off the ship." She gazed at red brick buildings crowding the street above the pier. "So this is Brisbane. It's larger than I expected . . . and modern looking."

"It's a first-rate city all right," Daniel said, wearing a broad smile.

"Thanks for yer help, mate," the crewman said, handing up Daniel and Rebecca's baggage.

"Glad to be of help." Daniel grasped two bags in one hand and one in the other. "They'll send on the rest of our things, then?"

"They'll be unloaded tonight and sent on over ta yer hotel, lad." The oarsman smoothed an overlarge mustache. "Ya been abroad?"

"Yes. Business in the States. And I picked up a bride while I was there." Daniel chuckled and hugged Rebecca with one arm.

An immediate blush heated Rebecca's face. "I wasn't just picked up . . ."

"Wal, of course not . . . ," the sailor said with a snicker.

"Nearly." Daniel grinned.

"Actually, it was all quite proper. You see . . ."

"Ah, don't worry 'bout it, lydie. As long as ya found each other . . . that's all that matters, eh?" The crewman tipped his cap. "Time I got back." He untied the ropes and pushed off. "Yer things will be brought 'round ta ya before dark. I'll make sure they're sent directly ta yer rooms."

"Thank you," Rebecca said, still wishing she could explain how she and Daniel had met. If only she could say they'd fallen in love.

She turned to Daniel. "You embarrassed me. You made it sound as if I were some little . . . strumpet."

"He knows better. It's obvious you're a lady." He kissed her cheek.

Rebecca felt uncomfortable with the familiarity.

"I'm sorry. Didn't mean to embarrass you." He glanced at the buildings along the quay. "Would you like to see some of the city before going to the hotel?"

"Yes . . . ," Rebecca said hesitantly, opening a small umbrella to ward off the sun. "Thank goodness for the breeze. It's awfully warm and humid."

"Right. It's always a bit sultry in these parts. Once we're over the mountains it won't be so bad." He turned and looked toward the street. "Come on, then." Juggling the luggage, he stepped toward the road.

"I'll carry one of those," Rebecca said.

"No worries. I've got it."

"I'm capable of helping. And you obviously have more than is comfortable. Please, let me help." She stopped and waited. "Why is it that men always have to be so gallant?"

"They don't always." Daniel sized her up. "And I guess you're quite able to help." He shifted the luggage. "Here you go, then," he said, handing her the smallest bag.

After stowing the baggage in the back of a carriage, Daniel helped Rebecca into a sturdy, but otherwise outdated, coach. A matched pair of stout horses stood calmly in the harness. The driver flicked the reins, and they plodded forward. *No doubt the heat has the animals worn down*, Rebecca thought as they moved through the streets of Brisbane.

They passed a three-story wood-paneled building with a broad veranda. An assortment of green plants provided ample shade. "Brisbane is quite civilized and lovely. Not exactly what I expected."

"What did you expect?"

"I'm not sure, really." Summoning her best Australian accent, she added, "I think I might quite like it 'ere."

"Roight, ya will," Daniel said. "But if ya want to become a local ya'll 'ave ta work on yer accent." He grinned, then looking at the house, he said, "Douloo isn't anything like Brisbane."

"Of course. I know that," Rebecca said, wishing it were. "This is a beautiful place though."

"Right. It is. And so is Douloo. You'll see."

☙

Rebecca didn't sleep well that night. Having grown accustomed to the movement of the ship, she thought it might be the stillness. More likely it was nerves. She would soon discover the truth about the life she'd chosen. The unknowns frightened her. After all, life on the station would be nothing like life in Boston. She'd done her share of traveling, but each new and interesting locale had always been temporary; this change would be permanent. And she'd face it with a man she knew only slightly and didn't love.

Heavy, broad-leafed plants outside their open window chafed in the breeze. That along with the cooler evening air finally soothed Rebecca into slumber.

☙

The following morning Daniel held Rebecca's hand as they stepped out of the hotel. Rebecca wished he was less demonstrative. After all, they were not the loving couple.

She breathed deeply, aware of an unfamiliar, sharp fragrance. The pace of the city seemed casual and unhurried compared to Boston. Rebecca liked that.

Travelers waited at an unpretentious train depot. People chatted amiably as if they were old friends. Boarding was done in a leisurely manner, yet everyone managed to get aboard before the train was scheduled to leave.

The coaches were even more uncomfortable than those in the States. Dust coated windowsills and the backs of shabby seats. They would travel by train to Jondaryan, then make the remainder of the four-hundred-kilometer trip by stagecoach. Rebecca felt shaky inside—anticipation and fear mingling.

"So are you ready to give it a go?" Daniel smiled encouragement.

"I'm looking forward to seeing your home."

"Our home."

Rebecca dusted off a seat. "I must admit to being a little nervous about meeting your family. After all, we married in such a hurry. I hope your father approves."

"Not to worry," Daniel said, but uncertainty lay behind his eyes. "Mum will take you into her heart. And if anyone can thaw out my father, it's you."

Apprehension swept through Rebecca as she sat on the stiff bench seat. She'd hoped that having a father-in-law would soften the pain of her own father's death. "What do you mean 'thaw'?"

"It's just that he can be a bit . . . severe from time to time."

Rebecca's anxiety grew. "You never talk about him. Please, tell me what he's like."

"He's a decent bloke. Everyone in the district admires him. And—"

The train jolted forward.

Without thought to his language, someone from the back of the car shouted his annoyance at the spilled luggage.

"Watch yer mouth," another man hollered.

Daniel rested a hand on Rebecca's arm. "Sorry, some blokes don't know how to mind their manners."

"It's all right," Rebecca said. And she meant it. She found the earthiness refreshing. The grime was another matter. She ran a finger along the edge of the windowsill, leaving a trail. "There's an awful lot of dust, don't you think?"

"That's the way of it 'round 'ere."

"I don't understand. It's lovely and green. Where is the dust coming from?"

"The train travels over the Great Dividing Range. On the other side it's a bit dry. But grand all the same—with its open spaces."

Rebecca wasn't sure she liked the idea of having a dry, open environment for a home. And the idea of a cantankerous father-in-law set her on edge. What if he disliked her, especially since she and Daniel had married in such a hurry?

The train moved out of the station. With regret Rebecca watched spacious homes with their broad verandas swamped with greenery disappear. Almost immediately the train plunged into a heavy forest.

"Is it all right if I open the window?" Rebecca asked. "That way I'll be able to see better."

"Why not," Daniel said, standing up and sliding open the filthy window. "After we get over the mountains it'll heat up a bit, and the fresh air will do us good."

The forest was an odd mix of tropical plants, curious-looking evergreens, and cedar. "I didn't expect to see cedar trees. They remind me of home."

"I'm partial to the cedars, but loggers are having a real go at them; I figure they'll be gone one day."

"They're beautiful." Rebecca pointed at a tree with smooth, nearly white bark and bunches of long, slender leaves. "What is that? I've never seen anything like it. It's splendid."

"It's a gum tree, or a eucalypt. We have more of those than just about anything, I'd say. Out on the flats they're not nearly so tall or full, and their bark can be very white—we call them ghost gums. On this side of the mountains they fare a bit better. You can smell them. Sometimes you can see a blue haze over the mountains—that's from the eucalypts."

The train continued inland and began to climb. Rebecca

was so taken by the surroundings, she forgot to worry about her new home and family. They traveled above the heavy forest. Below, the land looked like a lumpy green mat that rolled all the way to the ocean. Trees teemed with birds. Some had feathers that looked as if they'd been set afire; others wore deep blue cloaks. The air was alive with their squawks and shrieking calls. One variety was large, with white and gray feathers that looked like glossy coats covering the heavy bodies. Rebecca wished she could touch them to see how the plumage felt.

"I like it here," she said, exhilarated by the stimulating and interesting surroundings.

Daniel said nothing but smiled.

Rebecca settled back. Maybe living in Australia wouldn't be as challenging as she'd feared. It was different from home but fascinating. And Daniel had proved to be accommodating and kind.

They continued to climb. The train slowed, chugging as it covered the last miles to the mountain's crest. Rebecca worried they'd be forced to lighten their load by discharging passengers.

"Have a look at that," Daniel said as they rounded a bend. He pointed at giant boulders precariously balancing on one another. "Amazing, isn't it?"

"How do you suppose they got like that?"

"I figure God placed them there, but the blacks have their own tales. Woodman can tell you 'bout them."

"Woodman?"

"He's a half caste who works on the station. He's been there forever."

"What do you mean 'half caste'?"

"He's part black and part white. Good bloke though. He grew up on Douloo." Daniel studied the boulders. "Once when I was a lad, he took me on walkabout with him. When we needed water he went right to a water hole lying hidden in some rocks. All the blacks know 'bout them. When they go on walkabout they count on watering holes." He nudged his shoulders back. "I'm one of the few whites who knows 'bout the ones Woodman showed me."

"Why don't whites know about them?"

"Blacks and whites keep to themselves. They don't mix . . . and the blacks don't trust whites with their secrets."

"Why?"

"Just the way of it. Kind of like in America. Blacks don't like whites, and whites don't much like blacks. I'd say it's good to keep the races separate, eh?"

"I suppose so," Rebecca said tentatively. "But there's probably a lot we can learn from each other. Like the things Woodman taught you."

"He's different. Woodman's been on the station so long he's nearly like family. My father and him were chums." Daniel shrugged. "There's no reason to change the way things are between whites and blacks."

"I disagree." Rebecca met his eyes with a challenge.

"Now, don't go mixing things up. You'll only make trouble for yourself. 'Round 'ere the blacks have their place."

Rebecca was taken aback. She hadn't expected Daniel to be intolerant. "Don't you think change can be good?"

"Sometimes, but then again there are things a fella needs to leave alone. The blacks aren't a bad lot, but trying to change the order of things just causes trouble."

Rebecca knew now was not the time or place to have a discussion about such ideas. There would be time later. Instead, she asked, "What's a walkabout?"

"Well, it's when a black just up and leaves. They walk from place to place, sometimes for weeks or even months."

"Why?"

"I think they're searching for something . . . new experiences, a change of mind. Some of them are following song lines or something . . . it's in their souls."

"They just leave whenever they want?"

"Right." Daniel grinned. "We're used to it."

"What about their families, their jobs?"

"It's part of life for them. Even my father lets the workers go, and he's glad to have them back when they're done wandering."

"Seems strange."

"To us maybe, but the blacks know what they're doing." He shook his head. "Sometimes they leave in the middle of a job, and when they get back they take up right where they left off."

The train crested the mountains, and Rebecca turned and looked out the window. A broad plain stretched out below, disappearing into a hazy expanse. The air became discernibly hotter and dryer. The forests faded away, leaving a mix of brown grasses, gum trees, and brush. Patches of green dotted the flatlands. "What are the green areas?"

"Farms. They're properties that grow mostly vegetables."

"Do you have a farm?"

"No, we have a station. But we grow vegetables for our own use. There's not much water, but the land is good for grazing. That's why we raise cattle. Some stations have sheep. When my grandfather settled 'ere he decided to have a go at cattle. It was a right good decision too. We have the most prosperous place in the district."

"So your father decided to do the same, then?"

"No deciding to it. He did what his father did. No other course."

"A man should have a choice."

"My grandfather's blood and sweat went into making a go of things." He shook his head. "How could a son let a father's work die?"

Rebecca was reminded of her new father-in-law, and her stomach quailed. "You were going to tell me about your father."

Daniel glanced across the aisle at a chap sleeping with his chin resting on his chest. "He's a good man. Works hard and expects his family and his stockmen to do the same. There's nothing foolhardy about his running of the place. And he's a godly man, lives by the Bible. He watches out for everyone in the district, especially his family."

Although Daniel's words were complimentary, his voice lacked conviction and warmth. Something wasn't right.

⫯

The train made a short stop in Toowoomba, then hurried on to Jondaryan, a small community that sprang up because of the wool industry. Sheep were sheared there and the wool shipped out by train.

When Rebecca stepped off the train, she hoped for a reprieve from the oppressive heat, but there was none—no cooling breezes. "Is it always this hot?"

"This time of year, yes. And it'll be hotter out there." Squinting, Daniel nodded toward the west. "When we get farther out on the flats, it'll heat up." He grinned. "You'll get used to it."

Fanning herself, Rebecca doubted that.

After eating a light lunch, Rebecca and Daniel joined three others who were also traveling west. The small group waited in front of the only hotel. They'd barely arrived when a stagecoach moved down the street, pulled by two sets of horses. Dust enveloped it and continued to swirl about after it stopped.

An ill-tempered driver climbed down from the high seat.

Loading luggage, he said, "Ya better git on in. I got a schedule ta keep. Not even time enough for a middie," he grumbled.

Daniel helped Rebecca inside. "What's a middie?" she whispered, thinking that sometimes the Australian language wasn't English at all.

Daniel chuckled. "It's a medium-size beer. He's complaining because he's got to keep traveling—no time for refreshment." He grinned. Then, watching the driver through a window, he added, "Poor bloke. Probably choking on dust most days."

A couple in their middle years, a heavyset woman and her sparse-looking husband, sat across from Daniel and Rebecca. A man with a heavy beard and in need of a bath settled himself beside the older pair. He stared at Rebecca until she felt uncomfortable. She was glad when he turned his eyes outside as the coach lurched away from the hotel.

Rebecca was thankful for the movement. At least the hot air could circulate. She rearranged her skirts, wishing she could abandon her undergarments. She noticed that most women wore lightweight cotton dresses here. She'd have to make changes in her wardrobe. Exhausted, she longed to lean against Daniel and doze. Instead, she asked, "How much farther is it?"

"Nearly three hundred kilometers."

"I mean in miles."

"Two hundred or so."

Rebecca couldn't repress a groan. "How long will it take?"

"We'll be on the road all of today and two more days. There'll be places to stop for tea and something to eat and a bit of time for sleep."

Hot, dusty air suffocated, the springs in the seat pinched, and the coach rocked crazily. How would she tolerate three days of travel in this torture chamber? She closed her eyes, hoping sleep might blot out the discomfort.

"Won't do ya much good ta sleep," the man with the beard

said. "I swear these contraptions weren't meant for humans." He laughed, and Rebecca was reminded of a hen cackling over a freshly laid egg.

"Where ya from?" the man asked, peering at her through small blue eyes.

"Boston."

"America?"

She nodded.

"I could see that. A Yank." He laughed again, showing rotted teeth. "Wal, I'm from nowhere. Bushie I am." He gave his head a solid nod. "And what would a gal from Boston be doin' out 'ere?"

"My husband lives here." She glanced at Daniel.

"Wal, good ta meet ya. Name's Spud."

"Rebecca Thornton. This is my husband, Daniel."

Spud's eyes widened. The older couple leaned forward slightly, seeming interested. "A Thornton, eh?"

"Yes. Daniel Thornton. Good to meet you, Spud." Daniel offered his hand.

"Wal, I never thought I'd ride in a coach with a Thornton." Shaking Daniel's hand, the bushie looked genuinely pleased.

"It's an honor ta meet ya," the other man said. "I'm Carl Gray, and this is me missus, Lorraine."

"Nice to make yer acquaintance," Lorraine said.

"Yer father's Bertram Thornton?" Carl asked.

"That he is."

"Heard he's a good man."

"Honorable is what I heard. Ya must be roight proud," Lorraine said. "He's a help to the district."

"I'm proud of him, that's true." Daniel glanced down at Rebecca, then turned his eyes outdoors and gazed at the thirsty plain.

Rebecca's anxiety intensified. Who were the Thorntons

that strangers knew about them? *I'll find out soon enough*, she thought and leaned her head back, closing her eyes and feigning sleep.

⁂

Miles passed. Farms with vegetable patches and dark soil fell away. The land became wild and barren. Rebecca searched the emptiness for life, but there was little more than scrub and an occasional dwarfed gum tree. It wasn't anything like Brisbane. From time to time there was a windmill or farm-house and what Daniel explained were shepherd's huts. These were small huts built of wood.

The grasses in Toowoomba had been brown but tall and thick, and the gum trees green. Here the grasses were short and there were patches of bare earth where dirt swirled up and mingled with the dust raised by the horses and the wagon. Rebecca could taste the dust, and the desire for water became an affliction.

The coach rocked and bumped, and what little breeze was raised only carried in more dust. Rebecca felt sick. Her tongue stuck to the roof of her mouth, and she wondered how long it would be before they stopped for refreshment.

As she gazed at the naked plains, the fear that she'd made a mistake grew until Rebecca knew she shouldn't have come. She and Daniel shouldn't have married. She glanced at her husband. He was a good man. Pushing aside her disturbing thoughts, she imagined cool, damp forests like the ones at home and felt slightly better.

"What ya smiling 'bout, missy?" Spud asked.

Rebecca didn't realize she'd been smiling. "Oh, I was just thinking." She removed her hat and smoothed her damp hair, then dabbed at her moist face and neck with a handkerchief. "How much longer until we stop?"

"Not far. Mrs. Sullivan will have bread and stew waiting for us, and a bed too." Daniel rested a hand on Rebecca's arm. "You all right?"

Rebecca nodded. Then, taking in a tight breath, she said, "Just tired and thirsty."

"Ya'll get used ta it," Spud said. "Anyway, ya better or ya'll be takin' the next ship home."

Fighting gloom, Rebecca asked Daniel, "At the station is it like this?"

"Yes, but there are trees, and Mum keeps a garden." He gently tucked back a damp tendril of hair from Rebecca's forehead.

The gesture took her by surprise.

"It seems worse in this coach. It'll be better once we're home."

Rebecca nodded and hoped it was true.

"We have a good mob of horses. You can pick one out right away. We'll ride, often."

"I'd like that," Rebecca said, but she couldn't help thinking of all she'd left—the greenery, a cool sea breeze, Aunt Mildred. Had she made a terrible mistake?

"No worries, dear," Lorraine said. "It's always hard when ya first come over, but ya'll adjust. I came from Melbourne twenty years ago. It's much greener and cooler down there."

"And I suppose ya'll be gettin' off in Thornton Creek?" Carl asked.

The name Thornton Creek startled Rebecca. The town was named after her husband's family? Why hadn't Daniel told her? "Thornton Creek?"

"It's nothin'. My grandfather settled 'ere first, and they needed a name—they used his."

His nonchalant manner didn't reassure Rebecca. Something wasn't right. Daniel had been vague about his family, he hadn't told her about the town, and he'd hardly been honest about the beauty of Douloo. What else had he failed to mention?

She stared at the dismal scenery passing by her window. *It makes no difference. He's my husband, and I've vowed to be a wife to him . . . even if it means living in this place. We'll face the joys and hardships of life together.*

But the barren plains would not go away, and her troubled thoughts made her tremble.

7

The coach bucked as it moved through Thornton Creek, then lurched to a stop in front of the Thornton Creek Hotel. Daniel should have been pleased to be so close to home; instead, he could feel his anxiety intensify. He glanced at Rebecca. Her eyes were heavy with sleep. What would she think of Douloo? More importantly, what would his father think of her?

She sat up and smoothed her dress.

"We're just in time for midmorning tea," he said, forcing a smile.

"Thank goodness." Rebecca repositioned her hat and replaced a decorative pin. "I could do with something to drink."

His apprehension climbing, Daniel stepped out of the coach and offered Rebecca his hand.

She remained seated and looked at her traveling companions and then at Daniel.

"Don't ya worry none," Lorraine said. "All will be well."

"It was a pleasure to meet you," Rebecca said.

Lorraine offered a reassuring nod. "The same to ya. We may meet up again. Ya never know. And if we don't, well, then ya'll make new friends."

"I hope we do meet again."

Lorraine's husband said, "Take care of yerself." He looked at Daniel. "And you too, Mr. Thornton."

"We will," Daniel said.

Spud lifted his dusty cap. "Glad ta make yer acquaintance. Roight good ta see a Yank makin' a go of it. Good luck ta ya."

Rebecca settled a hand in Daniel's and stepped off the stage. The driver closed the door and climbed back onto his wooden seat. The driver hollered and flicked the reins, the horses set off, and the coach moved away in a swirl of dust.

Rebecca and Daniel watched until it disappeared. Daniel helped Rebecca up the steps in front of a two-story clapboard building. "Oh dear, my body feels stiff." She stopped and studied the hotel, which was in need of paint. Its windows were spotless.

Daniel settled an arm about her shoulders. "Perhaps a cup of tea and a biscuit will revive you, eh?" He tried to sound cheerful, but he couldn't release his apprehension. Since arriving in Brisbane, he'd been practicing what he would say when he faced his father, but even now the words didn't come easily. Nothing concerning his father was easy.

$\mathcal{D}$

A stout black man approached. He had a wide, friendly face and was mature in years. "Daniel, good ta 'ave ya home." He smiled.

"Woodman. Good to see you."

The two men clasped hands while patting each other on the back.

"How you faring?" Daniel asked.

"Roight good, lad. How 'bout yerself?"

"I'm fine. It's grand to be back."

"Roight fine ta see ya. Mrs. Thornton's been waitin' on ya, and yer father too."

Rebecca was taken aback at the warm greeting between the two men, especially after learning of her husband's intolerance toward blacks.

"I've got someone I want you to meet," Daniel said, stepping closer to Rebecca and circling an arm about her waist. "This is my wife, Rebecca. Rebecca, this is Woodman. Remember, I told you about him."

"I'm pleased to meet you."

Woodman smiled. His teeth looked white against dark brown skin. He lifted a shabby brown hat. "Nice ta meet ya, mum." He winked at Daniel. "She's a beaut, lad." Grabbing one of the trunks, he said, "We better get movin'. Yer mother's 'bout fit ta be tied, with the waitin'."

The men loaded the luggage, and Rebecca mourned the loss of a tea break. However, the thought of reaching their final destination was so enticing, she said nothing about it.

With the luggage loaded onto the back of a covered surrey, Daniel handed up Rebecca, then climbed in front with Woodman. "You don't mind if I drive, eh? I've been cooped up in the city a bit too long."

"Take the reins, then. Yer good with the horses."

They moved through the languid town of Thornton Creek, and Rebecca fought tears. She'd hoped for the bustle of people and the appeal of interesting shops. It was nothing like she'd expected. There was only a handful of establishments, and each looked similar to the hotel—clean and tidy but in need of paint for weatherworn siding. Most businesses had been named after the Thorntons—there was Thornton Creek Bank, Thornton Creek Livery, Thornton Creek Mercantile, and the Thornton Creek Pub. A seamstress shop seemed to be the only dissenter—the sign read, "Elle's," and below the name it said, "Fine Needlework and Mending." Rebecca didn't quite understand why, but she liked Elle, whoever she was.

Unable to keep her hands still in her lap, she gripped the armrest with one hand while fighting to keep her hair in place with the other.

Daniel glanced at her. "You all right? You look a bit pale."

"I'm just tired . . . and a little confused. Why are so many of the businesses named after your family?"

Woodman chuckled, then glancing back at Rebecca, said, "It doesn't mean so much 'round 'ere. Thorntons been 'ere from the first is all."

"Right," Daniel added. "Like I told you, my grandfather was the first to settle 'ere, so it was natural to name the town after him."

"That makes sense," Rebecca said, but she still felt uneasy, and she thought Daniel seemed edgy. Seeing her new last name plastered about felt peculiar.

A church stood at the edge of town. Although it was simple, a tall steeple with a bell made it a bit more striking than the other buildings in Thornton Creek. But like the rest of the town, it was in need of paint. Chipping paint and graying wood made the church look stark and inhospitable. Heaviness of heart settled over Rebecca.

"That's the family church," Daniel said. "We come every Sunday. It's not much to look at, but it will do. And the ladies will see that you're welcomed."

They moved past, and wishing it looked more like her church in Boston, Rebecca was glad to leave the building behind. She'd have felt better if it, or anything in this town, looked like home. *A gloomy disposition won't help*, she told herself. "We haven't far to go, then?" she asked.

"No. About an hour."

"You travel into town every Sunday for services?"

"Yes. My father wouldn't stand for anything less, except of course in the case of flood or fire."

Wouldn't stand for? A knot tightened in Rebecca's stomach. Was her new father-in-law as insensitive and rigid as he sounded?

The surrey moved along a dusty road leading into an empty, golden land. Except for an occasional grove of gum trees, there was nothing but blowing dust and dry grasses submitting to the wind. Rebecca had expected a creek; after all this was Thornton Creek. Finally she asked, "Daniel, why is the town named Thornton *Creek*? I haven't seen water of any kind."

"We've got a creek, all right. But this time of year it's dry. When the rains come it fills up. And sometimes it flows after a summer storm. 'Round these parts there's either too much moisture or not enough. Course, the real tough times are during a drought—everything dries up."

"Are you having a drought now?" Rebecca asked, thinking that would explain the aridness and the heat.

"Nah. It's dry all right, but this is no drought. Course, there will be. There always is . . . eventually."

Gazing at the open plains with their dun-colored grasses, Rebecca couldn't imagine the land being more parched. Using a fan she'd purchased in Brisbane, she tried to cool her overheated face. "Is it always this hot?"

"Ya'll get used ta it," Woodman said. "T'day's not so bad. There're days when it'll kill ya. Blacks sometimes dig in the ground alongside a mound and make themselves a little niche for shade 'til it cools off."

"We've a river of sorts on our place. And a billabong."

"What's that?"

"A nice shady place where the river pools up. I'll take you there." Daniel allowed the reins to go slack and rested his

84

arms on his thighs. "I thought Mum would meet us in town. I wired her 'bout Rebecca and our arrival."

"Yais, she wanted ta come along, but she's gettin' the place roight nice for 'er family." Woodman smiled, and his eyes disappeared in soft puffy folds of brown. "And ya know how yer father can be," Woodman added.

"Yah, I know." Daniel snapped the reins. He was silent a moment, then asked, "Where is my dad?"

"Up the north end of the station, checkin' the herds."

"He wired me 'bout the red water. How many have we lost?"

"None. The disease 'asn't touched our mob."

"But I thought . . . The wire said . . ."

Woodman shrugged. "Wal, ya know yer father. He's not one ta 'ave his sons runnin' off, eh?"

"Right." Daniel clenched his jaws and said nothing more. After a bit he handed the reins to Woodman, then climbed into the back of the surrey and sat beside Rebecca. "We'll be coming to Douloo soon, and I want to share your first sight of it."

The sun baked the dry earth, and although the surrey had a top, Rebecca started to feel that if they didn't get to the station soon, she'd arrive roasted. Letting out a slow breath, she gazed at a deep blue, cloudless sky.

"Right pretty, don't you think?" Daniel asked.

Rebecca didn't want to lie. "I've never seen a sky with such an intense shade of blue. It's quite pretty . . . but . . . well, it's a little stark here, don't you think?"

A shadow of disappointment touched Daniel's eyes. "I know it's not what you're used to, but it'll grow on you. Give it a fair chance." He smiled, his cheek dimpling.

"I don't mind, really. I'm sure everything will be fine." But Rebecca wasn't sure at all. She tried to think back to why she'd agreed to marry Daniel and move to this place. At this moment Boston and her aunt and uncle's small house crowded with children seemed tolerable.

The surrey rattled down the bank of a dry creek bed, bounced over ridges cut by previous water flows, then climbed up the other side.

"Does this have water in it when the rains come?" Rebecca asked.

"Yais," Woodman said. "Sometimes we get lots of rain. It's a sight all roight. Water's gushin'. Sometimes even this land is covered. And after, everything turns green and flowers pop up. Ya'll see." He winked.

Rebecca decided she liked Woodman. *Maybe he can be a friend*, she thought but quickly dispelled the idea. It would be inappropriate. But out here who was there? A dust cloud billowed in the distance.

"What's that?"

"I'd say a mob of mutton," Woodman answered with a grin.

The dust moved toward them along with the sounds of barking dogs and bleating.

"There must be an awful lot of sheep," Rebecca said.

When the animals could be distinguished from the dust, Woodman pulled back on the reins and stopped the horses. They waited while a dirty sea of wool and noise surged around them. Rebecca placed a handkerchief over her nose and mouth but couldn't keep the dust from penetrating. Her eyes watered, and she coughed, trying to clear the dust from her throat.

"I thought you said you had cattle," Rebecca yelled over the noise.

"We do. But a lot of our neighbors raise sheep. Like I said, my grandfather figured he'd have a go at cattle instead."

A drover tipped his hat and moved by without a word. Gradually the din and dust faded.

"I've never seen anything like that," Rebecca said, repinning her hat and wiping dust from her face. "I must be a sight. What will your family think?"

"No worries. They've made the trip—they understand." Daniel wiped a smudge of dirt from her cheek and planted a kiss there.

The gesture startled Rebecca. He acted as if he loved her, like a real husband. *He is my real husband*, she thought, remembering the kiss. It had been tender, and she felt a sense of being cared for. Her fears about her new home quieted.

"We've lived out 'ere a long while. We're used to the dust. Mum says it's a constant battle."

The idea of contending with unremitting dust swept away Rebecca's temporary ease. She'd hoped that by some miracle this thirsty world would disappear at Douloo. *Silly of me to believe that in the midst of this place a moist patch would simply appear.* She swallowed her disappointment and asked as cheerfully as possible, "How much farther?"

"We're nearly there. We'll see home soon, eh?" Daniel offered Rebecca a smile.

She managed to smile in return, but inside she quailed.

Woodman glanced back at Daniel. "Few days ago some blackfellas were caught poddy dodging down in the south end of the district."

"Whose place?"

"The McGregors'." Woodman clicked his tongue at the horses.

"They get away with many?"

"A fair number of cattle were lost. But they carted off them rustlers, they did. No one ever seen 'em again. Hanged, I figure."

His words reverberated in Rebecca's head. "What do you mean hanged? Without a trial? People don't just hang other people. What about the law?"

"'Round 'ere if ya get caught breakin' the law, ya pay for the crime, and more so if yer black."

"Even if they were black, they deserved a hearing," Daniel said, anger in his voice.

"Does this kind of thing happen often?" Rebecca asked, fear spiking through her.

"Roight often. But them blackfellas knew better. They shoulda kept their black 'ands to themselves."

Rebecca felt sick. "They had no trial?"

"Nah."

Rebecca fanned herself and stared out at the bleak surroundings.

"How's Mum been?" Daniel asked, as if he were trying to change the subject.

"Wal, she was real sorrowful in the beginning, but she's lookin' roight healthy these days." One of the horses stumbled, and he tugged on the reins. "Ah, steady there."

No one spoke for a moment; then Woodman said, "I had a dream 'bout Elton. He was racin' his horse across the flat, ya know the place down by that batch of ghost gums along the creek bed?"

"Uh-huh."

"He was runnin' one of the brumbies hard, goin' faster and faster, and then that horse just took into the air. He was flyin', he was. And Elton was happy. I could feel it. He's roight happy." Woodman steered the horses around a batch of scrub. "I told yer mum 'bout the dream, but it only made her sad. She's still grieven'."

Daniel gazed at the dirt road, with its waves of heat rising from the baked earth. His eyes moved across the fields, where buzzing hordes of flies enveloped piles of dried cattle dung. "Mum was heartbroken when Elton left, and then to lose him that way. I shoulda stayed home to be a comfort to her."

A sharp yip echoed across the open land. "What was that?" Rebecca asked.

"Dingo," Daniel said. "We've got plenty of them. You've no need to worry. They're nothin' but pests."

"What are they?"

"They're like a dorg, only wild," Woodman said. "Ya've no reason ta fear 'em. They keep their distance."

"They can be a blight on ranchers though," Daniel said. "Sheep and calves fall easy prey."

"Are they dangerous?" Rebecca asked, feeling a shiver move through her.

"They've been known to drag off and eat almost anything, but I've never seen one attack a human." Daniel offered an encouraging smile. "No need to worry."

Rebecca felt wretched. Queensland was nothing like she'd expected. What would her life be like in such a desolate place? What would she do with herself? There certainly wasn't a need for lawyers or teachers. There would be no trips to the philharmonic or to the theater and no quiet walks along the shoreline.

She didn't belong. *I'm truly a fish out of water*, she thought, picturing a gasping pike. She pushed the image from her mind, but a sense of helplessness and desperation lingered.

The surrey moved up a slight rise, and a dark shape seemed to grow up from the earth. They drew nearer, and Rebecca could see a house among a grove of trees. They moved past a huge barn, outbuildings, and cottages. The house was large, three stories, and had an angled roof with dormers in front. It was freshly painted white and looked bright beneath the brilliant sun. A broad veranda sprawled across the front and wrapped itself around both sides. A garden of roses, lavender, geraniums, and other, unfamiliar flowers hugged a walkway. Like an ocean swell, shrubs and wisteria washed up onto the foot of the veranda.

Relief enveloped Rebecca. It looked much like the homes in Boston. "It's lovely, Daniel. Really lovely."

Although reassured, Rebecca couldn't blot out the home's surroundings. It stood alone in the midst of thousands of acres of nothing but grass and scrub. There was no town, no neighbors.

"I knew you'd like it," Daniel said proudly. He stood and sucked in a deep breath. "It's grand to be home," he said without conviction.

A woman rose from a chair on the veranda and walked down the broad front steps. She was middle-aged, sturdy-looking, and had an attractive, friendly face. Long brown hair was caught back in a pale blue ribbon. Eyes alight, she hurried toward the surrey.

"Whoa," Woodman called, hauling on the reins. "I brought 'im safe and sound just like ya asked."

Tears spilled onto the woman's tanned cheeks. She held out her arms as Daniel stepped from the carriage. "It's so wonderful to have you home." She pulled him into a mother's embrace.

"I've missed you." Daniel kissed her cheek, then turned toward the cart. "I've got someone I want you to meet." He took Rebecca's hand as she stepped from the surrey. "This is my wife, Rebecca. Rebecca, this is my mother, Willa Thornton."

Rebecca barely managed to keep her feet. Her right leg had gone numb from the long ride. "It's a pleasure to meet you, Mrs. Thornton."

"Willa. Please call me Willa." Her sky blue eyes, so like Daniel's, smiled at Rebecca. Then the woman took her daughter-in-law's hands. "I'm very happy to meet you at last. Welcome to Douloo."

Willa turned to Daniel. "I've made some refreshments. I thought you would be thirsty and hungry after such a long journey."

Rebecca noticed that Willa's speech was crisp and clear, with only a bit of a lilt to it. Her diction was precise as if she worked at defining her words. *That must be from her years in England*, she decided.

"Right, Mum. I'm starved. I meant to have tea in town, but when I saw Woodman all I could think about was getting home."

Willa looked beyond Daniel toward the barn. "Your father," she said, her voice taking on an edge.

Rebecca turned to see a tall, broad-shouldered man striding toward them. He wore a somber expression, and his eyes seemed unfriendly.

Daniel and his mother waited silently, their bodies taut.

Rebecca was suddenly afraid.

8

Bertram Thornton carried himself with dignity and confidence. He was a striking man, even handsome, and his sun-damaged skin gave him a rugged appearance.

He offered Daniel a slight smile and shook his hand. "Good to see ya. It's been a long while, eh?" A well-worn hat shaded his eyes.

"Yes, sir. It has."

Rebecca thought the greeting rather formal for a father and son.

Removing his hat, Bertram turned to Rebecca. "And this must be yer bride, eh?" He smiled, but his light blue eyes remained emotionless.

"Yes, sir. This is Rebecca. We were married . . ."

"Good to meet ya, Rebecca. Welcome to Douloo. I hope ya'll be happy 'ere. Don't guess it's what yer used to."

"No, sir, but I'm certain I'll adjust," Rebecca said, doing her best to keep her tone cheery. "You have a beautiful home."

Bertram gazed at the house. "Finest in the district. My father brought every plank, every pane of glass, all of it, from England. He was proud of this house. And rightly so."

In spite of Bertram's sociable manner, Rebecca felt an underlying resentment. His words were amicable, but the look in his eyes remained indifferent. Even more disturbing, Daniel stood rigid and silent.

Bertram glanced toward the barn, where a man stood just outside the double doors. "Jim, I need yer help."

The young man's strong jaw and brown eyes were set as he walked toward the house. He wore dungarees and a short-sleeved cotton shirt. Rebecca couldn't help but notice his good looks. He exuded self-confidence . . . or was it arrogance? Brushing long brown hair from his forehead, he winked at Rebecca in a way that no one would notice, then turned to his boss. "What can I do for you, sir?"

"I need ya to carry the bags into the house. Woodman 'ere will give ya a hand."

"Happy to," he said, his tone belying his words.

He had no accent, and Rebecca thought he sounded American. Just knowing he wasn't Australian made her feel slightly less isolated.

Bertram placed a hand on Daniel's back. "I've got a filly I want ya to take a look at. She's new. Just brought her over from the Linnells'. Ya remember the Linnells, don't ya?"

"Yeah, I know them." Daniel sounded annoyed. He followed his father to the barn.

Rebecca watched them go, wondering why Bertram's words about the Linnells had been barbed.

"I'd like those trunks taken up to Daniel's old room," Willa said.

"Roight, mum." Woodman hefted a large bag off the surrey. "Happy ta do that for ya."

"I'll show you the way, Rebecca." Willa hurried up the front porch steps, the heels of her shoes making a hollow, clapping sound. "Right this way, dear." She opened the front door and disappeared inside.

Rebecca followed her into a tiled entryway that opened onto an expansive vestibule with a wooden coat rack and a long bench resting along one wall. To the right, an arched doorway opened to a sitting room, and straight ahead, a broad staircase led to the second level.

Just as Willa started up the stairs, the sound of shattering glass came from another room. "Glory be! Now, what was that?" She glanced at Rebecca. "You go ahead, dear. Your room is on the second floor. Just go up the staircase, turn left, and go to the end of the hallway."

Gingerly Rebecca placed her hand on the ornate wooden banister and started up. An intricately woven carpet of deep blue with gold and brown fibers cushioned her steps. One very much like it covered the wooden floor of the sitting room.

A bag in each hand, Jim brushed past her, thumping her leg with one of the pieces of luggage. He mumbled something and moved on.

Surprised at his rudeness, Rebecca stopped and watched him climb the stairs. Annoyance flared, and intending to give him a piece of her mind, she hurried after him. By the time Rebecca caught up to Jim at the end of the upstairs corridor, she had decided not to say anything about his discourtesy and simply asked, "Did Mr. Thornton say your name is Jim?"

"Yep. Jim Keller." He pushed through a doorway.

Rebecca followed him into a spacious bedroom. "Are you from America?"

"Yep. California." He strode to a large four-poster bed.

"I'm from Boston. It's good to meet another American."

"Means nothin' out here." Rebecca was taken aback, but before she could say anything, he continued, "In this territory we're all countrymen. We need each other. Can't be worrying about where a chap comes from." Jim set the bags on the floor.

Rebecca searched her mind for something more to say.

94

"Woodman's very friendly. I've never known a black man personally before. Is he an aborigine?"

"He's a half caste." Jim settled golden brown eyes on Rebecca. "Sorry to see the likes of you here."

"What?" Rebecca wasn't certain she'd heard him correctly.

"Nothin'." He moved toward the door. "Just watch out for them blacks. They've been known to eat white folks." Mischief lit his eyes.

Rebecca couldn't repress a gasp.

Jim smirked.

"You're teasing."

"I never tease."

"Do you like living here?"

"Yeah. I do." He removed his hat and picked at what looked like a burr stuck in the brim.

Rebecca glanced around the cheery room. Two windows draped with white lace curtains let in sunlight. The walls were papered in yellow floral that looked like Japanese silk crepe. On the wall opposite the windows hung two small paintings, each portraying an English garden. Rebecca felt a pang of homesickness. They reminded her of the grounds at home.

As she took in the rest of the room, a longing for home set in. Large, mirrored bureaus sat on opposite ends of the bedchamber. Each had a delicate lace doily draped over it. One had a pitcher of water and a bowl, and the other an ornate china clock. A small desk below one of the windows held a hand-painted vase filled with fresh flowers. *I'll write letters home from there*, Rebecca thought, a pang of sorrow pricking her—she had only her aunt now. A heavy armoire rested between the two windows. "This room is lovely, don't you think?"

"Yeah, real lovely," Jim said sarcastically, returning the hat to his head.

"Have I done something to annoy you?"

"Yeah, you moved here."

His tone raised Rebecca's ire. "And why is that a problem?"

"Yanks travel to Australia expecting adventure, thinking they're going to find a grand life. When they get here they kind of wither. Some of them leave." He gave her a once over. "Don't figure you'll manage well."

"How could you possibly know that?" Rebecca asked, anger building.

"I know your type. You won't stand up to the dust storms, the heat, or the critters. Soon you'll be cryin' for home. And home you should go. The sooner the better."

His rudeness stunned Rebecca. But more shocking than that was his precise statement of her fear—that she wouldn't endure. As calmly as she could manage, she said, "Please go. I have no need of you or your criticism."

"No, you don't understand. You need my criticism." His tone was softer now. "Be on your way. You don't belong here and you know it."

Does he know Daniel and I shouldn't have married? she thought in alarm. Then, feeling more put out than anxious, she asked, "What business is it of yours, my being here?"

He walked to the window and looked out. "The dried bones of those much tougher than you are scattered on these plains." He turned and looked at her, nudging his hat down in the front. "Go home, missy. While you can." Without saying more, he walked out of the room.

Rebecca fought fear and blinked back tears. His warning wasn't about her marriage. *I'm not going to cry over some drover's insolence.* She walked to the window and gazed outside, searching for calm. Hearing something behind her and thinking it was Jim, she whirled around, ready with a retort.

"Don't let 'im get under yer skin," Woodman said. "I think ya got what it takes." He smiled and set a trunk on the floor. "No worries."

"He said I should leave."

"And how do ya feel 'bout that?"

"My husband is here." She glanced at the surrey below. What she didn't say was that she was terrified and reasonably certain she should never have come and that although Daniel was her legal husband he felt more like a stranger.

Woodman shrugged. "I wouldn't listen to 'im then, eh?" He chuckled and walked out of the room.

Rebecca wandered into the hallway. There were several closed doors. Thinking them private, she didn't open any. Instead, she looked at paintings. She stopped in front of one piece she thought must have been painted in Venice. A man stood in a gondola, propelling himself down a waterway between stone buildings. She moved on, wondering if her new family had ever traveled there and remembering the holiday she and her father and aunt had spent in the exotic city. An ache settled in the hollow of her throat. There would be no more holidays with her father.

Moving on to the next painting, she studied a woman who looked like a young version of Willa. She sat on a bench amid a lush flower garden. The artist had captured a spiritual tranquility in the woman. Rebecca longed for the seemingly elusive serenity.

"My grandmother," a deep voice said.

Rebecca whirled around. "Oh, you frightened me. I didn't know you were there."

"Sorry. I didn't mean to," Daniel said stiffly.

Rebecca turned back and stared at the picture. "Did you say this is your grandmother?"

"Uh-huh."

"She looks so much like your mother."

"I never knew her. She died many years ago. I heard she and Mum were very much alike."

"Just like my mother and me."

Silence hung over the two.

"Have you seen our room?" Daniel finally asked.

"Yes. It's lovely."

His eyes serious, Daniel took Rebecca's hands. "I know this isn't the marriage you dreamed of, but I want you to be happy here. I'll do everything I can to make that happen."

Rebecca felt a tug at her heart. She'd married a fine man. If only she were in love with him. "Thank you, Daniel."

They walked toward their room. "Daniel, do aborigines really eat people?" Rebecca asked, remembering Jim's warning.

"Who told you that?"

"That Jim fellow. The one from America."

"It's true, all right. Some aborigines are cannibals. But you have no reason to fret about our workers. They're all top rate 'ere." He stopped, smiled down at his bride, and kissed her forehead. "No worries, eh?"

♫

That evening, the family gathered for an early supper in the formal dining room. Bertram bowed his head and then glanced up to see that everyone else had done so. He caught Rebecca's eye, and, embarrassed, she quickly dropped her eyes and bowed her head.

"Heavenly Father, I come to thee with a heavy heart."

Rebecca expected words about his dead son.

Instead, Bertram said, "Thy church is black with sin. I ask that thee show us our sin, force us to our knees before thee

98

so that we will be purified. We are a fallen people. Show us a better way. Gird us up with thy righteousness.

"I know and trust that thee hear me and that thee will have mercy on my family. I also ask that thee would bless this food to our bodies. Amen."

The room was quiet, the atmosphere tense. There had been no mention of Daniel's safe return or any word about his wife. Bertram looked at Rebecca; his pale blue eyes seemed to hold secrets. "And how was yer crossing?" he asked, unfolding his napkin and laying it across his lap.

"Very nice. The ship was quite magnificent." Rebecca followed his example and settled her napkin in her lap. "And, thankfully, the seas were calm most of the trip."

"Good." He took a sip of tea. "And from Brisbane?"

Rebecca believed in being honest, but she didn't want to start off on the wrong foot, so she decided not to mention the stagecoach trip. "I enjoyed the journey over the mountains. The country was beautiful and very interesting."

A smile creased Bertram's lips. "I know too well what it's like spendin' days on that rocking stagecoach, eh?" He glanced at Daniel, then leaned back slightly when an aborigine servant placed a bowl of soup on the table in front of him.

She served the entire meal silently, but her black eyes seemed to take in everything. Although she'd flattened down her wiry hair and coiled it into a bun, tufts of frizz sprang from her head. Her skin was darker than Woodman's but not the charcoal black of Lily, the kitchen maid Rebecca had met earlier.

"Callie, could you get us some tea, please?" Willa asked.

"Yais, mum." Noiselessly Callie disappeared into the kitchen.

The chink of silver utensils against china was the only sound in the pervasive silence. Finally Daniel said, "I think

99

I've found a mare for you, Rebecca. I'll bring 'er 'round to the barn tomorrow so you can get a look at 'er. She's not as grand as Chavive, but she's solid and steady."

"I'm sure she'll be fine," Rebecca said.

"Do you ride?" Willa asked.

"Yes. I used to ride nearly every day back home."

"This is yer home now," Bertram said, his voice stern.

Rebecca wet her lips. "Well, of course. I'm just not used to calling it that yet. I'm sure in no time it will seem like home to me."

She ate a spoonful of the hearty-flavored beef soup, but her throat felt tight and she wasn't at all certain she'd be able to swallow. She glanced at her new father-in-law. He looked angry. *What have I done?* she wondered, managing to swallow the broth. Maybe it was her poverty, her *need* of a husband.

Willa made a few more attempts at conversation, but each fell flat. Finally the last course was served and eaten and then the plates retrieved by Callie. The servant returned with tea and refilled the cups.

"Thank you, dear," Willa said.

"Yais, mum." Callie's voice was deep and soft.

Bertram sipped his tea.

Willa turned compassionate eyes on Rebecca. "Perhaps you'd like to retire early. You must be quite done in." She smiled warmly. "I'll have Callie turn down the bed for you."

"Thank you, ma'am. I am rather tired."

"Please, call me Willa. We're family now."

"Of course. I'd like that too."

Willa seemed to possess a character opposite of her husband's. Although both looked robust, Willa's tanned skin was smooth and vibrant, her demeanor warm and unpretentious, while Bertram's harsh exterior appeared to match his interior.

Rebecca liked Willa and felt certain she and her new mother-in-law would get along well.

Bertram laid his napkin beside his plate and pushed back his chair. "I'll have more tea in the library," he told Callie. With a grim glance at Daniel, he said, "I'd like a word with ya, lad."

"Right." Daniel finished off the last of his tea and set his napkin on the table. With a slight bow to his mother and a wink for Rebecca, he followed his father into the study.

"Would you like tea on the veranda?" Willa asked.

"Yes. That would be nice. It's probably cooler outdoors."

"That it is." Willa turned to Callie. "Could you bring tea and biscuits out to the veranda for us, please?"

"Yais, mum."

Following Willa through the double doors leading outside, Rebecca's mind remained with Daniel and Bertram. What were they talking about? She settled on a wicker rocker, savoring the touch of a gentle breeze. It cooled her hot skin and carried a sweet fragrance from the flower garden.

"It's so much nicer out here." Willa accepted a tray of tea and biscuits from Callie.

"Anything else I can do for ya, mum?"

"No. We're fine."

Callie returned to the dining room.

"She seems to go from place to place without even stirring the air," Rebecca said, mystified by the young woman's ability to move soundlessly.

"Almost all the blacks are that way. You never hear them, unless they want you to."

"It's a little unnerving."

"I dare say, but you'll get used to it. It's said the blacks see all the world as sacred and are careful not to disturb anything as they move through it."

"What a romantic thought. Most of us simply ramble

through without a care for the mystery of creation about us."
Rebecca rocked and gazed out at the open plains.

"That we do."

"Daniel told me you sometimes have summer storms?"

"Yes. I'm sorry to say they're rarely cooling, and the earth is like a dry sponge—the wetness is quickly gone."

"How much longer until winter?"

Willa filled a cup with tea. "One never knows for certain, but some months yet I'd say, if it comes at all. We're praying this year isn't so dry as the last." She poured tea into a china cup. "Would you like sugar?"

"Yes, just a bit, please."

Willa sprinkled a half spoonful of sweetener into the cup, stirred, and handed it to Rebecca. "I'm glad you've come. It will be nice to have another woman about the place." She offered Rebecca a biscuit.

Selecting one of the plain-looking sweets, Rebecca said, "At home we call these cookies." She took a bite. "It reminds me of the shortbread my aunt makes. Delicious."

"I'll tell Lily. She'll be pleased."

"I had no idea Douloo was so far from . . . civilization." Rebecca took another bite of biscuit.

"Indeed. It's quite a way into town, but I don't mind it a bit, really. I must admit that when I first arrived as a young bride the openness was disconcerting, but now when I travel east over the mountains I feel closed in. I truly love it here. I can't imagine living anywhere else."

Angry voices carried from inside the library. Willa glanced in the direction of the sound. "Those two, they've always had their spats. No worries though, dear. Everything will be just fine."

This time it's about me, she thought with certainty. Bertram hadn't seemed at all pleased to have her in the family. A puff of wind caught at her hair, and she smoothed it back into

102

place. "I must be a sight. All those hours on the train, then the stagecoach. I did manage to tidy up a bit, but . . ."

"You look lovely. Far prettier than any of the young ladies who've been after my son." She smiled. "And clearly more refined."

Before Rebecca could respond, Bertram's sharp voice boomed throughout the house and carried outside. "Yer a fool! No high-bred woman will do out 'ere. Ya knew it and still ya brought 'er 'ere. Ya would have done well to have stayed with Meghan. It was understood between ya two."

"She wasn't for me!" Daniel hollered, but the rest of his words were indistinguishable.

Alarm swelled in Rebecca. What if Bertram was right and she couldn't make it here? And who was Meghan? She stopped rocking to listen more closely.

Willa laid a hand on Rebecca's arm. "Don't worry. My husband doesn't take well to change, but he'll manage. Be patient. He'll come around."

Rebecca nodded, but inside she felt as if a storm had been set loose. *How can I live in a house with a man who doesn't want me here?* Why hadn't Daniel warned her? And what about Meghan? Would she have been a better choice?

"I'm very much looking forward to your meeting the women at the church," Willa said cheerily. "And they've been anxious to meet you. Ever since hearing about Daniel's wedding, they've been all a-twitter."

Would they feel the same if they knew why and how we married? Rebecca wondered. The men continued to quarrel, and she strained to hear. How could Willa simply ignore the squabbling going on between her husband and son?

"I'll not pamper her!" Bertram's voice boomed.

Pamper me! I never expected anyone to pamper me! Rebecca fumed, half inclined to storm into the study and defend herself.

"And," Bertram continued, "ya'd best make it clear she's expected to submit to her husband as well as to her father-in-law. I'll not have any women's suffrage types living under my roof!" For emphasis he continued, "God's Word is clear. Ephesians 5:22–24 says, 'Wives submit yerselves unto yer own husbands, as unto the Lord. For the husband is the head of the wife, even as Christ is the head of the church. . . . Therefore as the church is subject unto Christ, so let the wives be to their own husbands in every thing.' God placed man over woman. That's how it's always been, and that's how it will be in my house!"

Rebecca couldn't make out Daniel's response, but he didn't sound defiant. Her anxiety grew. What if Daniel stood with his father against her?

Callie's hands trembled as she cleared away the dishes. "Anything else, mum?" she asked, her voice tight.

"No. That will be all. Thank you." Carrying the tray with the teakettle and extra biscuits, Callie left the porch. "She's a lovely girl. We've had her since she was just ten. She's been a blessing to us." Willa's effort at cheerfulness only made the fractious atmosphere more palpable.

Willa added solemnly, "We're very lucky here. There are women who live alone on the flats with no female company or help. They contend with vermin and pray for water simply to survive. Everything here is lovely. Bertram makes certain we live in comfort, and he provides all I need for my garden."

Rebecca recognized Willa's need to defend her husband but wondered if compassion and brutality could exist within one man? And if so, which had the upper hand in Bertram?

Just then her father-in-law strode through the front door and stomped down the steps. Without even a glance at his wife or daughter-in-law, he headed for the barn.

"His bark is much worse than his bite, honestly."

Rebecca was unconvinced.

Daniel, who was visibly shaken, joined the women. Offering a forced smile, he crossed to Rebecca and stood behind her chair, resting his hands protectively on her shoulders. His strength reassured Rebecca. He would protect her.

"We've no worries, love. We'll be fine, eh?" He squeezed Rebecca's shoulders.

"Of course."

Nothing truly bad can happen, Rebecca told herself. They'd face his father together. *But I'm no soft, highbred woman*, she thought, remembering Bertram's harsh words. *I won't disgrace my husband. I'll show Mr. Thornton what it means to be a Williams.*

9

Daniel settled into a reed rocker, folded his hands in his lap, and thrust his legs straight out in front of him. "Nice out, eh?" He sounded relaxed, as if the argument with his father hadn't happened.

Rebecca gazed at the flower gardens and greenery growing along the veranda. "I'll be glad when the temperatures cool."

"I'm afraid the heat will last for a good while," Willa said. "But you'll get used to it."

Rebecca repressed a sigh. She'd been told more than once that she had no worries, which of course she did, and now she was being told she'd get used to the heat, which she highly doubted. She'd spent too many mild summers in New England.

She stood and moved to Daniel. Leaning close, she asked quietly, "Is there a necessary downstairs?"

A grin touched Daniel's lips.

"I'd rather not use the chamber pot," Rebecca explained, wondering at his humor. "You do have a water closet, don't you?"

Daniel smiled. "Oh, you mean the dunny. It's 'round the side of the house."

"Outside?"

"Right. We haven't got indoor plumbing, not for that kind of thing. We're still a bit behind Boston."

Rebecca straightened. "The . . . dunny will be fine."

Thinking she'd heard annoyance in Daniel's voice, Rebecca excused herself and walked around to the side of the house. The dunny stood several yards from the house. A fresh coat of white paint made it look bright in the simmering sunlight. It seemed tidy. Still, it was outdoors.

While traveling, Rebecca had been introduced to primitive Queensland, but after seeing the Thornton home she'd expected modern facilities. *One more difficulty to manage*, she thought, approaching the outhouse. "Stop your whining," she told herself. "It's not the first time you've had to use an outdoor privy."

She grabbed the door handle and pulled open the wooden door. It creaked on well-used hinges. She peeked inside. This was unlike the outhouses she'd been compelled to use on their journey. It was large, and all four sides had vents cut into the wood near the ceiling. Wallpaper with pink rosebuds covered the interior walls, and a shelf held a hand-painted vase, which had been filled with fresh flowers. *Willa*, Rebecca thought with a smile.

She stepped inside. In spite of Willa's efforts, the odor could not be overcome. Taking shallow breaths, Rebecca closed the door and latched it. The light in the small room dimmed, but Rebecca could see reasonably well.

She hitched up layers of skirt. *I'll have to purchase some light-weight gowns*, she thought as she saw something move along the floor near the doorway. Swiftly pushing her skirts back into place, she stared at the spot. There it was again! Something was definitely there! Heart thumping, she studied the shadows. The thing slithered across a shaft of light. Rebecca could see brown skin and a flick of a tongue. A snake!

Backing up against the toilet, she let out a shriek. "Help! Someone help!"

Several moments later the door jiggled. It was locked and wouldn't open. If she wanted to unlock it, she'd have to move closer to her unwanted visitor.

"Please hurry! There's a snake!" The door shook. "You'll have to break it. I can't get to the lock."

With a loud crack the door flew open. Using the barrel of a rifle, Jim scooped up the reptile and flung it outside. He turned, took aim, and shot twice. The snake bounced as bullets ripped through its body.

Pressing a hand to her chest and gazing at the lifeless reptile, Rebecca fought to quiet her breathing. "It must be eight feet long!" she gasped, studying the creature. "It doesn't look particularly dangerous. I'm sorry. I shouldn't have panicked. It was just so unexpected. And I've never been fond of snakes." She looked at Jim, wishing it hadn't been him who'd come to her rescue. "Thank you for being so gallant."

Jim lifted the reptile and grinned. "This here is a king brown. They're poisonous . . . deadly, in fact. Ought to make a nice meal though." He grabbed the snake and walked away.

Poisonous? Deadly? Rebecca thought she might faint. She gripped the edge of the doorway.

"What happened?" Daniel asked, striding toward Rebecca. He glanced at Jim strolling away.

"There was a snake . . . on the floor. There." She pointed at the place she'd first seen the reptile. She gulped down a breath; her heart still pounded. "Jim said it was deadly."

He looked back at Jim and the snake. "Looks like a king brown. I'm sorry, Rebecca. We don't generally get them 'round the house, but you never know 'round 'ere. You have to keep an eye out."

"Are there lots of snakes?"

"I wouldn't say lots. But they're about. You've just got to watch your step."

"But this one was in the . . . the outhouse."

Daniel grinned. "You'll do better calling it a dunny. Otherwise people won't know what you're talking about." Daniel draped an arm over her shoulders. "No worries."

No worries? Rebecca fumed.

"Everything's all right. You've had a long day. Why don't you go up to bed? You can use the chamber pot in our room. Callie will take it out in the morning."

Rebecca felt jumpy, not sleepy. "I don't feel tired."

"You must be."

"I suppose you're right. It's just the scare that has me on edge." Rebecca longed for human consolation but didn't feel comfortable leaning on Daniel.

"I'll be up soon," he said.

She nodded and headed toward the house. She couldn't help but watch the bushes for snakes, and when she approached the porch she gave it a once over before taking the steps.

D

Rebecca lifted a petticoat out of one of the trunks, carefully refolded it, and then placed the silk underskirt in a bureau drawer. She wondered if Daniel cared which dresser she used. A knock sounded at the door.

"May I come in?" Willa asked.

"Yes. Please."

The door opened and Willa stepped inside. "I'm so sorry about the snake."

"It's all right. I'm fine."

"I wanted to make certain you were settling in all right. And is there anything I can get you?"

"I'm fine, really. I was just putting away some of my things. This is a lovely room. Thank you for letting us use it."

"It's yours. Everything here is yours, or it will be . . . when Bertram passes on."

Rebecca hadn't given much thought to the endless stretch of days she'd be spending in this place. The enormity of what she'd done when she'd married Daniel swept over her. This wild territory was her home. This is where she would spend her life. Would it be loveless? How would she endure?

"I know the idea of it all can be daunting," Willa said.

You have no idea, Rebecca thought, closing the bureau drawer. "It is a bit intimidating," she said. "I had no idea . . . that Australia was like . . . this. Everything is so big, and . . . well, I'm not certain what I should or shouldn't do, or what my role here is."

"Indeed. Australia is a very large and handsome country. Hopefully, you'll have an opportunity to see more of it. There are wonders lying beyond this station. And I know it's hard for you to see now, but the flats have their own beauty."

She walked to a window and gazed out. "I marvel at the wonders of God's hand." She turned and looked at Rebecca. "And as for what you'll do here . . . well, I'm not so young anymore. I need help to run this household. There's a lot to oversee. Sometimes I find myself feeling a bit done in by it all."

Looking at the tanned and radiant woman, Rebecca couldn't imagine her being done in. "How many years have you lived here?"

"Thirty-four. I was just twenty when I met Bertram. My family lived in Melbourne. Like you and Daniel, we married quickly. Right off we knew we were meant to be together." She smiled at the memory. "When my eyes fell upon him my heart set to fluttering. Bertram was charming as a young man. And quite dashing. He absolutely stole my heart."

Rebecca couldn't help but wonder what Willa had seen in Bertram. As far as she could tell, there was nothing even remotely charming about him.

She felt guilty over her deception and said in a faltering voice, "Willa . . . I need to tell you . . ." She stopped and took a breath. "I admire Daniel very much. He's a fine man. But . . . I don't love him . . ." Her voice trailed off in embarrassment.

"I know."

"Daniel told you?"

"No. I have eyes." Willa smiled. "It's all right. Whatever the reason for your marriage, I know my son and he's not an irrational or stupid person. I trust his judgment." She gently cupped Rebecca's chin in her hand. "Love has a way of growing."

Rebecca gazed into Willa's sky blue eyes. "I want to believe that, but I don't. Admiration, yes . . . but love isn't something a person can summon at will."

"We shall see." Willa kissed Rebecca's cheek, then abruptly turned and crossed the room to the bed. She turned down the blankets and smoothed the muslin sheets. "I'll have Callie fetch you a bath." Willa stopped at the door. "It's splendid to have you here as part of our family."

Rebecca had no reply. She simply smiled courteously.

Willa left, closing the door softly, and with a heavy heart Rebecca returned to putting away clothing and setting out personal items. She placed photographs of her father and her aunt on the back corners of the bureau, her comb and brush on one side of the wash bowl, and a hat pin holder with her three favorite pins on the other side.

She lovingly set her Bible on the bed stand. She sat on the bed and for a long while stared at the black book, feeling comforted by its presence. It held the answers to all life's questions and quandaries. If only she could look through its pages and see what lay ahead.

✻

Rebecca stepped into a spacious bathing room. Two sconces were secured on either side of a table with a marble inlaid top and swivel mirror. Their light gave the ivory-colored floor tiles a soft sheen. Fresh soap and towels had been laid out. Steam rose from a four-legged tub half filled with water.

Just the idea of bathing made Rebecca feel more relaxed. The incident with the snake seemed far away as she removed her bathing robe and draped it over a Windsor chair. She stepped into the bath, lowering herself into the warm water. Resting the back of her head against the edge of the tub, she closed her eyes. A mild scent of lavender hung in the air. *This is nearly like home*, she thought, tension ebbing away.

✻

Dressed in a linen nightgown, Rebecca slipped between cool sheets. She plumped her pillows and lay back, feeling dreamy and content. She picked up the book *Little Women*. Her aunt Mildred had purchased it just before she and Daniel had married. It had been a pleasant distraction during the journey.

Opening to the place where she'd left off, Rebecca eagerly returned to the New England world of Meg and her sisters. The girls were skating. The scene carried Rebecca home to Boston, where fresh snow sheltered the earth and ice encrusted the ponds and rivers. The air would be so cold it burned your lungs. Rebecca felt the aching squeeze of sorrow in her chest.

"No," she said, pushing herself more upright. "I'm not getting maudlin over a bit of snow." She closed the book. "I'll have to adjust. It's as simple as that."

A knock sounded at the door. "Rebecca," Daniel said, then stepped inside.

She let her book rest in her lap. She'd hoped to be asleep before he came up.

Daniel stood just inside the doorway and gazed at her. "You look as if you've been dreaming."

"I guess I have been, in a way. I've been reading *Little Women*, and it's carried me home." She offered a tremulous smile. "I've had a lovely bath, and I'm feeling quite refreshed."

His eyes on her, he crossed the room and sat on the edge of the bed. "You're the most beautiful woman I've ever known."

Rebecca could see passion in his eyes. Her own response was confusion. She wanted him to stay, and she wanted him to go.

He leaned over and kissed her tenderly, then with more passion. Suddenly he straightened. "I can't stay."

"No?" Rebecca felt relief.

"I've business. My father and I are meeting with a man from another station. Seems there's been a real scare—more red water up north. We've got to decide what we're going to do if it moves into the district." He gazed at her. "I'd stay, but you know my father."

"No. I don't," Rebecca said, suddenly annoyed. "I've barely met him, but I know he hates me, and I know you don't want to tell me about him." She folded her arms over her chest.

"He doesn't hate you. He's just surprised at our getting married."

"And who is Meghan?"

"A long-time friend."

"And?"

Daniel grinned. "If I didn't know better, I'd say you were jealous."

Rebecca had no response. Maybe she was.

Daniel pressed her back against a pillow and pulled the sheet up under her chin. "Meghan and I have been friends since we were kids. There's nothing more to it than that." He kissed the tip of her nose. "I'll try not to wake you when I come in," he said and left the room.

In spite of her mixed feelings, Rebecca felt abandoned. She gazed at the ceiling for a long while, then returned to her book. A high-pitched yip echoed in the distance. *A dingo*, she thought, feeling satisfaction that she'd distinguished the voice of a local animal.

She threw back the covers, padded to the window, and gazed at a flaming sunset. Where the sky touched the earth it looked as if it had been washed with red paint. The color reached farther into the heavens, changing to a muted orange. Translucent clouds blushed gold. A breeze ruffled the grasses, and Rebecca felt the breath of the open land.

She stood there for a long while until the sun dipped beneath the horizon and the air cooled. An unusual thumping sound came from the darkening tablelands. She held her breath and listened. The sound came again, then again. "What can that be?" She stared at the dim landscape. A shadow moved just beyond the fence line. Rebecca felt a prickle of fear, and then she saw a kangaroo bound across the yard below. "So that's it," she said with a smile, feeling silly at her alarm.

A light glowed inside one of the cabins, and Callie stepped onto a tiny, railed porch. Skinny arms hugging her waist, she stared at the darkening plains. Rebecca sensed sorrow and loneliness in the woman.

A door banged closed, and Jim emerged from the barn. Rebecca watched him amble toward another cottage. *I wonder why he's so disagreeable.*

He glanced her way. Spotting Rebecca, he stopped. For a moment he gazed at her, then tipped his hat.

Rebecca could feel a flush burn her face. Embarrassed at having been caught watching him, she offered a barely discernible nod and backed away from the window.

When she was certain he was gone, she returned to the window and looked out. The yard was empty, but light radiated from inside several cabins. People she didn't know lived there. Rebecca felt alone and frightened. What was she doing here, so far from home? Then it struck her. She had no home.

She returned to bed, climbed beneath the sheets, and settled her head on soft pillows. The last hint of orange cast its light on the walls. The glow faded, and with the darkness came demons of doubt. Rebecca pulled the sheet up under her chin, as if she could hide from the uncertainties.

Angry voices carried from downstairs, adding to her disquiet. Were Daniel and his father quarreling about her? Bertram didn't want her here. But what could be done now? She was Daniel's wife. Nothing could change that.

10

Daniel sat on the edge of the bed and rested his elbows on his thighs. He rubbed his eyes, then looked at the darkness beyond the window. He was tired and discouraged. The previous night's debate with his father had gained him nothing except more condemnation. He'd known his father would disapprove of Rebecca, but he couldn't help but hope for better.

What if his father was right? What if he had made a mistake?

He looked at his bride. In the near darkness he could scarcely distinguish her features and her dark hair spilling across the pillow. He could imagine how her dark lashes rested against ivory cheeks and wanted to touch her, to press his lips against her cheek. He fought the impulse, still hearing his father's accusations.

"She's certainly no more than a spoiled socialite. How can ya expect 'er to have the heartiness needed to stand up to this country and its demands? Yer a fool, Daniel."

A fool. Well, maybe I am, he thought. He had doubts she would adjust to life on the flats. Most likely, Meghan would have been a wiser choice. After all, they'd known each other all their lives, and she was strong and well suited to life here. *But I don't love Meghan.*

He contemplated Rebecca and the troubles she'd faced since meeting him—her father's death and the loss of her home and all it contained. She'd held up well. When she'd married without love and moved from Boston to Queensland, she'd demonstrated sturdiness and a strong faith. *Right. She'll make it. She'll do fine*, he told himself.

However, in spite of his efforts at optimism, the truth that she didn't love him lay like an open wound. Would she ever? *What can I do to make her love me?* There was nothing he could do to *make* her feel that kind of devotion and passion.

Rebecca moved her hand onto the pillow. Daniel quickly looked away, not wanting her to catch him staring. He pushed up off the bed carefully so as not to disturb her. Rebecca's breathing remained steady and quiet.

Daniel crossed the room, stepped into the dressing closet, and took clothes off the shelf. Feeling his way in the darkness, he dressed quietly. If only his father weren't so demanding, he'd linger here with Rebecca. It would be pleasant to awaken and greet the day together. He smirked. It would never happen, not as long as his father had anything to do with it.

He grabbed his hat off a rack, moved toward the bedroom door, and opened it. Faint light from the hallway illuminated the room. He gazed at Rebecca. If it were possible, she looked even more beautiful than the day he'd first met her. "Love me, Rebecca. Please love me," he whispered before stepping into the corridor.

⁂

Still half asleep, Rebecca rolled onto her side. She opened her eyes and stared at the empty space beside her, then glanced about the room. Daniel was gone. She'd fallen asleep alone and had awakened alone. Is this how it would be?

She felt emptiness inside. Their partnership had quickly created interdependence. Without him, she felt alone.

Sitting up, she rested her arms on bent knees. Already she could feel the heat of the day, and her mind calculated the new wardrobe she'd need. A soft rap sounded at the bedroom door. "Just a moment." Rebecca threw off her lightweight blanket and sheet, dropped her feet over the side of the bed, and grabbed her robe off the bed post. Pulling it around her, she asked, "Who is it?"

"Callie. I brought yer breakfast."

Rebecca opened the door. "Thank you. Come in." Combing her fingers through a tangle of hair, she said, "I must be a sight."

"No, mum. Ya look well." Carrying a tray, Callie stepped into the room. "I didn't wake ya? I woulda waited, but Mr. Thornton believes in risin' early."

"I was awake. Thank you for bringing my breakfast. You didn't have to."

"That's me job." She set the tray on the desk. "There's more if yer of a mind."

Two slices of toasted bread, a poached egg, and a small teapot along with a cup and saucer rested on the tray. "This will be fine," Rebecca said.

"Good, then." Callie stepped out of the room and returned a moment later with a pitcher of fresh water. She laid out a clean towel and washcloth beside the washbowl. She moved silently; even the floorboards gave no sound.

Like a ghost, Rebecca thought, a ripple of apprehension moving through her. The aborigine servant wasn't like anyone she'd met before. Rebecca wondered if all the blacks were like her.

Callie picked up clothing Rebecca had laid over the chair the previous night and started for the door.

"Don't go," Rebecca said. Then she surprised herself by adding, "I could use some company."

Callie looked puzzled.

"Would you stay and visit? I haven't had a chance to meet anyone yet, except family of course."

Still wearing a look of surprise, Callie sat on a straight-backed chair, Rebecca's dress and petticoat resting in her lap. She stared straight ahead, clearly uncomfortable.

Rebecca bit into a piece of toast. "I suppose it can get lonely here—being so far from everything, I mean."

"Ya believe this a lonely place?"

"Well, it is kind of . . . stark."

"Douloo is what it is."

"Have you lived here all your life?"

"All me life on the flats, but 'ere only since I was ten, mum."

"Please call me Rebecca. I'd like to be friends."

Callie's eyes widened.

"I know it's probably not customary for people like us to be more than acquaintances, but it is allowed, isn't it? I mean . . . Daniel and Woodman like each other."

"Yais. They like each other well enough. Woodman is 'ere a long time, since he was a lad. But they not be mates."

"But . . . I thought . . . Well, after seeing them together yesterday, it's clear Daniel thinks highly of Woodman. They must be friends."

"Blacks and whites can't be friends."

Rebecca felt let down. She decided to change the subject. "How did you come to live here?"

"Long time ago me father traded with Mr. Thornton."

"You mean he traded *you*?"

119

"Yais. A good trade, it was." Callie almost smiled. "Me dad needed tools, Mr. Thornton needed a housemaid."

"How could a father do such a thing?"

Hurt flickered across Callie's face. "It was very good. I have a fine life, eh? I 'ave good clothes, a house, and good food. Mr. Thornton been good ta me. He says I'm worth a fair bit."

Rebecca choked down a bite of egg. How could a church elder trade a life for tools? She'd never understood men who felt they had the right to trade away human lives. It had happened in America—even in New England, but she'd not expected it here. This was something Daniel hadn't shared about living at Douloo. She set down her knife and fork, her appetite gone.

"Mrs. Thornton, she's a good lydie. I'm glad ta live 'ere."

Rebecca nodded and tried to think of something else to say. They seemed to share no common ground. "I met Daniel while he was in Boston settling Elton Thornton's affairs."

"Yais. I heard 'bout that." Callie glanced at the clothing in her lap. "I feel bad for Mrs. Thornton. She's real sad. Worse than when Elton had ta go."

"I thought Elton *wanted* to move to America."

Anxiousness touched Callie's face, like someone caught telling tales. "That's not for me ta talk 'bout, eh." She stood. "I got work ta do. G'day." Before Rebecca could object, Callie hurried out of the room.

A woman's screams and a child's wailing carried up from the front yard. *Oh, Lord, what now?* Rebecca crossed to the open window. Leaning on the sill, she gazed down. A black woman, her bare feet raising dust, ran toward the house. Shrieking in an unfamiliar language, she clung to a convulsing child. Falling at the foot of the front steps, she blurted out, "Mrs. Thornton! Help! Help me bybie!"

Rebecca heard footsteps tramp across the veranda; then

Willa appeared on the steps. She hurried to the woman and child. "Lord, have mercy."

The black woman held out the little girl to Willa, who examined a spot on the child's arm. "May I have her?" she asked, gently taking the youngster. Cradling the skinny little girl in her arms, Willa prayed and sang, then prayed some more. When the child vomited on the front of her dress, she paid no heed but continued to pray.

Finally the child quieted. A hand pressed to her mouth, Rebecca watched and pleaded with God to spare her life.

Though the girl went limp and didn't move for a long while, Willa continued to cradle her, rocking and singing. She gently ran her thumb over the child's forehead, brushed aside a wispy curl, then kissed her cheek.

Silently the mother picked up the little one and walked away. Willa remained on the steps.

Rebecca backed away from the window. "No," she said, wiping away tears. It had been so brutal, so swift. How could a child die such a death?

After quickly dressing, Rebecca hurried downstairs and out to the veranda. Willa sat on a cane-back chair. She'd changed her gown and seemed serene.

"I saw what happened," Rebecca said. "What was it? Has some horrible disease come to the station?"

"No." She rocked. "It was a funnel-web."

"And what's a funnel-web?"

"A funnel-web spider. The poor child had no chance."

"A spider did that?" Pressing a hand against her abdomen, Rebecca dropped onto a chair. She felt faint. "What kind of place is this?" she asked, not stopping to think how such a question might sound. "Yesterday I was nearly bitten by a deadly snake, and today a little girl dies from a spider bite?"

"I'm sorry, dear. I assure you, it's quite unusual. I'm not

going to pretend it never happens, but . . . rarely do people get bitten."

Rebecca glanced about, suddenly afraid that one of the poisonous spiders might be lurking on the veranda. "What do funnel-webs look like?"

Willa didn't answer right away, then said quietly, "They're quite large and nasty looking, actually. Their bodies are black, about the size of a man's thumb. They're easy to spot."

Rebecca shuddered.

"They're rather slow-moving creatures, so it's not difficult to kill them. In fact, Woodman likes to have a go at them whenever one's found."

Rebecca managed to nod and gave the porch another look.

"We're careful to keep the house clear of them."

Rebecca promised herself she'd never climb into bed again without checking between the sheets.

Callie appeared, carrying a tray with a teakettle and two cups and saucers. She set it on a wicker table between the women. Her face was an emotionless mask, all but her eyes. Rebecca was certain there was sorrow in their black depths. "Did you know her, Callie?"

"Who, mum?"

"The little girl."

"Yais. She was a good little girl." Her eyes misted, then resolve set in, expelling tears. "Now she's in a fine place."

"Heaven?"

"No. No blacks in heaven." She walked back inside the house.

Willa filled a cup. "Sugar?"

Rebecca felt the shock of Willa's quiet tone sweep through her. Did she believe blacks had no place in heaven?

"Rebecca, are you all right? You look troubled."

"I'm fine. But . . ." She wondered if she ought to say anything. After all, she'd barely arrived, and to voice an opinion over something divisive seemed disrespectful.

"What is it, dear?"

"I just think that blacks do have a place in heaven . . . like the rest of us," she said quietly.

"Of course they do. But they don't believe that. I've tried to convince Callie, but she refuses to listen. Now I wait on God to do the convincing." She smiled.

"Yes. I suppose that would be best." Rebecca's eyes swept over the flower garden, the yard, and then beyond to the barn. Everything seemed silent and empty. "Where is everyone?" she asked, accepting a cup of tea from Willa. "Daniel was gone when I woke up."

"He and the others are inspecting cattle. There's been an outbreak of red water up north. My husband's very careful with the stock. Daniel's a great help to him."

Two black women crossed the yard and entered the cottage where the aborigine mother had disappeared with her daughter.

"Daniel didn't tell me you had black servants. They look different from the ones in the States."

"Oh, how is that?"

"Their skin is darker, and they're smaller."

"They're indigenous. They weren't taken from Africa."

"Are they dangerous? That man . . . Jim, he said . . ."

"Oh, Jim. I dare say, he likes to stir up trouble now and then. Don't listen to a bit of what he has to say." Willa sipped her tea. "The blacks are our servants, not our slaves. Unlike in your country, we pay them."

"In America the Negroes are free, and they earn wages. They were liberated after the war."

"Really?"

Rebecca thought Willa's eyes didn't agree, so she continued, "Yes. The law says they're free. I've always considered slavery abhorrent."

"I must say, I've never been comfortable with the aborigines' plight either. It pains me. I'd like to see them truly emancipated. I see their distress every day."

"I've always believed the Holy Spirit speaks to us about such things," Rebecca said. "When I'm feeling unsettled about something or have a sense of assurance inside, that's him. He speaks to all his children, don't you agree? Even women and blacks?"

Willa smiled. "Yes. I believe he does." She fingered a button along the bodice of her dress. "Not everyone would agree, however." Worry touched her eyes. Then, returning to the subject of the aborigines, she said, "Here at Douloo we treat our blacks well." She gazed out over the open spaces beyond the house. "There are stories . . ."

"Stories? Could you tell me?"

"They're too horrible to speak of."

Although frightened by what she might hear, Rebecca wanted to know. "I feel out of place here. Maybe knowing more about things, even the bad things, might help."

"I doubt that." Willa set her cup on its saucer. "Some people, even in this district, hate the blacks. They kill them whenever they can, even the children."

Rebecca sucked in her breath. "Why?"

With a haunted expression, Willa said, "They're afraid. When I was a child in Melbourne, I witnessed a massacre— even the women and children. It was dreadful." She wet her lips. "Around here, though, most people treat their workers decently enough."

Callie reappeared. "Will ya be needin' me, mum?"

"No. We're fine, Callie." Willa turned back to Rebecca. "In truth, we need each other—blacks and whites."

Callie stood in the doorway.

Willa glanced at her. "No. That's not quite right. The blacks were doing quite well before we came along. We're the ones who need them."

Before Callie retreated indoors, a look of affection passed between her and Willa.

"Callie told me her father traded her for tools," Rebecca said.

"Indeed. That's quite right. Callie's a half caste. Her real father was white. I'd say the man who raised her was delighted to profit from his wife's indiscretion."

"What kind of people would trade away a child?"

"The kind who must survive." Willa's voice was firm. "The aborigines live a life of necessity and practicality. Most of the men value their wives and children, but there are some who see them as less than dogs."

"How horrible."

Willa's brow creased. "In our society how much value have we? Are we not our husbands' property?"

For a moment Rebecca was taken aback. "Why, yes . . . I suppose you might say we're 'property,' but Daniel would never . . ."

"No. Daniel wouldn't. But if he chose to, he has the right."

Rebecca suddenly felt vulnerable. She'd always lived safely under her father's protective shield. He'd never have allowed harm to befall her. Even so, she'd always known that many women in Boston society were viewed as little more than ornaments.

She looked directly at Willa. "I don't suppose our position is all that much different from Callie's, then." She picked up her cup. "And how does Mr. Thornton feel about such things?"

"About me or the blacks?"

"Both, I guess. Daniel has said very little about him."

125

Willa refilled her cup and offered Rebecca more tea, which she declined. "Bertram's a puzzle. He views the blacks much like the rest in the district do—as a necessary possession. But then there's Woodman. He and Woodman grew up together—they've been friends since they were lads. Bertram trusts him and on occasion even seeks out his advice."

Willa smiled. "And me? Well, he loves me and would never mistreat me. However, he takes his responsibility as husband and father quite seriously . . . too much so at times. Because of that, he can seem harsh—but never misinterpret that sternness as cruelty. He's always well meaning."

Rebecca hoped one day she'd be able to look beyond her father-in-law's severe exterior and see his heart. She'd begun to wonder if he had one. She wasn't at all certain he'd ever accept her presence at Douloo.

Willa set her tea on the wicker table, sat back, and clasped her hands. "Now then, I'd like to talk about the party."

"There's going to be a party?"

"Yes. We're having one in your and Daniel's honor—to celebrate your marriage. People from all over the district will be here. You'll meet our neighbors."

Rebecca scanned the open plain. "But you have no neighbors, not that I can see. They must be coming a great distance."

"It's not so far as you believe." Willa smiled. "Miles may separate us, but our lives are intertwined; we take care of each other." Her eyes flashed with affection. "Our friends have been anxious to meet you. We'll have a grand time. There will be music and dancing and, of course, first-rate food."

Rebecca felt anxiety bloom. Would these sturdy flatlanders accept an outsider? She wasn't like these people. *I don't fit*, she thought, and wondered if she ever would.

11

Rebecca wandered toward a covered pavilion, where an aborigine servant busily swept. Dust lingered in the air and tickled Rebecca's nose.

"It will look lovely once we get the decorations hung," Willa said, joining Rebecca.

"I'm sure it will."

Willa watched Callie set out dishes and flatware on a table while Lily settled one of two candelabra in the center. "No. No. That will never do." Willa walked to the table. "Perhaps if we set them here." She moved the candelabra farther apart, then stepped back and eyed the arrangement. "Yes. That's much better." She offered Lily a smile, then returned to the house.

Although dressed in a lightweight cotton gown, Rebecca still felt overly warm. *How will I adjust to this insufferable heat? If only there were a cooling rain.*

The unsettled feeling in Rebecca's stomach intensified. Guests would be arriving soon. She was about to meet long-time Thornton friends and neighbors. What would they think of the American woman who had married into the most prominent family in the district? Scrutiny would be acute.

Rebecca wandered the grounds, wishing she had something to occupy her mind other than the upcoming gathering. What if people knew about her father's financial indiscretions and thought the worst of her? *It is true. I did marry Daniel out of need.* She gazed at her husband, who stood among a group of men tending a side of roasting beef. Had she been wrong to marry him? Now neither of them would ever know true love.

Daniel and another man rotated the beef. Juices hissed as they dropped into a fire pit below, and the smell of roasting meat filled the air. He glanced at Rebecca and smiled. She smiled back, feeling a little less insecure. *He is handsome,* she thought. *I'm sure Meghan Linnell is very distressed. I wonder if she'll be here tonight. Certainly not.* The idea of meeting the woman who had meant to marry Daniel was unsettling. Rebecca hoped she would choose to stay away.

❦

Just as Rebecca found her way back to the table, Willa returned carrying a vase filled with roses from the garden. She smiled at Rebecca, then studied her daughter-in-law more closely. "I dare say, you seem a bit pale. Are you all right?"

"Yes. I'm fine. A little nervous."

"Try not to worry." Willa set the flowers on the table and approached Rebecca. "The people who will be here are friends. They won't bite, really."

"That's good to hear. Do they know?"

"Know what, dear?"

"About why we were married?"

"Oh, there is always speculation, but you've no need to worry. You and Daniel have done nothing wrong."

Rebecca glanced down at her skirt. "I wasn't certain this would be appropriate attire, but I couldn't bear the idea of wearing one of my heavy gowns in this heat."

128

"It's just right. And the soft green suits your complexion." She studied Rebecca a moment. "You're quite lovely, you know."

Rebecca felt a flush of pleasure and embarrassment. "Thank you."

"At the next opportunity we'll have you fitted for new dresses more appropriate for our warmer climate." She glanced at a seam of clouds lying in the distance. "We dare not hope for some cooling rains, eh?" She smiled.

"That would be pleasant. I must admit to not being used to the heat."

"When I first arrived here I was quite overcome by it, but one adjusts."

"It seems the temperature isn't the only thing I'll have to adjust to. Everything here is unlike Boston. I'm not sure what I'll talk about with your guests. I know very little about your country."

"I dare say, they'll be curious about yours." Willa took Rebecca's hand and patted it. "Just be yourself. You're a lovely person and obviously very bright. You'll make a fine impression. I'm sure of it."

"I wish I could be so confident," Rebecca said, taking a steadying breath.

☙

Guests started arriving, and Rebecca was reminded of the many cotillions she'd attended in Boston. Even then she'd much rather have hidden in the library unseen than socialize. Not that she didn't enjoy people, but she disliked the pretentiousness that seemed to accompany such gatherings. *Maybe this will be different,* she thought. *After all, this isn't Boston.*

The household help had been well trained. Each visitor was greeted, and after taking care of shawls and hats, which would be reclaimed for the ride home, the servants made certain every visitor had a cool beverage. Rebecca noticed that the blacks, except for the domestic staff, stayed out of sight.

Like any new husband, Daniel took Rebecca's arm and proudly introduced her around. Elvina Walker, a stout elderly woman with white hair and squinting eyes, joined Daniel and Rebecca. She made certain Rebecca knew she was the head of the women's guild at church, then gushed over Rebecca and tittered over what she called "Daniel's sweet surprise." Although Elvina seemed friendly enough, Rebecca didn't like her much. She knew instinctively that it would be unwise to get on Elvina's bad side.

There were many new faces, and soon Rebecca had their names mixed up. However, she guessed that if she were to call someone by the wrong name the blunder would be quickly forgiven. Everyone she'd met had been gracious and friendly.

When the sun hugged the horizon, lanterns were lit and food was laid out. There was roasted beef, casseroles, cheeses, breads, potatoes, and even fresh fruits and vegetables, as well as sponge cakes with clabbered cream and tarts for dessert. Men piled their plates high, while most women were careful not to overindulge.

Rebecca joined the line at the table. The sight and smell of food made her stomach rumble. She hadn't realized she was so hungry.

A tall, slender woman carrying an overly full plate sauntered up to Rebecca. "I'm Elle Taylor. I would 'ave said hello sooner except there was a crowd of people already waiting ta meet ya. It's a true pleasure ta meet Daniel Thornton's wife." She smiled warmly.

"I'm Rebecca. I'm pleased to meet you."

"Yer roight lovely. And I figure smart too."

"Thank you." Rebecca wasn't quite sure how to respond to such straightforward compliments.

Elle glanced over her shoulder at Daniel. "He's proud of ya. That's clear."

Rebecca looked at her husband. Was he?

Elle walked beside Rebecca; then when Rebecca sat she took the chair beside her. "So, ya settling in all roight?"

"Yes. But I'm still getting used to my surroundings. This is very different from home."

Elle took a bite of bread. "Just wanted ta let ya know I'm glad to have ya in the district. My niece, Cambria, is dyin' ta meet ya. I expect she'll come 'round before the night's over." She picked up a piece of beef and took a bite. Talking around the food, she said, "I run the dress shop in town. If yer ever in need." She turned her attention to a woman sparring with two youngsters. "Wal, looks like I've got a friend in need. I'll see ya 'round." She headed for the woman with the tussling children.

Rebecca watched Elle walk away. She was a lively sort, and Rebecca liked her. Elle walked past Elvina. Neither woman looked at the other. In fact, the two seemed to snub each other. Rebecca wasn't exactly surprised. They couldn't be more different.

A group of men assembled on a platform alongside the dance floor. One played a banjo, another a guitar, and the other a mouth organ. They started playing, and guests quickly finished up their food and gathered inside the pavilion. An occasional hoot and clapping of hands accompanied the music. Couples moved onto the dance floor.

Daniel approached with a woman on his arm. Rebecca felt an unexpected jolt of jealousy. The woman had very blond hair swept up carelessly off her neck. She was reed thin and had radiant blue eyes and an inviting smile. She walked as if she would have been more comfortable in trousers.

"I've someone I'd like you to meet," Daniel said. "This is Cambria Taylor—a neighbor and friend."

Cambria took Rebecca's hand and shook it heartily. "G'day. It's nice ta meet Daniel's bride."

Rebecca's jealousy evaporated. There was no deceit or threat in this woman.

"Hello. I believe I just met your aunt, Elle."

"Yais. She's me father's sister."

"Cambria's family owns a sheep station not far from here," Daniel said. "Our fathers were mates when they were lads, and their fathers before that."

"I've known him forever," Cambria said with a smile. "There was a time when I could give him a go at arm wrestling." She turned to him. "Then ya had to go and grow up. That was the end of that."

"I think I was sixteen before I could beat her," Daniel said with a grin. Two men grappled with what was left of the cooked beef. "Looks like I'm needed. Excuse me." He headed for the men and what looked like a disaster in the making.

"I've been dyin' ta meet the woman who stole Daniel's heart," Cambria said. With a mischievous grin she added, "Meghan Linnell is fit ta be tied."

"Yes. I heard she might be."

"Ya'll meet up with her sooner or later. I'm sure she'll be 'ere. She couldn't pass up the opportunity ta meet her rival."

Rebecca didn't like the sound of that.

"She's had her eye on Daniel for years. They were considered the perfect couple. When she heard the news of yer weddin', she was down 'ere in two flicks of a lamb's tail, askin' if he'd truly gone ahead and got married. She was so mad that . . . Well, let's say if ya'd been 'round 'ere ya would 'ave been roight smart to stay out of sight." She grinned, her eyes sparkling.

132

"Really?" is all Rebecca could say. She glanced about. "Is she here?"

"I haven't seen 'er yet." Cambria leaned in close to Rebecca and spoke softly. "To tell ya the truth, I'm glad Daniel married ya. I'd hate ta 'ave seen him saddled with someone like Meghan. She's roight spoiled and downroight overbearin'. He deserves someone better. He's a good sort, ya know."

"Yes. I do know." Rebecca remembered the touch of Daniel's gentleness as she said the words.

"Sorry," Daniel said, rejoining the women. "Those two blokes were about to drop the second helpings in the dirt." He laid a hand on Rebecca's arm. "Would you like to dance?"

"I'd love to." Rebecca turned to Cambria. "It was a pleasure meeting you. I hope we'll have a chance to visit again."

"Yais, me too. We'll make a point of it, eh?"

"Absolutely." Rebecca liked Cambria and hoped for a friendship.

Daniel guided her onto the dance floor. When he placed an arm around her waist, it felt natural. For the first time that day, Rebecca felt herself relax. He steered her through the other dancers, skillfully moving across the floor.

"You're a good dancer, Daniel," Rebecca said.

"You can thank my mum for that. She made sure Elton and I wouldn't embarrass the ladies. She was raised to believe in the social graces."

"We can all be grateful for that," Rebecca said with a laugh. She liked the feel of his large hand over hers and the closeness of his body. His blue eyes gazed down at her. Was it love she saw in them or only passion?

For a long while they danced without speaking. Rebecca's mind wandered back to Cambria, and she said, "I like your friend Cambria. She seems very nice. I met her aunt as well."

"She's a good gal. She and her family are well respected

in these parts. Except for Elle. She's another story—loved and hated, actually."

"Why is that? I liked her very much."

"Oh, she's one of those who believe in being just who they are, and that kind can sometimes be a burr under one's saddle. You'll see her in church occasionally, and Cambria's almost always there."

"Daniel," a woman said, stepping up to the couple. "How good to see ya. I meant to come by sooner."

The woman's voice was like silk, rich and smooth. Her brown eyes melded with Daniel's. She ignored Rebecca. Her reddish-brown hair had been swept up in a chignon, but tendrils caressed her face. She wore a vibrant blue gown, and it would have been stunning except that it was cut too low in front. Even in Boston it would have raised eyebrows.

Meghan, Rebecca thought.

Laying a possessive hand on Daniel's arm, Meghan tossed a smug smile at Rebecca. "I was hoping I might steal him from ya. Just for a few minutes." She looked back at Daniel. "It's been too long since we've seen each other, eh?"

"I'd like a visit, but right now I'm dancing with my wife."

"I haven't even been introduced to yer new bride." Meghan batted long lashes.

"Rebecca Thornton—Meghan Linnell."

"Lovely to meet ya," Meghan said. Before Rebecca could reply, she turned back to Daniel. "Please, just one dance?" Looking at Rebecca, she asked, "Ya wouldn't mind loanin' 'im to me for just a few minutes, would ya?"

"Of course not," Rebecca heard herself reply. It was the polite response but the last thing she wanted. Confronted by Daniel's past love, she felt a stab of resentment and jealousy.

"Wonderful. See, Daniel? She doesn't mind." Meghan stepped between the couple and took Daniel's hands. Daniel didn't move. Then finally, with a bewildered look at Rebecca, he stepped into the dance with his new partner.

Watching them, Rebecca felt miserable. *They dance well together. Obviously they're suited to one another—both Australians. They know what it means to live out here and to be part of this district—how to run a cattle station.* Rebecca didn't realize it, but she was clenching her jaw. Meghan probably would have been a better choice for Daniel. *If I hadn't agreed to marry him, he would have wed someone who truly loved him,* she thought sadly.

"I see you have no dance partner," Jim Keller said, stepping into Rebecca's line of vision.

"Meghan was insistent."

"I don't doubt it. She's used to getting her way." Jim offered Rebecca a small bow. "Would you forgive a bloke his bad manners and dance with me?"

Thankful to be rescued, Rebecca said, "I forgive you. And yes, I would like to dance. Thank you, Mr. Keller."

"Just Jim. Don't believe in formalities."

"I noticed," Rebecca said with a grin. "After our first meeting I was beginning to think . . ."

"Yeah, I know. I was rude. Sometimes I open my mouth when it ought to stay shut. I apologize. I was in a foul mood that day."

"Well, you're not now, and I must say, this mood suits you much better." Rebecca couldn't help but notice the strong line of his jaw and the penetrating brown eyes beneath perfectly shaped brows. He was quite handsome. "I prefer you when you're in a good disposition, sir."

Jim wasn't as good a dancer as Daniel, but he managed to maneuver Rebecca around the dance floor without stepping on her toes. For several moments neither spoke. Finally Rebecca said, "I believe you were in more than a bad temper

135

when I arrived. You seemed to take pleasure in frightening me."

"That's not exactly true."

"What was it then?"

Jim swung around, then stepped backward in time with the music. "Since you ask . . . well, I knew right off you didn't belong here. You're cultured and . . . soft. This country will kill you. Don't know what got into Daniel, bringing you here."

"I'm not as fragile as you think. I can take care of myself." Rebecca felt a stir of indignation. "Why is it that men always believe that because a woman is cultured and educated she's also weak? I've had a good upbringing, but I'm strong and can do whatever it takes to live alongside my husband. And I wouldn't say Willa Thornton is tough. She's genteel and well bred, but she's done well here."

"Whoa, simmer down. You've really got your dander up." Jim smiled. "Didn't mean to rile you."

"I won't apologize for my displeasure, Mr. Keller. I grew up in a society that demeans women. And to be perfectly honest with you, I've had just about enough of it. I'd hoped that here it might be different."

Jim shook his head. "It's no different here, especially not at Douloo. The women know their place. In fact . . ."

"Excuse me. May I cut in?" Bertram asked, wearing a charming smile. "I haven't had the honor of dancing with my new daughter-in-law."

"Of course, Mr. Thornton." Jim stepped back and bowed slightly to Rebecca. "It was a pleasure." With that, he turned and walked away.

A sense of strength emanated from Bertram. When he took Rebecca's hand and led her into the dance, she could feel the power and inner intensity of the man.

"So how do ya like Douloo so far?"

136

"It's remarkable, intriguing really. But I've barely had time to get acquainted. I've had no opportunity to explore the station yet. However, after I've been properly introduced, I'm sure to be impressed."

"I can't imagine living anyplace else. This is God's country, eh?"

Although Bertram smiled and chatted, the demeanor beneath the pleasantries frightened Rebecca. His power and authority were palpable, making her feel small.

Bertram's grip on her hand tightened, and his pleasant expression turned severe. "I know about your father and your reason for marrying my son. I won't mince words—I don't approve."

"It was your son who asked me," Rebecca said.

"Enticed by your beauty, no doubt." He squared his jaw. "Ya need to know yer not my choice for Daniel. 'Ere a man needs a strong woman, someone who knows and loves this country. Yer an outsider and will most certainly become faint at the first sign of adversity . . . as we've already seen."

Rebecca blushed at the reminder of her snake encounter. She compressed her lips and forced down mounting outrage.

"But . . . a marriage can't be undone. So I've decided the only way 'bout it is to accept ya, make ya part of the family. It's my intention to love ya like a daughter, like my own. And I expect ya to look at me as yer father. There's a lot to running a station, and my son will need a woman who's able to stand up to the hardships and support him. It's not just lawn parties where the big question is whether or not to serve crumpets or cakes."

"I never for a moment thought so," Rebecca said, her outrage spiraling.

He continued as if he hadn't heard her. "Ya'll answer to me like I were yer father."

She couldn't imagine Bertram as her father. But now wasn't the time to tell him so. Swallowing her indignation, Rebecca managed to say, "I'll do my best as Daniel's wife. I'll stand beside him. And just because we didn't marry for love doesn't mean we don't care about each other. I think a lot of your son." She met his eyes and held them. "And I'm not weak, sir."

"Well, that's something we can hope for, eh?"

At that moment Rebecca decided that she'd show Bertram just who she was. She'd be a good wife, and she'd learn about the station and what the cattle business was all about. She'd be the kind of helpmate Daniel—and Bertram—could be proud of. She'd show him that just because she was Boston born didn't mean she was delicate or cowardly.

Bertram steered her to the edge of the dance floor. "I look forward to knowing ya better. God has placed me over ya as yer guardian, then." He walked away.

"I thought it was Daniel God has placed over me," Rebecca said softly.

Bertram didn't hear. He wasn't meant to. Rebecca already knew it made little difference to him.

12

Rebecca reached beneath a rosebush and pulled a weed from the loose soil. She dropped it into a bucket. Working in the garden almost gave her a sense of belonging at Douloo. She liked the smell of earth and vegetation, and the sweet aroma of roses, lavender, and wisteria felt soothing.

However, there was always the thought of Bertram overseeing every soul in his household. Just the idea of his power made her feel weak. It might have been less intimidating if she felt Daniel were a dedicated and loving advocate for her. *I wonder if Bertram's ever considered the potential of independence? I'd like to be the one to teach him.*

"What are you thinking?" Willa asked. "You have a most curious smile on your face."

"I do?" Rebecca searched for a suitable reply. "I was just thinking about how much I enjoy working in the garden. It gives me a feeling of contentment. At home we had grounds-keepers. All I ever really got to do was cut flowers now and again."

"I've always found working with plants to be exceedingly uplifting. A garden appreciates a gentle touch and reliable workers." She gazed over the patch. "Indeed, I love it here.

The earth is cool and damp. It's like . . . nourishment to me."

Willa's eyes took on a misty look. "My mother always had a flower garden. Several times a week we worked in it together. Now I have my own." She leaned close to a red rose and smelled deeply. "I dare say, my favorites are the roses. Nothing in this world has a more refined fragrance." Her eyes sparkled with mischief. "Except, of course, the smell of a newborn baby."

It took Rebecca a moment to catch Willa's meaning; then she felt an embarrassed flush.

"Oh, I know I'm being meddlesome, but this place needs children."

Rebecca hadn't really thought about children. She'd had so much more on her mind. "Daniel and I hope to have children one day, but when . . . well, that isn't up to us."

"Indeed. But a mother-in-law can pray for such a blessing, eh?"

"Of course."

Rebecca wasn't certain she wanted a child. The idea of raising a family in this empty land gave her pause. And bringing children into a loveless marriage didn't seem quite right. And then of course there was Bertram. He was definitely not the kind of grandfather she'd envisioned for her offspring.

Since her arrival he'd managed to be polite part of the time and had remained reserved. He dominated the family. Rebecca didn't have to work hard to imagine that he could be cruel. She did her best to avoid him.

Pulling another stubborn weed, she asked, "How do you think Mr. Thornton would feel about having little ones in the house?"

"He'd be delighted. We've always talked about grandchildren and how one day our grandson would take over the

140

station." Willa shook dirt from the roots of a weed. "He loves children, truly."

Rebecca tried to imagine Bertram playing with a child. She couldn't conjure up the image no matter how hard she tried. The idea seemed preposterous.

Her doubts must have shown, for Willa said, "I know he seems stern, but he has a good heart. Bertram's father withheld his affections, so, sadly, Bertram learned to be reserved."

Reserved? Rebecca thought. *Brutal might be more fitting.*

Willa clipped off an unruly branch. "He cares deeply for his family. However, instead of revealing his feelings, he shows us in other ways. He's provided us with a nice home, he maintains a good reputation in the district, and he works exceedingly hard to maintain this station.

"It's been a burden he's carried well. Since he was a lad he knew that one day Douloo would be his to rule. He paid close attention to his father's handling of the place, and when his father died he took on the responsibility courageously."

The word *rule* had jumped out at Rebecca. *That's exactly what he does—rule.* She knew it was wrong, but it seemed everyone else was unaware of the potential harm.

Willa pushed herself up off her knees and brushed bits of vegetation from her skirt. "When Bertram was twelve he was required to go away to boarding school. It was excruciating for him. He told me how devastated he was. Indeed, he said he feared it would break his heart. All he thought of was returning home." Her sky blue eyes shone with pride. "And yet, he did as he was told without complaint, and he worked hard earning high marks in school. When he came home for good, that was the beginning of life to him. He relished the responsibility of safeguarding Douloo."

Rebecca felt a twinge of compassion for the boy who had

been sent away and then returned to face the responsibilities of a man.

Willa smiled tenderly. "Bertram's always taken a serious view of life. But that's part of what drew me to him. Of course, he *was* very handsome," she added, smiling. A dimple identical to Daniel's appeared in her cheek. "I believe I fell in love with him at first sight."

She turned serious eyes on Rebecca. "Don't be too hard on him, eh? His growing-up years were difficult. Too much, perhaps, was expected of him. And his father believed in swift obedience. If it didn't come about, the offender felt the sting of the belt. Mr. Thornton believed he had absolute authority over his family and that he was accountable for their sinful behavior or their righteous conduct."

Rebecca knew she was taking a dangerous step but felt compelled to ask, "Isn't that what your husband believes?"

Willa's eyes widened, the blue deepened. A moment passed. Then she said fervently, "Bertram loves us. He does what he believes is best. And he seeks God's will and direction in all things. He's a man of God, and I trust him to do what is right." She paused, then added, "Truly, a man carries the greater burden in a marriage. God holds him accountable for the way he takes care of his family."

Although Rebecca knew she might endanger the blossoming relationship between herself and Willa, she tentatively pushed on. "I agree a husband has an important role as head of his home, but God has placed him there as a protective covering, not as a monarch. There should be mutual respect and cooperation. And a man should never forget that God has provided his Holy Spirit to teach and guide *all* of his children. It has been my experience that growing as a Christian is often a series of errors. Our mistakes help us recognize our heavenly Father's voice, and hopefully, we will learn to listen and obey."

For a long moment Willa was quiet. Finally she said, "You're wise for someone so young, I dare say. And I agree with you. However, there are those who have ears to hear and those who do not. Indeed, wouldn't you agree it is wise to listen to the more mature, the ones who know God and his Word best? My husband is a fine example of maturity. I've never known a man more committed to prayer and to the study of our Lord's Word. He never misses his morning prayers." She clipped a rose and set it in a basket. "I trust him."

Rebecca smoothed the ground beneath a rosebush. It was true that some Christians needed more help than others, and it was always sensible to seek out advice from one more mature, but that was not an excuse for heavy-handed leadership.

"When someone loves deeply, he can be trusted." Willa looked over her garden. "My Bertram loves in just such a way. In fact, this garden is an expression of his affection. He allows it because he knows how much it means to me. Water is precious here. And if this garden is to live, we must keep the ground moist. Many men out here would consider it a waste to put water into a flower garden, but Bertram understands me well. And he loves me—so we have a garden."

Rebecca railed inwardly at Willa's use of the word *allow*. Did she make no decisions on her own? However, it was a man's world whether one lived in Queensland or Boston.

Hoping to avoid friction between herself and her mother-in-law, Rebecca decided to let go of the differences. "It's clear Bertram loves you. Who wouldn't?" She stood and kissed the older woman's cheek.

Willa placed a hand on Rebecca's shoulder. "I'm so happy you came to us. I've always wanted a daughter, and now I feel I have one. After Elton left . . ." Her eyes filled with tears. "Well, it hasn't been the same." She smiled painfully. "And you've helped fill the gap."

"I'm happy you feel that way. I've always missed having a mother, and now . . . well, now you're more than just a mother-in-law to me. I'm glad I'm here." Rebecca did feel a special bond with Willa. Maybe meeting Daniel had been an answer to more than one prayer. Not only had she found a man to rescue her, but perhaps she'd found a mother as well.

Even as the pleasant thought settled over Rebecca so did the shadow of Bertram. In spite of Willa's confidence, Rebecca doubted his wisdom. And moreover, she was confused. Clearly, he was a man of God, but she disagreed with him on many issues. Should she trust the one with years of experience or her own convictions? Could it be that she'd been misled all her life, that what she'd been taught about individual spiritual accountability had been wrong?

Pushing aside her turmoil, she leaned close to a rose, smelling its heavy, sweet fragrance. She bent the stem and broke it off and added the rose to the bunch in Willa's basket. She needed to feel some sense of independence, to breathe.

"When we first arrived Daniel said we would ride often, but he's been so busy there hasn't been time. I was wondering if I might go on my own."

"That would never do. It would be unwise, dear. This is a wild place, and you don't know your way about. It could be dangerous."

"I know a little bit of the area. We've been to church, so I know my way into town. I could keep to the road."

"You'll need more than that before you go too far afield. There are miles of open ground, and to the inexperienced eye it all looks alike. You could easily become lost. And to go unescorted . . ."

"At home I used to ride nearly every day. And I never required an escort."

"Perhaps with Bertram's permission. And you must give

yourself more time; there are dangers you know nothing about. There's the heat, and sometimes dust storms come up without warning. And what would you do if a lizard or snake frightened your mount and you were thrown? No. Bertram wouldn't allow it."

Bertram wouldn't allow it? Rebecca felt rising frustration. "Meghan Linnel rides alone. In fact, she's been here on several occasions." Just the thought of the arrogant young woman made Rebecca angry.

"She's not like other women."

"That's obvious," Rebecca said.

Willa cocked a brow. "Meghan grew up in the district and has always come and gone as she pleases."

Rebecca folded her arms over her chest and settled a challenging look on Willa. "You know as well as I do that Meghan comes here to see Daniel. I'm not sure she hasn't seen him more than I have."

Willa seemed to be struggling to stifle a smile. "Do I hear jealousy in your tone?"

"I think her behavior is disgraceful."

"I understand the difficulty for you, but you've nothing to fear from Meghan. Daniel's interest is completely platonic—they're no more than friends."

Willa clipped another rose. "Meghan has a mind of her own. I'll grant you, she's a bit forward at times. But you've no need to worry. She was raised properly and knows where the line of propriety is—she won't step past it." Willa moved to another rosebush.

"I'd still appreciate it if Miss Linnel would stay away from Douloo."

"She's simply having a bit of a tantrum. She knows her visits get under your skin. The smart thing for you to do is to not let on."

"I don't think it's proper for a woman to call on a married man."

"Indeed. But Meghan and Daniel have been friends since they were children. They're chums, actually." She smiled warmly. "And I know my son. He's an honorable man and will not shame you." She smiled. "I'm not certain, but I think he may actually love you."

Rebecca sighed. *If only we did love each other*, she thought. *Life would be more bearable.*

As if reading Rebecca's thoughts, Willa said, "Nothing is too difficult for God." She placed an arm around Rebecca's waist as they walked toward the porch. "Let's put these in water and then see if we can find a sweet treat for the children, eh?"

The two women quietly trimmed the flowers and arranged them in vases. Rebecca's mind remained with Daniel. Had her feelings for him changed since arriving at Douloo? She didn't believe so. She'd always held him in high esteem and still did. He worked long hours, and she often went to bed alone. In some ways, she wondered if their friendship hadn't wilted to some degree. His father kept him so busy that they had little time for conversation.

There were times during the day when she longed to see him, to share a new discovery or some inner thought. He seemed the only one who could satisfy the need for comradeship. Had she always felt that way?

Willa set one vase of flowers in the center of the dining room table and the other on a parlor stand in the sitting room. After that, she cut slices of sweet bread. "The aborigine children fancy this," she explained, arranging the bread on a plate.

146

"They do love the sweets, but I'm not so sure they don't enjoy the stories even more."

"That might be true, but their mothers are not so pleased." Willa frowned. "I pray that one day they'll hear with more than their ears." She carried the plate of bread and walked to the library, where she picked out a book from the case.

⚮

Willa sat on a bench beneath a gum tree, and children gathered about. An aborigine girl, no more than three years old, with wild yellow hair and skinny arms and legs, climbed into her lap. Willa hugged her and kissed her cheek, then handed her a piece of bread.

"Thank ya, mum," the little girl said.

"You're very welcome."

The rest of the sweet bread was handed around to the children and their mothers. Jim joined the group, leaning against a gum tree. When he caught Rebecca's eye, he winked. The aborigine adults stood and watched quietly, their expressions suspicious. The little ones settled on the ground and munched on bread, their faces eager. Willa opened the book and began reading.

"A carnival was coming to town, and a little boy named Johnny wanted badly to go," Willa began.

Rebecca sat on the ground with a young aborigine boy leaning against her. He ate his bread slowly, listening to the story. *This is wonderful*, Rebecca thought. *The children love tales. It's a good introduction to literature.* She gazed at the group of youngsters and their mothers, wondering if any knew how to read.

"Johnny worked very hard to earn the money for a ticket and a sweet roll." Willa smiled at the children, then continued.

A breeze rippled Rebecca's bonnet. She loosened the ties and let it drop onto her shoulders. After all, she was sitting in the shade. She glanced at Jim. He seemed taken with the story. His gaze was nearly as animated as the children's. *He's a puzzle*, she thought, wishing it weren't inappropriate to nurture a friendship between the two of them. *Daniel allows his familiarity with Meghan to continue. Isn't it the same thing?*

Jim glanced at her and tipped his hat. Rebecca nodded, then turned her attention back to Willa and the story.

"Johnny had almost reached the carnival when he saw an old woman sitting along the side of the road rocking back and forth and looking very sad. He didn't even want to look at her, for he knew there wasn't enough money left to help anyone else."

The little girl in Willa's lap tapped her arm. "Is he going to help her?"

"We'll have to read on and see," Willa said, then continued. "Johnny stopped and asked the woman what was wrong. 'I have no milk. And my children are hungry.'

"Knowing that if he gave her the last of his money there would be none for the carnival, the boy reached into his pocket and took out the remaining coins. He stared at them, then held out his hand and offered them to the woman. She smiled and with many thanks accepted the gift and hurried on her way."

"What's he gonna' do now?" one of the children asked. "He's got no money."

Rebecca watched the children's faces. Their black eyes shimmered in anticipation. *There should be a school for these youngsters*, she thought but knew better than to even suggest such a thing. It wasn't done.

"At the gate there was a man, and he watched Johnny as he stood looking in. Finally he asked him why he didn't buy a ticket, and when Johnny told him about the people he'd

148

met along the way, the man looked at the ground and in surprise bent and picked up a ticket from the dirt. Holding it up, he said, 'Well, what d'ya know—a ticket.' He looked about. 'I don't see anyone here looking for it. How about you use it?'

"Then the man dug into his pocket, pulled out a coin, and handed it to Johnny. 'Wouldn't be a carnival without a hot roll.'

"Johnny walked through the gate. Once inside he bought the hottest, biggest roll the baker had. There were painted clowns and acrobats, and he actually got to ride on a camel's back. Even though Johnny had given away all his money, it had turned out to be an exceedingly wonderful day."

Willa closed the book and studied the children's faces. "Johnny gave everything he had, but he wasn't sad. He felt happy inside because he was able to help the people along his way. And God had been watching over him. He was very pleased with the little boy and made certain Johnny got to enjoy the carnival after all."

"Can you read another story?" a little boy asked.

"I'll read you a story about Jesus."

The children turned quiet, and some glanced at their mothers, whose faces showed disapproval.

Willa was not put off. She opened her Bible and read the story about how Jesus taught at the synagogue while he was still a boy. Then she explained that he'd come to tell everyone who would listen all about his Father in heaven. And that every person, no matter how evil he might be, could one day live in heaven if only he believed in the Savior who had come to rescue him.

The children fidgeted, and when Willa finished they jumped up and ran off to play. All except the little girl who sat in her lap. She hugged Willa. "I like Jesus," she said, then walked away. The aborigine women returned to their work.

"Thank you, ma'am," Jim said, tipping his hat. "Reminds me of the days when I was a boy. We never missed church." He offered Rebecca a smile, then walked toward one of the corrals.

Willa stood. "He's a nice young man," she said. Then glancing at two of the aborigine women, she knit her brows. "They don't hear. And I don't know how to help them understand. I pray that the little ones will believe one day." She held the books against her chest. "If I could just get one to accept the truth, the others might too."

"I'm sure it will happen," Rebecca said.

Willa smiled. "I will continue to pray and to tell stories. The rest is up to God." She walked toward the house.

"I'll be along shortly," Rebecca called after her. She wanted to speak to Callie. Maybe Callie could explain why the blacks were so strongly set against Christianity. With a glance at the pale blue sky, she wiped moisture from her brow, then settled her hat in place and crossed the dirt yard to Callie's cottage.

Suspicion tightening the corners of her mouth, Callie met Rebecca at the door. "Why ya 'ere?"

"I wanted to speak to you. And I've never been to your house."

Holding open the door, Callie stepped back to show off the sparse interior of the single-room cabin. A table, two grass-woven rockers, and a bed were the only pieces of furniture. "Nothin' much ta see, eh?" She almost smiled. "Can I get ya a glass of water?"

"Yes. Thank you." Rebecca leaned against the porch railing and watched a woman scrubbing clothes alongside a nearby cottage. A baby lay in a pouch slung across her chest.

150

Callie dipped water out of a barrel and handed it to Rebecca.

"Thank you." Hoping the water was clean, she sipped. It was surprisingly cool. She emptied the cup, then handed it back to Callie. "That was refreshing. I was thirsty."

Callie returned the cup to the hook on the side of the barrel, then sat on the porch steps to watch three young boys playing with stones in the dirt. They tossed the pebbles, then cried out their joy or disappointment at the results.

Rebecca didn't understand the game, but she enjoyed watching.

"Mrs. Thornton is a good woman. She's kind ta the children," Callie said.

"She's always kind, which is why I'm a bit confused. Some of the women seem angry when she shares her Bible stories."

"It isn't Mrs. Thornton . . . We don't believe in Jesus. The God she speaks of isn't our God."

"There's only one God, the almighty God who created the heavens and the earth. Jesus was his Son."

"Yer God is only a tale spread by the white man."

"Callie . . ."

"We shouldn't speak of it anymore." She stood. "Ya should go now." Without even glancing at Rebecca, Callie walked past her and into the cottage.

Standing alone on the porch, Rebecca was dumbfounded. "I'm sorry," she said softly, then stepped off the porch, glancing at the nearly naked children with their dusky black skin.

She walked toward the house. The porch swing creaked, and she knew Willa would be sitting there, her sewing in her lap and a cup of tea at her side. This was a strange land—the cultured and the untamed living side by side. How would she ever find her place in this unruly country?

13

A knock came at the door as Rebecca pulled a brush through her dark tangle of curls. "Come in."

The door opened. "G'day, mum," Callie said, stepping inside. She carried a tray with tea and crumpets to the table near the window.

"Good morning, Callie."

"Feels like it's goin' ta be a hot one, eh?"

"Yes, very." Rebecca set the brush on the bureau. "Please stay and share a cup of tea with me."

"No time this mornin'. There's work ta be done. And ya 'ave church."

"Do you ever go? To church I mean."

"Oh no, mum." Callie filled a cup with tea, added a half teaspoon of sugar, and stirred. Handing it to Rebecca, she said, "It's roight hot. Be careful ya don't burn yer tongue." She started for the door, then stopped. She shifted from one foot to the other.

"Yes?"

"Well, mum, actually, me and some of the other lydies were talking . . . 'bout Mrs. Thornton and her readin' from the Bible. We like her roight fine, but . . . Wal, could ya ask 'er not ta tell no more stories 'bout Jesus? Yer close ta 'er, she'll listen ta ya."

"But why not?"

"Like I said yesterday, it's not our way. We don't want the children askin' 'bout it. The spirit god dreamed for many years of what he would make, and then he made everything—the rocks and trees, animals and people. We come from the land. We belong ta the land. And when we die, we go back ta the land. There's no place called heaven, and there's no Jesus."

"Oh, but there is. Please . . . let me show you." Rebecca walked to the bed stand and picked up her Bible. "God has so much to say to us. He loves us . . ."

"No. It's no good ta be lookin' at that book. There's no blacks what read it. The Boolyah man tells us what we need ta know."

"What's a Boolyah man?"

"One with great powers, and he's roight smart. No one goes against 'im, no one. And he can do things . . . things I can't speak of."

"Well, he's not God, and God can do *all* things." Rebecca looked at the Bible in her hands. "This is God's Word. He spoke straight to mankind so we would know the truth."

Callie stared at the leather-bound book in Rebecca's hand. Her eyes were hot with anger, but her voice remained steady and unemotional as she said, "There are white men who read that book . . . and still they kill blacks—even the by-bies. Mr. Thornton gives the blacks food and a place ta sleep. But he doesn't see us. He's a hard bloke. And he reads that book."

"Yes, that's true, but what about Mrs. Thornton? She's kind and good, and she reads it too."

"No matter if she reads or not—she be kind." Callie walked to the door. "Will ya speak ta 'er?"

"I will, but I can't promise anything will change."

Callie stepped into the hallway and silently closed the door. Rebecca dropped onto the chair at the desk, still gripping her Bible. Gazing out onto the yard below, she studied a clutch of hens scratching and pecking at the ground. *I have about as much sense as those chickens. I spoke up too quickly. Now Callie will never listen to what I have to say. I'm always blundering along ahead of you, Lord. Please forgive me. Help me to be useful to you and not a hindrance.*

She gazed at the Bible in her lap and ran her hand over the black leather cover, then watched as Callie carried a pail of leftovers and vegetables to the pigpen. Rebecca closed her eyes. "Father, help her to see you. Show Callie that you're real, that you love her, and that *you* created her, not some unknown god who supposedly walked the earth thousands of years ago."

Later that morning Rebecca walked up the church steps. Elvina Walker greeted her. "G'day," the white-haired woman said. "How's it been with ya?"

"Very well, thank you," Rebecca replied, hoping to avoid being trapped in a conversation with the well-known gossip.

"G'day to ya," Cambria said, taking the stairs.

"Hello," Rebecca said, grateful for the distraction.

"It's a lovely day, eh?" Elvina said.

"I figure we're in for a storm later though. Feels a bit muggy, wouldn't ya say?" Cambria smiled charmingly.

The bell chimed, calling everyone indoors. Cambria looped an arm through Rebecca's and walked in with her through the foyer. "Where's Daniel?"

"He had business of some kind. He'll be here shortly. I'm to save a place for him."

"Mind if I sit by ya, then? I'm here on me own today."

154

"Please do."

The two women walked down the center aisle between the heavy wood pews. The sanctuary was bare of any adornments except for a wooden cross at the front. Its one redeeming quality was the numerous windows on both sides. Sunlight slanted into the room, detracting from its otherwise somber tone. Rebecca sidestepped into a pew to her left and sat, careful to keep her eyes forward. It wasn't seemly to gape about.

"I'm so glad I caught ya," Cambria whispered. "Reverend Cobb's sermons are dry as dust. If I start ta nod, ya'll have ta wake me." She grinned.

Rebecca understood Cambria's sentiments. She'd not yet experienced a single inspiring sermon since arriving at Thornton Creek.

Reverend Cobb stood at a lectern in front, sorting through notes. She studied the man. He couldn't possibly be more ordinary looking. He was rather small and, she guessed, somewhere in his midforties. His brown hair was thinning but hadn't yet gone gray, and his pallid blue eyes seemed sad.

He continued to riffle through his notes. *There are a lot of them*, Rebecca thought with dismay. Last week he'd talked of hellfire and brimstone for nearly two hours, and the week before that he'd preached on the same topic.

Her eyes settled on the large cross behind the lectern. It was rough planed and slightly irregular. She wondered if the cross Christ had carried had actually looked like that. She wished Reverend Cobb would talk about such things rather than sin and hellfire.

He settled spectacles low on his nose and gazed over the rims at the congregation. "G'day. May the Lord bless ya." He smiled, then glanced at his notes.

Rebecca didn't exactly dislike Reverend Cobb. Although he

seemed somewhat stern, she'd caught glimpses of a compassionate disposition. However, he lacked spiritual vigor.

As the reverend began to speak, Daniel walked in with Cambria's aunt Elle on his arm. Rebecca liked Elle. She had a genuine, friendly nature. However, it was this same authenticity that often got her into trouble. Even Cambria had said she thought her aunt too outspoken at times, but she professed to loving her intensely. Elle was Cambria's father's only sister, and she'd never married, preferring to remain unfettered. She offered Rebecca and her niece a cheery smile as she sat on the other side of Cambria.

Daniel sat and grasped Rebecca's hand. "Sorry for being late," he whispered.

She offered him a smile, not unaware of the warmth of his hand. Rebecca glanced at him and felt unexpected tenderness for her husband.

She turned her attention to Reverend Cobb and wondered why he never talked about the joy and hope they had in Christ. While he rambled on about the terrors that awaited those who refused to repent and turn their lives over to God, Rebecca's mind wandered back to her morning conversation with Callie.

She tried to imagine Callie sitting here beside her. The image of the black woman with her frizzy hair and untamed spirit sitting stiff backed and proper in a pew didn't fit. *She would hate it*, Rebecca thought. *I nearly do, and I love the Lord.*

She glanced at the people around her—no blacks. They weren't allowed. *How will they ever come to a saving knowledge of Christ if they're not accepted in church?* She focused on the reverend. Could his sermons show anyone the hope they have in Christ? She doubted it.

Rebecca prayed, *Father, please help Reverend Cobb know the loving part of you. Fill him with expectations and foresight, so much so that it will overflow into this congregation and beyond to the rest of the district—to whites and blacks.*

Thankful the reverend had preached a relatively short sermon, Rebecca stood at the closing hymn. Daniel clasped her hand. He was being especially attentive. When the song ended he led the way through the parishioners and out to the porch.

Daniel looked down at her, his blue eyes intense. "It feels good to have you by my side," he said softly. "I've been missing you."

Rebecca felt a pang of longing. "You work too much," she said, trying to keep her tone light.

"True, and I have more work to do now. I've got business to take care of before we go home."

Rebecca loosed her hand. She'd known that. There was always work to be done.

"I won't be long," Daniel said and strode off to join his father, who stood visiting with Reverend Cobb.

"Cast off again, eh?" Elle said with a smile. She draped an arm around Rebecca's shoulders. "Why don't ya join me and Cambria for a bite? We're eating under that tree over there."

Rebecca looked for Willa. "I'll have to check with my mother-in-law."

Willa stood among a clutch of other women. "Oh, they'll never notice. She's already pally with 'er friends."

Rebecca hesitated.

"Come along, then."

"All right."

As Cambria laid out lunch she softly sang "Onward Christian Soldiers."

"You have a lovely voice," Rebecca said. "I think you ought to sing for the congregation someday."

"Roight," she said with a chuckle. "That will never happen."

"Why not? You're not afraid, are you?"

"Wal, a little, but even so it's just not allowed."

"For heaven's sake, why not?"

"The church lydies say it's improper."

Rebecca leaned against the back of the Taylor wagon. "Maybe someone ought to speak to them."

"No. Don't bother, really."

"Where's yer mum?" Elle asked Cambria as she joined her niece.

"She's home with me brothers. Ran was feeling poorly this morning, so she stayed home with the whole lot of 'em. It's just me and Dad today."

Elle climbed into the wagon bed and rested her back against the sideboards. A breeze ruffled her wispy blond hair. "Ah, now that feels good. I could do with cooler weather." She kicked off one shoe then the other. "Tomorrow it's back to work. This is me only day off. I might as well make the most of it."

Rebecca was surprised. It was improper for a woman to be barefoot in public.

Elle's eyes lit with mischief. She laughed. "If only ya could see yer face. Ya'd think I'd stripped of me dress."

Cambria laughed. "Don't mind Elle. She's just trying to get yer goat."

Rebecca smiled. "I don't mind, really. In fact, I agree it's a sensible idea to cool your feet."

The three women chatted while enjoying cold meat, cheese, fresh bread, and pastries.

"This is very good," Rebecca said.

"Ya can thank me mum. She's a right good cook."

"I will next time I see her."

Willa strolled toward the wagon. "G'day, Elle, Cambria. How have you been getting on?"

"Good," Cambria said. "Me mum told me to tell ya hello."

"I heard young Ran is ill."

"He's not terribly sick. Mum just thought it best to keep him home."

"G'day, Willa," Elle said. "I'll have another of those dresses finished this week."

"That's good news. I dare say, Rebecca needs something cooler. The gowns she brought from Boston are lovely but far too heavy for our hot summers."

Rebecca finished off a pastry. "I can't wait to see them. I hear you're the best seamstress in the district."

"Too roight. I am good, at that." Elle winked.

Willa looked at Rebecca. "I plan to stay for the women's auxiliary meeting. Perhaps you'd like to join us?"

"Yes, I would." Rebecca glanced toward the mercantile. "Do you know when Daniel will be finished with his business?"

"The men usually manage to finish up just as we complete our meeting."

"Course, there's an awful lot of 'em who conduct business at the pub," Elle said with a wry smile.

"Indeed. But I'm certain Daniel and his father aren't at the pub."

"Yer probably roight there."

Rebecca looked at Cambria and Elle. "Are you going to the meeting?"

"Don't believe I'd be welcome," Elle said. "I 'ave a habit of ruffling feathers."

"And I think me dad is about ready to leave," Cambria said. "But I'll see ya next Sunday." Cambria picked up the leftovers from lunch and returned them to the picnic basket.

"Next week, then."

159

Rebecca walked with Willa to the church. Although the wind had picked up and dark clouds were building in the east, it was only getting hotter. "You think there's going to be a storm?"

"Quite possibly. It's not unusual to have thunderstorms this time of year." Willa smiled. "I like the storms, but they can make a mess of the haying. That's why we're always in a hurry to get what's cut gathered in."

Rebecca followed her into the church, where a handful of women had gathered at a table in the foyer.

"Well, it's about time. We've been waitin' on ya lydies," Elvina said. She spoke lightly, but her face told them she was irritated at their tardiness.

"I apologize," Willa said, pulling out a chair and sitting. Rebecca took the chair beside her.

"We've been discussing what ought to be done for our up-coming Christmas celebration," Elvina said. "We've decided it ought ta be reverential. After all, it is the celebration of Christ's birth."

Silence settled over the women.

Now's as good a time as any, Rebecca thought. "What if Cambria were to sing a Christmas hymn? She has a lovely voice."

No one spoke.

Realizing she'd stepped into perilous waters, Rebecca pressed on. "I think it would be quite nice. We might even consider having a solo every now and again. There are others in the church with good voices."

"Absolutely not," Meghan said. "It can't be done."

"Pray tell, why not?" Rebecca asked.

"It's inappropriate. And I don't see why we ought to make any changes just because ya think it would be nice." Meghan folded her arms over her chest.

Willa's hands fluttered like dying butterflies as she tucked strands of loose hair into place. Finally they settled in her lap. "Perhaps we ought to give it a bit more thought."

160

"There's nothin' ta think on," Elvina said. "Solos are not done here." She leveled pale blue eyes on Willa. "And certainly if ya spoke to yer husband he'd give ya the same answer."

No more was said about the solo, and the women talked of other aspects of the Christmas celebration, which included special music, a potluck, and gifts for the needy. Long before the meeting was over, Rebecca felt like one of Willa's wilted roses. She wanted to go home. She glanced out at the surrey parked in the shade. Woodman sat in front, chewing on a piece of dried grass. She would prefer being in his company. Everywhere he settled peace seemed to be there as well. Unable to endure the meeting a moment longer, she excused herself and walked outside to the surrey. She was disappointed to find that the wind had quieted and the clouds she'd seen earlier seemed to have melted away.

"Ya 'ave enough of that tittle-tattle?" Woodman asked with a grin.

"Quite." She leaned against the front wheel. "Have you seen Daniel?"

"No. But he'll be 'ere soon enough."

"Woodman, I'm unclear about something. I know you don't attend church, but you seem to know about people in the district."

"Yais, I guess I do, at that."

"The women here are trying to decide what to do about Christmas. But they won't even consider trying something new. It's extremely frustrating."

"People get stuck in their ways. That's what I figure it is."

Rebecca nodded. "I suppose you're right. But I still don't think it's an excuse for being stick-in-the-muds." She gazed at a distant gum tree. Its twisted, gnarled limbs were captivating. Still looking at the tree, Rebecca said, "I have another question. Why aren't there any blacks in church?"

"Wal, blacks aren't allowed. That's how it's been, always will be. And most blacks wouldn't want ta go. Anyway, not to a white man's church." He grinned. "No insult ta ya, mum."

"None taken."

"I thought things with the blacks was the same in America as 'ere."

"Some things, yes. In America many of the Negroes are quite religious, but here . . ."

"We 'ave our own religion."

"Yes, I suppose so." She rested an elbow on the wheel. "I really don't know much about the Negroes. I never spent time with them. During the war there was quite a strong abolitionist movement in New England, however. I guess we might be considered free thinkers," she added with a smile. She studied him. "You're not like the others. Mr. Thornton and Daniel respect you. They trust you."

Woodman chuckled. "Wal, that depends on what's goin' on and who's 'round. I'm still just a blackfella. Only difference, me and Mr. Thornton grew up together. We were pally as lads." He scratched his head. "Guess I know 'im better than anyone 'cept for Mrs. Thornton."

He brushed something off his pants leg. "He understands me. When I go on walkabout, he knows I gotta go." He looked down at Rebecca. "Still, we're not mates. Can't be. Don't think Mr. Thornton even sees me as a whole human being."

Rebecca didn't know what to say, so she simply nodded.

⟡

All the way back to the house, Rebecca felt unsettled. She wished Daniel would ride in the surrey. Instead, he rode his stallion alongside his father. It would be nice if he paid a bit more attention to his wife than he did to his father. *What more could I have expected?* she thought miserably. *I thought things would be different.*

The surrey stopped in front of the house, and before Bertram turned his horse toward the barn, he settled a stern gaze on Rebecca. She felt her insides quake and glanced at Daniel, hoping for support. He offered no trace of reassurance.

"I'd like to see you in the study, Rebecca," Bertram said, then steered the horse toward the barn.

Daniel didn't follow but climbed down from his stallion and walked to the surrey. "No worries. I'm sure everything is right as rain."

"What do you suppose he wants?"

Daniel's horse stepped back, and he tugged on the reins. "I'm sure it's nothing. Don't look so stricken. He won't bite." He smiled, but his eyes told her he knew the truth—that Bertram may not bite, but he had a painful sting.

"Would you go with me?"

"Dad wouldn't like that."

"But you're my husband."

"He'll only send me out."

"Fine, then," Rebecca said, feeling rebuffed. She climbed down from the surrey. "I'll just freshen up." Keeping her back straight, she stepped past her husband and glanced at Willa as she moved toward the house. Willa's concerned expression made Rebecca's pulse pick up even more.

After tidying her hair and splashing her face with water, Rebecca headed downstairs. She walked decisively to the study. Stopping at the heavy door, she took a steadying breath and then knocked.

"Come in," Bertram called from inside. He sounded annoyed.

I've done something to displease him, Rebecca thought. Opening the door and stepping inside, she searched her mind for the blunder. "You wanted to see me?"

"Yes. Close the door, please."

Rebecca did as she was told, then approached her father-in-law's desk. She clasped her hands in front of her, hoping to quiet their trembling.

Bertram gazed at her from beneath heavy brows. "As I told ya, I believe my role 'ere is one of father to ya." His voice was gentle, belying his expression.

"Yes, sir, you did."

"And now I must take on another role—one of elder. As ya know, I'm an elder at the church, and as such I have clear direction to control my family."

Dread filled Rebecca. She couldn't imagine what she'd done that required a reprimand from an elder.

Bertram stood and leaned on his desk. "I was told of yer behavior in church today."

"My behavior, sir?"

"Ya went behind my back and tried to make changes in church procedure."

Flabbergasted at the accusation, she said, "I've done nothing of the kind."

"Seems ya requested there be solos during church?"

"Yes, but it was only a suggestion. The women didn't . . ."

"From now on ya come to me. I make the decisions 'ere at home and for the church."

"But . . ."

"I'm the principal elder, and all proposals come to me first." His voice was calm but firm. "It's a sign of disrespect to have someone in my own household go behind my back and seek authority from someone else."

"That's not what . . ."

"From now on ya'll ask me before ya speak to anyone."

Rebecca was trembling, as much from anger as fear. "Mr. Thornton, I've done nothing wrong. I didn't mean any disrespect. I simply thought it might be nice if someone like Cambria could sing . . . on occasion. She has a lovely voice."

"'Pride goeth before destruction, and an haughty spirit before a fall. Better it is to be of an humble spirit with the lowly, than to divide the spoil with the proud.' Proverbs 16:18–19. Would ya have yer sister filled with pride?"

Rebecca fumbled for his meaning.

"If we allow people to perform, we tempt them. They can too easily become prideful. And the Scripture is clear—pride brings destruction."

While she mulled over the idea, Rebecca said, "I hadn't thought of that."

"That's why ya must come to me. I have a great deal more experience in these matters. As ya know, I have daily devotions and prayer. God has blessed me abundantly. I have the finest station in the district. Therefore, I'm convinced he approves of my life."

"Yes, sir, that may be true, but I must say, Cambria doesn't seem the type to suffer from pride."

"No one's safe from it."

"Yes, I know, but . . ."

"Enough. Yer too young to know about such things. Plus, females lack the clear thinking needed for such judgments."

Rebecca's anger swelled.

Bertram reached out to her. "You can trust me. The Lord has made his face to shine upon me."

Rebecca allowed him to take her hand, but she disliked the control she felt in his grasp. He didn't seem the type to guide, but rather the type who forced people to do his will.

"I don't want to hear any more about this singing, eh? Things will stay as they are." He smiled. "And if ya have an inquiry about church, ya come to me."

Rebecca knew this was wrong. Bertram was not the only authority for this family. What about Reverend Cobb? What about Daniel? And what about God? His Word clearly stated that he spoke to his children whether they be male or female, old or young.

Her thoughts churned through all that had been said, then stuck on something. It was possible God was using Bertram to speak to her. After all, he did have more experience than she did, and he knew his Bible well. Why shouldn't she trust him?

"Rebecca, is there anything else ya'd like to say?"

"No, sir. I'll make sure to come to you first with any other ideas I might have."

"Good. I'm glad we had this chat. Now, on yer way." He sat down and picked up a book.

Rebecca was dismissed.

14

Rebecca stared at the open plains while the surrey sloshed over muddy roads and bounced through deep puddles. The last two days had brought needed rain, but rather than showers there had been a deluge.

It was Sunday, and as she considered the upcoming service, her mind traveled back to Boston and the kind of services she'd experienced there. Enthusiasm and vitality had always been part of being in church. Sunday had been a day she looked forward to, knowing there would be an inspired sermon and good fellowship.

Now she'd rather be heading almost anywhere else. Even during the Christmas holiday, there'd been little celebration. And Reverend Cobb hadn't seemed cheery at all.

Daniel walked his horse close to the carriage. "You look right surly this morning," he said, reining in his stallion to match the surrey's pace.

"She does look a bit peaked." Willa reached across the seat and patted Rebecca's leg.

"I'll admit to being a little down. I'd feel much better, though, if you'd allow me to ride," she teased, looking up at Daniel.

He glanced at his father, who had moved ahead. "You

know I don't mind, but . . . I don't have the last word 'round 'ere."

Daniel's deference to his father annoyed Rebecca. A spiteful retort hung on her tongue, but she bit it back and said instead, "Yes. I know."

"I've business after church today. So I won't be having a cuppa with you."

"Where are you going?"

"The Linnells'."

Jealousy nettled Rebecca. "Why the Linnells'?"

"They've got a grand bull. He's worth a fair bit, and he'd be a good addition to our stock."

Rebecca barely heard his reply. All she could think of was Meghan. She'd be there. *What difference does it really make, anyway?* she asked herself. *Daniel doesn't love me; I don't love him.* Rebecca felt miserable.

"Say hello to Mrs. Linnell for me," Willa said.

"Right. She's feeding the lot of us. There'll be others having a look."

Rebecca leaned back in the seat and folded her arms over her chest, considering if she might go along. She didn't suppose it was proper for a woman to join a group of men assessing a bull for breeding. And actually, when she thought of it, she'd rather not be there.

Using a handkerchief, she patted the moisture on her forehead. Even with the rain and clouds it was still overly warm. The humidity was worse than usual, making the heat more intolerable.

Jim rode up beside Daniel and tipped his hat. "Morning."

"G'day," Daniel said.

"Good morning, James." Willa smiled. "Are you faring well?"

"Yes, ma'am, I'm good."

"Will you be joining us at church?"

"No, ma'am. I've got friends waiting for me in town. After, I'll be going out with Mr. Thornton and Daniel to the Linnells'." A smile played on his lips as his eyes settled on Rebecca. "Figured they could use some company."

Thank you for that, Rebecca thought. He understood how she felt about Meghan and Daniel. She offered a smile.

The two men rode on ahead of the surrey, joining Bertram. Rebecca stood and rested her hands on the front seat. "Woodman, do you mind if I ride up front with you? I could use a change of scenery. And there might be a bit more breeze."

He looked back and smiled, showing off his surprisingly white teeth. "Ya come roight on up, then."

"Do you mind, Willa?"

"No. Of course not."

Modestly gathering her skirts, Rebecca clambered onto the front seat. "Thank you. I was feeling confined."

"It's a pleasure ta 'ave yer company." He clicked his tongue and flicked the reins. Gray mud had collected on the wheels, making travel slow.

Rebecca studied the horses. Their shiny, black rumps were well muscled, and they held their heads enthusiastically aloft. "They're good-looking animals."

"Too roight—a matched set. Morgans, they are. I'd say they're one of the nicest in the district. We're roight proud of our animals at Douloo."

"I can see that. They're well looked after."

Rebecca's mind returned to Meghan. She couldn't forget that Meghan had been Bertram's choice for his son. *I'm certainly a disappointment to him.* She looked at Woodman. He'd know about Daniel and Meghan. She gathered her courage and glanced back at Willa. Her mother-in-law seemed to be dozing.

Rebecca pressed gloved hands together, then cleared her throat. "You've known Daniel a long while."

169

"Yais. All 'is life."

"I suppose you'd know why Meghan Linnell appears to be . . . well, after him even though he's married."

"Wal, I know something 'bout it. She always figured he was 'ers—everybody did."

"You, too?"

Woodman settled dark eyes on Rebecca. "I figured that's the way it would go." He smiled. "A Yank wasn't my choice, but . . . yer roight good for Daniel. And I like ya fine."

"I like you too." Rebecca took a slow breath, then asked, "Why do you suppose Meghan can't accept that he's married?"

"She's always got what she wanted." He leaned forward and rested his arms on his legs. "Way I see it, no one belongs ta nobody."

"Don't husbands and wives belong to each other?"

"That's the difference between whites and blacks. Yer always hangin' on ta things 'stead of givin' 'em freedom. We come from the earth, and we go back to it. When we come we 'ad nothin', and when we go back we 'ave nothin'."

"Callie said nearly the same thing." Rebecca wondered if it was wise to question Woodman about his religion. Curiosity overcame her reservations. "Woodman, do you believe in God?"

"I believe in a creator all roight, the one who was in the dreamtime, but not the God yer talkin' of. Which is all roight with me. Ya can believe as ya wish."

Rebecca nodded. "Maybe we can talk about it someday?"

Woodman made no response but flicked the reins and kept his eyes forward.

Rebecca returned to her questions about Daniel and Meghan. "Don't you think it's wrong for Meghan to behave as she is? I mean, she's nearly throwing herself at Daniel."

"Roight. But then Meghan does as she pleases."

The knot in Rebecca's stomach tightened. If Meghan was used to getting what she wanted, would she continue to pursue Daniel until she got him?

Rebecca studied white puffs of clouds in an otherwise brilliant blue sky. Her eyes wandered over the open spaces. Tufts of green merged with dried grasses. "Will the plains turn green soon?"

"Not roight likely, not this time of year. We get our fair share of rain but not enough for real change." Woodman flicked the reins and guided the team through a gully.

Church was as Rebecca had expected. She was thankful when Reverend Cobb finished his dreary litany and the final hymn was sung. She decided to skip the women's guild meeting and share a lazy lunch with Cambria instead.

Sitting in the shade of a gum tree, the two friends ate and shared the latest news.

"I missed you the last few weeks," Rebecca said.

"I was sick, down with the bug me brother had. It went roight through the family—rough one it was too."

"I'm thankful you've recovered. You look well."

"I'm roight good now." She bit into a sandwich. "Ever since I got me appetite back, I've been starvin'. I'm liable to put on a few too many pounds."

Rebecca studied the slight young woman. "A little extra weight wouldn't hurt you any."

"Good. I like ta eat." Cambria grinned.

"I had a quarrel with my father-in-law. He was absolutely fit to be tied about my suggesting your singing a solo at Christmas."

"Really? Wal, I'm thankful I didn't 'ave ta do it. Just the thought makes me feel faint."

"He was outraged. I had no idea he'd be so upset. I thought it would be nice to listen to you sing." Rebecca sighed. "Doesn't seem I can do anything right."

Cambria slowed her chewing. "What did he say?"

"He told me I was never to make any suggestions without first getting his permission. And that allowing you or anyone else to sing was a temptation that might cause a person to become prideful." She tore off a piece of bread and put it in her mouth. "I've thought on it, and I'm certain you'd never be troubled by pride, especially over something like singing."

Cambria smiled. "Thank ya for yer confidence, but I struggle with pride now and again just like everyone else."

"I've been unsettled ever since. I'm not sure what I should or shouldn't do. I've been making every effort to be careful not to say or do anything that might upset Mr. Thornton. He can be very intimidating."

"I don't think ya 'ave anything ta fear from him. He's a fine man. Everyone in the district thinks highly of him. He's always doing a kindness for someone." She dabbed at her mouth with a napkin. "I know he likes ta oversee most things, 'specially important church decisions. And he's been known ta help people with their troubles and give them guidance. I can't think of a single time he's been wrong." She dropped the last bite of her sandwich into her mouth and chewed thoughtfully. "I think he might actually be a saint. But I must admit, he can be a bit frightening. I never know what ta say ta him. Can't imagine if I was ta live in the same house."

"It's not easy. I don't think he likes me much. But I suppose you're right. I should trust him. He's more learned than I, and he is my elder. But I think you've gone a bit far by calling him a saint."

Cambria shrugged. "I'm sure yer wrong about how he feels about ya. But I can see how he'd be disappointed, since he was counting on Meghan becomin' part of the family. Not that she was roight for Daniel."

"She's on my mind all the time. I know she and Daniel are spending time together."

"But it's not Daniel's doin'."

"I want to be more like Meghan, a true Australian."

Cambria laughed. "Oh no. Don't do that. She's a spoiled brat."

Rebecca nodded. "I can believe that."

Rebecca sat on the front porch and rocked while she embroidered the pocket of an apron. She'd decided to use an image of blue lupine. It was one of her favorite flowers from back home. Holding the apron away from her, she studied the emerging tapestry and was satisfied she'd caught the essence of the flowers.

With a sigh she set the apron in her lap and gazed out at the empty yard. It was hot; it was always hot. The thought of cooling rain showers at home sifted through her mind. She missed the fragrant, moisture-laden earth so common in New England.

"No rain, no cooling breezes," she said, gazing at a cloudless sky and dry, brown earth. The ground had dried up quickly after the brief rains. There was no activity in the yard or at the barn. Silence enfolded the grounds, and a hush pervaded the house. Daniel and his father, along with several drovers, were working a distant corner of the station. Willa had set off early to visit a sick neighbor. Rebecca wished she had something to do, but the day lay dreary and endless before her.

A dust cloud puffed into the air just below the rise at the end of the drive, then Rebecca heard the pounding of horses' hooves. Amid a swirl of dirt, a very short and skinny black man rode into the yard. When he reached the porch, he reined in his stocky mount. "G'day."

"Good day. What can I do for you?"

"I'm lookin' fer Miss Callie. She 'ere?"

"Yes. Around back."

"With a nod, the man kicked his horse and headed for the back of the house. A few minutes later Callie stepped through the front door and onto the veranda. She looked stricken.

"Callie, what is it?" Rebecca stood. "What's wrong?"

"It's me mum. She's sick. I'm needed at home. I was hopin' I could take a few days and go ta her."

"Of course." Rebecca was confused. She'd thought Callie had lost her parents when she'd been traded. "So you know where she lives, then?"

"Yais. When 'er man died she settled in Toowoomba. I won't be gone long, just a few days." Her eyes teared. "She's not long for this world, mum."

"You go right ahead. We'll manage just fine until you get back."

Callie nodded and headed for the steps.

"Is there anything I can do?"

"No, mum." She ran to her cottage and disappeared inside. The man on horseback followed and waited at her porch. A few minutes later Callie reappeared with a small bag, which she handed up to the man. He looped it over the pommel of his saddle, then offered his hand and helped Callie swing up behind him. The two rode off and disappeared beyond the rise.

Late that afternoon Willa returned. Woodman assisted her from the surrey. Looking hot and weary, she made her way to a chair on the veranda and lowered herself into it.

174

"You look exhausted," Rebecca said. "Are you all right?"

"Yes. But I dare say, I'm thankful to be home." She fanned herself. "That poor family is suffering so. Every last one of them is sick."

"What's wrong?"

"Fevers, fatigue, and terrible headaches. In this heat it's insufferable. I did what little I could." She closed her eyes and rested her head against the back of the chair. "It feels so much better here in the shade." She looked at Rebecca. "And how were you today? Any difficulties?"

"Everything was fine. Can I get you something to drink?"

"No. Callie can get it."

"She's not here."

Willa sat up, her brows raised in question.

"Her mother's gravely ill, and she's gone to be with her. She'll be away only a few days."

"Oh, poor Callie. I do hope her mother recovers."

"It didn't sound as if she would."

Willa brushed damp tendrils of hair up off her neck. "She came to you for permission?"

"Yes. There wasn't anyone else."

Willa nodded, then rubbing her left temple, closed her eyes again.

Shortly after Willa's return, Daniel and his father rode up and disappeared into the barn. A few minutes later, a weary Daniel ambled toward the house. He dusted off his hat and sat on the front steps.

Rebecca pushed out of her chair and crossed to him. "You look tired."

"Right. But it was a good day. We managed to get the whole mob moved into the corrals."

"Would you like something to drink? There's mint tea."

"No. I drank so much from the barrel down at the barn, it's sloshing around my gut." He grinned.

Bertram strode from the barn and up the steps. He didn't seem to notice anyone except Willa. He moved toward her. "Ya look done in," he said, his lined face showing concern.

"It's just this heat—it's insufferable with no breeze."

Bertram rested his large hand momentarily on her forehead, then smoothed back her hair. "Take care ya don't wear yerself out."

"I'm fine. Don't worry about me."

Daniel warmed to the exchange between his parents. *If only Dad was considerate more often*, he thought.

"I've got some paperwork to do," Bertram said abruptly and disappeared inside.

Willa pushed out of her chair. "I'll see if Lily needs any help." She moved indoors.

Daniel turned to Rebecca as she sat in her chair. "How did you fare today, being on your own?"

"Everything was fine, all except for Callie being called home to care for her mother."

"What happened?"

"Her mother's ill."

"Sorry to hear that."

Rebecca sipped her tea. "I'm glad you're back early," she said, then tentatively added, "I missed you."

"Missed me, eh?" Daniel asked jovially, trying not to allow the implication of affection to raise his hopes. "I was thinking about you too," he added more seriously, glancing at the open land surrounding the house. "I'd surely rather spend the day with you than with a mob of bawling cows."

"Well, that's quite a comparison," Rebecca teased. She set down her glass. "So Meghan Linnell didn't find you today?"

"No, as a matter of fact, she didn't. Does she distress you?"

"No. Of course not, but . . ."

"She's nothing more than a friend, Rebecca." *Actually, she's become something of a nuisance*, he thought.

"Meghan feels more than friendship, I can assure you."

Daniel wanted to keep the banter light but couldn't help but wonder why a woman who didn't love a man would be concerned about another woman. "You don't trust me?" he asked.

"Of course I do."

"Rebecca," Bertram's sharp voice called from inside.

Daniel could see Rebecca tense up, and immediately anger toward his father filled him. Why couldn't he treat her more kindly?

His jaw set and eyes angry, Bertram pushed open the front door and marched onto the porch. "I understand ya gave Callie permission to leave the premises?"

Rebecca stood. "Yes. Her mother . . ."

"Yer not to make such decisions on yer own."

"But, sir, Mrs. Thornton was gone and you were away."

Wishing he could protect Rebecca from his father's barbs, Daniel stood beside his wife.

Her hand trembling slightly, Rebecca brushed a strand of hair from her forehead. "Someone had to . . ."

"It could have waited until I returned. Yer too young to make important decisions."

"Her mother is sick; she's dying. I thought it . . ."

"Don't argue with me," he bellowed.

"Bertram," Willa said gently, joining her husband and resting a hand on his arm.

Without even glancing at his wife, Bertram continued, "Ya'll do as yer told! I won't have any disrespect!" Without another word, he turned and stormed back inside.

Staring at the door, Daniel seethed. He wanted to follow his father and tell him he had no right to speak to his wife the way he had. But he couldn't move. It would do no good. It never had. All intervention would accomplish was to make life more difficult for Rebecca. He placed an arm about her shoulders and pulled her closer. "He'll calm down. Just give him time."

Rebecca looked at him, her dark eyes revealing inner turmoil and the damage of fresh wounds.

Willa said nothing but momentarily rested a hand on Rebecca's shoulder before walking around to the side veranda, where she stopped and gazed out over the plains.

"I'm sorry about that," Daniel said. "But it'll be all right." He caught hold of her hand.

Rebecca clasped it tightly. "It'll never be all right, Daniel. I can't please him. He hates me." She looked at him through tears. "Why didn't you defend me?"

Daniel couldn't grab hold of an answer right off. "Well, I . . ."

"My father would never have spoken to anyone in such a manner, not even one of our servants. I would think that my own husband would shield me from such an attack."

"I wanted to. Truly. But it would do no good. I've watched this for many years. Nothing will change him. Just please try to get along. I'm sure he doesn't hate you." Even as he said the words, Daniel knew Bertram might very well hate his new daughter-in-law.

"Would you like to go for a ride?" he asked more lightheartedly. "It'll make you feel better, eh?"

Rebecca sniffed. "I suppose it would."

They walked toward the barn, and again Daniel reached for Rebecca's hand, but this time she moved it out of his reach and pretended she hadn't noticed. Daniel felt absolute frustration. There was nothing he could do. Things were as they were. *There must be some way I can shield her from my father's rage.*

"This is a nice mare," Daniel said, standing beside a small buckskin. "She's strong and steady."

Rebecca studied the mare, running a hand down the front of her face and nuzzling her velvet-soft nose. She patted her broad neck.

"She's not nearly the horse Chavive was, but she's smart and solid. And she seems eager for a ride."

"I like her." Rebecca studied the animal. "I think I'll name her Rena."

"Why Rena?"

"I have a friend in Boston with that name. It means 'peaceful.' And I think the name is appropriate for this mare."

"Good, then."

The horses were saddled, and Daniel helped Rebecca onto her seat. She fixed one leg around the tall pommel of the sidesaddle, then modestly arranged her skirts. "One day I would like to ride astride like Cambria . . . and Meghan."

"That's not for you, eh? They were raised among blokes."

"I can learn." Rebecca's horse sidestepped and tossed her head.

"You're a lady," Daniel stated flatly. "And ladies don't ride astride."

Rebecca gave him a questioning look. "You sound like your father, ordering me about."

"I didn't mean it that way," Daniel said, troubled by the comparison.

Once on the road, they cantered the horses until Rebecca's mare shied from a lizard skittering across the roadway. Her mount still fidgeting, Rebecca said, "It feels good to ride again. I've missed it terribly."

"I know I promised we would ride often. I'm sorry we haven't."

After that Daniel and Rebecca walked their mounts in silence, stopping now and then to gaze out over the empty plains. They moved alongside a small river. "I had no idea you had a stream on the station."

"It's one of the reasons my grandfather chose this place. Water's important. This one's stood up pretty well too. Only during the worst drought has it gone completely dry." Remembering the billabong, he added, "I have something I'd like to show you." He kicked his horse and loped ahead, continuing to follow the stream.

Soon a splotch of green appeared, an oasis in the middle of a dry plain. Trees and tall grasses surrounded a serene pool of water. "What is this place?" Rebecca asked.

"A billabong."

"So that's what it looks like," she said, allowing her horse to step into the shade of the trees.

Daniel followed, and suddenly they and their horses were surrounded by greenery and the cries of birds. "It's a place where the river bends and slows, forming a pool."

"It's wonderful." Rebecca scanned the area.

"My brother and I used to come here when we were lads." Daniel smiled at the memory, but a pang of sorrow followed. He missed Elton. He batted away a rope hanging from a tree. His mind turned back to the days when they would fling themselves out over the water and then let go and splash into the pool. "Elton and I had great fun 'ere."

Rebecca nodded. "I imagine it must have been grand."

"It was," Daniel said, unable to disguise the sadness in his voice.

"I'd like to come back. Perhaps we could have a picnic?"

"And maybe even go for a swim." Daniel managed a smile.

Reluctantly Daniel and Rebecca turned toward home. The sun blazed just above the horizon, a vibrant orange ball. The earth seemed to pause as it waited for the blazing orb to settle. There was not even a breath of wind to disturb the leaves of the gum trees.

Then the sun descended below the horizon and the evening sky turned a dusky pink. The world seemed serene and restorative. Daniel glanced at Rebecca. If only they could spend more evenings like this . . . maybe there could be a chance for real love between them.

A thumping came from the darkening expanse. Several kangaroos leapt across open grassland.

"Oh, how wonderful!" Rebecca said. "It's amazing how far they can leap!"

"They're quite spectacular," Daniel said, but his eyes were on Rebecca, not the kangaroos. He maneuvered his horse close and grasped her hand. "I've missed spending time with you."

"You're always working," Rebecca said, giving him only a glance before loosening her hand and looking back at the kangaroos.

Daniel breathed deeply and nodded. "I know. There's a lot to be done. And my father counts on me."

"If we're to have a chance . . . you must find more time."

Feeling the anguish of hopelessness, Daniel said, "I wish I could give you more."

"Do you?"

"Yes, I do."

Rebecca took a deep breath. "Your father's wrong about my letting Callie go to her mother's, and about other things as well. He's extremely domineering."

"It's just his way. He believes we're his responsibility." Daniel patted his horse's neck, then smoothed its dark coat. "He's a righteous man, and wise."

"That may be, but no one is right all the time," Rebecca said dryly.

Daniel knew she was right, but there was nothing to be done. What more could he say?

"God gave his followers gifts to be used in union with one another. If one makes all the choices and takes on all the responsibilities, there is no unity or reason for service."

Daniel clenched his jaw.

"We're to work together, Daniel. The Word says we are to be a body, working together. Where would I be if all there were to me was a hand? I need legs and eyes and my . . ."

"Right. I understand," Daniel said, feeling annoyance grow.

"Daniel, God can't do what he intends if your father is the only one making decisions. He runs the church, the lives of the people in the district, and his family's life."

"To him, the people in the district are his family. He cares 'bout us all."

"I know that. I'm not saying he doesn't, but . . . well, he's out of God's will. And you know it."

"There's no changing him. He is who he is."

"Is that why Elton left? Was he being strangled by your father's control?"

Daniel didn't answer right away. "Elton . . ." There it was again—the sorrow. Daniel didn't want Rebecca to see his pain. He said as lightly as possible, "He and Father used to go 'round a lot. He couldn't accept Father's way. Elton was like you; he didn't like authority." He offered Rebecca a half smile. "Finally he left. Actually, he and father had a row and he was ordered to go."

"I'm sorry, Daniel."

"They never spoke again."

"I don't mean to be rebellious, but it's time someone stood up to Bertram Thornton. And you're his only son."

Daniel turned his horse toward the house. "I can't change him. No one can."

15

Rebecca and Daniel lay back-to-back in their four-poster bed. Rebecca savored these rare mornings together. It was at times like this that she felt a glimmer of hope of achieving a complete marriage. She rested against him and said sleepily, "I wish you didn't have to work today and we could just have fun—maybe ride around the station. Go back to the billabong."

He rolled over and draped an arm on her side and intertwined his hand in hers.

You'd think we were in love. She left her hand in his.

"That would be grand," he said with a sigh. "But you know my father. He'll be quick to say, 'Yet a little sleep, a little slumber, a little folding of the hands to sleep: So shall thy poverty come as one that travelleth, and thy want as an armed man.'"

Rebecca rolled over and gazed into Daniel's blue eyes. "It's not a sin to enjoy life," she said softly. "I'd like to have more time with you."

Daniel's gaze was tender. What was it she saw in them? Love? *No*, she told herself firmly.

"I wouldn't mind having a go at some fun." Daniel pushed himself up and dropped his legs over the side of the bed. "But it will have to wait." He scrubbed his face with his hands before pushing off the bed. "I'll do my best to get back early."

Daniel dressed, splashed his face with water, then ran a brush through his thick blond hair. "I'm off, then," he said, leaning over Rebecca and resting his hands on either side of her head. He studied her. "You're beautiful, you know." He kissed her gently. "Maybe Dad can find work for me close to home."

Still feeling the touch of his lips on hers, Rebecca watched him walk to the door. A part of her longed for more than just companionship. She stretched her arms over her head. Of course, if she allowed herself to feel more, there were risks—he'd have greater power over her. "Can we go for another ride?"

"I might as well ask to go on holiday." He grinned. "Later, then." He stepped out and softly closed the door.

The room felt empty. Rebecca rolled onto her side and rested her cheek on her hands, staring at the place Daniel had been. What did she feel for him? In the months since their wedding, her emotions had changed—she cared deeply for Daniel, but was it love? *Would I stay if I had a choice?* She tried to imagine life without him. It felt empty, like the room without his presence. But the idea of Boston life was appealing.

"Enough woolgathering," she said, sitting up. What would she do with her day? She'd grown weary of embroidery, and although she enjoyed working in the garden, it didn't sound good either. *I want to ride.*

The sun had started its climb into the sky, and its light brightened the room. A rooster announced the new morning, and a calf bawled for breakfast. Rebecca climbed out of bed and walked to the open window. Callie tossed cracked corn to hungry chickens. She'd been home two days but hadn't spoken of her mother.

Jim stepped out of the bunkhouse and headed for the barn. He glanced up at Rebecca's window, then stopped and tipped his hat. "G'day."

"Good day to you," Rebecca said, leaning on the sill. "You're up early."

"I'm always up early."

She glanced at the sky. "Looks like another clear day," she said cheerily. "Will you be working with my husband today?" she asked, reflecting on the changes in Jim. At their first meeting he'd been downright surly. Now he seemed a different man.

"Nope. I've got work to do here. Maybe I'll see you around later?"

"Maybe."

Daniel strode up to Jim, then flashed Rebecca an unreadable expression. Not knowing exactly why she felt guilty over her banter with Jim, she offered Daniel a smile.

Turning to the American, Daniel snapped, "Don't you have work to do?"

"Sure do. I'll get right to it." Jim hurried toward the barn.

Daniel looked back at Rebecca, his expression cross.

He's jealous, Rebecca realized, feeling a momentary sense of satisfaction. Now maybe he'd understand her feelings about Meghan. "Have a nice day," she said.

Daniel didn't reply but walked back to the house. A few moments later footsteps sounded in the hallway and the bedroom door flew open. His tall frame filled the doorway. Gripping his hat in his hands, he glowered at Rebecca. "I don't want you talking to him."

"Jim? But why not?"

Daniel glanced around the room, looking as if he were searching for a reply.

"You're angry. Why?"

185

"He's always mooning over you, and every chance you get you flirt back."

"That's not true."

"You're married . . . to me. You're not to keep company with anyone else."

Outrage spilled from Rebecca. "How dare you accuse me of improper behavior! I would never! You know that."

"I know what I see. And I'll send him packing."

"Your eyesight is poor. And while we're talking about inappropriate conduct, I think we ought to discuss Meghan Linnell."

"We're talking about you and Jim Keller."

"Meghan's here at every opportunity. She hangs on your every word. She nearly salivates over you. It's disgusting and indecent."

"You know as well as I do there's nothing between me and Meghan. We're chums is all. Would you like me to cut off all my friendships?"

"No. Just that one." Rebecca folded her arms over her chest and turned her back to Daniel. She blinked away tears. *I won't give him the satisfaction.*

"If I see you with Jim again, I'll fire him. And I'll make sure no one in the district gives him a job. He'll have a hard go of it then, eh?"

Rebecca whirled around and faced her husband. "How can you punish someone for something he hasn't done? There's nothing between Jim and me." Daniel's face remained dark and angry. She continued, "There's barely anything between you and me, for that matter. We've a marriage of convenience, remember?"

Daniel stared at her, working his jaw. His words wrenched from his throat. "I thought it could be more than that."

"How so, Daniel? We barely knew each other when we

married, and you're rarely here. When would there be time for more?"

"We make love."

Rebecca's anger flared. She folded her hands over her chest. "Is that all men think is of importance? There's more. We need to know each other, how we think and feel and why. And if there is ever to be trust between us, there can be no others."

"Right. That means you're not to spend time with other men."

"Thinking there's something between me and Jim is pure nonsense."

Daniel ran the palm of his hand along the rim of his hat. "I suppose you're right. I'm sorry." He combed his fingers through his hair. "I married a handsome woman, and men are going to admire you—can't help themselves." He settled the hat on his head. "Foolish, I guess—faulting Jim for noticing beauty."

"He's an American, like me. We have something in common. It's nothing more."

"I'll try not to let it bother me. But you can't blame a bloke for getting upset." He stepped closer. "I realize Meghan's overstepped the limits of propriety." He stood close to Rebecca. "I know she fancies me. I'm not blind. I don't know how to tell her to stay clear . . . We've been chums so long. Even as kids we quite liked each other. Our fathers expected us to marry."

Rebecca wasn't certain how to respond. "I can't blame her for wanting you. You're a good man."

"But I'm taken, eh?" He smiled. "And I'll tell her so."

Rebecca nodded. "Be careful, Daniel. I don't trust her."

"I know how to handle Meghan Linnell. Don't you fret." He kissed her forehead and pulled her close. "We'll work on us. I promise." He released her. "Dad will be waiting on me, and I'll not hear the last of it."

Rebecca watched him walk away, then stared at the closed door. "Please be watchful; be wise." Disquieted, she dropped into the chair at her writing desk.

A longing for home engulfed Rebecca. She needed to settle into the leather chair in her father's office and have a long chat with him. But he wasn't there, would never be there. Opening the desk drawer and retrieving her writing materials, she decided a letter to her aunt would have to do.

She dipped pen into ink and started, "Dear Aunt Mildred, I miss you terribly. I hope you're in good health." She stared at the small paragraph and considered what else she should share. If she talked about her troubles, Mildred would worry, and there was nothing she could do about any of this. *Better she think all is well.*

Rebecca wrote about the interesting animals she'd seen since arriving and about Willa and her flower garden that reminded her of home. She explained the great distances people traveled just to go to town or to church and about her friendship with Cambria. She described the ride she and Daniel had taken and asked about Chavive. Did she ever see the mare and hear how she was doing in her new home?

She didn't mention lost hopes or dreams or fears about adjusting to her new life or the dreadful clashes with her father-in-law. She wanted badly to ask what God's Word said about a man's authority over his family, but she dared not. It would only stir up worry.

She sealed the letter, wishing she'd been able to tell Mildred that she felt imprisoned with no life of her own. *Dear Lord in heaven, this can't be what you wanted for me. There must be more. Show me what you have planned for my life.* She placed the letter on the top of her bureau. She'd drop it at the post office on Sunday. It would travel across the flats, over the mountains, and across the sea, then across another continent before reaching her aunt. She was so far away.

Rebecca's stomach rumbled, reminding her she'd forgotten about breakfast. A cup of tea and a crumpet would be just the thing. She dressed quickly and went down to the kitchen.

Callie stood at a sideboard. "I was just bringin' this up ta ya, mum."

"That's all right. I think I'd rather have breakfast on the veranda." Rebecca moved toward the door. "Where's Willa?"

"She's out at the barn. A calf was born in the night. Guess his mum had a hard go of it. He's a bit weak."

"Oh," Rebecca said, slightly disappointed she wouldn't have Willa's company during breakfast. She wandered onto the veranda. The air felt hot but seemed to be of no concern to the chirping birds darting among the greenery along the porch.

Callie set Rebecca's breakfast on the small table. "Anything else?"

"Thank you, no."

Silently Callie retreated.

Rebecca filled a cup with tea, added sugar, then sipped, contemplating the day. What would she do? It was too hot to work in the garden, she'd already written a letter, and the idea of spending a day sewing in the parlor was unbearable. She wished she could visit Cambria. She was such fun. *Maybe Woodman will take me.*

A nicker carried from the barn. *Rena*, Rebecca thought. *I'm an expert horsewoman. There's no reason why I shouldn't ride to Cambria's.* An image of Bertram's rage when he discovered her defiance of his rules filled her mind, and she cringed. Making him angry was not something to be taken lightly.

By the time Willa returned, Rebecca had finished her breakfast and sat drinking a second cup of tea. "Is the calf all right?"

"Quite. It's a lively little bull. I dare say, he's handsome too. I always like to visit the new ones when they're born in the barn." She sat in a chair opposite Rebecca, then used a

189

lace handkerchief to pat moisture on her neck. "It's already hot."

"I doubt I'll ever get used to the heat."

"Make certain to wear a hat and stay in the shade . . . Cool drinks help." She smiled. "My English ancestry rebels against such weather just as your Boston roots must. But in time you'll find it tolerable."

Rebecca nodded, her mind on horses. "Willa, do you ride?"

"I used to. I'm sorry to say my riding days are behind me. My back complains miserably if I spend much time in the saddle."

Rebecca's hopes of a riding companion evaporated. She pondered what to do. The idea of Bertram's anger was intimidating. *I could be back before anyone noticed.*

After a short rest on the veranda, Willa went inside to supervise the morning baking. Rebecca knew if she was going riding, it had to be now. She hurried to her room, changed into a riding habit, then walking as casually as her racing heart would allow, went straight to the barn. If she rode without mishap, there might be a chance of convincing her father-in-law it was safe for her to go alone.

The heat only seemed worse inside the barn. The smell of hay and manure reminded her of the stables back home and of Chavive. She peeked into the stall with the new calf. Solid brown with a white nose, he slept while his mother ground up a mouthful of hay.

Rena stood quietly in a darkened stall. Rebecca stepped through the gate, then keeping a hand on the mare's neck, she spoke softly. "Would you like to go for a ride?" The horse nickered. Rebecca ran her hand down the front of the animal's face. Rena nuzzled her. "Next time I'll bring you a treat. Do you like carrots?" She felt a growing companionship between herself and the mare.

190

Rebecca retrieved a bridle and blanket from the tack room. She put on the halter, tucking Rena's ears between the straps, then maneuvered the bit gently into her mouth. When she reached for the blanket, she heard a noise and turned to find Jim leaning on the gate, staring at her.

"Oh, you frightened me," Rebecca said with a nervous laugh.

"What do you think you're doing?"

Put off by his bossy tone, Rebecca replied haughtily, "I'm going for a ride."

"Mr. Thornton give you permission?"

Rebecca settled the blanket on Rena's back. "I'm my own person. I don't need permission."

"He'll have your hide and mine too if you go out alone. I can't let you."

"You have no say in what I do or don't do, Mr. Keller. In Boston I rode nearly every day. My horse Chavive and I spent hours on the grounds and exploring the woods near my home. And I don't intend to relinquish my freedom simply because I've moved."

Jim shook his head slowly. "You've more than moved. You're living in a different world. And as much as I disagree with Bertram Thornton's style of leadership, I agree with him in this. It's not safe for you to head out there on your own."

"Meghan does it all the time, and Cambria's been here to visit more than once on her own. I don't see why . . ."

"They've lived here all their lives. They know the troubles they might face and how to handle them. You don't."

"I'll learn."

"All right, then. Tell me what you'll do if you get lost?"

Rebecca didn't answer right away. She hadn't thought about that. "I won't get lost. I'll be very careful."

"The weather can get you, ya know. Do you have an extra canteen of water?"

Rebecca hadn't thought of that either. "I wasn't planning to go far."

"A person never sets out without plenty of water." His voice was sharp. "And just where were you planning to go?"

"I thought I'd follow the road and head toward town."

"Some places the road disappears. It's easy to get turned around out there."

"I'll manage." Rebecca strode to the tack room and picked up the sidesaddle.

Jim grabbed the saddle and returned it to its wooden frame.

Rebecca glared at him. "I'm going whether you like it or not."

Jim met Rebecca's stare. After a few moments he took a deep breath and his eyes softened. "All right. But I'm going with you."

Rebecca couldn't deny she'd like the company, but she knew full well that if Daniel discovered she'd gone riding with Jim he'd be furious. "No. I'll be fine."

"No you won't." A grin touched his lips.

Rebecca knew she wouldn't get away from the house without him following, and she wasn't about to give up her ride. "Fine, then. Suit yourself." She lifted the saddle and started for the door.

Jim watched as she trudged back to the stall. Once there, she realized that although Rena wasn't a large horse it would be extremely difficult to swing the saddle onto her back. She hesitated just long enough for Jim to step up and take the saddle. Effortlessly he settled it on the horse's back, cinched it up, then handed the reins to Rebecca.

"My horse is ready. We've already been working this morning." He walked out of the barn, and Rebecca followed, leading Rena.

Jim mounted while Rebecca led her horse alongside the fence. She used the bottom plank as a stepping stool and pushed up onto the horse's back. Settling onto the saddle, she straightened her skirts, then touched the horse's side with a riding crop and turned her toward the road.

Jim studied Rebecca.

"What are you looking at?"

"That tiny little hat isn't going to do you much good out in this sun."

"It goes with my riding habit. It's a riding hat."

Jim shrugged. "Don't say I didn't warn you. You're liable to get burned."

"I've never burned easily," Rebecca tapped Rena with the whip, and the horse trotted away from the house. By the time they'd cleared the trees and moved onto the road, the tension had left Rebecca's body. It felt wonderful to be riding, no matter who accompanied her.

Nothing was said for a long while; then Rebecca decided it was time to break the silence. "How long did you say you've been working here, Mr. Keller?"

"Ten years, give or take. Managed to find work the first month."

"Did you do this kind of labor before?"

"Nope. Grew up in New York City. My father was a longshoreman. But from the moment I got here I knew this was home." He gazed at the open land. "Either you love it or you hate it, there's no in-between. I hope to buy my own place. I've been putting money aside since my first paycheck."

"What about your family?"

A shadow touched Jim's eyes. "Never really knew my father. He worked most of the time, and my mother passed away a couple of years ago."

193

"I'm sorry."

Jim shrugged. "It's all right. We weren't close. My brothers live somewhere in the States. Just don't know where."

"How many brothers do you have?"

"Three. There's Eddie; he's the youngest. He was always in trouble. And then there's John. He's a year younger than me. I figure he's doin' good. He was kind of quiet and studious, you know the type."

Rebecca smiled and nodded.

"My older brother Robert lit out before me. The family never heard from him after he left. I figure he got killed in a fight somewhere. He was scrapping all the time." Jim was silent a moment, then asked, "How about you? Any brothers or sisters?"

"No. I'm an only child. My mother died when I was a five. My father and my aunt Mildred raised me." She gazed at a swirl of dust, then swept a fly away from her face. "My father died just before I married Daniel." The lone fly persisted and was soon joined by others.

"That why you married Daniel?"

Rebecca felt the question unsuitable, but there was something about Jim that provoked honesty. "Actually, yes. My father was a fine man but not a good businessman. When Daniel asked, I decided he offered the best option under the circumstances."

"You going to stay?"

"Of course." She swatted at the flies. "Marriage is not something I take lightly."

"I never said you did." Seemingly unaware of the flies, he added, "There are some who wouldn't stay. This is a lonely life." He adjusted his hat, still ignoring the horde of flies.

"I won't leave." She turned her horse around. "It's time we went back. This heat can't be good for the horses."

In truth, Rebecca knew the heat wasn't good for her. She

could feel the beginnings of a sunburn, and she was rapidly becoming overly warm. And the flies were another bother she'd rather do without. She grabbed her canteen, opened it, and took a large swallow.

"The horses are fine," Jim said with a smirk. "It's you who shouldn't stay out in this heat." He watched Rebecca swat at flies. "Bugs are bad right now."

They walked the horses back to the house, neither of them speaking. Rebecca didn't feel refreshed. Instead, she was sweating and fighting off flies. Back home in New England, riding had been much nicer.

"We should have gone to the billabong," she said.

"Would have been nicer there, I expect."

When they walked into the yard, Woodman met them. "Ya better git inside. Ya've been missed and Mrs. Thornton is upset. I'll take yer horse 'round ta the barn." He offered her a hand down.

Rebecca slid out of the saddle, then looked at Jim. "Thank you for accompanying me, Mr. Keller." She walked to the house and met Willa on the porch. "I'm sorry I worried you."

"Thank goodness you're all right, dear."

"You didn't need to worry. I'm an accomplished rider, and Jim was with me."

"Yes, well, that is reassuring," she said. "But, Rebecca, you must learn to tame this rebellious spirit of yours."

"It wasn't my intention to worry anyone. I simply needed to get out for a bit, and a ride seemed the right thing. I'm truly sorry I worried you."

Willa touched Rebecca's cheek. "You've picked up a sunburn, dear. You best come inside."

Rebecca knew when Bertram discovered her outing she'd face a harsh reprimand. His absolute authority over her life galled her, but what was she to do about it?

Remembering Daniel's earlier threats to fire Jim, she wondered if she'd lose her only connection to home. She hoped not. He made her feel less lonely.

⚘

As expected, Bertram called Rebecca into the library that evening. Although somewhat accustomed to the procedure, Rebecca couldn't quiet the butterflies in her stomach. She encountered Daniel in the hallway. He offered no encouragement but passed without speaking or even looking at her.

"Daniel?"

He kept walking.

His rebuff stunned Rebecca, but rather than give in to anxiety, she threw back her shoulders, straightened her spine, and stepped to the library door. *I did nothing wrong,* she told herself, turning the knob.

⚘

Bertram stood behind his desk. "Have a seat, Rebecca." His brow furrowed, he paced, then stopped and looked at her. "I understand you went for a ride today."

"Yes, sir. I did. I've been riding since I was a girl. I'm a competent horsewoman."

"Yais, well, not here. Ya don't know yer way 'bout. And there are dangers . . ."

"I was quite safe, sir."

"I won't have ya disobeying me. Ya've been warned and yet yer determined to be stubborn and foolish." He knit his brows and his voice deepened as he continued, "'Hear, ye children, the instruction of a father, and attend to know understanding. . . . Keep my commandments, and live.'"

His pale eyes boring into hers, he said, "Ya have a stubbornness 'bout ya that God will punish." He clamped his mouth shut and stood with hands clasped behind his back.

"May I be excused, sir?"

He continued to stare at her but finally nodded and turned away.

There would be no convincing her father-in-law that she'd done nothing wrong, and she didn't have the spirit to fight him. Rebecca knew her rebelliousness had carried her out of God's will many times. A hush lay over the house as she walked through dimmed corridors. When she stepped into her room, Daniel stood at the window staring out.

"Daniel, I assure you everything is fine. We left while it was still morning, before the heat got bad . . ."

"You won't go out again." He turned and looked at her. "Not unless you're with me."

His tone reminded Rebecca of Bertram. Inwardly she quailed at the possibility that Daniel might become like his father. She would never acquiesce as Willa had.

"Is that understood?"

Rebecca met Daniel's penetrating gaze. "No, it's not. I'll ride when I please. You can't lock me inside this house. I have nothing to do here."

"The garden needs tending, and you have your sewing. We go into town on Sundays. Isn't that enough?"

"No. It isn't. In Boston I was involved in my father's law practice, I rode nearly every day, I took part in the household responsibilities. And there was the symphony, the ballet, and the opera. I'm not used to inactivity. Here I'm cut off from everything and everybody."

"When you married me you knew life here wouldn't be like Boston. In fact, you made it clear that you frowned upon the posturing of Boston society and made it sound as if you wanted something different."

"There were aspects of society there I didn't approve of, that's true. But you didn't make it clear to me just how different it would be here."

The look in Daniel's eyes was baleful. "Are you saying you wished you hadn't married me?"

"No. I'm not saying that. But I have to be able to breathe. I need a certain amount of freedom." Rebecca knew her next words would most likely make matters worse, but she was powerless to stop them. "I won't be like your mother. Your father controls her every move. He tramples on her. You will not do the same to me."

"I don't want that either, but I won't have you embarrassing me. Your riding with Jim Keller today was like a slap in the face."

Rebecca had known that riding with Jim would be frowned upon, but in the midst of the battle she was unable to admit to the indiscretion. "I've been instructed that I can't ride alone. He offered. There seems to be no one else. And I can't bear to be locked up in this house any longer."

His jaw fixed, Daniel leaned on the window sill. "I'm sorry you find living here so difficult." He fixed his eyes on her. "Riding alone isn't safe. But if you ride with Jim, you endanger your reputation." He moved to the door. "I won't have you humiliating me." He walked out and closed the door hard.

Rebecca sucked in her breath. She'd been so insistent on doing things *her* way, having *her* freedom. She'd forgotten Daniel. He was right—riding alone with a man like Jim could damage her reputation and might very well disgrace her husband.

16

The Thornton household buzzed with activity as family and servants prepared for a competition of roughriders and local contenders at the town of Mitchell. It would be a full day's journey there and back, plus two overnights.

A week had passed since Rebecca's ride with Jim, but she still felt bruised from her argument with Daniel. Since that day, the tone between husband and wife had remained reserved. Although Rebecca made a point of being compliant and had avoided Jim, she and Daniel were more distant than ever.

"I'm feeling absolutely exhilarated," Willa said, joining Rebecca. "I quite enjoy these competitions."

"I've never been to a rodeo—that's what we call these competitions in America," Rebecca said. "It sounds a bit brutal."

"Oh no, not really. It's splendid fun. And rarely is anyone injured." Willa circled an arm around Rebecca's waist and gave her a quick hug. "I think it's just the thing for you and Daniel."

"I don't know what will help me and Daniel, but I doubt it's a rodeo," Rebecca said. "He's competing, you know."

"Oh yes. He always does. He's quite good."

Woodman drove the surrey up to the front porch steps. "Lydies, ya ready ta go?"

"Yes, quite ready," Willa said, walking down the steps. She smiled, and her wholesome, tanned face came alive. "I know we can trust you to miss as many potholes as possible?"

"No worries, mum. I'll give ya a smooth ride of it." He climbed down and gave Willa a hand into the surrey.

A wagon loaded with supplies, including tents and other necessities, rattled its way from around the back of the house. Jim sat in the driver's seat, while Callie and Lily sat in back. Rebecca felt a jolt of surprise at seeing Jim. She hadn't expected him to join the festivities. He lifted his hat and smiled at Rebecca, then at Willa. It just so happened that at that moment Daniel rode up.

His jaw set, he reined in his horse and turned sharply and rode toward his father, who sat on his heavy-bodied piebald.

Lord, can it get any worse? Rebecca wondered, accepting Woodman's assistance into the carriage. She settled on the seat beside Willa.

Bertram approached, his stallion blowing air from its nostrils and tossing its head. "Ya ready, then?"

"Yes. Absolutely," Willa said.

Bertram looked at the wagon with the servants and supplies. "Ya have everything, Callie, Lily?"

"Yais, sir," Callie said. "We do."

"Good." Bertram kicked his horse and turned it away from the house. Daniel rode alongside his father, and the two men led the small procession.

Rebecca would have preferred riding at least part of the way, but Bertram had made it clear that her proper place was in the surrey alongside his wife. Doing her best to be obedient, Rebecca had done what was expected without complaint.

"I thank the Lord for the coolness of the day," Willa said.

"It ought to make for a more pleasant trip." She settled back into her seat.

Rebecca felt a stir of excitement. The idea of a rodeo was enticing. She watched Daniel. He sat his horse well and looked especially handsome riding his chestnut stallion. Rebecca wondered if they could ever find their way to each other.

Maybe this weekend would help. Since he'd started preparing for the rodeo, his mood seemed to have lifted. He turned his horse about and rode toward the surrey, catching Rebecca's eye. She offered him a smile.

Daniel reined in his horse and walked alongside the surrey. "You ready for an adventure, then?" he asked Rebecca.

"Yes. I am, truly. I've never camped before."

Daniel looked relaxed. "I'm looking forward to sharing this with you. It should be grand fun." He lifted his hat, swiped his hand through blond hair, and resettled the hat.

"I hope so. I don't know anything about camping."

"No worries. I'll teach you," he said and rode off to join his father.

"Looks as if things are better already," Willa said with a smile.

"Yes. I think so." Rebecca kept her eyes on Daniel. His shoulders were broad, his waist narrow. His masculinity was appealing.

"Are you certain you wouldn't like to stay at the hotel with Bertram and me?" Willa asked. "It's more comfortable."

"Thank you, but I'd really like to experience camping. This is quite an adventure for me."

"Indeed. I remember when I was young . . . and in love," Willa smiled. "Those were good days."

Rebecca gave Willa a sideways glance. "You know Daniel and I don't love each other, Willa," she said quietly.

"Oh yes. I nearly forgot. You two act as if it's more than just need that brought you together." She smiled knowingly.

Rebecca didn't know what to say, so she silently watched the expansive grasslands move by. But she wondered if something was happening between her and Daniel. She had a sense of expectation and quiet joy inside when she thought of him. It wasn't something she'd ever felt before. Could it be love?

By the time they approached Mitchell, Rebecca wondered if she might not prefer the hotel room. A hot bath to wash away the travel dust would be nice, and a soft bed would ease weary muscles. However, it had been decided they'd camp, and she wasn't one to back out of commitments.

Bertram and Daniel rode on ahead. When the surrey made it into town, father and son had joined a mob of men clustered outside the corrals where livestock for the next day's competition had been confined.

Mitchell teemed with activity. People from all over eastern Australia had crowded into the small town. Women strolled along the dusty street. Men gathered in clusters where they smoked cigars and spit. Those who ran sheep stations discussed the quality of wool, the cost of shearers, and the number of lambs lost during the previous season. Cattlemen talked about the value of good bullocks, the heat, and withering feed. Men who planned to compete stood in line to register and size up the competition. There was much bravado among the men.

"This is definitely a man's event," Rebecca said.

Willa offered a knowing smile. "Oh yes, dear, that it is."

Daniel had joined the line of men waiting to register. Rebecca noticed that Jim had joined the procession as well. She wondered if he and Daniel would be competing against each other. She hoped not.

After Daniel registered he joined Rebecca and his mother. "I'll take you 'round to the camping area, then help the gals get set up."

"What are you competing in?" Rebecca asked.

"I'll be bronc riding and calf roping. I'm not crazy enough to ride the bulls."

"Thank the Lord for that," Willa said.

"Isn't riding wild horses dangerous?" Rebecca asked.

"Too right." Daniel grinned. "But I've been doing this since I was a lad. And don't mind saying I do right well." He smiled and nudged his hat up with his thumb. "You might have a go at the shops while we set up the tents."

"I'd like that." Rebecca stood. "Willa?"

"Perhaps later. I'd like to get settled in the hotel first. I'll join you for tea at the hotel eatery later?"

"That sounds nice," Rebecca said, allowing Daniel to help her down from the surrey.

Daniel kept hold of Rebecca's hand. "So I'll see you a bit later, then?"

"Absolutely," Rebecca said, suddenly feeling shy under Daniel's fervent gaze.

"G'day," Cambria said, striding up to Daniel and Rebecca. Her aunt Elle followed close behind. "It's grand ta see ya," Cambria said, her blue eyes bright.

"Hello." Rebecca smiled. "I believe just about everyone's here."

"It wouldn't be a rodeo without the whole of East Queensland 'ere," Elle said, the lines in her tanned face deepening with her smile.

She'd twisted her hair into a chignon, and blond wisps had escaped, causing a halo effect. Rebecca thought it looked attractive. "I've never taken part in anything like this before."

"I don't suppose, being yer from Boston," Elle teased. "And if yer going ta get a taste of a rodeo, this is the best." Elle glanced across the street at a cluster of men. "In truth, it's a chance for the blokes ta show off for the lydies." She chuckled.

"I believe they've more brawn than brains. They seem in a hurry ta do themselves in."

"Are there many injuries?" Rebecca asked, feeling a prickle of fear for Daniel.

"Some, but most blokes manage ta live through it all."

Sleeping on the ground turned out to be less exciting than Rebecca had imagined. She had a restless night, and by morning every muscle ached.

Daniel was up early. He paced while sipping a cup of coffee.

"You all right?" Rebecca asked.

"I'm fine. Just a bit antsy to get to it. Hope I do well."

"I'm sure you will. Please be careful," Rebecca said, realizing she couldn't bear the thought of his being injured.

Daniel stopped. "You really care?"

"Of course I do. You're my husband."

Daniel stepped closer. "I want you to be proud of me."

"I am proud of you. Truly."

He took her hands. "You know when I said I wasn't sure if I loved you . . ."

"They're about to start," Bertram called.

Daniel glanced at his father. "I'm coming." He looked back at Rebecca.

Her heart pounded. There *was* something between them.

"I love you, Rebecca. I'm sure of it." He gazed at her, waiting.

Rebecca knew he wanted to hear that she loved him too, but she didn't know what she felt. She was confused. "Please be careful," is all she could say.

Daniel leaned close and kissed her tenderly. When he straightened he searched her eyes, but she couldn't say what he wanted. Finally he walked off to join the other competitors.

⁂

Rebecca sat on rickety wooden stands, her hands clasped in her lap. Willa sat on one side, Cambria and Elle on the other.

The competition was about to begin. When the competitors rode into the arena, cheers rose from the spectators. Even atop their horses, the men swaggered. Rebecca thought Daniel the most handsome. He looked for her, and she waved, then settled back and prayed for his safety.

Other spectators, including Cambria and Elle, didn't seem to have qualms about injuries. They seemed only excited and animated. Willa, on the other hand, sat quietly, hands folded in her lap. She appeared tranquil in the midst of the uproar.

During the bull riding men were dumped, kicked, and trodded upon while onlookers whistled and cheered. Rebecca had to admit to enjoying the contest even with its violence. "I'm thankful Daniel isn't riding bulls," she told Willa.

"Indeed. He has more sense than that. His father, however, used to ride the bulls. I wanted to throttle him."

"I'd liked to have seen that."

"The bull riding?"

"No. You throttling him."

Willa chuckled. "Actually, I don't think I'd have dared to."

Calf roping followed the bull riding. As it turned out, Daniel and Jim were the two top contenders. By the final round Daniel was in first place. A calf was let loose, and his horse tore out of the chute, chasing down the calf. Daniel swung a rope over his head, then let loose. A loop dropped neatly around the calf's neck. Immediately the horse pulled up and stopped, the line went taut, and Daniel launched himself off the animal and, keeping a hand on the rope, ran to the calf. He picked up the bawling animal, dropped it on its side, and tied its hooves. While he returned to his horse, the calf lay still. It had been a good run. He'd be hard to beat.

Jim's turn came. And just as skillfully as Daniel he chased down his calf and tied him. He managed a faster ride, beating Daniel by two seconds to take first place. Daniel didn't seem discouraged and congratulated Jim with a handshake.

Daniel and Jim ended up in the lead at the last round of bronc riding as well. Daniel led by a single point.

Jim rode first. He'd drawn a good horse—a lanky, cantankerous stallion with a reputation for dumping anyone fool enough to climb on his back. Jim managed to stay with him until the whistle, then with seeming ease let go of the rope, pushed clear of the animal, and landed on his feet. He lifted his hat to cheering onlookers.

Daniel climbed atop his horse, a muscled white stallion. While still in the chute, the animal reared, nearly dumping Daniel.

Rebecca stood, pressing a closed fist to her mouth.

Resettling himself, Daniel fixed his grip and waited.

Help him have a good ride, Lord, Rebecca prayed.

"I always pray through these things," Willa said without taking her eyes off her son.

Looking at her mother-in-law, Rebecca realized Willa feared for Daniel. "Me too."

"Oh, but he loves this."

"I know," Rebecca said, feeling a rush of pride at her husband's courage and skill.

The gate swung open, and Daniel's horse blasted out of the chute, pitching first left, then right. Daniel managed to

206

maintain his seat. Determined to dispose of his passenger, the animal leaped, twisting and turning. He jumped straight up, then landed on straight legs before bounding sideways. The last move launched Daniel. He landed hard on his back.

The horse bucked his way across the arena. Daniel didn't move. "Dear Lord." Rebecca clutched Willa's hand.

Men hurried to the downed rider. Bertram knelt over his son. Finally Daniel pushed himself up on one elbow and managed to find his feet. He grabbed his hat from the dirt and offered the crowd a smile and a wave. Spectators cheered. Rebecca caught his eye, and although he managed bravado, she knew it was artificial. He was let down.

Daniel was quieter than usual that night and retired early. The following day he was up before Rebecca and had already left to meet with some of the men from other stations. She had no opportunity to speak to him.

"There's tea," Willa said, joining the family group.

"None for me," Rebecca said with a sigh.

"Daniel's pride is hurt, but he'll be fine."

"He won't speak to me."

"Be patient. He'll be right as rain in no time." Willa sat on a chair beside Rebecca. "He wanted to impress you. After all, it was the first time you've ever seen him compete."

"I'm proud of him. I want him to know that."

"You'll have your opportunity."

✠

All that day Daniel kept to himself. Once when he rode close to the surrey, Rebecca said, "You did well. I'm so proud of you."

"Yeah. But I lost to a Yank . . . twice. And it's a Yank with eyes for my wife." He rode off before Rebecca could reply.

That night Daniel stayed in Thornton Creek while Rebecca and the rest of the family traveled the last miles home. Confused and worried, Rebecca climbed into bed alone. She couldn't rid Daniel from her mind. Where was he? What was he doing?

To calm her fears, Rebecca read a few chapters from the book of Psalms, rereading Psalm 27 several times. The final words she read in a whisper, "Wait on the LORD: be of good courage, and he shall strengthen thine heart: wait, I say, on the LORD." Setting the Bible on the bed stand, she lay down and closed her eyes, feeling the promised strength. Sleep quickly overtook her.

Sometime during the night Daniel stumbled in. Something crashed to the floor, and Daniel let out an oath. "Can't someone put things where they belong?"

"Are you all right?" Rebecca asked, sitting up and staring into the darkness.

"Fine. Just fine," he said, slurring his words. He climbed into bed, the smell of spirits accompanying him. He nuzzled Rebecca. "I love you. I love you."

"You're drunk," Rebecca blurted.

"I had a few pints with the boys. No worries. Had a fine time." He kissed her.

"You smell like a pub."

"Too right." He laughed. "A bloke's got to get out and have some fun now and again, eh?"

Rebecca climbed out of bed, and Daniel followed, draping his arms around her. Rebecca pushed him away and managed to light the lantern.

"What's wrong?" Daniel swayed while he stared at Rebecca. "Not good enough for you, that's it. I'll never be good enough. Not for my father and not for you."

"Daniel, you're making no sense. What are you talking about?"

"Jim. That's what I'm talkin' 'bout. He's got eyes for you. And you like him. I can tell. After losing to that . . . that Yank . . . well, he'll never let me forget it. And he'll go after you too."

"What would make you think such things?"

Daniel staggered toward Rebecca. "He wants you." He stopped and deliberated as if he'd lost his train of thought. "You can't know what it means . . . to lose to a man who covets your wife."

"Daniel . . ."

"I know how he feels 'bout you. Any man in his right mind would want you."

This was a part of Daniel Rebecca had never seen. She was repulsed by this display. Barely able to keep her voice calm, she said, "Even if that were true, which it is not, that doesn't mean I want anything to do with him. And he's never done anything improper!" She folded her arms about her waist. "I thought we'd already talked about all of this. You know I have no interest in him. I explained—he's American, I'm American. We have our homes in common . . ."

"This is your home!" Daniel blurted.

"Yes, of course it is." Rebecca steered him toward the door. "Please, Daniel, you're drunk. We'll discuss this in the morning." While trying to avoid his embrace, she opened the door and pushed him through it. "And tonight you can sleep elsewhere."

She quickly shut the door, then leaned against it. Pressing a hand to her mouth, she wept. Everything was such a mess. For a moment yesterday she'd almost thought she might love him. Now . . . well, now she wanted nothing to do with him.

Daniel stood in the hallway, swaying and trying to understand what had happened. When the fog lifted just enough for him to comprehend, he yelled, "You can't do this to me." He pounded on the door. "Let me in! Rebecca! I demand that you let me in!"

"Daniel, people are sleeping. Please leave. We'll talk in the morning."

He leaned against the door. "Please let me in." There was no answer.

"What are ya doing, son?" Bertram asked in his most authoritative voice.

Daniel looked at his father.

Bertram stood in the center of the hallway, glaring at him. "What is this?" he demanded. "Ya smell like a brewery."

"I only had a few drinks with the fellas down at the pub."

"Yer drunk. And from what I can see ya've been put out of yer bed." He glanced at the bedroom door. "Can't say that I blame 'er."

Daniel stared at his father. How was it that he always felt small in his father's presence? He put his hand on the wall to steady himself.

"I'm ashamed of ya." A verse spilled from his mouth. "'Be not drunk with wine, wherein is excess; but be filled with the Spirit.'"

Daniel gaped at his father, trying to make sense of what he'd said.

Bertram's face turned red. "I want ya out of the house. Now! When ya've sobered up, then ya can return. And this will *never* happen again."

Still swaying, Daniel leaned against the wall. It would take a long while to recover from this. His father wouldn't forget.

"I don't want to see ya again tonight," Bertram said, then turned and stormed back to his room.

Daniel caught a glimpse of his mother as she peeked out at her son. Bertram ushered her inside and slammed the door.

Humiliated, Daniel turned and, gripping the balustrade, made his way downstairs. He reeled toward the front door, stepped into the cool night air, then staggered toward the barn.

Once inside, he didn't bother with a light. He knew where the hay pile was. He dropped into it and lay with his arms outstretched, willing the world to stop spinning. Filled with self-loathing, he could still see Rebecca's disappointment and disgust. She'd never forgive him . . . for this or for his accusations. And yesterday when he'd told her he loved her, she'd replied with a warning to remain safe, nothing more.

He squeezed his eyes shut. She didn't love him.

17

Rebecca awakened early. She ran her hand over the place where Daniel usually slept. The previous night's episode played through her mind, and she felt sick over what had happened. She threw back the blankets and climbed out of bed, then crossed to the window and gazed down on the empty yard. A soft breeze tickled the leaves of the trees. A cat lying at the corner of the barn uncurled and stretched. It all looked tranquil, so unlike the storm inside Rebecca. She needed to speak to Daniel.

After dressing, she hurried downstairs. Where had he spent the night? She stepped into the kitchen.

Lily patted out dough on a cutting board. "G'day ta ya. Yer up with the choox this mornin', mum."

"Choox?"

"Ah. Chickens is what I mean."

"Oh. I'm still learning." Rebecca glanced out the window. The sun was barely up, and the world looked fresh, almost dewy. She remembered Boston mornings—the moist air and wet droplets on plants and flowers. She'd often taken Chavive for a ride on such mornings. A longing for those days crashed over Rebecca. Sweeping the thoughts away, she reminded herself that she had more important things to think of now.

But maybe a ride would clear her mind. "Have you seen Daniel?" she asked Lily.

"No. Mr. Thornton's already up and gone. I figure Daniel musta went with him." She pressed the heel of her hand into the dough. "There're some scones if yer hungry."

Rebecca had no appetite. However, if she was going to ride, it would be a good idea to eat. She moved to the stove where the pastries rested on a warming shelf. "Do we have any clotted cream?"

"In the ice box," Lily said without looking up.

Rebecca retrieved the clotted cream, spread it on a scone, and took a bite. "Delicious. You must be the finest cook in all of Queensland."

Lily beamed. "Thank ya. I like cookin' well enough."

Rebecca filled a cup with hot tea from the stove, then between sips finished off the scone. She stepped onto the veranda, greeted by the raucous laugh of a kookaburra echoing across the fields. The morning coolness felt good.

As she leaned against the railing, the previous evening's argument tumbled through Rebecca's mind. The shock of Daniel's drunkenness and his accusations still felt fresh. How could he believe she could be unfaithful? Anger and sorrow merged, and like a ragged shawl draped itself about Rebecca. What was to become of this "practical" marriage? It wasn't working out. She considered speaking to Willa but pictured the submissive, genteel woman and discarded the idea.

A horse nickered from inside the barn, and Rebecca was again carried back to her morning rides with Chavive. *If only I could ride. I know it would help.* She finished off her tea. *If I'm careful no one will know.*

She pictured the stunning Meghan riding astride like a man, her mahogany-colored hair flying free in the wind. A longing for the same freedom grew inside Rebecca. *I'll wear britches and ride like a man. If Meghan can do it, so can I.*

213

Still upset with Daniel and driven by the desire for independence, Rebecca ignored her promises of compliance. Exhilaration and liberty was all she wanted to feel. She returned to the kitchen and set her cup on the counter. "I'm going out. I won't be gone long." She hurried upstairs.

Digging through her husband's pants drawer, she found his smallest pair of dungarees and pulled them on. They hung loosely on her. "Well, they're all I have for now," she said, bending to roll up the cuffs and thinking about purchasing a pair of her own. She guided a belt through the loops and pulled it snug, then fastened the buckle. Standing in front of a mirror, she chuckled. "I look positively ridiculous."

Thoughts of what her father-in-law would think disrupted her merriment. He'd be furious, not only because she'd ridden alone but also because she'd worn britches. "Don't worry," she told her reflection. "He won't know." *But what about Daniel?* She picked up a brush and ran it through her hair. *He's not willing to ride with me; what can he expect?* With resolve, she pulled on a pair of riding boots and laced them, then strode across the room. At the door she hesitated. If she was found out, she'd receive a tongue-lashing of the worst kind. *It certainly won't be my first,* she thought, opening the bedroom door and peeking out.

No one was about. She softly closed the door and hurried down the hallway and the stairs, then sped out the front door and ran across the yard to the barn. The pants felt peculiar, but she had to admit they did offer more freedom of movement than her gowns.

She ducked into the barn and headed for Rena's stall, stopping abruptly when she heard Bertram's voice. Her heart pounding, she pressed her back against a wall. He mustn't see her!

His voice sounded gentle. "There now, ya'll be right as rain in no time."

Rebecca moved behind some equipment and hunkered down in the shadows. He'd been kneeling beside one of the stalls. What was he up to?

Rebecca heard a whimper, then Bertram said, "I've got work ta do. I'll check on ya later."

Rebecca heard his steps. Making herself as small as possible, she held her breath until he strode past. She remained there for a few minutes, until she was convinced he wouldn't return, then stood.

Blowing out a breath, she said, "This is a foolish idea. I'll only get myself into more trouble." She wandered down the row of stalls. "Of course, it can't get much worse than it already is."

She stopped at the place where she'd seen Bertram. Just inside the stall lay one of the herding dogs. He was black with splotches of white. She'd seen him about the place and had admired him for his power and energy. Now he lay still, his left leg and hip bandaged. He watched Rebecca with dull eyes.

Bertram caring for a dog? I'd never have believed it. This animal would normally have been put down, yet Bertram had tended to him instead. Why? *Maybe he does have a heart.* Just the possibility made her warm toward the man. And she felt a morsel of hope that one day they might have a real relationship.

She patted the dog. He whimpered softly. "That's a good boy." Straightening, her thoughts returned to riding. She checked the paddock. Bertram's and Daniel's horses were gone. Most likely neither man would be seen until the end of the day. With nothing much to lose, she headed for Rena's stall.

Rebecca put a working saddle on the mare and cinched it tight. She grabbed hold of the saddle horn, placed her foot in the stirrup the way she'd seen the men do, then swung up and into the seat. Once steady, she pushed her right foot into the other stirrup. She felt a bit awkward but was certain she'd adjust. She pushed against the stirrups and raised herself off the saddle, then sat and seesawed sideways, getting a feel for this new way of riding.

Deciding she was ready, Rebecca turned Rena toward the barn door and clicked her tongue. The horse stepped into a trot, and almost immediately Rebecca slid sideways. She grabbed the saddle horn and pulled herself upright. This would be more difficult than she'd thought.

At the door she pulled back on the reins and stopped. The yard and the veranda were empty. Willa would still be reading her Bible and wouldn't find her way to the veranda for a while yet. Rebecca wasn't worried about Willa anyway. The only ones to be concerned about weren't anywhere around.

Nudging Rena in the sides, she moved out of the barn at a fast trot. Rebecca's backside bounced hard against the saddle. This would take some practice.

She passed by two aborigine boys playing in the shade of a tree. They looked up and stared, obviously shocked to see a mistress of the house riding astride. Rebecca smiled. "Good morning."

"G'day," one of the boys said.

Along the side of the main house, Callie beat a rug. She glanced at Rebecca, then acted as if she hadn't seen her. Rebecca thought she saw a smile on the woman's lips. *Callie and I are really not so different*, she thought with satisfaction.

When she'd neared the roadway, Rebecca gave Rena a kick with her heels, and the horse stepped into a canter. She squeezed her knees tightly against the mare's sides, enjoying the sensation of closeness with the animal. Rebecca could feel the power and energy of the horse. Rena wanted to run full out but obediently held back. "Soon, Rena, soon." Rebecca patted the mare's neck. When she felt comfortable riding astride, it was time to try a run.

The house disappeared behind the trees, and Rebecca leaned forward, touching Rena's flanks with the riding crop. The horse was ready and strode out, kicking up dry earth.

Hoping to avoid any chance encounters, Rebecca turned off the road and galloped across a field. Rena quickened her pace. The familiar sense of independence and exhilaration returned. Wind tugged at Rebecca's hat, and wisps of hair flew free. Her anxiety faded.

The more Rebecca rode, the more comfortable she became with riding astride. She felt more in control and better able to read the horse's intentions. The connection between horse and rider was much better riding astride than riding sidesaddle. Imagining Daniel's surprise at her new skill, she smiled, certain he would be amused. If only his father were. *There must be some way to convince Mr. Thornton that this is appropriate and acceptable.*

Her need for a run satisfied, Rebecca slowed Rena. Animal and rider walked. Wind whipped across the flats, cooling them. An occasional blast of air swirled up from the ground, carrying dust and twigs as it moved across the plains. Rebecca wondered if she could find her way to the billabong. It would be nice to spend some time in the cool of the shaded oasis.

She glanced about and felt a horrifying sense of being misplaced. Nothing looked familiar. The house was gone, along with its grove of trees. There were no barns or cottages. She couldn't see the trees that lined the roadway near the house. In fact, she had no idea at all which direction the road lay. After drinking from her canteen, she hooked its strap over the saddle horn and turned back the way she thought she'd come.

"I'll simply retrace my steps," she said. Her voice sounded hollow in the open terrain. Rena's trail was easy to follow for the first several yards. Then the hoof prints diminished and bit by bit vanished all together, whisked away by the wind.

Rebecca stopped, looked at the sun, and tried to figure out just where the house should be. *I'm in no danger*, she told herself. *There's no need to panic.*

Time passed, and the sun climbed higher into the sky, baking Rebecca's skin. Its heat penetrated her clothing, and she felt as if she were being cooked inside them. If only there were a shady place to rest. She thought about the veranda—its shade, breezes, and greenery. If not for her foolishness, she could be resting there now.

Stopping occasionally to drink from her canteen, Rebecca kept moving. Wind-swept dust turned gritty in her eyes and made her nose itch. It crept under the collar of her shirt and chafed her neck. She continued on but only became further confused. Finally she stopped and studied the landscape.

Everything looks the same. Have I come this way already? Panic washed over her. "Father, you know the way. Please show me."

She opened the canteen and drank, then poured a few drops of the valuable liquid into the palm of her hand and wet her burned face and lips. She was hot, too hot, and she knew she was in real danger. *I should have listened to Willa and to Daniel. Oh, Lord, why am I always so bullheaded?*

Draping the canteen over the saddle horn, Rebecca tried to think rationally. *How do others find their way? It can't be that difficult. Think.*

A goanna scampered across the ground in front of her. Rena danced, then hopped sideways. Rebecca pressed her knees into the horse's sides and pulled on the reins. The mare reared. Before Rebecca knew what had happened, she fell off backward and slammed into the ground. The impact knocked the wind from her, leaving her gasping for air. Pain in her back spread to her chest and arms.

Rena bolted and disappeared.

Rebecca rolled onto her side and hugged the earth. She lay there for a long while. When she finally caught her breath and the pain eased, she pushed to her feet, brushing earth and twigs from her clothes and hair. The wind sang a lonely song, sifting the earth and catching at Rebecca's snarl of curls.

She stood alone in the broad emptiness.

Fear seeped into her. She had no horse, no water, and no idea where she was. "Lord, what am I going to do?" Tears threatened, but she forced them back. They would serve no purpose. *Someone will come for me,* she told herself. But what should she do until then? There was no protection from the pitiless sun. Her mouth tasted of dirt, and she thought of the canteen still attached to her saddle.

Hands planted on her hips, she studied her surroundings. A slight knoll rose above the flat about ten meters from where she stood. Woodman had once told her that aborigines some-times dug out places in the earth to shelter in. "That's what I'll have to do," she said, searching for something to use for digging. A gnarled, nearly limbless and leafless ghost gum cast a narrow shadow on the dry ground. She crossed the parched land and scoured the earth near the ancient tree. A branch lay abandoned at its feet. Rebecca grabbed it, hoping it would be sturdy enough for digging.

Feeling weak and craving water, Rebecca walked to the rise. Using the sharp and narrowed end of the branch she started digging. The earth was hard, but she kept at it and inch by inch scooped away dirt. When the stick snapped, she found a stone and continued. Sweat dripped into her eyes. She wiped away the stinging moisture and kept digging.

Finally she managed to carve out an alcove just big enough to provide a shaded spot. She huddled inside, her knees bent and tucked close to her chest. Exhausted, she closed her eyes and tried to think pleasant thoughts, but thirst and a throbbing headache were pervasive.

"God, am I going to die here?" She thought of home. She should never have married Daniel and moved to this empty place. Living in someone else's home amid the disorder created by five children was preferable to this.

Her mind wandered to her husband. Their last words had been angry ones. Tears stung. She'd hoped for so much more. Her eyes closed, and in spite of the heat and thirst she slept.

"Aye! What are ya doin' in there?"

Rebecca lifted heavy eyelids and peered up. Cambria slid off her horse and hurried toward her friend.

"Thank the Lord I found ya." She kneeled beside Rebecca and put a water flask to her lips. "'Ere, 'ave some of this. It'll do ya good."

Rebecca gulped down the blessed water. "Thank you." She was more awake now.

"What are ya doin' out 'ere?"

"My horse threw me. And I didn't know where I was."

"Yer horse wandered into our place. Roight away I came lookin'. Me father and brothers are lookin' too." She offered Rebecca more water. "Come on, then, drink up."

Rebecca gulped down more of the precious liquid. Finally satisfied, she smiled and wiped her mouth. "You don't know how wonderful that tastes." Rebecca met Cambria's concerned gaze. "I thought I was going to die."

"Wal, and ya might 'ave too if I hadn't found ya." Cambria smiled. "Come on, then. I'll take ya back ta my place, then on home."

Cambria and Rebecca rode together to the Taylor station.

The house was small and unadorned. There were no flowers or broad verandas. The outbuildings were in disrepair and so were the corrals. Chickens roamed the yard, searching for tidbits in the dirt, and a scruffy cat lay curled in a wooden chair on a small front porch.

Weak and tired, Rebecca slid from the horse and followed Cambria inside. "Do you have ranch hands to help you with the work?"

"Nah. Me and me brothers are all there is. We manage." Pushing open the front door, she said, "I found 'er. Horse threw 'er, but she's fine. Mostly just hot and thirsty."

"And I'll bet hungry," Mrs. Taylor said, hustling to Rebecca and gently pressing her hands on the young woman's cheeks. She studied her face. "And yer a bit sunburned too. Poor thing. 'Ave a sit. Ya look done in. I'll get ya somethin' to eat, then." She dipped a ladle into a pot on a hot stove, filled a bowl with what looked like stew, and set it on the table in front of Rebecca.

Cambria brought a cup of water. "A little more won't hurt ya."

"Thank you," Rebecca said. Her head pounded and she felt sick to her stomach, but she ate.

"Anything I can do ta help a Thornton," Mrs. Taylor said. "Yer father-in-law's a fine man, a saint I'd say. He's always been 'ere ta give us a hand when we needed it. I'm always pleased ta help out a Thornton."

Rebecca took a bite of stew, thinking on the woman's words. Cambria had said the same thing. She couldn't imagine her father-in-law as a saint.

"Why, there's been more than a time or two that he was the only reason we were able ta hang on ta this place. Without 'im we'd 'ave lost it." She smiled, and her eyes crinkled with pleasure.

"I didn't know," Rebecca said, sipping her water.

221

"Most people don't. He's quiet about his charity. But he's a real fine Christian, eh?" She glanced at Cambria. "Why don't ya hitch up the wagon. I'll not 'ave her riding home on horseback in such a condition."

"How well do you know Mr. Thornton?" Rebecca asked, puzzling over what seemed to be a contradiction between what she was hearing and what she'd experienced. He'd shown kind consideration toward Willa, and she had to take into account what she'd seen that morning in the barn. Now Mrs. Taylor was expressing high regard for the man. Just who was he, really?

"We've known 'im for years. Always has been a fine person." Mrs. Taylor smiled.

Rebecca's mind moved ahead to the confrontation she knew was coming. She'd never be able to sneak home. In fact, there were probably people searching for her. Bertram must be furious. Just the thought made her throat tighten. She'd have to face him, dungarees and all.

I deserve it. I was foolish to leave the way I did. I have no excuses.

18

Rebecca could hear preparations being made downstairs for a day at the races, yet she remained at her desk. The Bible lay in front of her, and she continued reading, hoping to shut out the world, if just for a time. *He that dwelleth in the secret place of the most High shall abide under the shadow of the Almighty.* Rebecca's eyes traveled to the book and chapter, Psalm 91:1. She wanted to remember where to find this verse. It was a comfort.

Over the years, and more so since coming to Douloo, she'd been told of the sovereignty of God and of his wrath. Contrary to that, so much of what was written in the Bible spoke of a God of love and compassion—the God she knew. Closing her eyes, she felt the reassurance of his presence. She longed to remain with him.

Bertram's accusing eyes intruded on her peace. The day she'd been lost, he'd been one of those looking for her. After returning with Cambria, she'd stood before him, still wearing britches. He'd stared at her a long time, then in a quiet, venomous voice had said, "I expect ya to change yer clothes. Ya know the wrong ya've done. It won't be mentioned again. And it won't happen again. Is that understood?"

Rebecca had glanced at Daniel, seeking solace, but there had been none. An ache swelled in her throat at his remoteness.

Willa had placed an arm around Rebecca's shoulders. "We're thankful to have you home safe and sound. You scared us half to death." She had gazed at her husband. "It's natural for a young woman to wander a bit. And here it's especially difficult, with little for a well-bred, educated woman to do."

Bertram's countenance had remained harsh. "Foolishness, rebelliousness, disobedience—God does not look kindly on such behavior."

"I'm sure she meant to do none of those things," Willa had argued.

Bertram had throttled her with his eyes. "God has placed men over women. And a wife is to be a helpmate to her husband. Is standing against yer own husband being a proper helpmate?"

Willa had kept her arm around Rebecca, but she'd said no more. Rebecca had felt her mother-in-law's annoyance.

"Sir, I know what I did was foolish," Rebecca had said. "I really didn't understand how dangerous it could be. I should have listened to you and Daniel. I'm very sorry."

"I might be able to excuse that. Yanks don't understand this country. But the clothes? Riding astride?" The tenor of his voice had risen with each question.

"Other women wear trousers, and they ride astride—Meghan and Cambria . . ."

"Yer not other women. Yer my son's wife, a Thornton. Thorntons aren't like other people. We're held to a higher standard."

A call from outside carried Rebecca back to the present. *It was the clothes*, she thought. *He only cared about what I was wearing. I hate him.* Her mind turned to Willa. *How does she stand it? Is being like Willa what's expected of me? I can't do it. I won't.* Another thought throttled her. *If Daniel had married Meghan, would she have had to change?*

She closed her eyes to pray, but she saw Daniel, standing beside his father, a shadow of a man. Many times Bertram had reprimanded her, and not once had Daniel come to her defense. Would he ever? Or would he become his father?"

The bedroom door opened. "Rebecca," Daniel said. "It's time to go."

She wiped away remnants of tears, then turned to look at him.

"Are you all right?"

"I'm fine. I was just reading."

"Well, we're waiting. Mum's already in the surrey."

Rebecca stood and smoothed her gown. "I suppose I'm ready, then."

Rebecca sat beside Willa. She didn't feel much like visiting. In fact, she felt little interest in this outing, or anything else for that matter. She'd rather have stayed home.

"It's a lovely day for the races," Willa said. "Right perfect. Not too hot, not too cold, and no rain. Not just yet, anyway." Her eyes sparkled with mischief. "This time of year we get storms on occasion. And soon it will be March, and the temperatures shall become cooler."

"I'm looking forward to that," Rebecca said.

The entire household accompanied the Thorntons. It was a short jaunt to the track. A picnic lunch had been prepared ahead of time and would be shared by all. There had been a carnival atmosphere to the preparations.

Woodman looked back at the women. "Ya ready, then?"

"Indeed, we are," Willa said cheerfully.

With a flick of the reins and a click of the tongue, Woodman moved the horses out, and the procession of one surrey, two wagons, and several riders proceeded. Daniel rode alongside his father. Rebecca watched him, resentment growing. *He has no spine when it comes to his father.* In Boston he'd been different, more fun loving. *I suppose that's what comes from being out from under his father's authority.* At Douloo it was as if he'd been dragged onto a stage where he played out a chosen role.

She could feel the sting of tears. If only he could stand up to his father. *As long as he continues to yield, he'll not know freedom . . . and neither will I.*

"I should like to make a trip to Brisbane," Willa said. "And I was thinking it might be wise to go before the weather turns wet."

"What? I'm sorry. I didn't hear what you said."

"Oh, I was just speaking about going to Brisbane. I try to travel there at least once a year. Would you like to go?"

"That would be wonderful," Rebecca said, remembering how charming the city had been. "I liked it there."

"I do as well." Willa studied Rebecca. "How are you feeling, dear?"

"My sunburn is much better."

"I wasn't speaking of your physical health."

"Oh." Rebecca didn't know just what to say. "I don't know, really. I guess I'm a bit sad and a little afraid."

"Afraid? Whatever of?"

Rebecca knew better than to speak honestly about her fears, but she needed to tell someone. "I'm . . . afraid . . . Daniel will become like his father and that I'll be like you."

Willa looked stunned.

"Please don't misunderstand. You're a dear woman. And I love you. But I can't be like you." Rebecca tried to gather her thoughts. Once again, she'd said more than she ought. "Certainly, I should be somewhat like you. I'm often too

226

mutinous for my own good. But I don't believe life is to be lived by a list of rules overseen by one's husband."

Willa kept her hands clasped in her lap; her eyes held a mix of hurt and irritation.

"I'm not saying this very well, but please hear me out." Rebecca took a deep breath and tried to relax. "My father was a godly man, a good man. He was the authority in our home, but he led gently . . . usually." She offered a half smile. "We had our battles, but never did he make me feel as if I were of little value. And when he said something in anger, he was always quick to apologize. He never seemed to lose sight of God's sovereignty and the fact that we must allow room for God's will in our lives."

Still looking wounded, Willa remained silent. Rebecca understood she'd thrown a barb, but there were things that needed to be said. She continued, "I've never lived in a home like this. Truly, I'm confused. I see your husband reading his Bible and praying, and I hear him quoting Scripture, but I don't see God's love in him."

Willa unfolded then refolded her hands. "Your words have cut into my heart. It pains me to realize how unhappy you are. But I don't know that I can do anything to change the circumstances.

"I love my husband, but I'm not blind. He can be a hard man. But that's not his heart. He does his utmost to obey God's call as overseer and protector of his family. He sees it as his duty to make certain they remain on the narrow path to redemption." She glanced at her husband, then looked at Rebecca. "I know he sometimes loses his way, but I also know he's God's servant. And the Lord loves him and us; therefore, we can be assured the path Bertram follows is the one ordained by God."

She rested a hand on the top of the surrey door. "Many

years ago I vowed to be his helpmate and to obey him. I won't betray that vow. It's my duty to pray, to love, and to obey."

A smile of reminiscence touched Willa's lips. "I remember the tenderness, and I still see it from time to time. Please don't give up on him. He's a good man and he'll come 'round."

Rebecca wanted to believe her mother-in-law, but more and more she'd come to think her father-in-law had strayed from the truth of God's Word. The memory of him in the barn tending the wounded dog puzzled her. He did possess compassion. She laid her hand on Willa's. "I didn't mean to hurt you, only to help you understand my distress. I haven't lost hope. All things are possible with God."

Daniel rode up to the surrey. "It's a good day for a race, eh?" He smiled as if he were happy with the world.

"Absolutely," Rebecca said, trying to be cheerful.

"Cambria will be there. You two will have time for a chat." He chuckled. "And I'm sure she'll be glad to see you in a dress this time."

Rebecca's disposition turned sour. "I seriously doubt she cared a whit about what I was wearing when she found me. She cared only about my welfare. As you should have."

"I was . . ."

"If I had my way I'd buy a dozen pairs of trousers," Rebecca snapped. "It seems someone in this family would care more about my nearly dying in this godforsaken country than whether or not I was wearing britches!" Folding her arms over her chest, she squared her chin and looked directly in front of her.

"I was sick with worry," Daniel explained. "But you wouldn't speak to me when you returned."

Rebecca kept her eyes forward.

Daniel continued to ride alongside the surrey. "You're the most hardheaded woman I've ever known," he finally sputtered and rode off.

"In his defense," Willa said, "he was fit to be tied. And not about your trousers. He was worried about your safety. You're being unfair."

"I suppose." Rebecca dropped her arms to her sides. "Sometimes I can't seem to keep from being contentious." She watched Daniel urge his horse across the dry grasslands.

"How do you feel about being Daniel's wife? Have your feelings for him changed?" Willa asked softly.

Rebecca sucked in a deep breath and blew it out. "Yes and no. I care for him, but I don't believe it's love I feel."

"Give yourself time." Willa patted Rebecca's hand. "Try not to be so hard on him. He's doing his best." She raised an eyebrow. "It's not easy for him—living under a man like Bertram."

"If he was so frightened about what had happened to me, why didn't he speak up?"

"Maybe the barbs you wore kept him from telling you how he felt."

Rebecca remembered how angry she'd been and mortified during her confrontation with Bertram, and finally furious with Daniel for not defending her. She had refused to speak to him. "I still think he should have said something in my defense."

The racing grounds were jammed with businessmen, horse traders, gamblers, and plain folks from all over the district. Excitement permeated the place.

Rebecca found Cambria, and the two of them strolled the grounds, admiring horses and eyeing other women's apparel. It seemed that even in Queensland women dressed up for the races.

Men from around the district studied the horses; some

made deals for future breeding or made outright purchases of animals. Men were taking and making bets. Rebecca was surprised at the amount of money changing hands.

Woodman handed a wad of bills to a man. "Now, why would he do that?" Rebecca asked. "He's not much on possessions."

"The other man's takin' bets. Seems Woodman's makin' a bet."

"But he wouldn't."

Cambria shrugged. "It's all very excitin' don't ya think?"

"Yes, but I'm not sure why we're here, exactly. Mr. Thornton is set against gambling, and that's what this racing business is all about, isn't it?"

"Yais and no." Cambria nudged back her bonnet and rubbed her forehead. "There's a lot of gambling going on, but there are some 'ere who are more interested in findin' good breedin' stock."

"It's all very interesting. I've always loved horses. My father believed in owning only the best quality animals."

"We've never had such luxuries."

"I'm sorry . . . I didn't mean . . ."

"No worries." Cambria smiled, and her blue eyes looked bright. "I'm quite content on me father's station. Money never was of much interest ta me."

"I've never been much interested in it either, but then I've always had all I needed." Rebecca chuckled and offered an apologetic smile.

"How did it go with ya after I left the other day?"

"Not well. Mr. Thornton was angrier than I've ever seen him. And Daniel . . . well, he sided with his father. Willa, bless her heart, stood up for me—what little good it did."

"It is true, ya made a poor choice headin' out into the bush the way ya did. It takes time to learn yer way about."

"I know. And I apologized, but Mr. Thornton seemed more

upset about my trousers than my well-being." She managed a crooked grin. "I don't understand. Sometimes you and Meghan wear pants."

"Yais, but we're not lydies the same as you. We're more like one of the blokes 'bout 'ere. We ride and work alongside the drovers."

Rebecca stopped and leaned against a wooden fence encircling the track. She peered between the rails, watching a black stallion dance as he was being led around the arena.

"I can see your point, but why do I have to be so different?"

"Yer a Thornton."

"Hmm. That's what Mr. Thornton said." She straightened and said with a sigh, "I'd be happier if my name wasn't Thornton." She shrugged. "Although I must admit, some of my difficulties have more to do with my personality than my name. Even when I lived in Boston I felt trapped by the proprieties of society. I'd hoped things would be different when I married Daniel. I thought he was different and would understand and accept me as I am."

"Daniel's a good bloke. He loves ya. But he's a Thornton and has responsibilities. And he's learned ta listen ta his father." Cambria pressed her forehead against a railing. "Rebecca, Mr. Thornton's a fine man." She turned and settled serious eyes on her friend. "God speaks ta him. Sometimes he can be frightening, but he's righteous and wise."

"I don't know what to think about that." Rebecca watched Meghan saunter toward Daniel, who stood visiting with some men farther down the fence line. "My life in Boston was very different. In my church there, I was taught to respect the elders and, of course, my parents, and I sometimes sought counsel from those more spiritually mature than me, but . . . well, no one has ever dictated my every step."

Meghan leaned on the fence beside Daniel. *Too close. The*

hussy, Rebecca thought, struggling to keep her mind on her conversation with Cambria. "Of course, there have been people who felt strongly about certain things, especially my father. But in most ways he allowed me to be myself. And nearly always permitted me to make up my own mind about things. He instructed me to seek God's will. Mr. Thornton decides he knows God's will, then tells you what it is. That's not right."

"All I know is that he makes good decisions, and he's looked out for me family. We owe 'im a great deal."

Rebecca nodded. "I know. That's what I've heard. And to be honest, that's what's confusing me."

A woman's laughter carried above the racing din. *Meghan.* Rebecca looked and found the Australian beauty standing very close to Daniel. She rested a hand on his arm. The two seemed to be sharing some private joke. Meghan glanced at Rebecca, triumph in her eyes.

Rebecca seethed inwardly. No matter what she felt for Daniel, Meghan had no right.

"It's shameful the way she fawns over 'im. If he were me husband, I'd tell 'er how I felt."

Rebecca agreed, but did she have the right? Daniel professed to loving her, but their marriage was still one of convenience. Again Meghan flashed Rebecca a triumphant smile. "I think I will have a word with her."

Rebecca waited until Daniel and the men walked away and Meghan was alone. "Pray for me," she told Cambria and headed toward Meghan.

With her back against the fence, Meghan rested her elbows on a rail. Her brown eyes wore a challenge. "Wal now, how are ya' feelin'? Heard about yer close call the other day. Can't imagine someone having so little sense as to go wanderin' about when they don't know their way 'round."

"I was fine until my horse threw me," Rebecca said, struggling to maintain her composure. "But I didn't come here to talk about that. It is my opinion that you need to be reminded that Daniel is married. It would be a shame if such an oversight were to ruin your reputation."

Meghan smiled, and her almond eyes turned into slits. "Yer husband likes me. He always has. And whether he's married or not doesn't matter ta me. He belongs ta me, and one day he'll come back ta me."

"Whatever you had with Daniel is part of the past. I'm his wife now—and you will stay away from him."

"Yer his wife all right, but it's not what was meant to be. Even Mr. Thornton wishes Daniel had married me. When things are set aright, Daniel will be much happier and so will 'is father."

"Bertram Thornton is a righteous man and would never accept divorce."

Meghan seemed undaunted by Rebecca's words. "It's been understood Daniel and I belong together. Ya might as well get used to the idea."

Before Rebecca could reply, Meghan strutted away. She longed to give her a more thorough tongue-lashing, but to run after her and force her to listen would only create a scene and bring more condemnation from Bertram. Her fury boiling, Rebecca watched Meghan seek out Daniel and slip an arm through his as he walked toward one of the horses being groomed. She wanted to slap her.

Rebecca realized she was afraid. What if Daniel really did belong with Meghan and regretted marrying her? *Well, then it would all simply have been a mistake. Just as I've thought.* The words made sense, but Rebecca didn't feel comforted.

"She's something, isn't she?" Jim said, joining Rebecca.

Barely able to speak, Rebecca said, "She certainly is."

"Don't let her get under your skin. She's used to getting her way, and she's jealous—can't seem to make anything happen. She and Daniel may have had something once, but no more."

"How do you know that? He seems . . . taken with her."

Jim grinned. "I know because of the light in his eyes when he looks at you. Wish I had someone who felt that way about me."

Cambria joined them. "G'day, Jim. Nice ta see ya."

"Good to see you." He flashed a smile. "Well, I've got work to do." He tipped his hat to the ladies and walked away.

"Good lookin' bloke, that one, eh?" Cambria said, watching him go.

"He is, at that," Rebecca said. "From what I hear he's looking for someone to love."

"Roight. A lydie, not someone like me."

Cambria went to help her mother, and Rebecca wandered the grounds alone. Occasionally she'd stop to study an animal or watch a race. It would have been enjoyable if Daniel had shared the time with her. He was busy studying horseflesh and flirting with Meghan.

Callie joined Rebecca late in the day. "Mum, Mrs. Thornton was wonderin' if ya would like ta join 'er. She's over yonder." Callie nodded at a tree where Willa sat in the shade, chatting with a friend. "She's thinkin' ya might be wantin' some company."

"Yes. Tell her I'll come visit shortly."

Instead of returning to Willa, Callie remained. "I seen ya wanderin'. Somethin' troublin' ya?"

Rebecca was surprised at Callie's concern. "No. I'm fine. The horses are beautiful, aren't they?"

"Yais. Roight fine." She watched a group of men swapping bets. "Seems the men 'ave a good time of it."

"They do. But from what I've seen, they're here to gamble more than anything else. A lot of money has changed hands. I must say, I was surprised to see Woodman making bets. He doesn't seem the type."

"He never bets."

"But I saw him."

"He don't care for possessions. They mean nothin' ta black-fellas." She paused. "I'd say the bet was for Mr. Thornton."

"But I've heard him preach about the evils of gambling. He said he visits the races only so he can get a look at the horseflesh in the district."

"What a man say and what he do is not always the same, eh?" Callie smirked. "Whitefellas always want things, need ta 'ave goods. I wonder sometime, is it something ta do with yer God?"

"Certainly not. It's simply human nature. God's Word states clearly that man's not to store up treasures on earth but rather in heaven. And he tells us not to fret over what we're going to eat or wear. His Word says he feeds even the birds, and he cares for us more than he does a bird—we're to trust him."

Silence settled between the two women, then Callie said, "Mr. Thornton 'as much treasure. If yer God says this is bad and not to store up, why is he rich?"

Rebecca was momentarily stumped. Clearly Callie had given this some thought. It was important she offer a sensible answer. "I don't believe God is saying that being rich is bad but that the desire for riches should not hinder our verve for him. Nothing should be more important than God."

"Wal, I see Mr. Thornton doing what yer God says not ta do. He says God loves, but sometimes he don't love very well." She shook her head. "No. I don't believe what's in his black book."

"No one can live a perfect life, Callie. Not even Mr. Thornton. The Bible talks about so much more than what you see in his life."

Callie took a step away. "I don't want to talk no more 'bout this. What ya believe is for fools."

Rebecca watched Callie as she walked away. How would she ever know God's presence and his forgiveness if those around her didn't live out what they believed? She glanced at Meghan and knew that being a living example in this place would be a challenge.

19

Tea in hand, Rebecca stepped onto the veranda. A storm rumbled from the east, and the smell of rain was in the air. Wind caught at her hair and dress. Anticipation coursed through her. "Rain, wonderful rain," she said, closing her eyes and breathing deeply.

Although squalls sometimes visited the flats during the summer, they generally released little moisture before moving on. It had been weeks since they'd had any real precipitation.

Woodman had explained they could pretty much count on an occasional storm in March. And just that morning he'd predicted one was on its way.

Rebecca was ready—ready for green grasses, the smell of moist earth, and the charm of fields sprinkled with flowers.

Willa joined her, then stood watching the eastern sky. "We're in for it, I'd say." She pointed at a gray curtain in the distance. "See there, it's coming down in sheets." Her voice was filled with anticipation. Distant thunder rumbled.

The wall of water moved closer. The first splatters plopped on the ground, leaving wet dimples in the dry earth. Big drops splashed the porch steps. Lightning fractured the sky and thunder boomed. Then all of a sudden the downpour moved across the yard and to the house in a drenching deluge.

Exhilarated, Rebecca gazed at the display. "It's marvelous! I hope it rains for days!"

"You may get your wish," Willa said. "Once the heavens open up, it sometimes takes days to turn off the spigots." She smiled. "We never know quite how much we'll get. Indeed, there may even be flooding."

The rain continued for five days. It splattered the windows and drummed against the roof. The yard turned to mud, and the garden plants sagged beneath the weighty wetness. Rivers filled and some flooded, and reports were that some of the streets of Thornton Creek flowed with muddy water. The Thorntons sheltered indoors, and for the first time since Rebecca had arrived, there was no church meeting. However, she'd heard that in spite of the flooding, seats at the Thornton Creek Pub were filled. Men in the district had little to do.

Rebecca spent contented hours indoors. The sound of rainfall brought an ease she hadn't felt since arriving at Douloo. One afternoon while curled up in a large chair reading *Jane Eyre* and listening to the downpour, Rebecca was struck at the similarities she felt between herself and the novel's heroine.

She hadn't grown up orphaned or in poverty, but she now lived in a house with a fierce man who possessed absolute authority. He was sometimes frightening and always a puzzle. She could only wish for a happy ending.

Callie dusted around her. "Why do ya read?"

Rebecca looked at her. "For lots of reasons."

"Why that book?"

"I don't know. It's an adventure; I admire the main char-

238

acter. She has a deep reverence for God and a strong spirit of service. And there's a hint of a romance. I like that." She pressed the book against her chest.

"It talks about those things?"

"Yes. You don't know how to read?"

"No. Blacks don't read. I never knew any blackfellas who could."

"Would you like to learn?" Rebecca felt the stir of excitement. Reading could open up the world to Callie.

"No, mum."

"But why not?"

"I'm not smart enough."

Rebecca set her book in her lap. "Of course you are. In fact, I think you're quite intelligent."

"Ya do?" Callie's face brightened for a moment before the mask of disinterest returned. "Wal, readin's not for blacks."

Rebecca stood. "Why don't you let me teach you? It would be fun."

Callie looked at the dust cloth in her hand, then at the door leading into the main house. "Ya think I could learn?"

"Yes. Absolutely."

"Wal, then . . . maybe."

In the days that followed, Rebecca spent time each day teaching Callie. The servant was bright and learned quickly. She moved from the basic alphabet to rudimentary words in no time. As she grasped the written language, her hunger for knowledge grew.

Rebecca thoroughly enjoyed the time they spent together, but she knew Bertram would disapprove, so the lessons were kept a secret. The two women waited for snatches of time, then met in Rebecca's room.

One day Callie looked up from her studies, a puzzled expression on her face. "Mum, what am I ta do with this readin'? I like it, but me life won't change."

Rebecca was stuck for an answer. "I don't know for sure, but I'm certain God does. And knowledge is always a good thing. One day you'll be able to read the Bible."

Callie compressed her lips. "I don't wish ta read yer Bible."

"What about a novel, then? There are many good ones—*Vanity Fair*, *Jane Eyre*, or even *Uncle Tom's Cabin*." She smiled. "Of course, that one you'll have to read in secret. It's somewhat controversial, and I don't think people around here would approve."

"They'll be mad about any readin'. I'm tellin' no one, eh?" She grinned. "But I'll keep learnin'."

"Absolutely. Now, you better get back to your duties before you're missed."

"Roight." Callie closed the book she'd been working on and walked to the bedroom door. She stood there a moment, her brow creased. "Mum, I think Mr. Thornton knows. A coupla days ago he found me lookin' at this." She held up her elementary reader. "He said nothin', but I could see his inside anger."

"Try not to worry. I'm sure everything will be fine," Rebecca said, but inwardly she quaked.

"Yais, mum."

Rebecca closed the door behind Callie and walked to the window. What would Bertram say? "I'm probably in for another tongue-lashing," she said, gazing out across the open plains.

Just as Woodman had said the day she first arrived in Thornton Creek, the rain transformed the plains. The grasses were thick and green, and patches of wildflowers had blossomed, looking like brightly colored jewels. It reminded her of spring back home. As the thought penetrated her mind, she realized Boston didn't seem as much like home as it once had. *Curious,* she thought, then picked up her bonnet, settled it on her head, and tied it. "I'd say it's time to enjoy some of this springlike weather."

☞

Rebecca stepped out the front door and walked across the porch, breathing deeply. The air smelled of damp vegetation and floral sweetness. Rain had beaten down the garden, leaving the delicate domesticated flowers and plants more than a bit undone. The roses had suffered most and clearly longed for more sunlight and heat. *Willa and I will have to prune them back,* Rebecca thought.

Stepping on patches of new grass and avoiding puddles, Rebecca walked toward the barn, hoping Daniel would be working inside. Since the weather had changed he'd kept closer to home. They had even spent mornings drifting from sleep to wakefulness. Sometimes they would lie in each other's arms and talk about their future—the hope of children and one day even grandchildren. On such mornings Rebecca could imagine she loved Daniel.

Her mind carried her to the previous day. Again she felt the pang of regret.

Daniel had climbed out of bed and gone down to bring up their morning tea. When he returned he handed her a cup and saucer.

"Thank you," Rebecca had said. "I could have gotten it, or Callie would have brought it up."

"Sometimes it feels good to do something nice for the one you love." He'd climbed in beside her, careful not to spill his own tea.

Rebecca had leaned against propped-up pillows. She was

still unable to tell him she loved him. She knew he longed to hear the words. *I can't lie about something so important,* she'd thought. Taking a sip of tea, she'd said, "It's moments like this that I'm glad I came to Australia."

"And the rest of the time?"

"I'm still adjusting, but I'm getting used to it." She'd set her cup in the saucer. "There's something I've been wanting to tell you. I've been feeling a bit guilty."

"And what is that?"

"Well . . ." Rebecca had hesitated, fearing Daniel's reaction. Still, he needed to know. "I've been teaching Callie to read. She's doing very well," she'd hurried on. "She's quite bright."

Daniel had sat up straighter. "Now, why would you waste your time teaching a black?"

"Why not?" Rebecca had felt her defenses rise.

"She's a grand person, all the blacks here at Douloo are. They're loyal and hardworking, but they don't have the intelligence they need for learning things like reading and writing."

"But she *is* learning. She *can* read."

"It's either some kind of trick or it's the white blood in her. That must be it. She has a white father, you know."

Rebecca had been outraged. She'd sat up so quickly she'd spilled her tea. "You really believe that? I know Callie's smart, and it's not because her father's white. Aborigines can learn just like we can."

"Well, you can waste your time if you like," Daniel had said, rolling out of bed. "But all your hard work will lead nowhere. And, hopefully, you'll soon be too busy caring for our own child to spend time with her." He'd leaned down and kissed Rebecca. "I'll see you at afternoon tea."

In just a few moments, Daniel had managed to extinguish Rebecca's kind thoughts about him and Australia. His prejudice was a disappointment. How could an intelligent, compassionate man believe such things?

And what about children? He'd mentioned his expectations more than once. Watching him disappear into the dressing room, her mind had ruminated over why she wasn't pregnant. They'd been married nearly six months. What if there were no babies?

With a sigh Rebecca wandered into the barn, unconsciously resting her hand on her abdomen. There was no one about. The smell of animals and hay wafted over her. Birds flitted among the eaves, and one of the barn cats rubbed against a wooden barrel. Rebecca's eyes traveled to a pile of hay. A memory from childhood tickled her thoughts. Should she dare? She crossed to the hay pile, turned her back to it, and with her arms outstretched, dropped straight back, falling into the soft, sweet-smelling pile. It gave beneath her, nearly burying her in the fragrant dried grasses.

Smiling, she lay quietly looking up into the rafters. The barn was well built. There were no cracks or gaps. She watched a bird dart back and forth. Was it trapped or searching for a nesting spot? For some reason, Rebecca felt she needed to know its mission.

A noise came from the back of the barn. Quickly Rebecca pushed to her feet, brushing hay from her dress and hair. She didn't want to be caught in folderol, as her aunt Mildred would have called it. Bertram would certainly think such behavior foolish.

When she considered herself presentable, Rebecca followed the sound to the back of the barn. Jim was mucking out a stall. Rebecca stood quietly and watched him. Their budding friendship had faded. Both knew Daniel and his father disapproved of any tie between them. *What can a friendly chat hurt?* Rebecca thought, stepping up and leaning against the gate.

Jim glanced up. "Oh, Rebecca. Hello." He straightened and leaned on his pitchfork. "How long have you been here?"

"Not long."

He lifted his hat and, using his shirtsleeve, wiped sweat from his forehead. "Seems like it's cool until you start working. Then the humidity gets to you."

"I'm beginning to doubt it will ever truly be cool." Rebecca stepped up onto the lowest board on the gate. "Can I help? I don't have anything to do right now."

"That probably wouldn't be a good idea. I'd hate to see Mr. Thornton's face if he caught you mucking out a stall."

Rebecca nodded, then said, "He won't find out. I didn't see him or Daniel anywhere near the house. And it would give me something to do." She fiddled with the gate latch. "I envy Cambria. I even envy Meghan. They can ride when they want, and they work alongside the men. They're real Australians. I want to know what that's like."

"It's overrated," Jim said with a crooked smile. "I'm sure there's more you can do besides this."

"I used to work with Willa in the garden, but the rain drove us out. And of course there's needlework and reading, but that's becoming tiresome. Even cooking with Lily is growing tedious. Riding is out of the question—the weather, plus I rarely have anyone to ride with."

"This weather won't last long. It'll soon dry out."

Rebecca sighed. "When I lived in Boston I thought my life was restricted. I had no idea what that really meant. Mr. Thornton barely lets me breathe. He expects things should be done a certain way—his way. It . . ." Rebecca knew she was about to stray beyond what was proper, but she hadn't talked to Cambria in days and she needed to share her burdens. "It might change if Daniel would stand up to his father. And defend me."

"Never happen," Jim said matter-of-factly.

"Why not?"

"Daniel's a good bloke. I like him. But he doesn't have the strength to tackle his father. It's always been this way . . . always will be." He jabbed the pitchfork into the filthy hay. "Daniel's not the type to take to the road the way Elton did."

"What really happened? No one's ever told me."

Jim compressed his lips. "I probably shouldn't either." He rocked the handle of the pitchfork from one hand to the other. "Elton and Daniel were always very different from one another. Daniel was the 'good son' and Elton, a thorn in his father's side. He was kind of like you." Jim grinned. "He wanted his own life."

"I don't see anything wrong with that."

"I didn't say there was." Jim pushed the pitchfork deeper into the hay. "Anyway, one day Elton and Mr. Thornton had an argument. It was one to beat all." He dumped a pitchfork full of hay into a wheelbarrow. "Started out civilized enough, but grew and grew until the two of them were screaming at each other. Mrs. Thornton tried to intervene. It didn't do any good. The whole thing ended with Elton leaving and Mr. Thornton disinheriting him. Elton never returned. And Mr. Thornton's never mentioned his name since."

"How awful!"

"Yeah. Real sad." Jim scraped the sole of his boot against one of the pitchfork tines. "Daniel's a good man, but he won't chance that happening to him. He's not about to let go of his inheritance. He loves this place too much." He lifted the pitchfork. "I better get back to work. Hate to be caught lollygagging."

"And I've got to get back to . . . well, nothing in particular."

Feeling down, Rebecca wandered toward the house. Daniel said he loved her, but was the station more important to him than she was? *I guess if it were me and I knew my husband didn't love me, I'd make sure to keep my estate a priority.*

Her mind wandered to their conversations about children. If she and Daniel did have children, would Daniel allow his father to bully them like he did everyone else? Could Daniel stand up for his children?

No matter what Daniel thinks, I will never allow Mr. Thornton to rule my children. Not ever.

❦

That night at supper Bertram seemed in a worse temper than usual. Willa made an unsuccessful stab at conversation, then conceded there would be no banter and ate quietly.

Callie started clearing away the soup bowls when Bertram said, "There's no wisdom in teaching blacks, ya know. Waste of time. They lack intelligence." He looked at Rebecca.

A tremor traveled through her. Taking a breath, she said, "Well, sir . . . that's not exactly true. In fact—"

"Yais, yais. I know. Ya've been teaching Callie. Well, ya'll stop. There's no good purpose in any black knowing how to read or write."

Callie showed no emotion.

"Sir, I must differ with you," Rebecca said. "There is good reason. All people should know how to . . ."

"Did ya hear me? I said no teaching the blacks. It's a waste of yer good time."

"I don't have anything better to do," Rebecca said, taking another track. "You've given me no responsibilities."

"There's plenty of work to be done, woman's work." He watched Callie walk toward the kitchen. "Ya'll have our neighbors up in arms before ya know it. They don't hold with educating blacks any more than I do." He stood. "And furthermore, I don't like ya keeping company with a black.

246

They're heathens and hold to beliefs that can contaminate yer Christianity."

Willa turned pale but said not a word.

Allowing herself time to think, Rebecca slowly let out her breath. "I respect your opinion, sir, but in this I must protest. In God's Word it's clear that Christ spent time with the wicked, even eating among thieves and beggars. He came to save the lost. Aren't we to do the same?"

"If God meant ya to be a missionary, ya wouldn't have married my son. And I don't believe God called the blacks to salvation. He is sovereign, and we must respect his choices." Bertram squared his jaw and knit his brows. "It's my responsibility to protect my flock."

Rebecca was flabbergasted. "You can't possibly believe the blacks have no hope for salvation."

"What I believe is . . . it's God's sovereign choice who is saved and who is not."

"But, sir—"

"Not another word."

Rebecca couldn't keep quiet. "Sir, you and Woodman have been friends since you were boys. He's your friend. Don't you care about his eternity?"

"Woodman has nothing to do with this."

Rebecca looked to her husband. "Daniel? Do you agree with this?"

Daniel sat stone-faced.

"Please, say something."

He looked from Rebecca to his father. Finally he shoved back his chair and stood. "I have work to do," he said and trudged out of the dining room.

In disbelief Rebecca stared at his back as he left.

❦

Daniel settled on his chestnut stallion and touched his flanks with his heels. The animal trotted through the corral gate and into the yard. The evening air was cool, the near darkness welcoming. He leaned forward and clicked his tongue, and the horse broke into a canter, heading toward the road.

A butter-colored half moon hung in the sky, providing enough light for a leisurely ride but not enough to give his horse his head. He longed to escape into the open, dark emptiness where he could yell and shriek away his frustrations and anxieties.

Rebecca's brown eyes haunted him. When he'd first met her, they'd been filled with the sparkle of anticipation and mischief. Now they were pensive and troubled. Rebecca was unhappy. The conflict between her and his father was growing, just as it had with Elton. And she didn't love him. If she did, she would have said something.

He'd hoped love would grow. She still treated him as a friend rather than a husband. Her response to his lovemaking was obedient rather than passionate. And he knew she expected him to stand up to his father. How could he? He'd never stand for it. *And if I don't will she leave?*

"Lord, what am I to do? My father's squeezing the very breath from us." His mind reeled back over the years—countless confrontations, countless disappointments, and countless agonies. His father had never held him in high regard, and Daniel had never learned to stand his ground. All his life he'd existed within his father's shadow. While he worked, Bertram was there; while building his reputation, he was there; while . . . loving, he was there. His father was overseer of his life—every move, every thought.

Daniel rested his hands on the saddle horn and closed his eyes. A groan rose from deep beneath his ribs, growing into an agonizing bellow. The chirruping of cicadas quieted. Then stillness fell over the plains once again, and they took up their song. Daniel opened his eyes and gazed at the stars. A flicker of a boyhood memory touched his heart. He and Elton and his father had lain beneath this same sky counting stars, a fanciful goal for sure but one attempted just the same.

"Father, my dad is a godly man. He seeks you at every turn. And your Word is always on his lips. That Word says I am to listen to him and obey him. But I'm a man. How do I live fully as a man and still obey my father?"

The sight of Rebecca's plaintive eyes wrenched his heart. How many times had he seen that same look on his mother's face? This night Willa had disagreed. He'd seen it. Yet as always, she'd remained quiet, obedient. Is that what he wanted from Rebecca? Is that what he expected of her?

From the beginning, her bold spirit had drawn him. If she was forced into a mold of his father's making could that spirit survive? *No*, came the whispered reply.

If he wanted her, what choice did he have but to leave Douloo? Even as the thought touched his mind, he knew he couldn't go.

20

With the passing days and weeks Bertram became more dicta-
torial and, seemingly, more angry with Rebecca. She couldn't
please him. And the harder she tried, the angrier he became.
Gradually resentment moved into her heart, and she closed
herself off to the possibility of a congenial relationship.

For the most part, the two avoided each other. However,
there were essential activities that forced them to interact.
Evening meals were the most difficult. Hostility between
Bertram and Rebecca often bristled, and supper was wrought
with, at the very least, uneasiness and, at the worst, open
hostility.

One evening after supper Daniel stopped Rebecca in the
foyer. "This must stop."

"What must stop?" she challenged.

"This . . . thing between you and my father." He rested his
hands on her upper arms. "I know he can be difficult, but
can't you simply relent and obey?"

"How can you expect me to bow to him? You saw how I
tried to comply with his wishes week after week. It made no
difference. He sees what he wants. The only thing that will
satisfy him is if I forfeit my very soul to him." She straightened
her spine and folded her arms over her chest. "I refuse."

"You're making too much of all this. He can be overbearing, but you're wrong about the rest; he doesn't want your soul. He wants what's best for you."

"No. He wants what's best for him. And as for overbearing? I'd say tyrannical is a more accurate description."

"Please, Rebecca. He won't give in. I'm telling you."

"If you stood with me, he might."

"No. He won't. He believes he's doing God's will. And in that he's unwavering. To him you're a rebellious child who needs disciplining." Daniel took Rebecca's hands. "Please, do it for me. I can't stand to see you hurt."

"You say you love me? Then stand up to him." Rebecca disengaged her hands. "If you don't, he'll always control your life—you'll never be free."

"This isn't about me."

"Yes, it is. He's been angry with me from the moment I arrived, but it began long before that, and only you can stop it."

"It's not that simple. And if you follow this course, it's you who will suffer."

"I admit, I may have deserved some of his barbs. I have done some things wrong. I know I can be bold, even rebellious, but I can't fit into your father's mold, and neither should you. I need your partnership. When we married we were united, and we are to esteem one another above *all* others."

Daniel stared at Rebecca, then took a deep breath and said, "I can't go against him. No one can change him. It would take an act of God."

Rebecca stepped back. "Then so be it. We'll leave it in God's hands." Tears blurred her vision. "What hope is there for us?" With a resigned shake of her head, she turned and walked away.

This was not the conversation she'd intended to have. After supper she'd planned to tell him about the baby. She'd missed

251

two cycles. There was no other explanation but that she was pregnant. Now she didn't feel she could tell him anything.

⯏

The following afternoon Rebecca stood on the veranda. Heavy clouds hung over green fields. The weather had been cool, with occasional rain showers. The fields had been cut, but lush grasses had already shot up. Cattle grazed in a nearby pasture, and a foal kicked up its heels in one of the corrals.

She contemplated how she would tell Daniel about the baby. After last evening's quarrel, it all felt so complicated. They'd not spoken to each other. Resting a hand on her abdomen, she wondered how she could raise a child in this house.

Her eyes continued to roam over the landscape, and she breathed in clean-smelling air. Douloo was beautiful. And when one looked at it from the outside it must appear serene. She knew better—there would be no serenity here as long as Bertram was alive.

Daniel, his father, and a man who lived on the east end of the district emerged from the barn. Mr. Connor had been at the station before. She recognized him by his red hair and heavy beard. His young son, Kieren, bounded ahead of the men. A heavy-muscled bull moved from an indoor stall into the corral. He stopped in the center of the enclosure and with his head lowered, glowered at the men. Mr. Connor was considering buying the impressive animal.

Bertram chatted amiably with his guest. *I wish he could be like that with me*, Rebecca thought, a longing for a father spreading through her. It could happen . . . if she'd completely submit to his authority. *How do I maintain my self-respect and still please him?* Watching the two men, she couldn't help but wonder if she'd done all she could.

252

Kieren ran back toward the barn and picked up a ball, then dropped it to the ground and kicked it. He sprinted after the toy, then picked it up, tossed it again, and chased after it. His face was alight with pleasure as he captured the ball and rolled it across the ground.

Rebecca smiled and glanced down at her abdomen. One day she'd watch her child play. Would it be a boy or a girl? *Daniel would love to have a son.* She imagined him, blond headed and blue eyed, his hand clasped in his father's.

Kieren giggled, once more catching Rebecca's attention. He threw the ball hard, and it rolled under the corral fence. He raced after it. Alarm coursed through Rebecca. She was relieved when the youngster stopped at the fence and peered at his prize. The white-faced bull gazed at the ball; then as the lad straddled the bottom railing and climbed inside the enclosure, the brute turned his gaze on the intruder.

"No!" Rebecca shouted.

Absorbed in conversation, the men didn't hear. Kieren moved toward the ball, which had rolled several yards inside the corral.

The bull dropped his head and blew air from wide nostrils.

"Help him!" Rebecca cried, heading for the porch steps.

Daniel looked at Rebecca.

"There!" She pointed at Kieren.

Almost instantaneously Daniel ran for the corral. In one smooth motion he catapulted over the fence, sprinted to the child, and picked him up. Facing the bull, he hollered and waved at the powerful animal, then took cautious steps backward toward the fence.

Rebecca lifted her skirts and ran. *Lord, protect them.*

The bull kept his head down and pawed the dirt.

Daniel kept moving.

The bull charged.

Daniel turned for the fence and raced toward it. With the boy tucked under one arm, he clambered over. The bull pulled up short, then trotted around the enclosure, occasionally glancing at the intruders.

Daniel looked at the animal and then laughed with relief. "You're getting slow, old man." He carried Kieren to John Connor and handed him over.

The man embraced Kieren, then shook Daniel's hand. "Thank ya. Yer a good man."

"Glad the lad's safe," Daniel said.

Rebecca's heart hammered. "I was so frightened," she said, running up to Daniel. "You could have been killed."

"Yer lucky. That boy was nearly killed. What was in yer mind?" Bertram stormed. "Why would ya leave the animal in the corral? Ya know better." He glanced at Kieren and pointed at him. "That child nearly died because of yer irresponsibility."

Daniel stared at his father, incredulity on his face. Without a word he strode to his hat lying on the ground and picked it up. He dusted it off on his pants, pushed it down on his head, and walked away.

Rebecca wanted to throttle Bertram. How could he shame Daniel that way? He'd risked his life to save Kieren. Couldn't he see the goodness and courage in his son? Before she said something she'd regret, Rebecca swung around and watched Daniel disappear inside the barn. *Lord, why doesn't he resist? Why doesn't he say something?*

Her child would not be raised in this venomous environment. *We must return to Boston,* she decided.

⌘

That evening Rebecca read while she waited for Daniel to come to bed. When he finally climbed in beside her, she put away her book and rolled onto her side, facing him. "You look tired," she said.

"I am for sure."

"I was proud of you today. What you did was very courageous."

"Not according to my father."

Maybe now wasn't the right time to tell Daniel. He seemed in a sour mood. Still, he needed to know. "I have some news that ought to brighten your day." She met Daniel's eyes. "We're going to have a baby."

Daniel's face flushed and his blue eyes widened. "A baby? You're sure?"

She nodded.

He smiled and pulled her into a tight embrace. "A baby!" He sat up. "Well, I'll be; I'm going to be a dad." He rolled off the bed and stood. "What do you think it is? Can you tell?"

"No, of course not. We won't know until it gets here."

"When? When will it arrive?"

"I'm thinking late December or early January. I haven't seen a doctor yet, so I don't know for certain."

Daniel pulled Rebecca out of bed and danced her around the room. When he stopped he was out of breath. He cradled her face between his hands. "I love you."

Rebecca wanted to say she loved him. At this moment she could nearly believe she did. He was so exultant.

A flicker of disappointment touched Daniel's eyes, and then he hugged her. "You'll be a wonderful mother."

"I hope so," she said. *I might as well ask while he's in a jubilant mood.* "I was thinking . . . well, you know how difficult your father can be and how we're always quarreling." She chewed her lip. How could she ask him to leave his home? She looked down at her clasped hands. "I don't want our child to live here . . . with your father. I was hoping we could move . . . maybe back to Boston?"

"Move? I can't move."

"But you know how your father is, how could you . . ."

"I have an obligation—to my dad and to our child. This station is an inheritance, and it will go on only if I stay to work it. One day I'll pass it on to our son." He smiled. "I know my father has been in a bit of a mood lately, but this news will set him to rights." He kissed Rebecca. "He loves and honors God. That's a grand heritage to pass on." He kissed Rebecca again. "Do you think I turned out so badly?"

"No," Rebecca said, but she thought, *You don't see the shadow you live in.*

"Then don't you think my father did something right?"

"Of course he did, but I would venture the gentleness you possess came from your mother."

"He hasn't always been this bad. It's just since I came back from the States."

"Yes. When you brought me. He's angry because of me. How can you expect me to live with that? And to have our child watch as his mother is treated badly by his grandfather?"

"The baby will change everything. I know it. You'll see. Just give my father some time."

Rebecca knew there would be no changing Daniel's mind. She would have to accept that her life would be lived out here on Douloo. But how would she shield her child?

"I'll try, Daniel. Maybe if I give him a grandson, he'll accept me." She managed a small smile. "Would you consider moving into a house of our own close by?"

"I suppose that could be done, but there's no call for it. I don't see how it would change anything. And you'll be needing help from Mum after the baby comes."

Rebecca nodded. "I suppose so." It was no use. They would remain under Bertram's thumb.

"Let's tell them. Now."

"Who, your parents?"

"Right. Come on, then." Before Rebecca could stop him, Daniel rushed into the hall and strode to his parents' room. "I've got news!" he said loudly, standing outside their door.

⟠

Bertram and Willa were overjoyed. And true to Daniel's word, his father did change. He was like a new man—even tempered and congenial. More than once he actually placed an arm about Rebecca as if he were truly proud of her. When he made an announcement at church, he included both Daniel and Rebecca in his blessings.

Bertram talked about the joys of grandchildren and how he intended to be splendid at grandfathering. He spoke of the things he would do with his grandson—teaching him to ride and to rope—and how he'd show him all of Douloo.

Rebecca felt as if she were holding her breath, waiting for Bertram to return to his prior self. She wanted to believe he'd changed but couldn't completely convince herself.

The doctor confirmed that January was the expected time of confinement. Willa and Rebecca set about sewing baby clothes, blankets, and bonnets. Aside from her morning sickness, those were good days, and Rebecca decided she could be happy at Douloo.

⟠

One Saturday morning she felt quite ill. She joined the family for breakfast but knew tea was all she could tolerate. Bertram and Daniel sat at the table in the kitchen, eating hot cereal.

Willa bustled about, working alongside Lily. She glanced at Rebecca. "You look a little peaked, dear. Are you all right?"

257

"Oh, a bit queasy. Thought a cup of tea might help."

"Perhaps a bit of dry toast too. There now, sit down. I'll get it for you." Willa retrieved toast from the oven and poured a cup of tea. She set the cup in front of Rebecca, then placed a plate of toast on the table.

"Thank you, but I can't eat, really. Tea will be fine."

"All right, then."

Bertram studied his daughter-in-law. "Ya should try to eat, for the baby."

"The doctor says it's normal to feel queasy, and the baby will be just fine if I can't manage breakfast."

"And since when are doctors always right?"

"I'm sure the tea will help. I'll have something later."

"Ya need to eat."

"Bertram," Willa said. "She's not up to it."

"Ya can do what ya set yer mind to." His tone had turned harsh.

Rebecca felt a stab of apprehension. Was this the moment she'd feared?

"Ya'll feel better if ya have a bite." He stood and grabbed a piece of toast off the plate, buttered it, and held it out to Rebecca. "Here. Now eat it."

Rebecca took the toast, knowing he wouldn't give in until she at least took a bite. She nibbled a corner while Bertram returned to his seat. Just the taste of it set her stomach to churning. She broke out in a cold sweat and set the toast down.

Bertram watched her while he finished his breakfast. "I thought ya were going to eat."

"I just can't, sir. I've tried. I'll have something later. I promise."

"Ya'll have something now. I won't have ya starvin' my grandson. I've watched ya, day after day skipping breakfast. I don't care what the doctor said, it'll do him harm. Ya'd

258

think there would be enough love in ya to put up with a little stomach upset. Trust in the good Lord to help ya."

"Bertram—" Willa started.

"Enough!" He pushed away from the table. "I won't have my grandchild injured because his mother's character is too weak to do what's best."

"I am doing my best."

"Father," Daniel said. "Let her be."

Rebecca felt sick in her soul. Here was the man she'd known. He'd been hiding. He hadn't truly gone. Rebecca stood, resting her hands on the table. "Daniel, just as I said, he'll never change." The room swirled and Rebecca thought she might faint. "I won't have my child raised in a house without mercy." The room spun, but Rebecca managed to find her husband's face. "I'm returning to Boston, with you or without you."

Willa dropped into a chair. Daniel stared at her, clearly stunned by the ultimatum.

Bertram walked around the table until he stood directly in front of Rebecca. He towered over her. "You won't go," he said evenly.

"I will," Rebecca fired back, meeting his harsh gaze.

"Ya best remember who yer dealing with, young lady. I control what happens in this district, and if I say ya'll stay, ya'll stay. After the baby's born, ya may leave with my blessing. But the child will remain."

Rebecca couldn't believe what she was hearing.

"And if ya think I can't do it, then ya haven't been paying attention these last months. People in this district do as I say." He raised an eyebrow. "And that includes the law."

Like a wildfire out of control, fear spread through Rebecca. She knew he spoke the truth.

"You can't do that," Daniel said. "I can't believe that even you would be so cruel." Daniel turned to Rebecca. "She'll stay. We'll work it out, eh?"

Rebecca shook her head. There was nothing more to be said. Too angry even for tears, she walked out of the room.

They won't hold me captive. I'll escape, she thought, already formulating a plan.

21

Rebecca sat straight backed in the pew. Something was wrong. When she'd arrived at church that morning, she'd been greeted by whispers and disdainful looks, even pointing fingers. She glanced at Cambria, who sat across the aisle. Even she had avoided her.

This is not my imagination. Something is terribly wrong. She looked to see if Daniel was anywhere about. He'd gone off with his father and hadn't returned. She tried to focus on the minister's words.

"Let the wicked forsake his way, and the unrighteous man his thoughts: and let him return unto the LORD." Reverend Cobb stopped and looked directly at Rebecca before continuing. Several parishioners turned and looked at her.

Rebecca wanted to disappear. What had she done that had them all in a dither? Throughout the rest of the sermon, there were several instances where she felt the reverend's condemnation. *What have I done?*

At the closing song Rebecca hoped for a quick exit. The intensity of the minister's words and the atmosphere in the sanctuary frightened her. She wanted out. As the song came to an end, she moved quickly to the center aisle but was un-

261

able to escape before people crowded around her, forcing her to become part of the flow.

Reverend Cobb stood at the door. He smiled and took her hand, but judgment lay behind his eyes. "You may come and talk to me, Rebecca. That's why I'm here. Remember, God asks that we let go of our sin and seek his forgiveness. He's faithful and just to forgive us our sins."

"Yes, thank you, Reverend," Rebecca said, feeling heat in her cheeks.

Why was he talking to her about sin and forgiveness? Taking back her hand, she hurried down the steps. Meghan stood at the foot of the stairway and offered Rebecca a look of triumph as she passed. *What does she have to do with this?* Trying to avoid eye contact with other parishioners, Rebecca hurried toward the surrey.

Willa approached her. "Rebecca, dear, would you like to join us for lunch?"

"I'm not hungry." Remembering the incident over not eating breakfast, she added, "I'll have a little bit, thank you. And something to drink would be nice."

"Splendid," Willa said and sat on a blanket Woodman had spread out. She opened a basket and removed a sandwich. "These look wonderful. I'll have to thank Lily when we get home."

Hesitantly Rebecca sat across from Willa and accepted half a roast beef sandwich. Gingerly she took a bite.

"I wonder where Daniel is. Do you know?" Rebecca asked.

"I believe he and Bertram had business to discuss with one of the merchants in town." Willa offered Rebecca a cup of water.

"Thank you." Rebecca took a drink, washing down a bite of sandwich. Glancing about, she noticed the other women were keeping their distance. Usually several sat with Willa. She took another bite, but it felt heavy as it hit her stomach.

"This is nice," Willa said. "It's just you and me today."

"Yes. I suppose. But don't you think it peculiar?"

"Now that you mention it, I suppose so." She glanced at Cambria, who sat in the back of her family's wagon, legs hanging off the back. "You usually eat with Cambria."

"She's not very friendly today."

"Hmm."

Cambria picked at a piece of bread and glanced at Rebecca.

"Very out of character for her," Willa said.

Elvina ambled toward Rebecca and Willa. As the head of the church guild, she always made certain to visit with all the ladies. Rebecca didn't care for Elvina, seeing her as critical, and it was well known she was a gossip. Elvina always managed to make Rebecca feel uncomfortable.

"G'day, Willa."

"Good day. You look well, Elvina. How is your family?"

"We're all fine, thank ya." Elvina settled cool eyes on Rebecca. "And yer well?"

"Yes. Very." Rebecca felt as if a snake were looking at her and was ready to strike.

"Well, after discussing, uh, yer condition with the women in the guild, we've decided it will be too taxing for ya to remain part of the group. For yer own health we're advising ya to step down as a member of the guild. Ya can wait outside while we have our meetings."

"I'm fine, really," Rebecca said, knowing instinctively there was another reason for her dismissal.

Willa's usual calm expression had been replaced by one of surprise. "I wasn't told about this."

"It was decided just this morning."

263

"Rebecca's in fine health. I see no reason to exclude her from the meetings."

"I'm thankful for her health, but the decision has been made." Elvina walked away.

"Well, I'll not go, then," Willa huffed. "Have you been feeling poorly and not told me?"

"No. I've been fine, except for queasiness in the morning." Rebecca watched as Elvina joined a group of women. They looked as if they were discussing something of importance. An occasional glance was cast her way. "Willa, something's wrong. I'm certain people are angry with me. But I can't think of what I've done to cause their ire."

"That's nonsense. Whatever could they be angry about?" Willa stood and smoothed her skirt. "Indeed. I'll just have a talk with them." She glanced at Rebecca. "We'll have this straightened out in no time." Looking very much like a tranquil saint, Willa strolled toward the group of women.

As if they had something of great consequence to discuss with her, the ladies gathered around Willa. Some appeared regretful, others eager.

Rebecca glanced at Cambria. She'd never avoided Rebecca. "She knows what this is all about," Rebecca said and pushed to her feet.

☙

"G'day," Cambria said, offering a weak smile.

"It doesn't feel like a good day." Rebecca rested a hand on the side of the wagon. "It's not lovely at all. There's something wrong. Everyone is acting strangely toward me . . . even you. What have I done?"

"I'm not upset with ya."

"And ya've done nothin' wrong," Elle Taylor said, joining

the two. She threw an arm over Rebecca's shoulders and gave her a hearty squeeze. "I'd say those old hens are bored and looking for trouble is all."

"What does it have to do with me? Everyone seems angry with me, and they've been avoiding me."

Elle shook her head. "There's no need ta speak of it. It's only gossip."

"That's roight, eh?" Cambria said. "I know ya wouldn't do such a thing."

"Do what? What is it I'm supposed to have done?"

Cambria and Elle looked at each other. With a sigh Elle said, "Well, the truth of it is, there's talk . . . about ya and that Jim Keller fella."

"What kind of talk?" Rebecca asked, understanding dawning.

"Wal, that the two of ya . . ." Elle set her jaw and looked directly at Rebecca. "That the two of ya are keeping company."

"That's preposterous!" Rebecca glanced at the clusters of people chatting over their afternoon meals. "They believe that Jim and I . . . ?"

"Yais. Sorry ta say they do. They're always ready ta believe the worst about a person." Elle's blue eyes were full of fire as if ready for a fight.

"That's not true, Aunt Elle. Not everyone believes it. It's Elvina and Meghan."

"Yais, well the others seem to be going along, I'd say." Elle offered Rebecca a comforting smile. "And that's not all of it."

"Yais . . . There's gossip about who the father of yer baby is."

Stunned, Rebecca looked at those standing about. "How could anyone . . . How could they . . . It's not true, none of it."

"We know that," Elle said.

What did Daniel think? Had he heard the gossip? She glanced around. He wasn't anywhere. He'd missed church. "Have you seen Daniel?"

"I did," Cambria said. "He was heading into town earlier. I'm afraid he looked angry."

Had he believed the lies? "He should have come to me and asked me. I would have told him the truth."

"People believe what they want."

"Aunt Elle, ya can't be so pessimistic. Most folks want ta be fair. They're willin' ta hear from the family."

Rebecca turned to Cambria. "What about you? What do you believe?"

"How can ya ask me such a thing? I know ya too well ta believe such folderol. Ya'd never do such a thing."

"Thank you," Rebecca said, but she felt only a measure of relief.

Willa's face looked stormy as she walked away from the ladies. She marched toward Rebecca.

"Oh no. She believes them," Rebecca said.

"We're leaving," Willa snapped. "I'll have nothing to do with people who are . . . no more than . . . than . . . gossips." She rested a hand on Rebecca's arm and offered a reassuring smile.

"Thank the good Lord," Rebecca said. "For a moment I thought you might believe them."

"Of course I don't. I know you would never be unfaithful to Daniel." She glanced toward town. "I only wish my son had as much sense."

"He believes it?" Rebecca felt as if the ground had dropped out from beneath her. She grabbed hold of the wagon wheel. "How can he?"

"I don't know, dear. Sometimes men have no more sense than a wild boar." She took Rebecca's arm. "Woodman will take us home." She nodded at Cambria and Elle. "Good day to you, ladies."

Once settled in the surrey, Rebecca could feel the sting of tears. She blinked hard and kept her eyes straight ahead. As they moved away from the church, people stared, their expressions laden with condemnation. A handful offered encouraging nods or smiles. At least some didn't believe the lies.

Daniel and his father joined the family. His jaw squared and back straight, Daniel rode ahead of the surrey, unwilling to even look at Rebecca.

"Willa, how can I make him listen to me?"

"You can't, not right away. Give him time. His good sense will return."

Rebecca settled back. Anger was beginning to override her shock and her hurt. *How can he believe I would be disloyal? I'm an honorable woman—he knows that.*

When they arrived at Douloo, Daniel rode ahead, left his horse in the corral, marched toward the house, and disappeared through the front door.

"Don't worry 'bout 'im," Woodman said. "He'll find 'is way soon enough. Just needs time, eh?"

"Time to what?" Rebecca asked, her anger boiling. "Either he believes me or he doesn't." She stepped out of the carriage and followed Daniel indoors and up the stairs to their room.

Standing in the bedroom doorway, she watched Daniel pack his clothes into a traveling case. He ignored her.

Finally she asked, "What do you think you're doing?"

"I'm moving to another room. I'll not share a bed with a . . . with a whore." His eyes bore into hers.

"How dare you speak to me in such a way! You're my husband!"

Daniel stopped packing and stared at Rebecca. "Maybe you should have remembered that sooner."

"You know I'd never do such a thing. I've never been interested in Jim . . . Mr. Keller."

"I've tried to deny it. But I've seen the two of you. He hangs around you like a moth about a lantern. You share a heritage. And we both know you've never belonged 'ere. You've never really belonged to me."

"Up until this moment I've valued your character and have been proud to call you husband. And I've believed that as your wife my place was here."

Daniel shook his head. "There's nothing I can do to change what's happened." He shoved a pair of socks into the bag, then turned anguished eyes on Rebecca. "I can't even be certain the child you're carrying is mine."

She rested a hand on her abdomen. "Of course it's yours. I've never been unfaithful. Never."

"I want to believe you. But I've seen too much."

"Talk to Jim. He'll tell you."

"You really think I'd trust the likes of him?" He stuffed more socks into the bag. "Anyway, he's gone. My father fired him."

Rebecca felt lightheaded and gripped the door frame. What could she say that would make him hear?

"Maybe you'd like to go with him." Daniel pushed past her.

Gazing through a pool of tears, Rebecca stared at her husband's back as he stormed down the hallway and disappeared down the staircase.

She stumbled into the bedroom and sat on the bed. Heavy sobs shook her body. This couldn't be happening.

Spent, Rebecca lay on her side, her knees bent and tucked in close to her abdomen. If only she could sleep. A floorboard creaked, and she pushed herself up on one arm. Bertram stood just inside the door.

For a long while he stared at her. "I'd like to have ya thrown out, but . . . we can't always have what we want. Ya've broken my son's heart . . . mine too. But worse, ya've broken God's heart. His condemnation will come upon ya."

Sitting up straight and squaring her shoulders, Rebecca said, "I don't expect you to believe me, but I'm innocent. It's all lies—utterly and completely untrue." She met his hostile gaze. "I'll be returning to Boston on the first ship. Soon you won't have to worry about me." The words sounded empty; Rebecca felt empty.

"That's not possible. The child yer carrying may be my grandchild. We won't know until after it's born. Ya'll stay until we do know. I can tell a Thornton when I see one."

Rebecca couldn't think of anything else to say. She was powerless.

Bertram turned and walked out.

22

Suppressing a shiver, Rebecca stood at the sitting room window and stared out at a soggy world. The air felt chill and damp. She was dismal, alone. Callie and Willa seemed to be the only two in all of Queensland who hadn't charged her with the crime of infidelity. Even Cambria hadn't visited.

She missed Daniel. He rarely made it in before dark, filling his days and evenings with work. When he managed to make an evening meal, he said only what was necessary, then retired to his room or to the library.

In spite of her justifiable anger, she couldn't help but notice the dark smudges beneath Daniel's eyes and the considerable amount of weight he'd lost. She worried about him. The handsome, fun-loving man she'd met in Boston had departed. She longed to see his mischievous smile, the wink of an eye. Instead, he remained aloof, speaking to Rebecca only when necessary.

"Mrs. Thornton was hopin' ya could join 'er," Callie said, startling Rebecca.

Rebecca turned and looked at Callie. She didn't feel like visiting, but Willa might help shake off the doldrums. "I guess I could use a bit of company," she said, offering a smile.

She took a sweater from the coat rack, draped it over

her shoulders, and stepped outside. The air was heavy with moisture. Plants and flowers drooped beneath the weight of rain. Droplets like jewels rested on broad-leaved plants, and miniature ponds dotted a muddy yard.

"Rebecca dear," Willa said. "Come, have a cuppa with me. I've missed our chats."

Rebecca moved to a chair across from Willa and sat. "I haven't felt much like talking. I apologize."

"No need. I understand."

A small table with a teakettle and matching saucers and cups sat between the two women. "Tea?" Willa asked.

"Yes. Maybe something hot will drive away the chill."

Willa filled a cup and handed it to Rebecca. "I dare say, you look tired. Are you all right?"

"I'm fine," Rebecca said. Nothing could be accomplished by sharing her misery.

"And the baby?"

Rebecca glanced at her slightly rounded stomach. "Its growing, but I haven't felt any movement yet." *Daniel and I ought to be sharing the joy of this child*, she thought, sipping her tea and watching the rain. "I'm beginning to wonder if the rain will ever cease."

"It will, soon. The men are planning to move a mob of cattle south to the railroad station as soon as the sun reappears. The grasses will be plentiful along the way. The animals should be in good condition when they arrive. We've done right well this year. The calves are strong and healthy, and so is the herd."

Only half listening, Rebecca nodded. How could she be concerned about cattle when her life was in shreds? The entire district thought her an adulteress, including her husband. Each passing day her desire for home grew stronger. Aunt Mildred would believe her. In Boston she would be safe and loved.

"Rebecca, you can't let your mood continue to be so sullen. It's not good for you or the child."

Rebecca's anger churned. "If it's not a Thornton as people claim, why would anyone care?" Setting her cup down hard on the table, she stood and walked to the railing. She glanced at Willa. "If your husband believes me an adulteress, why won't he allow me to leave?"

"He explained that." Willa's eyes radiated tenderness. "Not everyone believes the rumors."

Willa's kindness deflated Rebecca's anger. "I'm sorry. I didn't mean to be rude. You have been kind." She leaned a hip against the balustrade. "But . . . I can't stay. I must return to Boston soon. You understand, don't you?"

"Yes, I suppose I do."

"Couldn't you speak to your husband?"

"I already have. He won't budge. I'm sorry. I know this is dreadful for you, but you must trust God to work it out. He knows the beginning and the end of all things." She offered a small smile. "I'd miss you terribly if you were to go, and I'm so looking forward to meeting my grandchild."

Rebecca returned to her chair. "Have you spoken to Daniel about any of this?"

"He doesn't want to talk about it."

"Why won't he believe me?"

"I can't be certain." She raised an eyebrow slightly. "Perhaps it has to do with your marrying him out of need. I'm quite certain he loves you."

"Yes. He told me so. But it seems he should know me well enough to realize I'd never betray him."

"Sometimes men are reasonable and strong and brave. I'm grateful for that, but . . . there are times when they allow uncertainty to rule their minds. Daniel's always had difficulty with confidence. I fear his father had much to do with it. He was hard on the boys."

Her eyes took on a look of reminiscence. "Elton wasn't like Daniel. Right off he was stubborn. As he grew older he became defiant. That's what got him into trouble." Her eyes shimmered.

Rebecca held her breath. Willa had never spoken about her eldest son.

"He had too much brass for his father's liking. The two never got on well. Of course, when he was a boy it was different. They'd tussle and play." She smiled at the memory. "I can still hear Elton's giggles." She was silent for a long moment. "Right around the time he turned thirteen, things began to change. He stood up to his father and refused to do as he was told." She shook her head. "The skirmishes began and continued until the day Elton left." Her voice fell off, and sorrow lay in the lines of her face.

"What about you, Willa? Do you ever stand up to your husband?"

"My, yes. We've had our rows now and again. But I know my place, and I never push too hard. Over the years I've watched and prayed while Bertram carried his family's and community's burdens." Her eyes settled on Rebecca's. "He has overstepped the bounds, but he doesn't understand that."

"Have you told him?"

"Indeed, but he doesn't see, and I can't make him. He must be willing to open his eyes." She set her cup on its saucer. "One day he'll know the truth. I pray it won't come at too great a price."

A rider approached. It was Meghan. Rebecca's annoyance immediately flared. Ever since Daniel and Rebecca's falling out, the brazen interloper had stepped up her visits to the Thornton home. This time she dismounted, tied her horse to the corral fence, and strode into the barn.

"What is it she needs today?" Rebecca asked, her voice dripping with contempt.

Willa didn't answer.

Rebecca eyed her mother-in-law. Something was wrong. "What is she doing here?"

"She's helping the men prepare for the drive."

"And?"

"She's going with them."

"I thought it was a man's job."

"It is. But Meghan's not like other women. She's joined them every year since her twelfth birthday." Sympathetic eyes rested on Rebecca. "You have no need to worry."

⚶

The rain stopped and the temperatures warmed. The drovers set out. Her arms folded over her chest, Rebecca stood at her bedroom window and watched while Meghan and Daniel rode away. Her heart ached. Was it merely jealousy or something more?

He didn't even bother to say good-bye, she thought. Resting a hand on her abdomen, she considered what should have been, and the hurt grew. Pressing the palm of her right hand against her stomach, she opened her fingers wide. "Little one, I'm so sorry. I wanted better for you. I never meant for this to happen."

Closing her eyes, she sought God, but he felt far away. "Lord, I ask for your mercy. You are able to do all things. I beg you to soften Bertram's and Daniel's hearts—help them to see the truth. Show them that this child belongs to Daniel and me." She opened her eyes and watched the dust rising from the riders. "And help me to love my husband."

⚶

Although Rebecca did her best to fill the days with activities, they seemed long and meaningless. She worked in the garden when the weather allowed, helped Lily in the kitchen, and visited Callie. They chatted while feeding the chickens and collecting eggs. Rebecca even helped make up beds. And of course there was always needlework. One afternoon she rested on the settee in the sitting room, embroidering a spray of roses on a handkerchief. The ticking of the clock seemed loud, and Willa rocked and stitched in rhythm to each stroke of the pendulum.

When the chair's creaking stopped, Rebecca looked up from her work. Willa was asleep, a nearly completed baby's blanket in her lap. Rebecca reached for a coverlet draped over the settee and gently covered Willa. *You are a treasure*, she thought. *If only the rest of the world was like you.*

She walked out to the veranda. Sunshine brightened the yard and paddocks. How could the world look washed and clean when life was so foul? *Maybe a walk will help*, Rebecca thought, stepping off the porch and strolling toward the corral. Rena stood munching hay. *A ride would settle me*, she thought. But there would be no riding. She knew better than to go alone. Plus, the doctor had stated she was not to sit a horse until after the baby was born.

The mare trotted to her mistress and nuzzled her arm. Rebecca ran her hand down the front of the animal's face, then caressed her soft nose. "I know, girl. I wish we could ride. I'll give you a good brushing though. That's nearly as good." She walked into the barn to get a currycomb and a brush.

After the brightness of the yard, the inside of the building seemed especially dark. Rebecca knew her way and didn't hesitate. She walked into the tack room and took the comb and brush off a shelf. When she turned to leave, her eyes fell upon a black man who worked at the station. He appeared to be sleeping on the floor. Then she saw it—a spear. It penetrated his stomach.

Rebecca suppressed a scream and hurried for the door, where she stopped and turned to study the man. He wasn't moving. Was he dead? She stepped closer, then reached out and touched him. His skin was cool and unyielding. The spear protruded from his back. Rebecca dropped the comb and brush and ran for the house.

"What is it?" Willa met her at the bottom of the front steps. "You're white as a ghost."

"There's a man—he's dead." Rebecca pointed toward the barn.

"Oh my Lord." Willa glanced about. "Woodman. Where is he?"

"He's gone into town," Callie said from the porch.

"All right, then," Willa said with resolve and hurried toward the barn. Callie and Rebecca followed.

Willa gingerly stepped into the tack room, then knelt and examined the man. "Gandji," she whispered. "Someone's murdered him!" She stood and looked at Callie. "Why would anyone do such a thing?"

Callie's eyes seemed to hold a secret, but she said nothing.

"Do you know what happened?" Willa asked.

"No, mum." She turned and started to walk way. "I'll 'ave someone fetch Woodman."

ᗡ

Rebecca couldn't rid herself of the image—Gandji, blood seeping from the wound, the spear. Later that day she sought out Callie, certain the servant knew what had happened. She found her working in an upstairs bedroom. Standing in the doorway, Rebecca watched quietly. Callie glanced at her but continued her dusting without comment. Finally Rebecca said, "You know what happened, don't you."

"Why ya say that?" Callie picked up a photo and dusted it.

"It's in your eyes. Tell me. I need to know."

"There's nothin' ta tell ya." She set the photograph back on the bureau. "He's just a dead fella."

"Callie . . ."

Callie studied Rebecca as if taking stock of her. Finally she walked to the doorway and glanced up and down the hall. She whispered, "If I tell, ya will say nothin'?"

"I promise. Not a word."

Callie closed the door. Speaking in hushed tones, she said, "The Boolyah man says he must die."

"But why?"

"A spirit tells him of an evil done by Gandji's ancestor. Gandji must pay."

"I don't understand."

"If an ancestor breaks a taboo, there is a penalty. The man chosen to kill Gandji cannot refuse."

"Do the Thorntons know about this?"

"Yais. Thorntons know. It happens before. No one can stop it. It's our way." Callie walked to the window and gazed outside. "Sometimes I'm afraid. What if my ancestor did evil?"

"Oh, Callie. How awful." Rebecca paced the room. "The whole idea is barbaric. Why does everything here have to be so primitive? I can't grasp how anyone can tolerate such things." She stopped pacing and cast a fierce look at Callie. "Well, I won't. I won't stay in a place like this. And my child won't be raised here."

Rebecca didn't know just how she would escape, but she knew it must happen before the men returned.

A bawling white-faced black calf wandered from the herd. Daniel secured a handkerchief over his nose. There'd been little rain this far south, and the dust was bad. Leaning forward and pressing his feet into the stirrups, he lifted himself a few inches off the saddle. "Back ya go," he said, swinging a rope over the calf's head and whistling. The calf tried to dart away. "'Ere, none of that, now." Daniel's horse quickly maneuvered around the calf and directed it back. "Stay with the mob, eh?"

The calf and its mother managed to find each other, and Daniel settled back to follow the herd. His body ached from long hours in the saddle, and his eyes stung from the grit in the air. He'd hoped working on the drive would be a distraction from his heartache, but the discomforts only seemed to magnify his painful thoughts of Rebecca. He missed her, the smell of her, the feel of her. How long had it been since he'd heard her laugh?

Then the memory of what she'd done pierced him. How could he forgive her? He could never trust her again. Briefly the bitter fog lifted. *What if she's telling the truth and has done nothing?* When he remembered the way Jim had looked at her, the moment of clarity evaporated. *She liked him fine too.*

For weeks Daniel had avoided Rebecca. He couldn't bear to look at her. Her unhappiness was stark, and it tortured him. He knew she needed his forgiveness. But each time he saw her rounded belly, he thought about who the father might be and his empathy dissolved.

What if the child is mine? What will I do then, eh? And what if I never know?

Daniel remembered how it had been in the beginning. The day she'd marched into her father's office, he'd been stunned by the beautiful, intelligent American. At first, infatuation had driven him to seek her out, but over the weeks love had grown. He'd prayed she would return that love. Sadly, it seemed the more passionate his love became, the more she withdrew.

And then there was Jim.

Makes sense. They're both Americans. She never really took to Australia . . . or me.

Pushing aside the gossip and his own jealousy, he thought of Rebecca the woman. She was strongly moral and principled. Could she have done what she was accused of? There was a time when he'd never have believed it, but his father wasn't one to toss about false accusations. He might be a hard man, but Bertram wouldn't lie about such a thing.

Meghan galloped up to Daniel. "G'day. How ya faring, eh?"

"Good. It's a fine day," Daniel said, keeping his eyes on the cattle and hoping she'd move on. Every day since leaving home, she'd sought him out, making attempts at conversation, occasionally finding subtle ways to remind him that he could no longer trust his wife. He knew she wanted more than a friendship with him. Her desire had frayed the camaraderie they'd shared for so many years. She'd become something of a pest. He wanted to be alone.

She rode alongside him. "Thankful for good weather. Hope it holds."

"Right."

"It's kind of like the old days, eh?" she smiled coyly. "You and me . . ."

Daniel kicked his horse and moved ahead. "It would be good if ya could ride along 'ere while I go up and speak to my dad," he called over his shoulder. "Watch that one there." He pointed at the black calf. "He's in the habit of wandering off." He tipped his hat and rode away, leaving Meghan looking out of sorts.

🌀

Meghan wasn't about to be put off. That night at the campfire, she sat beside Daniel. Rather than asking for help, she leaned across Daniel to reach for a billy sitting among the hot ashes. She pressed her leg against his. After pouring tea into a tin cup, she repeated the familiarity when returning the pot to its place among the embers.

"Cattle are holding up well. We covered a good number of miles, eh?" she said.

"Yah. Won't be long 'til we'll be heading home." Normally Daniel looked forward to home; now all it meant was facing Rebecca and her betrayal.

"Ya have to stop feeling so sad 'bout yer wife. If it was me, I'd divorce her. And the sooner the better. Ya have the right." Meghan poked a stick in the fire. "Best thing for 'er would be to go home to Boston where she belongs, eh?"

Meghan's unpleasantness was too much for Daniel. "What happens between me and my wife is none of your concern."

The fire reflected in Meghan's brown eyes. She looked stunned. "Why, I . . ."

"I've had enough." Daniel stood. "I won't have you speaking badly of my wife."

He walked away from camp, hoping for solace in the darkness.

As he moved through the brush, something scuttled across the ground in front of him. He ignored whatever it was and kept walking. Feeling sick inside, he wondered if there was a way to fill the gaping hole he felt. For the first time he could see himself through Rebecca's eyes. He'd allowed Meghan's flirtations and had even flirted back. Maybe what had happened was his fault. Had he driven Rebecca to Jim?

Finally he stopped and sat on a fallen tree. The emptiness burned in his gut. What was to be done about him and Rebecca now? He leaned his elbows on his thighs and rested his face in his hands. *I should never have brought 'er 'ere. She told me straight out that she didn't love me. I was a fool to believe she'd be satisfied with Douloo and with me.*

23

Rebecca made plans to escape. The first step was to learn
how to harness the horses to the surrey and how to drive the
team. She fabricated reasons for trips into town and made
sure to watch while Woodman harnessed the horses. She
even convinced him to teach her to drive.

It would have been great fun had she another reason
for learning. In spite of all that had happened, the idea of
sneaking away weighted her with guilt. Bertram had left her
with no recourse.

Tormented over the idea of leaving Daniel, she nearly
decided to stay. However, each time she contemplated the
circumstances, she came to the same conclusion—there was
no place for her at Douloo and no hope for her and Daniel.
Even if he changed his mind and believed her innocent, how
was it possible for her to love a man who had so little faith
in her?

On one of her excursions to town, she stopped by Elle's
shop, hoping to meet up with Cambria. She'd not seen her
friend since the rumors spread through the church. Since
that day Rebecca refused to attend. The accusing stares and
whispers were more than she could endure.

A bell hanging from the door jingled as Rebecca stepped

into the shop. "I'll be roight with ya," Elle called from a back room. When she stepped through a door leading from the back of the building, her eyes lit up. "How grand ta see ya." She hurried to Rebecca and hugged her. "It's been too long."

"I've missed you."

Holding Rebecca away from her, Elle turned serious. "How ya been?"

"I'm managing. But I've missed seeing you and Cambria."

"Ah, Cambria. She's deeply grieved over all of this. Ya need ta know she 'asn't turned 'er back on ya. It's 'er father, me fool brother . . . he won't let 'er see ya. If I'd known ya were coming in today, I could 'ave told 'er. I'm sure she could 'ave found a way ta make a visit."

Heartened, Rebecca nodded. "Tell her hello for me . . . and that I miss her dreadfully." She wanted to say a proper fare-well, but she couldn't trust her secret with anyone. "I better be on my way. I hope we'll see each other again someday."

"Wal, of course ya will. This ugliness will blow over, and things will right themselves." She studied Rebecca closely. "Or is there something else brewing?"

"No. Nothing." Rebecca clasped the woman's hand. "Thank you for your kindness." She blinked back tears.

Elle scooped her into a hug. "Ya just keep rememberin' that ya know the truth, and so does the one who really counts. Mind ya don't forget that."

"I'll remember."

Rebecca left and walked across the street to the bank. She needed money. However, women couldn't make withdrawals without their husbands' consent. She hoped that since Daniel was out of town, Mr. Oxley would make an exception.

She stepped inside the small establishment. Dark wood floors matched dark cabinets and counters. Mr. Oxley, who always wore a suit and bow tie, stood at one of two teller windows. Ignoring her, he counted bills into neat little stacks. Hoping to get his attention, Rebecca cleared her throat. He continued to count. Finally she said, "Mr. Oxley, I would like to make a withdrawal."

He stopped and looked at her through insolent eyes.

"Presently my husband is out of town, but I need to make a withdrawal."

"You know our policy—only clients are allowed to withdraw money. You are not on your husband's account."

Rebecca could feel herself growing angry. The bank's policy was ridiculous. "I understand, but Daniel is on a cattle drive. He can't sign for the withdrawal."

"Well, then there's nothing I can do about it. You'll have to wait until he returns, eh?" He compressed his lips and went back to counting money.

"I can't wait. I need the money now. And I know Daniel wouldn't mind."

"Look here, young lady, I told you what our policy is, and if you don't like it you can take it up with your husband when he gets home. I'm sure Mr. Thornton didn't leave the house without providing for his family. I recommend you speak to Willa Thornton." He picked up a stack of currency and placed it in a drawer.

Rebecca knew it was no use and walked out. *There must be money in the house somewhere*, she thought, but the idea of taking it made her uneasy. She'd never stolen anything in her life. *It isn't exactly stealing—more like borrowing, really. And besides, what choice do I have?*

$\mathcal{D}$

It was midafternoon and the house was quiet when Rebecca returned. Probably everyone was napping. Rebecca walked quietly toward the library and stopped at the door.

Glancing about to make certain no one saw her enter, she turned the knob and stepped inside.

Every nerve on end, she closed the door softly and moved to her husband's desk. The room seemed hushed.

She quickly opened the top drawer and scanned the contents—pen and ink, a smattering of papers and envelopes, and a letter opener. Reaching toward the back, her fingers closed on a bulging envelope. She held it up to the window light. There didn't seem to be any money inside. She rifled through the other drawers. Nothing.

Standing with hands on hips, she scanned the room. *Where would they keep household money?* Her eyes rested on Bertram's mahogany desk. She hadn't wanted to invade his property.

"He must have left money for Willa," she said, moving to the desk. She rested her hands on the dark wooden surface, blew out a breath, then willed herself to explore. As she pulled open a drawer, she imagined Bertram stepping into the room and discovering her intrusion. The hair came up on her arms. *You're being silly. He's nowhere about. I'll be on my way before he discovers I've borrowed the money.* She'd return what she'd borrowed even if it meant paying on the loan the rest of her life.

She searched through a collection of pens and business papers and discovered a small key. She picked it up and wondered what it might belong to. A cash box perhaps? She gazed about the room. Where could he have hidden it? She saw nothing that even faintly resembled a money box. She pulled open another drawer—more papers, but beneath them was a leather pocketbook. She searched through it—nothing.

"There must be funds somewhere," she muttered.

The library door opened and Callie stepped in. Rebecca quickly pushed the desk drawer closed and straightened. "Why, Callie, I thought you'd already cleaned this room."

"Nearly. I just need ta do a little dusting." Callie studied

Rebecca, a question on her face. "What might ya be doin' in 'ere, mum?"

"Oh, I was just looking for . . . a letter. I'm sure I left it here somewhere." She feigned a search.

"In 'ere, mum?"

Rebecca knew her charade was easy to see through. She dropped into Bertram's chair and rested her hands on the large armrests. *Maybe Callie can help.* She looked at the aborigine. Could she trust her? Deciding she had no other choice, Rebecca took a calming breath.

"In truth, Callie, I'm not looking for a letter." She glanced at the drawer she'd just searched. "I need money."

"Why, mum? Ya 'ave everything ya need."

"I'm leaving Douloo and returning to Boston."

Callie's eyes widened. "And Mr. Thornton's all right with that?"

"He doesn't know." Rebecca stood and moved around the desk. "Callie, I need your help. You work all over this house. You must know where Mr. Thornton keeps . . . things."

Callie didn't respond.

"I need money for passage. As soon as I arrive in Boston, I'll return what I've borrowed."

"Can ya go ta the bank?"

"I tried that. They wouldn't give me any money . . . not without Daniel's signature." Rebecca clasped Callie's hands. "Please. Help me."

"Why can't ya stay? There's the bybie . . ."

"That's why I *must* go. I can't have Mr. Thornton dealing with my child the way he's dealt with his own. And I don't think this wild place is a fit home for a child. It's much too uncivilized."

"I can't say 'bout Mr. Thornton, but what happened to Gandji . . . Wal, ya don't need ta fear such things. Ya won't never be touched."

285

"It's more than that . . . it's everything. I simply can't stay. I won't."

"Yer brave ta go on yer own, but . . . I can't help ya. If Mr. Thornton found out . . . Wal, I'm 'fraid what he'd do." Callie glanced at the floor. "I'm roight sorry." She walked to the door, then stopped and looked at Rebecca. "I'm proud ta 'ave known ya. Yer a fine person."

I'm not fine. I'm a thief and a coward, Rebecca thought, watching Callie retreat and realizing how much she'd miss her aborigine friend. *I've no time to think about such things now.*

Hoping Daniel might have left money in his bedroom, she went there next. She sneaked into the room, hurried to his bureau, and opened the top drawer. She rummaged through socks; then her hand closed over a bundle. Pulling it from the back of the drawer, she realized she held a leather pouch. She loosened the drawstring and looked inside. A wad of paper currency had been stuffed inside, and coins lay at the bottom. Taking only what she thought she'd need, she shoved the money into her dress pocket and returned to her room. *I'll send him a letter from the ship,* she decided. She could post it from San Francisco.

"Tomorrow. I'll go tomorrow," she said aloud to bolster her courage. But the idea of leaving didn't feel the way she'd expected. Rather than anticipating liberty, she was frightened and uncertain. Sorrow pressed down on her. Most likely, she'd never see Daniel again.

※

The following morning the taste of dust and a sighing wind woke her. Curtains fluttered, and outside grit was carried inside.

Rebecca scrambled out of bed and ran to close the windows. Dust sifted in along the bottom lip and around the edges of the window. Rebecca stuffed towels around the frames, then turned to survey a cloud of dust hovering in the room. There was nothing more to be done here. She hurried downstairs.

Willa, Callie, and Lily busily moved from window to window, door to door, sealing off cracks, anyplace dust and dirt might find its way indoors.

Callie hurried to Rebecca, leaned close, and whispered, "It's a bad one, mum. Ya'll be stayin' home for a while."

Disappointment swept over Rebecca. She must leave before the men returned. "How long do these storms usually last?"

"Never know. Day, maybe more."

Carrying a damp towel, Willa stepped in from the kitchen. "There's only one thing I detest about living here, and this is it." She pressed the towel along the bottom edge of a window. "It seems that no matter what we do, the dirt finds its way inside. We'll be tasting it long after the wind stops."

"Callie said it could last more than a day," Rebecca said.

Straightening and brushing a loose strand of hair off her forehead, Willa said, "My, yes. I've seen it go on for days and days. I pray this one will be short-lived." She gazed out the front window. "And may the Lord watch over our men and provide them with shelter. They must be close to home by now."

The wind and dirt roiled around the house for three days. Trapped, Rebecca paced and waited. Now that she'd made the decision to go, she felt driven to leave. And with each passing day, she feared the men's return. *Surely they must have found shelter somewhere*, she thought. *They couldn't possibly travel in this weather.* Still, she watched.

Finally the wind quieted and the air cleared. Rebecca made plans to leave the following morning. She'd packed only two bags; the rest of her things could be shipped later or replaced.

That day the men returned.

Daniel walked from the barn to the house. His step seemed to have more life to it than it had when he'd left. Rebecca felt a sense of the old Daniel. She longed to sit and chat. Memories of mornings spent in his arms haunted her.

Bertram stepped out of the barn. He looked at the house, then settled his gaze on Rebecca. It lingered on her abdomen, and Rebecca felt heat in her cheeks. Although innocent, she felt the reproof of his accusation.

Daniel stepped onto the porch. "G'day. Hope you fared well during the storm."

"Yes. We were fine, thank you."

He stood there a moment longer as if he had something more to say, then walked inside the house.

At supper Bertram was animated, talking about the journey, the fact that few animals were lost, and the good prices they'd managed to get. Rebecca, on the other hand, remained quiet and was barely able to choke down her meal. Afterward, Bertram went to the library and Daniel said something about going out. Willa and Rebecca moved to the parlor.

The clock ticked away the minutes. Rebecca tried to read, but the words couldn't penetrate her mind as she contemplated what lay ahead. When it was time for her to go up to bed, she longed to say a proper farewell.

Willa sat in the glow of a lantern, continuing her work on the baby's blanket. She held up the nearly finished piece. "It's coming along quite nicely, don't you think?"

"Yes. It's beautiful," Rebecca said, swallowing past a lump in her throat. The baby would never use it. "I'm tired. I think I'll go to bed."

She gazed at Willa. She'd accepted Rebecca into her home, then loved her as she would her own daughter. Rebecca bent and kissed her cheek. "You're a lovely person, Willa." She dared not say more.

"Why, thank you, dear." She took Rebecca's hand. "I'm so glad you're here. I know it's not been easy for you, but life has a way of working out. You'll see."

Rebecca squeezed Willa's hand and retreated.

⚘

Feeling miserable, Rebecca climbed beneath the covers and tried to relax. Hoping for a few hours' sleep, she closed her eyes. Her mind reeled with plans and fears. Finally she lay staring into the darkness, working through the process of hitching the horses to the surrey and the techniques of steering the team. What if she couldn't handle the horses, or what if she lost her way in the early morning gloom? What if . . . The questions went on and on.

She pushed aside her worries, but they were only replaced by thoughts of Daniel.

Memories tumbled through her mind—how she'd met him, their days in Boston, and the plans they'd shared. She pictured his handsome face and sympathetic blue eyes. The heavy weight of loss felt suffocating. She would raise her child in Boston, alone. Daniel would live here on the plains of Queensland. Never again would she know his tender touch. Darkness pressed in, and tears slipped from the corners of her eyes.

⚘

More than once Daniel had started up the stairs. He and Rebecca couldn't go on as they had been. He must speak to her.

Everyone had gone to bed, leaving the house dark and quiet. *She's no doubt asleep,* he told himself and sat on the bottom step. *What good will it do to talk? What have I to say? I don't even know how I feel.* He scrubbed his face with his hands. He was weary, not the kind of weariness that comes from hard work but the sort that evolves from emotional emptiness.

"I love her," he said to the quietness. He stood and gripped the handrail. *I can put her indiscretion behind me. We'll begin again.* He took a step, then stopped. Could he really put it behind him? *Yes,* he told himself.

With a feeling of urgency, Daniel headed up the staircase and walked toward Rebecca's room. The closer he got, the heavier his steps became and the less confident he felt. Finally he stood in front of her door. He didn't knock but stared at it. He could see Jim and Rebecca . . . together. The knot in the pit of his stomach ached. *I've no choice. I can't stop loving her.* He knocked.

"Who is it?" Rebecca asked.

"Daniel. Can we talk?"

"It's awfully late." There was a long pause, then Rebecca said, "Tomorrow after breakfast?"

"No. It can't wait."

"All right. Just a moment."

Daniel waited until Rebecca opened the door. She had a bathrobe pulled tightly about her, and dark hair cascaded over her shoulders. Her eyes looked wide and anxious. A wave of love and desire crashed over Daniel.

"I didn't mean to awaken you."

"It's late, Daniel."

"Yes, I know. But I just need a few minutes." When Rebecca didn't respond, he stepped inside and closed the door.

Clutching her robe close, she moved to the window. "What is it you want?"

He knew she'd shut him out and felt the chill of her scorn.

"Right." He glanced at his feet, then continued, "While I was gone I did some thinking."

"Oh, what about? You and Meghan? Did you enjoy her company?"

"Rebecca, don't. There's nothing between 'er and me." He worked to gather his thoughts. He had to do this right. "I may have misjudged you a bit. Perhaps I've been too hard on you."

"Too hard, you think?" Rebecca's tone was bitter. She turned scornful eyes on him. "You believed the lies without even allowing me the courtesy of defending myself."

"You're right. I did. I just kept seeing you two, and I knew how much you liked Jim, and you both being Americans, well . . . I'm like any other bloke, I guess. I got a bit carried away. But I saw the two of you together . . . more than once. What was I to think?" He forced a smile. "I want to put all that behind us, eh? I've decided to give you another chance. I've forgiven you. We can begin again."

"You've forgiven *me*? I did nothing wrong." Rebecca swept a hand through her hair. "You believed the lie. You gave no thought to who I am or my promise to you. If you knew me, you would have known I could never do such a thing. And this baby, you still don't believe it's yours, do you?"

Daniel couldn't answer right away. He didn't know what he thought.

"I see. And what kind of life can a child have when his own father won't claim him?" Rebecca sighed heavily. "We have nothing to talk about, Daniel."

"I need a bit more time is all. I'll come 'round. I do believe you." Even as Daniel said the words, he knew they weren't true. He didn't believe, not completely, anyway.

"You can say the words, but they don't come from your heart. Until they do, we have nothing to say to each other."

"All right, it's true. I don't know what I believe, but I'll manage."

"I refuse to live in a house where my own husband, not to mention my father-in-law, can't trust me." She met his eyes squarely. "There's only one way I'll believe you're ready to at least try. You must stand up to your father. Be the man God intended you to be. Go to him and tell him I'm innocent of the accusations. Tell him he will no longer bully me, and tell him I'm not his daughter but your wife! You'll have to choose, Daniel—me or your father." Rebecca folded her arms over her chest.

Daniel couldn't say what she wanted to hear. "It doesn't have to be a choice. We can have a fine life and still get along with my father." He glanced at the burning lantern. "He'll not listen. He'll quote Scripture and tell me that a man is the head of his wife and that I'm to control you. He'll not change. And I can't make him—this is his house," Daniel said, knowing he'd put an end to his marriage.

"It seems you and your father have conveniently forgotten an important part of what God has to say about marriages. Your father likes to quote Ephesians 5:22, but he fails to mention the part that says a man is to love his wife as Christ loved the church—as Christ loved the church, Daniel. Jesus Christ died for the church. He gave everything, including his life. He made the ultimate sacrifice, and all that was required of the church was to love him in return. I had hoped to love you. I've even wondered a time or two if I might . . . love you. But that's not enough anymore. You and your father have seen to that." Her voice turned soft, the fight seeping from her.

Daniel was confused. He'd never paid any mind to the portion of Scripture Rebecca mentioned. And his father had never brought it up. He took a step toward Rebecca and grasped her hand. "I love you. I ache for you. But there's nothing I can say that will change my father's mind. He is who he is. We must accept that. If we live 'ere, then we must do things his way."

"Why must we live here?"

"You know I can't leave."

Rebecca closed her eyes and wrenched her hand out of Daniel's. "Please go."

Daniel felt powerless. He couldn't please his wife; he couldn't please his father. All his life he'd answered to Bertram. He tried to imagine what it would be like to defy the man. It would be an all-out war. *There must be another way.*

Rebecca turned her back on Daniel. "Good night."

Revolted at his own weakness, he walked to the door. What more could he say? What could he do? There was no way to save his marriage and preserve his relationship with his father. He would have to choose.

24

Rebecca woke with a start. She pushed up on one elbow and looked about. Already morning light illuminated the room. She hadn't meant to sleep so long. Was the staff up? What about Bertram?

She listened for activity. There was only silence. "Thank you, Lord," Rebecca said, throwing off the sheets. Her feet found the floor. While removing her nightdress, she hurried to the armoire.

Pulling a chemise over her head, she was struck by the magnitude of what she was about to do. Her fingers felt clumsy, and her hands shook while she dressed. It took several tries to manage the buttons on her gown. In the semi-darkness, she pulled on stockings and pushed her feet into sensible shoes. If she was to spend the next several days traveling, comfort would be important.

Opening the bedroom door just a crack, she listened. The house was still. She peeked out into the dimly lit hallway. It was empty, but soon the family would be up. She must hurry or be found out.

Leaving the door ajar, she moved to the closet and retrieved the two bags she'd packed. It would scarcely be enough, but she had little choice. After taking another glance up and down the corridor, she cautiously set the bags in the hallway and stepped out, closing the door with care. Her heart pounded hard beneath her ribs. Pressing a hand to her chest, she took in a deep breath, then started toward the staircase.

A loud pop from the floorboards startled her. She stopped and pressed her back against the wall. *Lord, help me to move soundlessly, like Callie.* The thought of her aborigine friend brought a pang of regret. She would miss her.

Rebecca started down the stairway but stopped when she heard noise coming from the kitchen. Sitting on a step, she pressed close to the wall and listened. The grate on the kitchen stove rasped as it was moved; then the crunch of paper being shoved into the firebox disrupted the quiet of the house. Lily was up and already at work.

Rebecca pushed to her feet and swiftly took the final steps. Her eyes swept over the parlor as she passed, hesitating on the chairs where she and Willa often sat and visited while doing their needlework. Sadness pressed down on her. From the start Willa had been family. Losing her daughter-in-law and grandchild would leave a painful wound. *I'm so sorry, Willa. I wish there were another way.*

Ghosts of those she loved and cared about followed her as she crossed the foyer. She remembered her first day—Woodman's friendship and Jim's contrary behavior. Her friendship with Jim had been a pleasant surprise. She hadn't had any premonition of the heartache that would come from it. *I should have seen the danger. It's too late now,* she thought, realizing that no matter what she'd done both Daniel and Bertram would have eventually rejected her.

At the front entryway Rebecca set down one of her bags and opened the heavy front door. It groaned. She was certain someone would hear. Holding her breath, she waited. No one came. With a small sense of triumph, she stepped onto the veranda, picked up her bag, and closed the door.

The sun touched the edges of the morning sky, reminding her of evenings spent with Daniel on the veranda, watching as a descending sun burned the heavens with vibrant color. They had often stayed until the sky went black and stars emerged to wink down at them as if encouraging love.

How could it all have changed so completely? She'd started to hope there could be love. Tears threatened, but she blinked them away and walked down the steps, a bag in each hand.

When Rebecca was several paces from the porch, she turned and looked at the house. It glowed in the coming dawn. It didn't look at all evil.

She stared at Daniel's bedroom window. A curtain trembled in the breeze. What would he think when he discovered that she'd gone? Would he be bereft or relieved? She would have liked to say good-bye.

Her resolve wavered. Was there another way? She thought over all that had happened and where the events had led—her relationship with Bertram, Daniel's lack of trust. *No. There's nothing I can do.* With fresh determination, she hurried toward the carriage house.

The horses stood quietly in their stalls, tails swishing, teeth grinding the last of the previous day's hay. Rebecca took only a moment to give the matched set of Morgans a pat before running to the tack room to get the harnesses. A bird trapped inside during the night fluttered past in a flight for freedom. Startled, Rebecca stopped and caught her breath. She watched as the bird soared through the open door.

Grabbing pads and collars, she hurried back to the stalls. Setting some of the gear on the floor, she stepped in beside one of the Morgans. With a soothing stroke, she placed a blanket on his back, then reached under his chest, lifted the collar, and fastened it at the top of his neck. After doing the same with the other horse, she grabbed a light driving harness and, careful not to tangle it, placed it along the Morgan's back, then fastened the harness strap to the collar. Hands shaking, she pulled the breeching over the gelding's rump and lifted the animal's tail, then dropped the breeching into place.

She returned to the tack room for the remainder of the gear. Then, once back with the horses, she closed her eyes and struggled to remember the next step. What had Wood-man done? She'd watched him so many times. *Lord, help me remember.*

Taking a deep breath, she hooked one end of the belly strap to the pad, then leaving it hanging, moved around the gelding, grabbed the belly strap, and hooked it to the other side of the pad. Finally, she placed a headstall on the animal, guided the bit into his mouth, and made sure the blinders were in place.

Out of breath and shaking, she hurried to do the same with the other horse. A feeling of success began to grow. She'd nearly done it. She led each horse to a hitching post and tied them side by side. Well trained, they stood quietly.

She glanced at the sky. It was becoming brighter. There was little time.

Half running, Rebecca returned to the carriage house and pulled the surrey out. It was lighter than she'd expected, and the large wheels made it easy to maneuver. She lined it up behind the Morgans and hooked the traces to the harness and ran them back to the surrey, then grabbed the pole and moved it into place between the team. She lifted it up and hooked it to the neck strap of each horse. Out of breath from her efforts, she ran the tugs down the sides of the horses and connected them to the chain links on a wooden doubletree at the front of the surrey.

She'd done it!

Taking a quick glance at the horizon, she realized the sun was up. She was out of time. After quickly checking the lines to make certain everything was in order, she loaded her bags and climbed into the surrey. Carefully backing up, she turned toward the road. With a soft flick of the reins, the team moved away from the carriage house.

A light glimmered in Callie's cabin, and Rebecca wished she could say good-bye. She didn't dare stop. She walked past, hoping to catch a glimpse of her friend, but Callie didn't step outside.

The horses tossed their heads. Rebecca gripped the reins tightly but dared not yank on them for fear of distressing the animals. The sound of jangling harness and the creaking wagon seemed exceedingly loud. *Everyone will hear.* She glanced at the house.

Rebecca continued on and managed to make it to the road without anyone sounding an alarm. She turned and studied the house. Something glimmered in Bertram and Willa's window. "Lord, keep me hidden from sight," she prayed.

Facing the team, she clicked her tongue and flicked the reins. The horses stepped into a lively trot. Rebecca hoped she'd mastered driving well enough to keep the Morgans under control.

In some places the road was well marked, and in others it disappeared altogether, seemingly becoming a part of the expanse of grasslands. She couldn't afford to make any errors. The stagecoach leaving Thornton Creek was due in less than two hours. She barely had enough time to make it into town and purchase tickets. It would have been best if she could have bought a ticket in advance, but it was too great a risk. Thornton Creek was a small town, and word would have gotten out.

"Hah, get up there," she called, feeling an urgency. The

horses gladly obliged, picking up their step. Rebecca was uncertain if she was holding the reins too tightly or too loosely. She didn't want to hold the animals back, and yet she had to be careful not to let them get away from her.

She'd always taken coachmen for granted, never giving any thought to how much skill was required to properly drive a carriage. Now she wished she'd paid more attention throughout the years or had gotten more practice driving. She leaned forward, doing her best to hold the reins loosely. The ground seemed to pass too quickly beneath her.

Wind blew her dark hair free of its pins, allowing curls to fall into her face. She brushed back the tendrils and studied the surrounding grasslands. The breeze whipped tall, thick blades of grass into a dance. She felt the thrill of accomplishment and a sense of command and thanked God for her freedom, at the same time grieving all that she'd lost.

By the time a kilometer had passed beneath her wheels, Rebecca had relaxed. She felt confident in her driving abilities, and it seemed she'd managed to get away undetected. She'd made it.

Rhythmic pounding echoed from behind her. The sound was like that of hooves striking the earth. Her skin prickled in apprehension. She glanced back and her mouth went dry. Her heart kicked into a rapid beat.

Bertram was following!

Leaning over his stallion's neck, he whipped the animal. Rebecca couldn't see his face clearly, but she knew the hardness in his eyes and the set of his chin. He'd be resolute.

Why won't he let me go? She grabbed the whip and flicked it over the horse's backs. "Hah. Get up!" she yelled. *He can bluster all he wants. I'm not staying. He can't force me.*

She allowed the horses their head. The surrey bounced precariously as it passed over the rough roadway. A wheel rolled over a large stone, and the carriage swayed. Dust bil-

lowed out behind her. As they plowed through a deep pot-
hole, Rebecca was nearly unseated.

She looked back. He was close! The big stallion continued
closing the gap until Rebecca could hear its labored breathing and the strike of each footfall. He strode alongside the
surrey.

"Stop!" Bertram hollered.

Rebecca ignored him.

"I say stop! Obey me at once!"

Rebecca kept her eyes forward.

"Ya'll do as I say!"

"Leave me alone!" Rebecca yelled. "I'm going home . . .
where I belong. You can't make me stay!"

"Ya will stay!" He rode close to the surrey and acted as if
he might climb aboard.

Shocked at herself, Rebecca swiped at him with her whip.
"Go away!" She hit him across the neck, and he grabbed for
the lash. He closed his hand over it, but it slipped from his
grasp.

Leaning forward, Rebecca snapped the reins. The wheels
bounded over a ridge, and the cart felt as if it might come
apart. *Sovereign God, may your hand of help be upon me.*

"Stop. Ya'll kill yerself. Be reasonable," Bertram shouted.

As if being chased by demons, Rebecca kept on. Yielding
was not an option. She continued to give the horses their
head.

"Yer a fool!" Bertram raged and pushed his horse for more
speed. Overtaking the surrey, he matched the Morgans' pace.
He reached for one of the horses' halters but missed. Leaning farther away from his horse, he tried again and missed
again.

"Who's the fool now?" Rebecca asked between clenched
teeth. "Let me go! Stop!" He continued to ride alongside the
team. "Go away!" Rebecca screamed.

The horses labored. A frothy, white sweat appeared between their hind legs. Rebecca knew it was dangerous to push them. Why wouldn't he give up? A small stone kicked up by his horse stung her cheek, and she wiped at the stinging slash. Blood came away on her hand. "This is all so ridiculous," she muttered. "I'm a grown woman. No one has the right to hold me prisoner."

Reaching for the Morgans' headgear, Bertram leaned away from his horse. He managed to grab the halter of one gelding and hauled back on it. The animal thrust his head forward, pulling hard. The excitement and panic drove the horses—they wouldn't stop. Bertram heaved on the leather line. The horse threw his head back, then pulled forward sharply, yanking Bertram out of his seat.

Clinging to the side of his saddle, he fought to maintain his hold on the halter. Without warning, his stallion veered away, and Bertram grabbed the surrey harness with both hands.

His added weight panicked the Morgans, and they charged wildly on, heads down. They kicked and bucked in the harness, moving away from the road and through a patch of brush. With each stride the horse's powerful shoulder pummeled Bertram, its hooves thrashed his legs. Bertram's feet and ankles were battered against the ground.

His grip slipped, and Rebecca watched in horror as he fell beneath the horse's hooves. The animal plowed over him, and its full weight came down squarely on Bertram's back.

Rebecca gripped the edge of the seat as the surrey bounded over Bertram's body. For a moment she thought the carriage would tip, but it righted itself and she grabbed the reins and fought to slow the horses.

Rebecca glanced back. Her father-in-law lay face down in the dirt, a motionless lump. She expected to see him push himself up and yell at her, but he didn't move.

He's fine, she told herself, still fighting the team. Winded and sweating, the animals finally slowed to a trot. Rebecca looked back. Bertram still hadn't moved.

She steered the team back to the road and continued toward town. Her conscience told her to go back. She kept on. *This is my chance.*

She took another look at her father-in-law. He must have been badly hurt. Otherwise he'd have gotten up. She slowed the team. It could be a trick. The horses kept moving. *No self-respecting person would leave a man lying in the dust, no matter how much he deserves to be there.*

"Someone will come after him," she said out loud, as if to convince herself. "They will." But even as she spoke, Rebecca knew the someone would be her. She couldn't go on, not if he was badly injured.

She stopped the horses and climbed down, leaving them to chew on their bits. Reluctantly she walked toward Bertram.

He might be fine and this is all a trick, she thought. However, the closer she got to him the more certain she was that he was seriously hurt. Bertram's face was pallid, his breathing shallow. He didn't move, not at all.

"Father in heaven, what have I done?" She ran the last few yards. Dropping to her knees, she rolled Bertram onto his back. He groaned but didn't open his eyes. He looked as if someone had beaten him, and he struggled for every breath.

Rebecca wiped dirt from his forehead. *This is my fault*, she thought. *He's dying and it's my fault.*

25

His mother's voice and a knocking intruded on Daniel's restless sleep. He forced open his eyes.

"Daniel," Willa said, opening the door and stepping into his room.

"What is it? What's wrong?" Daniel asked, pushing himself up on one elbow.

"It's your father."

"Is he sick?"

"No. He's gone after Rebecca."

"What do you mean? Where's she gone?" He sat up and dropped his legs over the side of the bed.

"I'm not certain. It appears she's run away." Willa's eyes filled with tears. "I'm afraid something dreadful is going to happen. Your father's in a terrible state. He left a few moments ago, riding hard." She rested a hand on Daniel's arm. "Go after him. I . . . I don't know what he might do. I've never seen him so angry."

"Right. I'll get him. No worries, Mum," he said, although his own anxiety was intensifying.

Daniel quickly dressed and rushed downstairs.

Willa stood at the front door. "Please, be careful."

"I will." He kissed her cheek. "Everything will be fine."

With the reality of what had happened sinking in, Daniel sprinted for the barn. *Rebecca's leaving. That's the truth of it.* He'd known it was coming but had hoped she wouldn't actually go. And now his father would only make things worse. Daniel's anger flared. *This wouldn't have happened if not for his bullying.*

All his life Daniel had submitted, even yielding his responsibility as husband to his father. It had been his duty to care for and protect Rebecca, not his father's. Years of frustration and resentment filled Daniel with rage. "I'll see to her now!"

He strode into the barn, his mind churning through all that had happened since he'd brought Rebecca to Douloo. In truth, he couldn't blame his father for everything. *This is as much my fault as his. I should have taken charge of my family. I shouldn't have let him rule over her or me. I pray it's not too late to convince Rebecca to stay.*

Woodman already had Daniel's chestnut stallion saddled. Handing over the reins he said, "Figured ya'd be out roight soon. I saw 'er go. She's not too far ahead. Stop yer father and bring yer lydie back." He grinned.

"I'll do my best," Daniel said, swinging into the saddle. He kicked his horse in the sides and urged him forward. He couldn't overtake his father, but if Bertram managed to stop Rebecca, he'd catch up soon enough, hopefully before too much damage had been done.

As Daniel rode, his mind reeled with scenes of the past several months. He saw even more clearly his mishandling of things. *Lord, forgive me. Help me explain it all to Rebecca. Give me a chance to be the kind of husband you meant me to be.*

Kicking up dust, he moved away from the house and over the rise leading to the road. It stretched out in front of him, and in the distance he could see the surrey bustling along amid a puff of dust. His father followed.

Bertram closed the distance. *She's going too fast*, Daniel

thought, fear piercing him. The surrey careened to one side, and for a moment he thought it would tip over. "Slow down. He won't hurt you. It's not worth your life," he shouted, but of course she couldn't hear. *It's not worth the baby's life . . . my baby's life.*

All of a sudden he knew. There'd never been anything more than friendship between Rebecca and Jim. He'd believed a lie. And it was that assumption more than anything that had driven Rebecca away. Shame pressed down on him.

His father pulled up even with the surrey, then moved ahead and tried to stop the horses. "You fool. You'll kill yourself." The words were barely out of his mouth when Bertram was dragged off his horse. Daniel leaned forward and whipped his horse with the reins.

Rebecca continued on while Bertram lay motionless in the dirt. Daniel felt sick. This was his fault. If only he'd stood up to his father. If only he'd listened to Rebecca . . . and believed her. How deep must be her misery—to take such a chance and then to leave an injured man lying in the dirt.

The surrey finally slowed and stopped. Rebecca climbed down and warily walked toward Bertram. She didn't notice Daniel. He kept riding hard.

Rebecca was kneeling beside Bertram when Daniel rode up. She looked at him, her face stained by tears and dirt. "I never meant . . . I didn't know he would come after me. This wasn't supposed to happen. I'm so sorry."

Daniel's stomach dropped. "Is he dead?" He dismounted and hurried over to Rebecca and his father.

"No. He's alive. But he's badly hurt. He's not moving and he's unconscious."

Daniel dropped to his knees beside his father. "Dad, can you hear me?"

"I'm so sorry," Rebecca said again.

"This isn't your fault." Daniel's voice was sharper than he'd intended.

He laid a hand on his father's chest. "Dad, you all right?" There was no movement. "Dad." Still no response. "We've got to get him back to the house and send for the doctor. You'll have to help me." He strode to the surrey, took hold of the horses, and led them back to where his father lay.

"I'll need you to take his feet. I'll grab hold of his shoulders."

"We could injure him further."

Daniel met Rebecca's gaze squarely. "We have no choice." He bent and, placing his hands under his father's arms, gently lifted. Rebecca grabbed hold of Bertram's feet. "All right, then, on three," Daniel said. "One . . . two . . . three."

Rebecca let out a groan with the effort, and Bertram moaned. She stopped.

"Keep moving," Daniel said. He walked backward, looking over his shoulder as he placed his foot on the step of the surrey. He pushed up and in one fluid motion moved into the carriage. Rebecca managed to follow, still holding Bertram's legs. Together they maneuvered him onto a seat.

Breathing hard, Daniel leaned forward and rested his hands on his thighs. Straightening, he wiped sweat from his forehead with the back of his hand. "Right, then. I'll drive and you can tend him."

After tying the two stallions to the back of the surrey, he climbed into the front and took the reins. Rebecca kneeled on the floor beside Bertram, resting a hand on him to keep him still. His breathing was labored, and he still hadn't moved. "Lord, please heal his body," Rebecca prayed.

By the time they reached the yard, Bertram had started to stir. "I think he's waking up," Rebecca said.

Daniel glanced back.

Willa, Woodman, Callie, and Lily ran out to meet them. "What's happened?" Willa asked.

"Dad's been hurt. We need to get him inside."

Woodman was the first in the surrey. He leaned over Bertram. "Mr. Thornton, sir?"

Squinting, Bertram peered up at Woodman. "What ya lookin' at?" His voice sounded raspy. "I'll be fine; just give me a few days." He started to push himself upright, then cried out and lay back down.

Standing outside the surrey, Willa stood close to Bertram. She smoothed his hair. "You behave yourself, now. Lie right there and let Woodman and Daniel help you."

She glanced at Woodman. "Do be careful."

Bertram looked at his son. "Ya keep yer hands off me. It was you who brought 'er 'ere."

"Now's not the time," Daniel said.

Bertram flinched away from Daniel when he reached for him.

"All right, then," Daniel said. "We'll talk about it now." He nudged his hat back. "I did bring 'er. And it's a good thing too." He glanced at Rebecca. "She's added color and life to this place. She's been good for us. Good for me. I love 'er. And you'll show 'er respect." He folded his arms over his chest. "And while you're laid up, I'm in charge. You'll do as I say. You're in no condition to be giving orders."

Bertram looked as if he might protest, but he said nothing and closed his eyes instead.

Daniel bent over his father, then looked at Woodman and said, "Right, then. We'll carry him to his room, and then I'll go for the doctor."

Woodman grabbed Bertram's feet, and the two men lifted him and carried him out of the surrey.

"You'll be just fine," Willa said, walking beside her husband. "God will see to you." Just before the men carried him up the front steps, she rested her hand on his chest. "I love you."

Bertram managed a smile, but it looked more like a grimace.

Daniel went for the doctor, and Willa tended Bertram. She lifted a washcloth from a pan of warm water and wrung it out. "You made a mess out of yourself, Mr. Thornton—you and your temper." She dabbed at a deep wound on his chin.

Bertram winced but said nothing.

Willa cleaned the dirt from his face and cared for his other wounds. Callie swapped the tepid water for cool, and Willa continually changed the cool compresses on his forehead.

Not knowing just what she ought to do, Rebecca hovered. She stood at the window and prayed, then sat at a table by the foot of the bed and prayed, and finally paced in the hallway and prayed. This was her fault. It had been her reckless behavior that had set Bertram off.

Callie appeared, carrying a fresh pitcher of water and a clean pan. She stopped in front of Rebecca. "This isn't yer fault, mum. Ya did what ya had ta do. That's all."

Rebecca smiled at her friend. "You always seem to know what I'm thinking."

"It's not so hard ta see." Callie stepped into Bertram's bedchamber, and Rebecca followed.

Willa poured the fresh water into the pan and dipped a clean cloth into it. She removed a compress from Bertram's forehead and handed it to Callie, then gently replaced it with the clean rag.

"The doctor will be here any moment. I dare say, he'll probably have you up and out of that bed before the week's out."

"Willa," Bertram croaked. "I don't think it's going to be that easy. I . . . I can't feel my legs. I can't move them."

Willa remained stoical. "Perhaps it will pass. God hasn't forgotten you. I haven't ceased praying. Nor have Daniel and Rebecca."

"I don't want to hear her name," Bertram snarled weakly. His eyes found his daughter-in-law, and he stared until Rebecca couldn't take his revulsion any longer and escaped to the hallway.

I'll have to stay . . . at least until he's begun his recovery, Rebecca thought, starting down the stairs. The stage must have left Thornton Creek by now.

⅏

When Daniel returned he only glanced at Rebecca before guiding the doctor up the stairs. She waited in the parlor. *He hates me. Of course he must; this is my fault.*

Woodman stood in the entryway, his face creased with concern, his black eyes pained.

Callie came down the stairs and walked into the parlor. Leaning against the door frame, she studied Rebecca, then said, "Mr. Thornton's a stubborn man. He decided ta go after ya. Ya didn't make 'im chase ya down or go after them horses. It was his choice."

"Listen to 'er," Woodman said. "She's roight. Ya'll drive yerself crazy if ya take on burdens that don't belong ta ya."

Rebecca took in a deep breath and slowly blew it out. "I'll do my best to remember that."

It seemed a long while before Daniel and Willa followed

309

the doctor downstairs. Willa sat in an overstuffed chair, and Daniel stood beside her, his hand on her shoulder.

The doctor swiped thinning hair back, then rested troubled eyes on Willa. "It doesn't look good." Nudging round wire-rimmed glasses farther up onto his nose, he continued, "The head injury is pretty serious, but it will heal. He's got a couple of broken ribs. They're going to cause him a great bit of pain, but they'll heal as well. It's his back I'm most concerned about. There's swelling there, and he's got a monster of a bruise. And since he can't feel anything from his waist down, I fear he's broken his back."

"Oh no," Willa said, pressing a handkerchief to her mouth.

The doctor looked from Willa to Daniel, then back to Willa. "He's strong. If he makes it through the next couple of days, he might recover."

Willa looked pale. She sat quiet and placid, but the spark hadn't gone out of her eyes. "All right, then. I'll just go on up and see to him. He'll need someone with him."

"Now, Willa, I don't want you wearing yourself out." The doctor eyed Daniel. "You make certain she takes care of herself, lad."

"I'll do that."

"Someone must stay with Bertram at all times. He can't be left alone. Right now there's nothing he can do for himself." He took a step toward the door, then stopped. "If the feeling comes back into his legs, don't let him out of bed. Send for me right away." He offered a kindly smile and continued toward the door. "I'll be back tomorrow," he said before stepping outside.

"I'll help care for him," Rebecca offered.

Daniel frowned. "He won't take kindly to that."

"It's the least I can do."

Through the night it felt as if the house itself were holding its breath. Bertram endured until the morning light. And throughout that day and the next three, he managed to hang on to life. After that his strength waned, his will weakened. He even stopped snapping at Rebecca.

Neighbors and friends came to visit, but Bertram wouldn't see anyone. Once Rebecca caught sight of Meghan with Daniel. Jealousy flared. Then, remembering that her marriage was over, she told herself, *I've no right to worry about those two. I'll be leaving, and Daniel will begin a new life.*

Cambria stopped in and chatted with Rebecca. She apologized profusely for not coming sooner, explaining that her father had forbidden her to visit.

But even her apologies and her pleasant chitchat did little to lift Rebecca's spirits.

On the sixth day Bertram seemed to perk up. He tried to eat and went back to ordering Rebecca and Daniel about. The doctor explained that even if Bertram survived, he would probably never walk again or regain full use of his arms and hands.

While the household staff, Willa, and Rebecca looked after Bertram, Daniel put his energies into running the station. By all accounts, he did a grand job. The days were full, and Rebecca and Daniel found no time to discuss what had happened or what lay ahead.

One day while standing at the window in Bertram's room, Rebecca wondered what life would hold for her now. She held out little hope for anything grand. She would return to the States and become a teacher. It's what she should have done in the beginning rather than foolishly running off to Australia in search of a romantic adventure.

She gazed outside, seeking some sort of solace, but the empty land offered her little. She turned and looked at the man sleeping in the bed. Bertram was a shadow of who he'd

311

once been. He was thin, and the color had gone from his sunken face. He was weary and beaten, and his life seemed to be fading.

In the weeks since the accident, Rebecca had changed too. She felt wrenching heartache as she studied her father-in-law. Hatred and fear had been transformed, and what had started as an obligation had become a mission of devotion. *If only he would live.*

Rebecca realized she loved him. When and how the transformation had occurred she didn't know, but it definitely had. And Rebecca was certain it had nothing to do with her will. It was a gift from God. There was no other reasonable explanation. Since his accident Bertram had become more cross with her than he'd been before, and he scolded her relentlessly. She refused to counter the darts he hurled, understanding that Bertram's bristles came from fear and regret. He knew his life would never be restored to what it had once been. Rebecca was certain he'd have preferred death to dependence.

How frightening life can be, she thought. *We never know what is to come. This might be exactly what Bertram needed. Lord, reveal your grace and mercy to him.*

"What ya staring at?" Bertram bellowed.

Rebecca was startled. "Oh, was I staring? I'm sorry. I was just thinking."

"I need something to drink." He struggled to push himself up on one elbow. "What were ya thinking 'bout?" He eyed her suspiciously. "Were ya trying to figure how to do me in? I'm an easy target." He chuckled sardonically.

"What a terrible thing to say." She eyed him with a half smile. "I was thinking about you." She filled a glass with water and held it to his lips.

He sipped, then fell back against his pillows. "And what were ya thinking? Couldn't be good."

"In truth? I was thinking about how much I've grown to love you."

A light flickered in his eyes, but his voice was gruff as he said, "Love me? I don't want yer affection. I can't stand the sight of ya. Ya deceived my son, and ya'll take his life too."

"I didn't deceive him. You know that."

"I know no such thing. I wish my son could see the truth."

"If you're worried about Daniel, you have no need. And I'll be leaving just as soon as you're well."

"Don't let me stop ya."

Rebecca shook her head. "You can bellow all you want. It won't change anything." Inwardly Rebecca marveled at her calm. *It must be God.*

"Ya feel sorry for me, that's what it is. Well, don't. I'll get up out of this bed. Ya'll see."

"I feel badly about what's happened to you, but I don't feel sorry for you, Mr. Thornton. God has a plan."

She really did love this cantankerous old man. How marvelous to be able to love without requiring love in return. She'd never truly experienced what it meant to love an enemy.

"This is no plan—it's simply yer doing. I'll die in this bed because of ya."

Rebecca winced inwardly. "I am sorry, but . . . you played a part in this too. I know that what you're experiencing must be excruciating, but we know that all things work together for good to them that love God, to them who are called according to his purpose. You do believe that, don't you? They're God's words."

Bertram glowered but said not a word.

26

Bertram groaned, then with trembling arms pulled the sheet down to his waist. "I can't abide this any longer."

"What can't you abide?" Rebecca asked.

"Just lyin' here—day in and day out. It's been weeks. I've got a station to run."

"Daniel's handling it very well. You've no need to worry about that."

"Can ya get Willa? My back aches and I need a rub."

"She's taking a well-deserved nap. I'll do it for you."

"Ya don't do it right."

"That may be so, but I'm all you have right now."

"I'd say yer a bit free with that mouth of yers, young lady."

"And I'd say if you continue to give me trouble, I can walk right out of here."

Bertram clamped his mouth shut and stared at the ceiling.

Rebecca moved to the bed stand and picked up a bottle of liniment.

"Roll onto your side. I'll help you." She pressed her hand against his back and pushed while Bertram pulled with his weakened arms.

"I pray the Lord will take me home. I don't want to live like this."

"What would Willa do without you? And the rest of us?" The pungent pine scent of the liniment burned Rebecca's nose.

"No one cares, except Willa." He closed his eyes as Rebecca massaged his sore muscles. "She's a right lovely jewel. And doesn't deserve this." He smiled slightly. "I remember the day we met. She was in the garden with 'er mum. I knew the moment I saw 'er she was for me. She was a beaut, all right."

"She loves you still. I'd like to see you get well, at least for her." Rebecca pressed the palms of her hands against his upper back. "God makes the decisions about life and death. You don't know yet what plans he has for you."

"I'd say he's pretty much done with me."

Rebecca worked the liniment into his shoulders. She could feel Bertram relax beneath her touch.

"That stuff draws the flies, ya know."

"I'll make sure to pull down the mosquito netting." Rebecca continued rubbing. Soon Bertram's breathing was deep and steady. He was asleep.

Daniel stepped into the room. He offered Rebecca a smile, then asked in a whisper, "He sleeping?"

She nodded.

"Thanks for taking such good care of him." His eyes held hers. "I'll see you at supper?"

"Yes. I'll be there."

Daniel walked out. Rebecca wished he'd stay, but he never did. These days neither of them said much to the other. However, Daniel's hard shell had softened. His tone was softer, and now and then he even smiled or tossed out a laugh.

What is he thinking? Rebecca wondered. She hoped he'd forgiven her for the accident. And there was the matter of

Jim. Daniel still believed she'd been unfaithful. In truth, it mattered little what he thought. They couldn't find their way to each other now. Too much had happened.

Daniel might put on a front, but he would never completely believe her innocence. He'd always see her as an adulteress. And she could never forgive him for that.

✵

Willa walked into the bedroom. She dabbed at her neck and forehead with a handkerchief. "I dare say, it's terribly hot. And summer hasn't actually arrived yet. I'm not much for this heat."

"Did you get a nap?"

"Just a bit of one." Willa looked at Bertram. "I feel just awful watching him swelter in that bed. When he wakes up I'll wash him down with cool cloths."

"I'm sure he'll appreciate that." Rebecca smiled at Willa. "He told me about your first meeting. He said he was smitten immediately. I wish Daniel and I . . ." There was no use in wishing. She compressed her lips and blinked back tears.

"It will work out for the two of you. You must have faith."

"I don't think any amount of faith can help us." Rebecca rearranged the netting about the bed, then walked to the window and opened it completely. "I wish a breeze would come up."

Willa sat on the chair beside her husband's bed and stroked his hand. "He was such a fine man."

"Was?"

"Did I say that?" Willa sniffed. "He's still wonderful, but the years have changed him a bit. And now . . ." Willa stopped. Her eyes brimmed with tears. "Now I can't bear to see him like this. To him it's worse than death."

316

"God will do what's best," Rebecca said. "We must trust him."

Willa lifted weary eyes to Rebecca. "You're such a dear. I don't know what I would do without you."

"You don't hold me in reproach in any way?"

"Indeed not. I love Bertram, but I know him well. He was in a rage when he went after you. He behaved recklessly. You couldn't have known this would happen."

Rebecca looked at Bertram. "I wish I'd never left that morning."

"Perhaps God has a plan and this is all part of it."

"Perhaps." Rebecca rested a hand on Willa's shoulder. "I worry about you. You're spending too much time cooped up in this room."

"Where else am I to be except at my husband's side?"

"Why don't we have Callie come in and stay with him while we have a cuppa on the veranda."

"That's a lovely idea."

⟡

"This is much nicer," Rebecca said, stretching out her legs and wiggling bare toes. "Is being barefoot on a veranda in Queensland improper?" She chuckled.

"Indeed it isn't. You may do whatever you wish on your own veranda."

"It feels good."

"There is independence for those who seize it." Willa settled understanding eyes on Rebecca. "I believe you can do that."

"I'd like to think so. But you're the one who's been brave and who has worked so hard to build a life here." Rebecca dunked a biscuit into her tea and took a bite. She chewed

317

thoughtfully. "I feel discourteous asking this question." She hesitated.

"Please, go right ahead."

"How is it that you've allowed Bertram to rule over you as he does?"

Willa set her tea aside, then folded her hands in her lap. "It was something I decided upon many years ago. I accept the Bible as being literal. And in the matter of a woman's place, my role is clear. I've prayed and trusted that the quietness and peace offered by God would be seen in me. In this wild and rough place, where would Bertram see such qualities if not in his wife?

"God has honored my prayer. He's given me peace that only he can give. My mission in life has been to my husband." She grinned. "As you can imagine, it hasn't always been easy. Bertram can be inflexible. But he's always treated me with absolute devotion and respect, and the love we felt for each other in the beginning has grown stronger.

"I must say, however, the course I chose is not necessarily the only way for a woman to be a helpmate to her husband. It's the path God chose for Bertram and me. You and Daniel must find your own way." She glanced at Rebecca's stomach. "You and Daniel, and your child."

"I'm afraid its heritage is in doubt."

"I have no doubts."

"Thank you, Willa, for your faith in me." Rebecca rested a hand on her abdomen. "When the baby moves I sometimes lose my breath at the wonder of it."

Willa's eyes warmed. "Indeed. I remember." She picked up her cup and took a drink of tea. "I wish you could have met Elton. He was rather like you—his own person and something of a rebel. But . . . wonderful." Her words became a whisper, and she choked back tears. "I pray it's not time for Bertram to join him. It would be too much to lose both of them." She took a handkerchief out of her dress pocket and dabbed at her eyes. "Bertram always regretted the estrangement, but he's stubborn."

She cleared her throat and looked directly at Rebecca. "Enough of that. There's something I wanted to speak to you about—you and Daniel. Am I correct in assuming you haven't reconciled?"

"We haven't, and I see little hope that we will. Daniel seems less angry, but he still believes the lie. How can I forgive him?" Rebecca watched a bee hover about a red rose. "And there's this business with Mr. Thornton, which seems to have no resolution. I've grown to love him, but it's clear that if he had his way he'd never lay eyes on me again."

"So you're still planning to leave us?"

"Yes. As soon as Mr. Thornton is well enough."

"Please reconsider. God has the power to put things right. Daniel loves you, but it's hard for a lad . . ."

"He's not a lad."

"No, not to you, but to his father he is . . . and will always be." Willa let her gaze drift over the garden. "It's difficult to stand up to Bertram."

"I know. But that doesn't eliminate Daniel's responsibility. I can't live here with the present situation."

"Daniel has done better recently."

"For a day or so, yes, and then he steps back into his role as son but not husband."

Silence settled over the two women.

Rebecca caressed her rounded abdomen. "I'll have to leave soon. It won't be long before I'll be big as a barn and won't be able to travel."

Sadness touched Willa's eyes. "I will truly miss you. I can't imagine Douloo without you."

"I'll miss you too. But I never really belonged here. We both know that."

"Do we?"

Rebecca set her cup on the table. "I'm a bit tired. I think I'll lie down." She stood. "I'll sit with Mr. Thornton during supper and stay until you come up."

"That will be fine." Willa stood. "Rebecca, I must say that I don't believe this thing between you and Daniel can't be sorted out. God is the healer of all wounds." Her eyes held a hint of mischief. "If I'm not mistaken, I believe you're the one who reminded me of that."

Rebecca didn't know how to reply. She knew God could do anything. In fact, she'd seen his healing touch most recently in her change of heart toward Bertram. But the hurt over Daniel went much deeper. "I suppose you're right," she said. "But there are some offenses that can't be forgiven."

"Do not limit God. He's greater than we can comprehend."

"He's in a foul mood," Callie said when Rebecca walked into the room with Bertram's dinner tray.

"We'll be fine. I've brought his favorite meal." She winked at Callie. "If he won't cooperate, I'll eat it myself."

"May ya fare better than me," Callie said as she walked out.

"I'm not hungry," Bertram growled. "I'm tired of the pitiful excuse for food ya bring up 'ere." Bertram feebly folded his arms over his chest.

"It's the same thing we all eat. It's just cut into small bites so you can swallow. We don't want you choking." Rebecca sat on the chair beside the bed and set the tray on the bed stand. She lifted Bertram's folded arms and set them at his side, then unfolded a napkin and lay it over his chest. "Do you need the pillows propped up more?"

"No. I'm fine. And I'll feed myself, thank ya."

"Good for you." Rebecca placed the fork in his hand, then held the plate in front of him.

His arm shaking, Bertram clumsily maneuvered a lifeless-looking hand toward the plate. He pushed the fork into a pile of mashed potatoes, then directed it toward his mouth. Before it made it there, however, the fork and potatoes dropped into his lap.

"Merciful—"

"Now, Mr. Thornton, I know you don't want to use the Lord's name in vain." Rebecca quickly picked up the fork. "Try again."

Setting his mouth, Bertram asked, "Why not curse him? He's done little for me."

"Why, he's given you so much. Look at this home, the land, and your family . . ."

"My family? My son left and then died half a world away, Daniel doesn't have enough bristle in him to oversee this place, and you . . . well, ya've been a thorn in my side since ya got 'ere."

"I never meant to be a thorn," Rebecca said. "I must say, I've done my best to get along, and I've put up with the likes of you."

"Yer an ungrateful wretch, that's what ya are. Ya come 'ere with yer high and mighty ways figuring ya didn't have to listen to the likes of me or anyone else. I'd say yer a spoiled brat and a shame to yer own father. No wonder he shipped ya off."

"I beg your pardon, sir. You know my father is dead. He was a fine man who loved me very much." She choked back tears. "I tried my best to learn your ways—while you wagged your finger at me, I might add. I couldn't do anything right; nothing suited you."

"Yer husband should have throttled ya."

"And if I had, then what would you have done?" Daniel asked, striding into the room.

"Well, if ya had she might have listened to ya, lad."

"Why would she do that? You did everything in your power to usurp my authority. I have no influence in this house."

"Nor should ya."

Daniel stared at his father, then said sternly, "I've had enough of your overbearing, oppressive rule. And I demand your respect for me and for my wife. You're not to say another unkind word to her. She's been at your bedside for weeks, and I've yet to see a kindness or hear a word of thanks from you."

"I owe 'er nothing. She spat on me and my family when she went off and got herself pregnant by another man!"

"I didn't. I was never unfaithful to Daniel. And I won't stay here and listen to your accusations." Humiliated, Rebecca turned and marched out.

⟨⟩

"You won't speak to her that way, never again. Nor will you speak to me in that manner. I've listened to you roar at us for too many years. I don't see anywhere in the Scriptures that Jesus Christ ever bellowed. If he were standing 'ere now, you'd have good cause to be ashamed. He may be the reason you're in this bed. You needed humbling." Daniel gripped the bedpost with his right hand. "I'll not pity you. In that bed or not, your tyrannical behavior will stop. I won't allow it."

"*You* won't allow it?"

Years of hurt and frustration flowed from deep inside Daniel. He ignored his father's interruption and continued, "All these years Mum's stood by you while you whipped us with the belt and with your tongue. And it wasn't just Elton and me. You may not have used a belt on Mum, but you might as well have. I see nothing in God's Word that allows a man to mistreat his wife."

"I never—"

"It says," Daniel said loudly, "a man is to love his wife as Christ loves the church. Have you ever thought over just what that means? It was my own wife who helped me see the verse. You best be contemplating the Lord's words.

"I believe your behavior to be a far greater sin than mistakes made by those who try to do their best in life. An error in judgment is far different than a deliberate act of cruelty. I won't make excuses for you any longer."

"Ya'll mind yer manners. The Bible says—"

"Right. The Bible says. Over the years so much of what you've pounded into me and what you've done has been founded on the words of the Good Book, but you've misquoted and misused those words. No more. You'll stop, or Rebecca and I *will* leave. And you'll not have anything to do with us or your grandchild. Which, by the way, I'm certain is *your* grandchild." He took a step closer to his father. "I believe Rebecca. I love 'er, and if it comes down to it, I'll let go of you and this station to keep 'er."

"Then yer a fool!"

"Maybe so, but I rather think you're the fool."

Bertram tried to push himself upright, but his arms failed him and he slumped back. Weakly he hollered, "Ya dishonor me. Yer to honor yer father."

His tone firm, Daniel said, "Yes, honor thy father." He settled serious eyes on Bertram. "You have not honored *the* Father."

With that, Daniel turned and walked out, his step light for a man who may have just lost his inheritance. However, Daniel knew he'd finally laid hold of something far more significant—himself.

27

Daniel walked into the parlor. "I'm sorry about that. The old duffer's just in one of his moods."

Old duffer? Rebecca had never heard Daniel refer to his father in such a disparaging way. "No need to apologize," she said.

"I expect he'll be a bit better from now on . . . after our little . . . chat."

"I'll go back up, then. He might need me."

"He doesn't deserve you, you know. Then, neither do I."

Puzzled at Daniel's compassionate tone and personal manner, Rebecca responded to his first comment. "I'm just doing my part to help. And sometimes I get angry. He can still set me off."

Daniel chuckled. "He can set off just about anybody."

Rebecca settled dark eyes on her husband. "Daniel, God's changed my heart toward your father. He's given me a look at who Bertram Thornton really is. And he's not so difficult to love."

Daniel seemed taken aback for a moment, then said, "Sometimes it's difficult to remember his attributes, eh?" More seriously he added, "He's been hard on you, Rebecca."

"God didn't say we're to love only those who love us in

return, but we're to love even our enemies." As she said the words, Rebecca couldn't forget the bitterness she harbored toward Daniel. *That's different,* she told herself, then said briskly, "I better go on up."

🍂

Rebecca stopped at Bertram's door, took a deep breath, and tried to clear her thoughts of Daniel. It was Bertram she needed to think about. She doubted he had long to live, and she'd started to believe that in spite of his knowledge and his prayers, he didn't truly know God but rather knew *about* him.

Grasping the doorknob, she prayed, *Place the right words in my mouth, Lord. May I say only what you allow.*

Rebecca walked into the room, and Bertram acted as if he hadn't heard her come in. He lay rigid, staring at the ceiling. Finally he asked, "What are ya doing here? I don't want ya."

"I know. And that's all right. I won't say a word. I'll just sit here and read. If you need anything let me know."

"I want ya out. Now." His voice sounded raspy and weak.

Rebecca walked to the desk and picked up Bertram's Bible. He hadn't touched it for many days. "I know I said I'd be quiet, but there's something that needs to be said. It seems to me you've read this book many times, correct?"

"The Bible? Right. Ya know I have."

"But you haven't read it lately."

He didn't answer.

"God loves you. Do you know that?"

"Don't try ta teach me. I know that Bible better than ya ever will."

"I'm sure you do." Rebecca walked toward the bed. "But do you know the author?"

Bertram looked flabbergasted. "What are ya trying to say? Of course I know the author."

"All these years you've been studying and doling out your 'wisdom,' but you missed the most important part of God's Word—his heart. He loves in a way no living creature can. He wants you to know that love, to understand that he created you out of love, and he wants you to be like him by loving others."

"I do my best," Bertram said, tight lipped. He glanced at the Bible. "He's also a God of wrath. He punishes those who disobey his Word. And he's not always charitable—if he were, then why am I in this bed? I'm a righteous man. I don't deserve this."

"I don't know why this happened, but I do know God is sovereign and allows what he chooses to allow. His Word says he sendeth rain on the just and on the unjust."

Bertram didn't respond.

Rebecca sat in the chair beside the bed and opened the Bible to John 3:16. "For God so loved the world, that he gave his only begotten Son, that whosoever believeth in him should not perish, but have everlasting life." She turned to Romans. "For I am persuaded, that neither death, nor life, nor angels, nor principalities, nor powers, nor things present, nor things to come. Nor height, nor depth, nor any other creature, shall be able to separate us from the love of God, which is in Christ Jesus our Lord."

She let the book rest on her lap. "His love is so great that nothing can separate us from it. I can't comprehend such a love. Can you?"

"I know the verses. Ya don't have to read them to me." Bertram scowled.

"Bertram Thornton," Rebecca said in a tone a mother might use when correcting a naughty child, "God is speaking to you. But you haven't been listening, not for years."

Bertram opened his mouth to respond, but Rebecca cut in.

"You've been reading this book like it's a book. It's more than that; it's God's Word, his very words spoken to us." Reverence filled her voice. "God speaking to us," she said in little more than a whisper.

"It pains me to see you suffer, but I can't help but wonder if you're in this bed because God is trying to get your attention."

Bertram jutted out his lower jaw.

Rebecca set the Bible on the bed stand. "I suggest you spend time reading, only this time use your heart, not your mind." She stood and walked out.

Callie had been watching from the doorway, and when Rebecca moved past her, she followed. "Miss," she said. "What is that yer sayin' ta Mr. Thornton? I don't understand yer lovin' him when he's been so cruel ta ya."

Rebecca stopped. She pressed her back against the wall and closed her eyes a moment. "I know you don't understand. I'm not sure I do. All I can say is that I feel God's presence. And he's telling me and showing me how to love Mr. Thornton. He has shown me his heart. There is so much more to Mr. Thornton than what he says. He's not cruel, not really." She smiled.

"I still don't understand."

"I'm sinful, you're sinful, we're all sinners, including Bertram Thornton. And yet God loves me and you, and Bertram. And we're to love others in the same way." She looked at Callie. "It's not me you see, but God in me."

Callie walked toward Bertram's room, shaking her head. "I think yer crazy, mum."

"Maybe I am," Rebecca said and walked toward the staircase.

A few minutes later Callie showed up in the parlor. She looked distraught.

Rebecca set the book she was reading in her lap. Willa glanced up from her mending. "What is it?" she asked, her voice tight.

"Mum, Mr. Thornton says I can't come into his room no more. He said only you and Woodman can help him now."

"Oh dear. I'll go on up," Willa said setting her sewing in a basket.

Rebecca's heart sank. He hadn't heard what she'd said. Would he ever?

Although Bertram wanted only Willa and Woodman to care for him, he spent countless hours reading his Bible. Willa said it seemed as if he were seeing it for the first time and delighting in newly discovered verses.

Five days after Bertram refused all visitors except Willa and Woodman, Willa joined Rebecca on the veranda and dropped into a chair with a sigh.

"You look weary. I'm worried about you."

"No need. I'm fine." She closed her eyes and clasped her hands in her lap.

"You and Woodman need help. Can't you convince Mr. Thornton to allow Callie and me to assist you?"

"No. I'm sure not. Something is happening to him, and it's important, so important he trusts his emotions only with the two people he's closest to. He reads and reads his Bible, then stops to pray. Sometimes he catches my hand and reads me a verse, his voice filled with wonderment." Tears pooled in her eyes. "I haven't seen him like this, not ever."

Rebecca smiled. "It's happening. His eyes have been opened, and he's discovering God."

"But he's known the Lord for years."

"I don't think so, Willa. He knew *about* God."

Willa kicked off her shoes and wiggled her toes. "Whatever is happening, it's good. He's enthralled."

"And his health? How is it?"

"Oddly, deteriorating. He grows thinner and weaker every day." She took a handkerchief from her pocket and dabbed at her eyes. "I don't know that I can bear his going. He's always seemed indomitable. I was certain I'd be the first to go."

Rebecca reached for Willa's hand and gently squeezed it. There was nothing she could say to ease her pain.

⚘

The following day Bertram sent for the minister. For hours the two men closed themselves off in Bertram's room. When the reverend came downstairs, he looked as if he'd been weeping.

"Is everything all right?" Willa asked.

"Yes, fine. Bertram's in good hands." He settled compassionate eyes on Willa. "He moves closer to the Creator every moment. He wants you."

"Oh," Willa said, a fluttering hand resting on her throat. "Could someone send for Daniel?"

"I will," Rebecca said.

⚘

Willa was the only person with Bertram when he died. It was a bittersweet moment. "Bertram was ready to meet his Savior," she said, managing to maintain an appearance of serenity.

Sadly, Daniel didn't arrive in time to say farewell, but Willa assured him his father loved him and had been proud of him.

All that day an unearthly hush hung over the house. Willa and Rebecca made arrangements.

At the burial Willa, though obviously grieved, remained composed. Daniel stood at her side. When they walked to the burial site, Willa leaned against him. Rebecca walked close behind.

"He's with God," Willa said. "At the end he was filled with hope and love."

Rebecca took comfort in her words. She'd prayed for just that.

A man Rebecca had seen but had never been introduced to walked up to her. He said, "Ya should 'ave stayed in America where ya belong. He'd still be with us if ya 'ad."

"He's roight," Elvina muttered as Rebecca walked past her.

Willa slowed and took Rebecca's hand. "Don't listen, dear. They're speaking out of grief."

Rebecca knew it was more than that. She'd seen contempt on many people's faces. They blamed her for Bertram's death. They hated her. She kept her eyes lowered and looked at the ground.

When they reached the grave site, Cambria joined her and placed an arm about her shoulder. She offered a smile. "I've been prayin' for ya and the rest of the family. It's a crushin' weight when someone ya love dies. I'm so sorry."

Rebecca rested a hand over her friend's. "Bless you, Cambria."

She looked at the casket, and her eyes pooled with tears. How was it possible that a man like Bertram was dead? He'd seemed invincible. Now all that was left of him in this world was a decaying body laid out in a box. The person, the man Bertram had been, lived on, only now he was in God's presence. It all seemed such a mystery.

The minister said that those who might like to say something in reverence to Bertram should do so. Many spoke up, telling stories about their youth, or the times he'd paid to cover a lost crop, or the days he'd shown up with needed food or supplies. It seemed Bertram had been a very generous and thoughtful man.

No wonder the people love him, Rebecca thought.

When the last person had finished speaking, the minister shared his insights about Bertram. He talked of his life, his dedication to the people in the district, his family, and his commitment to the accurate teaching of God's Word, as well as his love of Australia and especially of Douloo Station.

After pausing and taking a quieting breath, he continued, "On the day of his death, Bertram asked me to his home. His heart was troubled. He asked that what he shared with me remain confidential until this moment."

Mourners grew silent. Wind whispered across the open plains, and a bird trilled.

Even in death he must have the last word, Rebecca thought.

"Bertram knew his Bible. And all these years he believed that it was all he needed," the reverend said. "Not until the end of his life did he realize it wasn't enough and he met his loving Lord and Savior.

"By the power of the Holy Spirit, his sin was revealed to him. He asked that I share with you, family and friends, what he discovered about himself and about God.

"Many years ago, he set out to be a help to this community and to take good care of his family, but he lost his way. In his final days he realized that he'd taken on the role of a god, deciding what was right and what was wrong for everyone, including me." The reverend grinned. "He had a bit of a habit of revising my sermons.

"The day he died he asked for my forgiveness and yers." The minister shook his head. "He was a good and wise man, and told me that he'd shortchanged the work of the Holy Spirit in yer lives, expecting ya to listen to and obey him rather than the Lord."

The minister paused, then looked up and scanned the faces. "Bertram was willing to take the blame for this, but we all share in it. We allowed him to tell us what to do—it was easier that way, requiring no faith of our own."

He closed his Bible. "In addition, there was something Bertram wanted me to set straight. There have been rumors . . . about Rebecca Thornton."

Rebecca's heart beat hard, and she felt as if her breath were caught in her throat.

Willa's hand clasped hers, and she felt stronger.

"When Bertram heard the rumors about his daughter-in-law's misconduct, he knew they weren't true, but he accepted them anyway. He was angry with her, so he used the gossip to hurt her."

Eyes turned to Rebecca. She wanted to hide.

"He wants ya all to know that Rebecca would never do such a thing. He wants ya to know she's moral and upstanding, a woman of faith. And he wants ya to know he admires her, even her spunk." The minister's eyes rested on Rebecca. "He loved ya. He asked me to tell ya that."

Tears pooled in Rebecca's eyes and spilled onto her cheeks. She made no attempt to wipe them away.

"Bertram told me he knew who started the rumors, and he asked me to keep it a secret, saying there was no good purpose served in exposing that person. He figured the Holy Spirit would deal with them."

Murmuring moved through the crowd. Then, one by one,

people looked at Meghan. They knew who had started the lie. Her face reddened, and she backed away from the group, then finally turned and walked toward town.

"Mr. Thornton wanted me to tell ya he loves ya all. Maybe that's why he tried so hard to help. He asks that ya love one another. He was ready and eager for eternity and the reunion he would have with his son Elton. It's long overdue." He smiled. "We have a Lord who has provided his Word and his Holy Spirit to guide and teach us. May we all find the joy of discovery, together."

Willa, Daniel, and Rebecca clasped hands. Bertram had been a good man and would be sorely missed.

28

Rebecca set her Bible in the top of her trunk. It was the final thing to be packed. She straightened. "That's it," she said, glancing around the room with a heavy heart. This would be her last evening at Douloo. She'd thought returning home was the right thing to do, but now she wasn't sure. *It's too late to change my mind*, she told herself, looking over her belongings.

She had everything packed away except for her night-clothes and clothing for the next day's travel. Woodman would collect her bags first thing in the morning. Sitting on the bed, she reflected on what lay ahead, and the gloom intensified.

"Mum," Callie said from the doorway.

"Yes? Come in."

The servant quietly stepped into the room. An awkward silence settled over the two women. Callie tucked tufts of curls inside her bandanna.

"I'll miss you," Rebecca finally said.

"I'm gonna miss ya too. Yer different from most whites. Yer like Willa." Her brown eyes shimmered. She blinked hard, then said, "I don't think ya should go. And I know it's not me place ta say so, but I had ta."

334

"I wish things had turned out differently. I really do."

"Daniel, he's a good bloke. Ya ought ta give 'im a chance."

"I haven't made up my mind completely yet. I'll go home where I can think more clearly. I'll have the baby . . . and I may return."

"No, mum. If ya go back we won't see ya again. Ya 'ave Boston in yer blood, just as I 'ave this place in mine."

A fluttering at the window caught the women's attention. A small brown bird stood on the window ledge. A breeze ruffled its feathers. A few moments later it darted away.

Callie looked at Rebecca. "It's a sign, mum—that wild bird. It wanted in. Yer ta stay."

"It was just a bird. There are a lot of them here at Douloo. It means nothing."

"No, mum. It's a sign, I know it is." Her voice plaintive, Callie continued, "I 'ave never seen Daniel so sad. Not even when Elton died. Ya must pray ta yer God for help in loving 'im."

"It's not that I can't love him . . ."

"Then what, mum?"

"Things will never be right. I can't . . . forgive him." Rebecca could barely say the words after all she'd said about God's mercy and how she'd forgiven Bertram, plus all that had been forgiven her. She blinked back tears and told herself, *This is different.*

"I don't understand yer God, then. Ya say he can do anything, but he can't do this? He must be a small god."

"No. It's not him. It's me." Rebecca walked to the window. "I don't understand my feelings just yet. When I do I'll write and explain it," Rebecca said, ashamed of her feeble faith. She turned and looked at Callie. "I'll think of you often. I'm grateful for your friendship. I hope the miles separating us won't change that. Maybe one day you can come to Boston."

Callie's eyes grew large. "Oh no, mum. I couldn't do that. It's too far away. I wouldn't know how to live there."

"I was just thinking you might visit. I know how it is to feel lost in a foreign place."

"Don't think I can visit neither." Callie looked at Rebecca's abdomen. "Ya take care of that bybie now, eh?"

"I will."

"Wal, I 'ave work ta do." Callie moved toward the door, "Oh, I was told yer ta come down for supper."

"I'll be right there."

Callie waited a moment. "Do ya think the bird will come back, mum?"

Rebecca looked at the empty sill. "No," she said. "It doesn't belong here."

With the setting of the sun, Rebecca's uncertainty grew. *Am I doing the right thing?* She crossed to her trunk and lifted out her Bible. She'd keep it with her. Clasping it against her abdomen, she walked to the window and gazed out on the yard and barns. Resting her hand on the sill, she remembered the bird. She *was* like that bird. She couldn't change who or what she was or where she belonged.

A wind blew off the flats, and Rebecca closed her eyes, relishing the smell of burnt grasses and eucalyptus. Opening her eyes, she gazed at the dusky rose-colored sky. *It is beautiful here.* A dingo yipped, and she was reminded of the many lessons she'd learned since arriving. Now it was over.

A knock sounded at the door. "Yes, who is it?"

"Daniel."

Rebecca turned, then smoothed her skirt. "Come in."

The door opened, and Daniel stood in the doorway, his shoulders back and his spine straight. His misery couldn't be hidden. She remembered their first meeting in her father's office in Boston. It seemed so long ago. He'd been full of life then.

He smiled, but there was no light in his eyes. And why should there be? He'd lost his brother, his father, and now his wife.

"Is there anything you need?" he asked.

"No. I'm fine, thank you."

He glanced at her bags and two trunks. "Seems you're all packed, then, eh?"

"Yes."

"I'll take them down for you."

"That's not necessary. Woodman will do it."

Daniel stood there, seemingly rooted to the floor. Silence fell over them.

"Right. Is there anything else I can do, then?"

"No. Really, everything's been taken care of."

Again, silence.

"Rebecca, please reconsider. I love you, and I believe you love me. That should be enough. It's a start."

"Too much has happened. I must leave. I need to be home . . . well, in Boston anyway. Maybe I can think more clearly there. Just as you love Queensland, I love New England; I long for the cool greenness and my aunt's company. I don't want to hurt you, but—"

"I was thinking that maybe we might go together. There are a few things I need to finish up here, but then I would be—"

"No, Daniel." Rebecca walked to the bureau and pushed closed a drawer that was partially open. "I need time alone."

"There must be something I can say or do that will change your mind. I know if you go you won't come back. I'm sorry for all that's happened, but things will be different now. I promise you."

337

Rebecca looked at him. "I wish I could believe that. There might have been a chance for us, but . . . you believed Meghan's lie. What will keep you from believing the next one? I'm not certain you'll ever be completely sure of me again." She slowly shook her head. "I just can't do it. I don't want to live like that, and I refuse to accept that kind of life for our child."

She brushed a strand of hair off her face. "And then there's this place. It's wild and unpredictable. Much too dangerous a place for raising children. Plus, they'll never know what it's like to sail on the bay or attend a symphony or the opera. There's so much more than this."

With a spark of revolt in his voice, Daniel said, "And I want my children to know how good it feels to put in a day's hard work, to look upon a bronze sky at sunset and the open canvas of stars at night. I want them to watch a group of roos leap across an open field. There's so much *here*."

"Not enough."

Daniel squared his jaw. "I won't see you off, then." He turned and walked out.

⌀

Woodman loaded the last of Rebecca's bags into the surrey, then waited alongside the carriage.

Willa stood quietly.

"It seems the time has come," Rebecca said. She hugged her mother-in-law. "I shall miss you."

"I don't suppose there's any changing your mind?"

"No. I must go, at least for a while."

Willa was silent a moment, then said softly. "I've been praying diligently about this. And just this morning I was reading Matthew 18. I'm sure you know the story about the servant who owed a large debt to a king. The king had the right to have the servant sold, along with his family. But the man begged his master for patience, promising to repay the debt. The master was moved with compassion and forgave all the man's debt."

Rebecca knew the story. Her heart winced.

"The man who'd been forgiven his debt turned right around to one of his fellow servants who owed him money and demanded payment. And although the servant begged for patience and time, the man refused and had him thrown in prison. When the king discovered this, he delivered the servant over to the torturers."

"I know the story, Willa," Rebecca said softly, taking a ragged breath. "I'm not being cruel and unforgiving. I'm just being practical. There will always be a rift between Daniel and me. How can we ever find peace and love? The damage is too great."

Willa retained her calm countenance. Quietly she said, "God is greater than our offenses and able to heal all wounds." She reached out and gently laid her hands on Rebecca's upper arms. "You will discover his true power and presence only if you offer up your needs with faith." She smiled and stepped back. "I know you will find God's path. May our Lord go with you, Rebecca dear. I pray you will return."

Rebecca brushed aside fresh tears and nodded, then with Woodman's assistance stepped into the surrey. He took his place on the front seat. Callie and Lily moved onto the veranda and watched the surrey pull away. Jim stood in the barn door and saluted her. Surprised to see him, Rebecca offered a small wave and asked Woodman, "Why is Jim here? I thought he'd been fired."

"Roight, but Daniel thought better of it and hired 'im back."

Rebecca settled into the seat. Maybe Daniel did believe her after all. She studied the house. Its white paint looked brilliant beneath the morning sun, just as it had the day she'd arrived. Daniel stood at a window on the second floor. Their eyes met and held, and Rebecca's heart constricted. The horses headed for the road, and the house disappeared behind the rise.

Rebecca gazed at the open plains. They no longer seemed hostile or unfamiliar. *I've grown accustomed to this place.* Cattle grazed, flicking away flies with their tails. A calf bucked across the grassland. Rebecca smiled at his antics. *Some things I will miss*, she thought, but the vision of cool weather and the green forests of home played through her mind. Its allure was strong. Boston was home, not this place. It would be best to accept the truth of it and go on.

Willa's words about forgiveness tickled the edges of her mind. What if this was all about forgiveness and she was walking away from God's plan because she was unwilling to forgive Daniel? And unwilling to believe he'd accepted the truth without conditions?

The thought of life without him felt bleak. *I do love him. But it's not enough, not anymore.*

※

The trip into town seemed shorter than usual. Before Rebecca knew it, they were pulling up in front of the Thornton Creek Hotel. Woodman gave her a hand down, then unloaded the trunks and bags.

Rebecca walked into the hotel to make certain everything was in order. She didn't relish the long days of travel ahead. The journey had been difficult enough when she'd had Daniel at her side and the anticipation of a new life.

Her thoughts wandered to the nights when the sound of the didgeridoo echoed over the flats, its haunting tones resonating through the darkness. It had once frightened her, but now it seemed to offer peace and permanence.

"Everything is in order," the clerk said, "and the stage should be on time." He handed her the ticket. "We'll miss ya, Mrs. Thornton. I'm right sorry 'bout what's happened. And I know I speak for everyone. We'd like ya ta stay. Give it some thought, eh?"

"Thank you, Michael, but it's time I went home." Rebecca placed the ticket inside her purse.

"I was told that if ya showed up I was ta tell ya ta stop by Mr. Stacy's office."

"Do you know why?"

"No."

"Do I have time before the stage?"

"Yais, I'd say."

Rebecca couldn't imagine what Bertram's attorney would want with her. All the papers had been taken care of. She stepped out of the hotel. Woodman sat on the edge of the wooden sidewalk. "I'll return shortly. I have an errand to run," she said.

"Roight, then. Don't be too long, mum."

"I won't." Rebecca headed toward Mr. Stacy's office, her curiosity growing with each step.

She walked into the small, tidy office. It smelled of cigar smoke. Mr. Stacy sat at a large oak desk and quickly stamped out his cigar and stood.

"G'day," he said. "So you're traveling, eh?"

"Yes. My coach is due any moment. I was told you wanted to see me?"

"Yes." The small man crossed to an oak cabinet. Pulling open a drawer, he searched through the files and pulled out an envelope. Pushing the drawer closed, he returned to the desk. "Mr. Thornton instructed me to give this to you if you decided to leave Douloo. That is your intention?"

341

"Yes. At least for now."

"Right, then. Well, this is yours." He offered Rebecca the envelope.

Taking it, she asked, "What is this about?"

"I'm not allowed to divulge any information. You'll have to read it." He offered her a kindly smile.

"Thank you," she said, puzzling over what Bertram could possibly have left to say to her.

"G'day."

Rebecca sat on a bench just outside the door and opened the envelope. Bertram had written the letter himself. She recognized the writing, even with the shaky, uneven lettering. He'd been so weak in his last days.

"Dear Rebecca," he began. "I write to you knowing that the moment of my passing is near. There is so much that must be said, yet I fear I will not have the vigor to write it all."

He must have the last word, she thought. Had he carried his need to control even to the grave? A flicker of disappointment touched her.

She returned to the letter. Bertram spoke of his youth, the dreams he and Willa had shared for Douloo and for the family they would one day have. He talked about love and hate, as well as grief and the importance of mending relationships, and how he longed to go back and reclaim the day he had thrust Elton out of his life.

He went on to explain how much he admired Rebecca—her courage and stamina. He spoke of how her loyalty and her compassion had impacted him. He continued, explaining that these qualities were needed in the person who would help watch over Douloo.

"I know God chose you for Daniel," Bertram wrote. "In the beginning I was certain he'd been foolish. But I know now that it is I who have been foolish. You possess the strength and courage needed by all those who live at Douloo, but especially

342

my son. You can be part of carrying a greater awareness and understanding of who God is to our family and our community. Sadly, I interfered in God's plans, spoiling so much. I am grateful for his mercy and know that, if you allow it, God will use you to help make a proper path for his work."

Rebecca let the letter rest in her lap. She felt breathless, and the sting of tears burned. Even after all she'd heard at the funeral service, she could barely believe what she was reading. *This is just a dying man's desire; it's not true*, she told herself. Yet she felt the stirring of the Holy Spirit's conviction. *For so long I thought I didn't belong, yet he's saying this is precisely where I should be, precisely where I'm needed.*

Rebecca turned back to the letter. "You and Daniel, together, will make the station better than it's ever been. Together you will be strong, enduring hardships while also praising God for his blessings. And together you will bring harmony—a song, if you wish." Rebecca smiled, wondering if his reference was to suggest that church solos might be all right?

"I ask that you forgive my son's weaknesses. I'm responsible. Year upon year I tore him down, robbing him of his independence. Only now is he discovering who he is and how he is to live out his own destiny. He needs you beside him; I'm certain that is God's will. I beg you to think again about the Lord's greater plan and to see beyond your own pain to what you and Daniel can become."

Rebecca closed her eyes. He'd signed the letter with love. She folded it and placed it in her purse. She stood and walked back to the hotel. Raising dust, the stagecoach rattled down the street and stopped in front of the hotel.

The driver leaped down, and Woodman handed him one of Rebecca's bags.

"Wait. I'm not going," Rebecca said.

Woodman gave her a questioning look, then grinned.

343

"Too roight, mum." He took back the bag and set it on the sidewalk.

Daniel stepped out of the hotel. "Rebecca?"

She hadn't expected him. "I thought you weren't going to see me off."

"I changed my mind."

Rebecca stared at Daniel. His blue eyes were lit with hope, and a smile touched his lips. She stepped closer, searching his eyes. She loved him; she had for a long while. God had a plan of restoration—she was to be a part of it.

"I may not love Australia yet," she said, "but I do love you. And this is where I belong."

Bonnie Leon dabbled in writing for many years but never set it in a place of priority until an accident in 1991 left her unable to work. She is now the author of more than eleven historical fiction novels, including the best-selling *Journey of Eleven Moons*. She also stays busy teaching women's Bible studies, speaking, and teaching at writing seminars and conventions. Bonnie and her husband, Greg, live in Glide, Oregon. They have three grown children and four grandchildren. You can contact Bonnie at www.bonnieleon.com

Coming in May 2005 . . .

BOOK 2

IN THE

QUEENSLAND

CHRONICLES

Excerpt from Book 2

The Thornton kitchen smelled of stew and rising bread. Rebecca pressed the heel of her hand into a lump of dough, then folded the resilient mass and pressed again. "What time is it?"

Willa's blue eyes sparkled with mischief. "I'd say about ten minutes later than the last time you asked." She crossed the kitchen, placed an arm around Rebecca's waist, and gave her a squeeze. "I thought baking might take your mind off your aunt's arrival. I should have known better."

"The minutes are passing too slowly." Rebecca rolled the dough into a ball and set it in a ceramic bowl.

"She'll be here soon enough, I dare say." Willa smiled.

"I can't stand this waiting." Looking into her mother-in-law's kind eyes, Rebecca said, "It's been three months since I received word that she would be visiting. I've been anxious ever since." She glanced out the kitchen window. "I can't imagine Aunt Mildred traveling all that way by herself. If only I could have gone along to meet the stage."

"It appears boldness runs in your family." Willa steered Rebecca to the table and sat her down. "Now, you know what the doctor said. And if I don't keep you close to home, he'll have my hide."

Rebecca leaned an elbow on the table. "I know . . . no trips into town, keep my feet up . . . rest." She laid a hand on her rounded abdomen. "The baby isn't due for another few weeks." As a familiar pain pulled at her lower back, she said, "Maybe the doctor's right. I haven't been feeling quite myself today."

"Are you unwell?" Willa eyed her.

"I'm fine, but I think the baby is preparing for its arrival." She stared at her stomach. "It will be nice to have my body back to myself." The pain subsided, and she let out a slow breath.

"Are you laboring?"

"No. I don't believe so."

"You're sure you're all right?"

Rebecca nodded. "You worry too much."

Lily, the cook, picked up the bowl with the dough Rebecca had prepared and placed it on the warming shelf of the oven. "Looks just roight. Ya done a good job." She grinned, revealing two spaces in front where teeth belonged. Lily's smiling, dark eyes were spaced far apart in her square black face, giving her a friendly appearance.

"I thought myself a fair cook when I arrived, but you've taught me so much more. Aunt Mildred will be pleased, I'm sure."

"Ya've learned roight well. Daniel 'as every roight ta be pleased with ya."

"Only because you took the time to teach me." Rebecca gazed out the window at the dusty yard. Her eyes rested on the place where the drive disappeared over a small rise. "Woodman must be driving especially slow today. The stage was supposed to be in two hours ago."

"I expect he's being exceedingly careful with your aunt," Willa said, walking to the stove.

"Aunty must be exhausted," Rebecca said, remembering her own arrival more than a year ago. The ache in her back returned, and she rubbed at it.

Willa placed a cup of tea on the table in front of Rebecca. "Maybe this will help some." She settled a gentle hand on

Rebecca's shoulder. "Your aunt will be here in no time, you'll see."

Rebecca placed a hand over her mother-in-law's. "You're so good to me."

"You're a love, so it's easy." Willa returned the teakettle to the stove, then removed a lid from a hefty pot. Steam puffed into the air. She stirred the contents, then peered inside. "This looks wonderful, Lily. And smells heavenly."

"Just a stew, mum. Hope it's ta yer likin'." She looked at Rebecca. "And I hope yer aunt will like it. It's one of me specialties."

"I'm sure she will," Rebecca said. "In fact, it seems to me that when I lived in Boston, Aunty made a rather good stew." Rebecca stirred a half teaspoon of sugar into her tea. "They must be nearly here, don't you think?" She looked at Willa.

"Perhaps."

Rebecca set the spoon on the saucer and sipped her tea. Stretching out her legs, she cradled the cup in her hands and closed her eyes. "That's better. I practically feel calm. How is it tea nearly always seems to help?"

"Can't say, dear, but it's what my mother always gave me—whether it was a stomach ailment or nerves, it would be just the thing."

Rebecca took another drink. "I can hardly believe more than a year has passed since I've seen my aunt. I wish my father were alive," she added sadly. "I miss him terribly." She rested a hand on her abdomen. "He would have made a wonderful grandfather."

In the distance a swirl of dust rose into the air. Setting her cup in its saucer, Rebecca stood. "That must be her!" She pushed out of her chair, and as quickly as her added girth allowed, she walked to the front door. Pushing open the screen, Rebecca stepped onto the veranda.

Callie, the housemaid, hurried down the broad staircase

leading from the second story. "They're comin', mum! I saw them from the upstairs window!" She joined Rebecca on the porch. "They're not far."

Keeping her eyes fixed on the drive, Rebecca moved toward the steps.

The front door opened and closed again, and Willa stood with Rebecca and Callie. "I wish Bertram were here."

"We all do," Rebecca said, remembering her powerful father-in-law, Bertram Thornton. Their first meeting had been painful, but in the end they'd learned to love one another.

"I dare say, I feel badly for your aunt—I know how miserable the trip from Brisbane can be."

Rebecca's mind reeled back to the days she'd spent traveling from Brisbane. The journey had been nearly unbearable—dust, heat, and several days in an uncomfortable coach. "I arrived just about this time of year. Remember?"

"Indeed I do," Willa said, her eyes soft with the memory.

Dust churning, the top of the surrey appeared just above the rise. Then a set of stallions and Woodman sitting in the driver's seat came into view. Rebecca strained to catch a glimpse of her aunt. She sat beside Daniel.

"There they are, mum," Callie said, sounding nearly as excited as Rebecca felt.

Gripping the handrail, Rebecca walked down the front steps and waited at the bottom. Her heart drummed. Smiling broadly, she waved and called, "Aunty!" She hurried toward the surrey.

Daniel stepped out and offered Rebecca's aunt a hand. She looked a bit undone and worked to straighten her bonnet before taking the proffered hand. Then she stepped out with as much dignity as she could muster.

When her eyes found Rebecca, the weariness evaporated. "Oh, Rebecca! How wonderful you look!" She folded her niece in thin arms and held her tightly. A few moments later